D0377926

Dear Reader,

Welcome to the world of the incomparable Nora Roberts! In this special volume of classic novels, Nora demonstrates her mastery of romantic storytelling. Both loyal fans and new readers are sure to enjoy *Rules of Play,* which features two exciting tales of reunited couples who learn to live—and love—by breaking all the rules.

She was known as the ice princess. He could set hearts ablaze with a single glance. When old flames Asher Wolfe and Ty Starbuck reunite after years apart, *Opposites Attract* once more. While their chemistry is undeniable, secrets from their past soon threaten to tear them apart. Can they set aside old hurts and misunderstandings and start a new life—before it's too late?

After spending years away from home, beautiful photographer Cynthia "Foxy" Fox couldn't help but focus on her girlhood crush, Lance Matthews. Lance had never looked twice at Foxy before, but suddenly he's seeing his best friend's kid sister in a whole new light. Could this mean *The Heart's Victory* for them both?

Enjoy!

The Editors
Silhouette Books

NORA ROBERTS

rules of play

Silhouette Books

Published by Silhouette Books

America's Publisher of Contemporary Romance

SILHOUETTE BOOKS

RULES OF PLAY

Copyright © 2005 by Harlequin Books S.A.

ISBN 0-373-28511-6

The publisher acknowledges the copyright holder of the individual works as follows:

OPPOSITES ATTRACT
Copyright © 1984 by Nora Roberts

THE HEART'S VICTORY
Copyright © 1982 by Nora Roberts

This edition published by arrangement with Harlequin Books S.A.

® and TM are trademarks of Harlequin Books S.A., used under license. Trademarks indicated with ® are registered in the United States Patent and Trademark Office, the Canadian Trade Marks Office and in other countries.

Visit Silhouette Books at www.eHarlequin.com

Printed in U.S.A.

CONTENTS

OPPOSITES ATTRACT

For Joan Schulhafer,
leader of tours, handler of details and good friend

CHAPTER 1

"Advantage, Starbuck."

Isn't it always? Asher mused. For a moment the large arena held that humming silence peculiar to indoor sports events. There was an aroma of roasted peanuts and sweat. The overhead lights heated the scent somewhat pleasantly while the crush of bodies added enforced camaraderie. A small child sent up a babbling complaint and was hushed.

Seated several rows back at mid-court, Asher Wolfe watched Ty Starbuck—tennis master, Gypsy, eternal boy of summer and former lover. She thought again, as she had several times during more than two hours of play, that he'd changed. Just how wasn't yet completely clear. More than three years had passed since she'd seen him in the flesh. But he hadn't aged, or thickened, or lost any of his characteristic verve.

Rarely over the years had she watched a televised match—it was too painful. Too many faces were familiar, with his the most strictly avoided. If Asher had chanced to come across a write-up or picture of him in the sports pages or in a gossip column, she had immediately put it aside. Ty Starbuck was out of her life. Her decision. Asher was a very decisive woman.

Even her decision to come to the U.S. Indoor Tennis Championship had been a cool-headed one. Before making this trip, she had carefully weighed the pros and cons. In the end logic had won. She was getting back into the game herself. On the circuit, meetings with Ty would be unavoidable. She would see him now, letting the press, her colleagues and fans see clearly that there was nothing left of what had been three years before. Ty would see too, and, she hoped fervently, so would she.

Ty stood behind the baseline, preparing to serve. His stance was the same, she mused, as was his sizzling concentration. He tossed the ball up, coming back and over with the wicked left-handed serve that had become synonymous with his name, a Starbuck.

Asher heard the explosion of his breath that forced the power into it. She held her own. A lesser player than the Frenchman, Grimalier, would never have gotten a racket on the ball. His return was quick—force meeting force—and the rally began.

The crowd grew noisier as the ball smashed and thudded. Echoes bounced crazily. There were cries of encouragement, shouts of appreciation for the prowess of the two players. Ty's basic entertainment value hadn't decreased since Asher had been out of the game. Fans adored or detested him, but they never, never ignored him. Nor could she, though she was no longer certain which category she fell into. Every muscle of his body was familiar to her, every move, every expression. Her feelings were a confused jumble of respect, admiration and longing, which swirled to reach a vortex of pain, sharply remembered. Still, she was caught up in him again. Ty Starbuck demanded every last emotion and didn't really give a damn if it was love or hate.

Both men moved quickly, their eyes riveted on the small white sphere. Backhand, forehand, drop shot. Sweat poured down unheeded. Both the game and the fans demanded it. A tennis buff wanted to see the effort, the strain, wanted to hear the grunts and whistling breaths, wanted to smell the sweat. Despite her determination to remain dispassionate, Asher found herself watching Ty with the undiluted admiration she'd held for him for more than ten years.

He played with nonchalant flash—contradictory terms, but there it was. Strength, agility, form—he had them all. He had a long, limber body, seemingly elastic until the muscles flowed and bunched. His six-two height gave him an advantage of reach, and he could twist and turn on a dime. He played like a fencer—Asher had always thought a swashbuckler. Graceful sweeps, lunges, parries, with an almost demonic glint in his dusk-gray eyes. His face was that of the adventurer—narrow, rakish, with a hint of strong bone vying with an oddly tender mouth. As always, his hair was a bit too long, flowing wild and black around a white sweatband.

He was a set-up, and held advantage, but he played as though his life depended on this one point. That hadn't changed, Asher thought, as her heart pounded at double time. She was as involved in the match as if she were the one with the racket in her hand and the sweat rolling over her skin. Her palms were slick, her own muscles tight. Tennis involved its onlookers. Starbuck absorbed them. That hadn't changed either.

Ty smashed the ball crosscourt at the sideline. It careened away even as the Frenchman dove toward it. Asher sucked in her breath at the speed and placement of the ball.

"Wide," the line judge said dispassionately. A loud complaint poured out of the crowd. Asher fixed her eyes on Ty and waited for the explosion.

He stood, breathing hard from the punishing rally, his eyes fixed on the judge. The crowd continued to roar disapproval as deuce was called. Slowly, his eyes still on the judge, Ty swiped his wristband over his brow. His face was inscrutable but for his eyes, and his eyes spoke volumes. The crowd quieted to a murmur of speculation. Asher bit hard on her bottom lip. Ty walked back to the baseline without having uttered a sound.

This was the change, Asher realized with a jolt. Control. Her breath came out slowly as the tension in her shoulders diminished. In years past, Ty Starbuck would have hurled abuse—and an occasional racket—snarled, implored the crowd for support or berated them. Now he walked silently across the service court with temper smoldering in his eyes. But he held it in check. This was something new.

Behind the baseline Ty took his time, took his stance, then cracked an ace, like a bullet from a gun. The crowd screamed for him. With a quiet, insolent patience he waited while the scoring was announced. Again, he held advantage. Knowing him, and others like him, Asher was aware that his mind was occupied with his next move. The ace was already a memory, to be taken out and savored later. He still had a game to win.

The Frenchman connected with the next serve with a blazing forehand smash. The volley was sweating, furious and blatantly male. It was all speed and fire, two pirates blasting at each other across a sea of hardwood. There was the sound of the ball hitting the heart of the racket, the skid of rubber soles on wood, the grunts of the competitors as they drew out more force, all drowned beneath the echoes of cheers. The crowd was on its feet. Asher was on hers without even being aware of it. Neither man gave quarter as the seconds jumped to a minute, and a minute to more.

With a swing of the wrist the Frenchman returned a nearly impossible lob that drove him behind the baseline. The ball landed deep in the right court. With a forceful backhand Ty sent the ball low and away from his opponent, ending the two-and-a-half-hour match, three sets to one.

Starbuck was the U.S. Indoor Tennis champion, and the crowd's hero.

Asher let the enthusiasm pour around her as Ty walked to the net for the traditional handshake. The match had affected her more than she'd anticipated, but she passed this off as professional admiration. Now she allowed herself to wonder what his reaction would be when he saw her again.

Had she hurt him? His heart? His pride? The pride, she mused. That she could believe. The heart was a different matter. He would be angry, she concluded. She would be cool. Asher knew how to maintain a cool exterior as well as she knew how to smash an overhead lob. She'd learned it all as a child. When they met, she would simply deploy his temper. She had been preparing for the first encounter almost as religiously as she had been preparing to pick up her profession again. Asher was going to win at both. After he had finished with the showers and the press, she would make it a point to seek him out. To congratulate him—and to present the next test. It was much wiser for her to make the first move, for her to be the one prepared. Confident, she watched Ty exchange words with Grimalier at the net.

Then Ty turned his head very slowly, very deliberately. With no searching through the crowd, no hesitation, his eyes locked on hers. The strength of the contact had her drawing in a sharp, unwilling breath. His eyes held, no wavering. Her mouth went dry. Then he smiled, an unpleasant, direct challenge. Asher met it, more from shock than temerity as the crowd bellowed his name. *Starbuck* echoed from the walls like a litany. Ten seconds—fifteen—he neither blinked nor moved. For a man of action he had an uncanny ability for stillness. Boring into hers, his eyes made the distance between them vanish. The smile remained fixed. Just as Asher's palms began to sweat, he turned a full circle for the crowd, his racket above his head like a lance. They adored him.

He'd known, Asher thought furiously as people swarmed around her. He had known all along that she was there. Her anger wasn't the hot, logical result of being outmaneuvered, but small, silver slices of cold fury. Ty had let her know in ten seconds, without words, that the game was still on. And he always won.

Not this time though, she told herself. She had changed too. But she stood where she was, rooted, staring out at the now empty court. Her thoughts were whirling with memories, emotions, remembered sensations. People brushed by her, already debating the match.

She was a tall, reed-slim figure tanned gold from hours in the sun. Her hair was short, sculptured and misty-blond. The style flattered, while remaining practical for her profession. Over three years of retirement, Asher hadn't altered it. Her face seemed more suited to the glossy pages of a fashion magazine than the heat and frenzy of a tennis court. A weekender, one might think, looking at her elegant cheekbones in an oval face. Not a pro. The nose was small and straight above a delicately molded mouth she rarely thought to tint. Makeup on the courts was a waste of time, as sweat would wash it away. Her eyes were large and round, a shade of blue that hinted at violet. One of her few concessions to vanity was to darken the thick pale lashes that surrounded them. While other women competitors added jewelry or ribbons and bows to the court dress, Asher had never thought of it. Even off the court her attire leaned toward the simple and muted.

An enterprising reporter had dubbed her "The Face" when she had been eighteen. She'd been nearly twenty-three when she had retired from professional play, but the name had stuck. Hers was a face of great beauty and rigid control. On court, not a flicker of expression gave her opponent or the crowd a hint of what she was thinking or feeling. One of her greatest defenses in the game was her ability to remain unruffled under stress. The standard seeped into her personal life.

Asher had lived and breathed tennis for so long that the line of demarcation between woman and athlete was smudged. The hard, unbendable rule, imposed by her father, was ingrained into her—privacy, first and last. Only one person had ever been able to cross the boundary. Asher was determined he would not do so again.

As she stood staring down at the empty court, her face told nothing of her anger or turmoil—or the pain she hadn't been prepared for. It was calm and aloof. Her concentration was so deep that the leader of the small packet of people that approached her had to speak her name twice to get her attention.

She'd been recognized, she discovered. Though Asher had known it was inevitable, it still gave her a twist of pleasure to sign the papers and programs thrust at her. She hadn't been forgotten.

The questions were easy to parry, even when they skirted close to her relationship with Ty. A smile and double-talk worked well with fans. Asher wasn't naïve enough to think it would work with reporters. That, she hoped, was for another day.

As she signed, and edged her way back, Asher spotted a few colleagues—an old foe, a former doubles partner, a smattering of faces from the past. Her eyes met Chuck Prince's. Ty's closest friend was an affable player with a wrist of steel and beautiful footwork. Though the silent exchange was brief, even friendly, Asher saw the question in his eyes before she gave her attention to the next fan.

The word's out, she thought almost grimly as she smiled at a teenage tennis buff. Asher Wolfe's picking up her racket again. And they'd wonder, and eventually ask, if she was picking up Ty Starbuck too.

"Asher!" Chuck moved to her with the same bouncy stride he used to cross a court. In his typical outgoing style he seized her by the shoulders and kissed her full on the mouth. "Hey, you look terrific!"

With a laugh Asher drew back the breath his greeting had stolen from her. "So do you." It was inevitably true. Chuck was average in almost every way—height, build, coloring. But his inner spark added appeal and a puckish sort of sexuality. He'd never hesitated to exploit it—good-naturedly.

"No one knew you were coming," Chuck complained, easing her gently through the thinning crowd. "I didn't know you were here until…" His voice trailed off so that Asher knew he referred to the ten seconds of potent contact with Ty. "Until after the match," he finished. He gave her shoulder a quick squeeze. "Why didn't you give someone a call?"

"I wasn't entirely sure I'd make it." Asher allowed herself to be negotiated to a clear spot in a rear hallway. "Then I thought I'd just melt into the crowd. It didn't seem fair to disrupt the match with any the-prodigal-returns business."

"It was a hell of a match." The flash of teeth gleamed with enthusiasm. "I don't know if I've ever seen Ty play better than he did in the last set. Three aces."

"He always had a deadly serve," Asher murmured.

"Have you seen him?"

From anyone else the blunt question would have earned a cold stare. Chuck earned a quick grimace. "No. I will, of course, but I didn't want to distract him before the match." Asher linked her fingers—an old nervous habit. "I didn't realize he knew I was here."

Distract Starbuck, she thought with an inner laugh. No one and nothing distracted him once he picked up his game racket.

"He went crazy when you left."

Chuck's quiet statement brought her back. Deliberately

she unlaced her fingers. "I'm sure he recovered quickly." Because the retort was sharper than she had intended, Asher shook her head as if to to take back the words. "How have you been? I saw an ad with you touting the virtues of a new line of tennis shoes."

"How'd I look?"

"Sincere," she told him with a a quick grin. "I nearly went out and bought a pair."

He sighed. "I was shooting for macho."

As the tension seeped out of her, Asher laughed. "With that face?" She cupped his chin with her hand and moved it from side to side. "It's a face a mother could trust—foolishly," she added.

"Shh!" He glanced around in mock alarm. "Not so loud, my reputation."

"Your reputation suffered a few dents in Sydney," she recalled. "What was that—three seasons ago? The stripper."

"Exotic dancer," Chuck corrected righteously. "It was merely an exchange of cultures."

"You did look kind of cute wearing those feathers." With another laugh she kissed his cheek. "Fuchsia becomes you."

"We all missed you, Asher." He patted her slim, strong shoulder.

The humor fled from her eyes. "Oh, Chuck, I missed you. Everyone, all of it. I don't think I realized just how much until I walked in here today." Asher looked into space at her own thoughts, her own memories. "Three years," she said softly.

"Now you're back."

Her eyes drifted to his. "Now I'm back," she agreed. "Or will be in two weeks."

"The Foro Italico."

Asher gave him a brief smile that was more determination than joy. "I've never won on that damn Italian clay. I'm going to this time."

"It was your pacing."

The voice from behind her had Asher's shoulders stiffening. As she faced Chuck her eyes showed only the merest flicker of some secret emotion before they calmed. When she turned to Ty he saw first that his memory of her beauty hadn't been exaggerated with time, and second that her layer of control was as tough as ever.

"So you always told me," she said calmly. The jolt was over, she reasoned, with the shock of eye contact in the auditorium. But her stomach muscles tightened. "You played beautifully, Ty…after the first set."

They were no more than a foot apart now. Neither could find any changes in the other. Three years, it seemed, was barely any time at all. It occurred to Asher abruptly that twenty years wouldn't have mattered. Her heart would still thud, her blood would still swim. For him. It had always, would always be for him. Quickly she pushed those thoughts aside. If she were to remain calm under his gaze, she couldn't afford to remember.

The press were still tossing questions at him, and now at her as well. They began to crowd in, nudging Asher closer to Ty. Without a word he took her arm and drew her through the door at his side. That it happened to be a woman's rest room didn't faze him as he turned the lock. He faced her, leaning lazily back against the door while Asher stood straight and tense.

As he had thirty minutes before, Ty took his time studying her. His eyes weren't calm, they rarely were, but the emotion in them was impossible to decipher. Even in his relaxed stance there was a sense of force, a storm brewing. Asher met his gaze levelly, as he expected. And she moved him. Her power of serenity always moved him. He could have strangled her for it.

"You haven't changed, Asher."

"You're wrong." Why could she no longer breathe easily or control the furious pace of her heart?

"Am I?" His brows disappeared under his tousled hair for a moment. "We'll see."

He was a very physical man. When he spoke, he gestured. When he held a conversation, he touched. Asher could remember the brush of his hand—on her arm, her hair, her shoulder. It had been his casualness that had drawn her to him. And had driven her away. Now, as they stood close, she was surprised that Ty did not touch her in any way. He simply watched and studied her.

"I noticed a change," she countered. "You didn't argue with the referees or shout at the line judge. Not once." Her lips curved slightly. "Not even after a bad call."

He gave her a lightly quizzical smile. "I turned over that leaf some time ago."

"Really?" She was uncomfortable now, but merely moved her shoulders. "I haven't been keeping up."

"Total amputation, Asher?" he asked softly.

"Yes." She would have turned away, but there was nowhere to go. Over the line of sinks to her left the mirrors tossed back her reflection…and his. Deliberately she shifted so that her back was to them. "Yes," she repeated, "it's the cleanest way."

"And now?"

"I'm going to play again," Asher responded simply. His scent was reaching out for her, that familiar, somehow heady fragrance that was sweat and victory and sex all tangled together. Beneath the placid expression her thoughts shot off in a tangent.

Nights, afternoons, rainy mornings. He'd shown her everything a man and woman could be together, opened doors she had never realized existed. He had knocked down every guard until he had found her.

Oh God, dear God, she thought frantically. Don't let him touch me now. Asher linked her fingers together. Though his eyes never left hers, Ty noted the gesture. And recognized it. He smiled.

"In Rome?"

Asher controlled the urge to swallow. "In Rome," she agreed. "To start. I'll go in unseeded. It has been three years."

"How's your backhand?"

"Good." Automatically she lifted her chin. "Better than ever."

Very deliberately Ty circled her arm with his fingers. Asher's palms became damp. "It was always a surprise," he commented, "the power in that slender arm. Still lifting weights?"

"Yes."

His fingers slid down until they circled the inside of her elbow. It gave him bitter pleasure to feel the tiny pulse jump erratically. "So," he murmured softly, "Lady Wickerton graces the courts again."

"Ms. Wolfe," Asher corrected him stiffly. "I've taken my maiden name back."

His glance touched on her ringless hands. "The divorce is final?"

"Quite final. Three months ago."

"Pity." His eyes had darkened with anger when he lifted them back to hers. "A title suits you so well. I imagine you fit into an English manor as easily as a piece of Wedgwood. Drawing rooms and butlers," he murmured, then scanned her face as if he would memorize it all over again. "You have the looks for them."

"The reporters are waiting for you." Asher made a move to her left in an attempt to brush by him. Ty's fingers clamped down.

"Why, Asher?" He'd promised himself if he ever saw her

again, he wouldn't ask. It was a matter of pride. But pride was overwhelmed by temper as the question whipped out, stinging them both. "Why did you leave that way? Why did you run off and marry that damn English jerk without a word to me?"

She didn't wince at the pressure of his fingers, nor did she make any attempt to pull away. "That's my business."

"*Your* business?" The words were hardly out of her mouth before he grabbed both her arms. "*Your* business? We'd been together for months, the whole damn circuit that year. One night you're in my bed, and the next thing I know you've run off with some English lord." His control slipped another notch as he shook her. "I had to find out from my sister. You didn't even have the decency to dump me in person."

"Decency?" she tossed back. "I won't discuss decency with you, Ty." She swallowed the words, the accusations she'd promised herself never to utter. "I made my choice," she said levelly, "I don't have to justify it to you."

"We were lovers," he reminded her tightly. "We lived to-gether for nearly six months."

"I wasn't the first woman in your bed."

"You knew that right from the start."

"Yes, I knew." She fought the urge to beat at him with the hopeless rage that was building inside her. "I made my choice then, just as I made one later. Now, let me go."

Her cool, cultured control had always fascinated and in-furiated him. Ty knew her, better than anyone, even her own father—certainly better than her ex-husband. Inside, she was jelly, shuddering convulsively, but outwardly she was com-posed and lightly disdainful. Ty wanted to shake her until she rattled. More, much more, he wanted to taste her again—obliterate three years with one long greedy kiss. Desire and fury hammered at him. He knew that if he gave in to either, he'd never be able to stop. The wound was still raw.

"We're not finished, Asher." But his grip relaxed. "You still owe me."

"No." Defensive, outraged, she jerked free. "No, I don't owe you anything."

"Three years," he answered, and smiled. The smile was the same biting challenge as before. "You owe me three years, and by God, you're going to pay."

He unlocked the door and opened it, stepping back so that Asher had no choice but to meet the huddle of reporters head-on.

"Asher, how does it feel to be back in the States?"

"It's good to be home."

"What about the rumors that you're going to play professionally again?"

"I intend to play professionally beginning with the opening of the European circuit in Rome."

More questions, more answers. The harsh glare of a flash causing light to dance in front of her eyes. The press always terrified her. She could remember her father's constant instructions: Don't say any more than absolutely necessary. Don't let them see what you're feeling. They'll devour you.

Churning inside, Asher faced the pack of avid reporters with apparent ease. Her voice was quiet and assured. Her fingers were locked tightly together. With a smile she glanced quickly down the hall, searching for an escape route. Ty leaned negligently against the wall and gave her no assistance.

"Will your father be in Rome to watch you play?"

"Possibly." An ache, a sadness, carefully concealed.

"Did you divorce Lord Wickerton so you could play again?"

"My divorce has nothing to do with my profession." A half-truth, a lingering anger, smoothly disguised.

"Are you nervous about facing young rackets like Kingston and old foes like Martinelli?"

"I'm looking forward to it." A terror, a well of doubt, easily masked.

"Will you and Starbuck pair up again?"

Fury, briefly exposed.

"Starbuck's a singles player," she managed after a moment.

"You guys'll have to keep your eyes open to see if that changes." With his own brand of nonchalance, Ty slipped an arm around Asher's rigid shoulders. "There's no telling what might happen, is there, Asher?"

Her answer was an icy smile. "You've always been more unpredictable than I have, Ty."

He met the smile with one of his own. "Have I?" Leaning down, he brushed her lips lightly. Flashbulbs popped in a blaze of excitement. Even as their lips met, so did their eyes. Her were twin slits of fury, his grimly laughing and ripe with purpose. Lazily he straightened. "The Face and I have some catching up to do."

"In Rome?" a reporter cracked.

Ty grinned and quite deliberately drew Asher closer. "That's where it started."

CHAPTER 2

Rome. The Colosseum. The Trevi fountain. The Vatican. Ancient history, tragedy and triumphs. Gladiators and competition. In the Foro Italico the steaming Italian sun beat down on the modern-day competitors just as it had on those of the Empire. To play in this arena was a theatrical experience. It was sun and space. There were lush umbrella pines and massive statues to set the forum apart from any other on the circuit. Beyond the stadium, wooded hills rose from the Tiber. Within its hedge trimmings, ten thousand people could chant, shout and whistle. Italian tennis fans were an emotional, enthusiastic and blatantly patriotic lot. Asher hadn't forgotten.

Nor had she forgotten that the Foro Italico had been the setting for the two biggest revelations in her life: her consuming love for tennis, her overwhelming love for Ty Starbuck.

She had been seven the first time she had watched her father win the Italian championship in the famed *campo central*. Of course she had seen him play before. One of her earliest memories was of watching her tall, tanned father dash around a court in blazing white. Jim Wolfe had been a champion before Asher had been born, and a force to be reckoned with long after.

Her own lessons had begun at the age of three. With her shortened racket she had hit balls to some of the greatest players of her father's generation. Her looks and her poise had made her a pet among the athletes. She grew up finding nothing unusual about seeing her picture in the paper or bouncing on the knee of a Davis Cup champion. Tennis and travel ruled her world. She had napped in the rear of limousines and walked across the pampered grass of Wimbledon. She had curtsied to heads of state and had her cheek pinched by a president. Before she began attending school she had already crossed the Atlantic a half dozen times.

But it had been in Rome, a year after the death of her mother, that Asher Wolfe had found a life's love and ambition.

Her father had still been wet and glowing from his victory, his white shorts splattered with the red dust of the court, when she had told him she would play in the *campo central* one day. And win.

Perhaps it had been a father's indulgence for his only child, or his ambition. Or perhaps it had been the quietly firm determination he saw in seven-year-old eyes. But Asher's journey had begun that day, with her father as her guide and her mentor.

Fourteen years later, after her own defeat in the semi-finals, Asher had watched Starbuck's victory. There had been nothing similar in the style of her father and the style of the new champion. Jim Wolfe had played a meticulous game— cold control with the accent on form. Starbuck played like a fireball—all emotion and muscle. Often, Asher had speculated on what the results would be if the two men were to meet across a net. Where her father brought her pride, Ty brought her excitement. Watching him, she could understand the sense of sexuality onlookers experienced during a bullfight. Indeed, there was a thirst for blood in his style that both alarmed and fascinated.

Ty had pursued her doggedly for months, but she had held him off. His reputation with women, his temper, his flamboyance and nonconformity had both attracted and repulsed her. Though the attraction was strong, and her heart was already lost, Asher had sensibly listened to her head. Until that day in May.

He'd been like a god, a powerful, mythological warrior with a strength and power that even the biased Italian crowd couldn't resist. Some cheered him, some cheerfully cursed him. He'd given them the sweat they had come to see. And the show.

Ty had taken the championship in seven frenzied sets. That night Asher had given him both her innocence and her love. For the first time in her life she had allowed her heart complete freedom. Like a blossom kept in the sheltered, controlled climate of a hothouse, she took to the sun and storm wildly. Days were steamier and more passionate—nights both turbulent and tender. Then the season had ended.

Now, as Asher practiced in the early morning lull on court five, the memories stirred, sweet and bitter as old wine. Fast rides on back roads, hot beaches, dim hotel rooms, foolish laughter, crazy loving. Betrayal.

"If you dream like that this afternoon, Kingston's going to wipe you out of the quarter-finals."

At the admonishment, Asher snapped back. "Sorry."

"You should be, when an old lady drags herself out of bed at six to hit to you."

Asher laughed. At thirty-three, Madge Haverbeck was still a force to be reckoned with across a net. Small and stocky, with flyaway brown hair and comfortably attractive features, she looked like an ad for home-baked cookies. She was, in fact, a world-class player with two Wimbledon championships, a decade of other victories that included the Wightman Cup and a wicked forehand smash. For two years Asher had been her doubles partner to their mutual satisfaction and success. Her husband was a sociology professor at Yale whom Madge affectionately termed "The Dean."

"Maybe you should sit down and have a nice cup of tea," Asher suggested while tucking her tongue in her cheek. "This game's rough on middle-aged matrons."

After saying something short and rude, Madge sent a bullet over the net. Light and agile, Asher sprang after it. Her concentration focused. Her muscles went to work. In the drowsy morning hum the ball thudded on clay and twanged off strings. Madge wasn't a woman to consider a practice workout incidental. She hustled over the court, driving Asher back to the baseline, luring her to the net, hammering at her by mixing her shots while Asher concentrated on adjusting her pace to the slow, frustrating clay.

For a fast, aggressive player, the surface could be deadly. It took strength and endurance rather than speed. Asher thanked the endless hours of weight lifting as she swung the racket again and again. The muscles in the slender arm were firm.

After watching one of Asher's returns scream past, Madge shifted her racket to her left hand. "You're pretty sharp for three years off, Face."

Asher filled her lungs with air. "I've kept my hand in."

Though Madge wondered avidly about Asher's marriage and years of self-imposed retirement, she knew her former partner too well to question. "Kingston hates to play the net. It's her biggest weakness."

"I know." Asher slipped the spare ball in her pocket. "I've studied her. Today she's going to play my game."

"She's better on clay than grass."

It was a roundabout way of reminding Asher of her own weakness. She gave Madge one of her rare, open smiles. "It won't matter. Next week I'm playing center court."

Slipping on a warm-up jacket, Madge gave a hoot of laughter. "Haven't changed much, have you?"

"Bits and pieces." Asher dabbed at sweat with her wristband. "What about you? How're you going to play Fortini?"

"My dear." Madge fluffed at her hair. "I'll simply overpower her."

Asher snorted as they strolled off the court. "You haven't changed either."

"If you'd told me you were coming back," Madge put in, "we'd be playing doubles. Fisher's good, and I like her, but…"

"I couldn't make the decision until I was sure I wouldn't make a fool of myself." Slowly Asher flexed her racket arm. "Three years, Madge. I ache." She sighed with the admission. "I don't remember if I ached like this before."

"We can trade legs any time you say, Face."

Remembering, Asher turned with a look of concern. "How's the knee?"

"Better since the surgery last year." Madge shrugged. "I can still forecast rain though. Here's to a sunny season."

"I'm sorry I wasn't there for you."

Madge hooked her arm through Asher's in easy comradeship. "Naturally I expected you to travel six thousand miles to hold my hand."

"I would have if…" Asher trailed off, remembering the state of her marriage at the time of Madge's surgery.

Recognizing guilt, Madge gave Asher a friendly nudge with her elbow. "It wasn't as big a deal as the press made out. Of course," she added with a grin, "I milked it for a lot of sympathy. The Dean brought me breakfast in bed for two months. Bless his heart."

"Then you came back and demolished Rayski in New York."

"Yeah." Madge laughed with pleasure. "I enjoyed that."

Asher let her gaze wander over the serene arena, quiet but

for the thud of balls and hum of bees. "I have to win this one, Madge. I need it. There's so much to prove."

"To whom?"

"Myself first." Asher moved her shoulders restlessly, shifting her bag to her left hand. "And a few others."

"Starbuck? No, don't answer," Madge continued, seeing Asher's expression out of the corner of her eye. "It just sort of slipped out."

"What was between Ty and me was finished three years ago," Asher stated, deliberately relaxing her muscles.

"Too bad." Madge weathered Asher's glare easily. "I like him."

"Why?"

Stopping, Madge met the direct look. "He's one of the most alive people I know. Ever since he learned to control his temper, he brings so such emotion to the courts. It's good for the game. You don't have a stale tournament when Starbuck's around. He also brings that same emotion into his friendships."

"Yes," Asher agreed. "It can be overwhelming."

"I didn't say he was easy," Madge countered. "I said I liked him. He is exactly who he is. There isn't a lot of phony business to cut through to get to Starbuck." Madge squinted up at the sun. "I suppose some of it comes from the fact that we turned pro the same year, did our first circuit together. Anyway, I've watched him grow from a cocky kid with a smart mouth to a cocky man who manages to keep that wicked temper just under the surface."

"You like him for his temper?"

"Partly." The mild, homey-looking woman smiled. "Starbuck's just plain strung right, Asher. He's not a man you can be ambivalent about. You're either for him or against him."

It was as much inquiry as statement. Saying nothing, Asher

began to walk again. Ambivalence had never entered into her feeling for Ty.

On his way home from his own practice court Ty watched them. More accurately he watched Asher. While she remained unaware of him, he could take in every detail. The morning sun glinted down on her hair. Her shoulders were strong and slender, her gait long, leggy and confident. He was grateful he could study her now with some dispassion.

When he had looked out and had seen her in the stands two weeks before, it had been like catching a fast ball with his stomach. Shimmering waves of pain, shock, anger, one sensation had raced after the other. He had blown the first set.

Then he had done more than pull himself together. He had used the emotions against his opponent. The Frenchman hadn't had a chance against Ty's skill combined with three years of pent-up fury. Always, he played his best under pressure and stress. It fed him. With Asher in the audience the match had become a matter of life and death. When she had left him she'd stolen something from him. Somehow, the victory had helped him regain a portion of it.

Damn her that she could still get to him. Ty's thoughts darkened as the distance between them decreased. Just looking at her made him want.

He had wanted her when she had been seventeen. The sharp, sudden desire for a teenager had astonished the then twenty-three-year-old Ty. He had kept a careful distance from her all that season. But he hadn't stopped wanting her. He had done his best to burn the desire out by romancing women he considered more his style—flamboyant, reckless, knowledgeable.

When Asher had turned twenty-one Ty had abandoned common sense and had begun a determined, almost obsessive pursuit. The more she had evaded him, the firmer she refused, the stronger his desire had grown. Even the victory, tasted first in Rome, hadn't lessened his need.

His life, which previously had had one focus, then had re-aligned with two dominating forces. Tennis and Asher. At the time he wouldn't have said he loved tennis, but simply that it was what and who he was. He wouldn't have said he loved Asher, but merely that he couldn't live without her.

Yet he had had to—when she'd left him to take another man's name. A title and a feather bed, Ty thought grimly. He was determined to make Asher Wolfe pay for bringing him a pain he had never expected to feel.

By turning left and altering his pace Ty cut across her path, apparently by chance. "Hi, Madge." He gave the brunette a quick grin, flicking his finger down her arm before turning his attention fully to Asher.

"Hiya, Starbuck." Madge glanced from the man to the woman and decided she wasn't needed. "Hey, I'm late," she said by way of explanation, then trotted off. Neither Asher nor Ty commented.

From somewhere in the surrounding trees Asher heard the high clear call of a bird. Nearer at hand was the slumberous buzz of bees and dull thud of balls. On court three, some-one cursed fluently. But Asher was conscious only of Ty be-side her.

"Just like old times," he murmured, then grinned at her expression. "You and Madge," he added.

Asher struggled not to be affected. The setting had too many memories. "She hit to me this morning. I hope I don't have to face her in the tournament."

"You go against Kingston today."

"Yes."

He took a step closer. In her mind's eye Asher saw the hedge beside her. With Ty directly in her path, dignified re-treat was impossible. For all her delicacy of looks, Asher didn't run from a battle. She linked her fingers, then dragged them apart, annoyed.

"And you play Devereux."

His acknowledgment was a nod. "Is your father coming?"

"No." The answer was flat and brief. Ty had never been one to be put off by a subtle warning.

"Why?"

"He's busy." She started to move by him, but succeeded only in closing the rest of the distance between them. Maneuvering was one of the best aspects of Ty's game.

"I've never known him to miss one of your major tournaments." In an old habit he couldn't resist nor she prevent, he reached for her hair. "You were always his first order of business."

"Things change," she responded stiffly. "People change."

"So it seems." His grin was sharp and cocky. "Will your husband be here?"

"Ex-husband." Asher tossed her head to dislodge his hand. "And no."

"Funny, as I recall he was very fond of tennis." Casually he set down his bag. "Has that changed too?"

"I need to shower." Asher had drawn nearly alongside of him before Ty stopped her. His hand slipped to her waist too quickly and too easily.

"How about a quick set for old times' sake?"

His eyes were intense—that oddly compelling color that was half night and half day. Asher remembered how they seemed to darken from the pupils out when he was aroused. The hand at her waist was wide-palmed and long-fingered—a concert pianist's hand, but it was rough and worked. The strength in it would have satisfied a prizefighter.

"I don't have time." Asher pushed to free herself and connected with the rock-hard muscles of his forearm. She pulled her fingers back as though she'd been burned.

"Afraid?" There was mockery and a light threat with the overtones of sex. Her blood heated to the force she had never been able to fully resist.

"I've never been afraid of you." And it was true enough. She had been fascinated.

"No?" He spread his fingers, drawing her an inch closer. "Fear's one of the popular reasons for running away."

"I didn't run," she corrected him. "I left." *Before you did,* she added silently. For once, she had outmaneuvered him.

"You still have some questions to answer, Asher." His arm slid around her before she could step back. "I've waited a long time for the answers."

"You'll go on waiting."

"For some," he murmured in agreement. "But I'll have the answer to one now."

She saw it coming and did nothing. Later she would curse herself for her passivity. But when he lowered his mouth to hers, she met it without resistance. Time melted away.

He had kissed her like this the first time—slowly, thoroughly, gently. It was another part of the enigma that a man so full of energy and turbulence could show such sensitivity. His mouth was exactly as Asher remembered. Warm, soft, full. Perhaps she had been lost the first time he had kissed her—drawn to the fury—captured by the tenderness. Even when he brought her closer, deepening the kiss with a low-throated groan, the sweetness never diminished.

As a lover he excelled because beneath the brash exterior was an underlying and deep-rooted respect for femininity. He enjoyed the softness, tastes and textures of women, and instinctively sought to bring them pleasure in lovemaking. As an inherent loner, it was another contradiction that Ty saw a lover as a partner, never a means to an end. Asher had sensed this from the first touch so many years ago. Now she

let herself drown in the kiss with one final coherent thought.
It had been so long.

Her arm, which should have pushed him away, curved up
his back instead until her hand reached his shoulders. Her
fingers grasped at him. Unhesitatingly she pressed her body
to his. He was the one man who could touch off the passion
she had so carefully locked inside. The only man who had
ever reached her core and gained true intimacy—the meeting of minds as well as of bodies. Starved for the glimpses of
joy she remembered, Asher clung while her mouth moved
avidly on his. Her greed for more drove away all her reserve,
and all her promises.

Oh, to be loved again, truly loved, with none of the emptiness that had haunted her life for too long! To give herself,
to take, to know the pure, searing joy of belonging! The
thoughts danced in her mind like dreams suddenly remembered. With a moan, a sigh, she pressed against him, hungry
for what had been.

The purpose of the kiss had been to punish, but he'd forgotten. The hot-blooded passion that could spring from the
cool, contained woman had forced all else from his mind but
need. He needed her, still needed her, and was infuriated. If
they had been alone, he would have taken her and then
faced the consequences. His impulses were still difficult to
control. But they weren't alone. Some small part of his mind
clung to reality even while his body pulsed. She was soft and
eager. Everything he had ever wanted. All he had done without. Ty discovered he had gotten more answers than he'd bargained for.

Drawing her away, he took his time studying her face.
Who could resist the dangerous power of a hurricane? The
wicked, primitive rumblings of a volcano? She stared at him,
teetering between sanity and desire.

Her eyes were huge and aware, her lips parted breathlessly.

It was a look he remembered. Long nights in her bed, hurried afternoons or lazy mornings, she would look at him so just before loving. Hot and insistent, desire spread, then closed like a fist in his stomach. He stepped back so that they were no longer touching.

"Some things change," he remarked. "And some things don't," he added before turning to walk away.

There was time for deep breathing before Asher took her position for the first serve. It wasn't the thousand pairs of eyes watching around the court that had her nerves jumping. It was one pair, dark brown and intense, seventy-eight feet away. Stacie Kingston, age twenty, hottest newcomer to the game in two years. She had energy, force and drive, along with a fierce will to win. Asher recognized her very well. The red clay spread out before her, waiting.

Because she knew the importance of mastering the skittish nerves and flood of doubts, she continued to take long, deep breaths. Squeezing the small white ball, Asher discovered the true meaning of trial by fire. If she won, here where she had never won before, three years after she had last lifted a racket professionally, she would have passed the test. Rome, it seemed, would always be her turning point.

Because it was the only way, she blocked out the past, blocked out tomorrow and focused wholly on the contest. Tossing the ball up, she watched the ascent, then struck home. Her breath came out in a hiss of effort.

Kingston played a strong, offensive game. A studied, meticulous player, she understood and used the personality of clay to her advantage, forcing Asher to the baseline again and again. Asher found the dirt frustrating. It cut down on her speed. She was hurrying, defending herself. The awareness of this only made her rush more. The ball eluded her, bouncing high over her head when she raced to the net, dropping

lazily into the forecourt when she hugged the baseline. Un-
nerved by her own demons, she double-faulted. Kingston
won the first game, breaking Asher's serve and allowing her
only one point.

The crowd was vocal, the sun ferocious. The air was thick
with humidity. From the other side of the hedge Asher could
hear the games and laughter of schoolchildren. She wanted
to throw aside her racket and walk off the court. It was a mistake, a mistake, her mind repeated, to have come back. Why
had she subjected herself to this again? To the effort and pain
and humiliation?

Her face was utterly passive, showing none of the turmoil.
Gripping the racket tightly, she fought off the weakness. She
had played badly, she knew, because she had permitted Kingston to set the pace. It had taken Asher less than six minutes
from first service to defeat. Her skin wasn't even damp. She
hadn't come back to give up after one game, nor had she
come back to be humiliated. The stands were thick with
people watching, waiting. She had only herself.

Flicking a hand at the short skirt of her tennis dress, she
walked back to the baseline. Crouched, she shifted her weight
to the balls of her feet. Anger with herself was forced back.
Fear was conquered. A cool head was one of her greatest
weapons, and one she hadn't used in the first game. This
time, she was determined. This time, the game would be
played her way.

She returned the serve with a drop shot over the net that
caught Kingston off balance. The crowd roared its approval
as the ball boy scurried across the court to scoop up the dead
ball.

Love-fifteen. Asher translated the scoring in her head with
grim satisfaction. Fear had cost her the first game. Now, in
her own precise way, she was out for blood. Kingston became
more symbol than opponent.

Asher continued to draw her opponent into the net, inciting fierce volleys that brought the crowd to its feet. The roar and babble of languages did not register with her. She saw only the ball, heard only the effortful breathing that was hers. She ended that volley with a neatly placed ball that smacked clean at the edge of the baseline.

Something stirred in her—the hot, bubbling juice of victory. Asher tasted it, reveled in it as she walked coolly back to position. Her face was wet now, so she brushed her wristband over her brow before she cupped the two service balls in her hand. Only the beginning, she told herself. Each game was its own beginning.

By the end of the first set the court surface was zigzagged with skid marks. Red dust streaked the snowy material of her dress and marked her shoes. Sweat rolled down her sides after thirty-two minutes of ferocious play. But she'd taken the first set six-three.

Adrenaline was pumping madly, though Asher looked no more flustered than a woman about to hostess a dinner party. The competitive drives she had buried were in complete control. Part of her sensed Starbuck was watching. She no longer cared. At that moment Asher felt that if she had faced him across the net, she could have beaten him handily. When Kingston returned her serve deep, Asher met it with a topspin backhand that brushed the top of the net. Charging after the ball, she met the next return with a powerful lob.

The sportswriters would say that it was at that moment, when the two women were eye to eye, that Asher won the match. They remained that way for seconds only, without words, but communication had been made. From then Asher dominated, forcing Kingston into a defensive game. She set a merciless pace. When she lost a point she came back to take two. The aggressiveness was back, the cold-blooded warfare the sportswriters remembered with pleasure from her early years on the court.

Where Starbuck was fire and flash, she was ice and control. Never once during a professional match had Asher lost her iron grip on her temper. It had once been a game among the sportswriters—waiting for The Face to cut loose.

Only twice during the match did she come close to giving them satisfaction, once on a bad call and once on her own poor judgment of a shot. Both times she stared down at her racket until the urge to stomp and swear had passed. When she had again taken her position, there had been nothing but cool determination in her eyes.

She took the match six-one, six-two in an hour and forty-nine minutes. Twice she had held Kingston's service to love. Three times she had served aces—something Kingston with her touted superserve had been unable to accomplish. Asher Wolfe would go on to the semi-finals. She had made her comeback.

Madge dropped a towel over Asher's shoulders as she collapsed on her chair. "Good God, you were terrific! You destroyed her." Asher said nothing, covering her face with the towel a moment to absorb sweat. "I swear, you're better than you were before."

"She wanted to win," Asher murmured, letting the towel drop limply again. "I *had* to win."

"It showed," Madge agreed, giving her shoulder a quick rub. "Nobody'd believe you haven't played pro in three years. I hardly believe it myself."

Slowly Asher lifted her face to her old partner. "I'm not in shape yet, Madge," she said beneath the din of the still-cheering crowd. "My calves are knotted. I don't even know if I can stand up again."

Madge skimmed a critical glance over Asher's features. She couldn't detect a flicker of pain. Bending, she scooped up

Asher's warm-up jacket, then draped it over Asher's shoulders. "I'll help you to the showers. I don't play for a half hour. You just need a few minutes on the massage table."

Exhausted, hurting, Asher started to agree, then spotted Ty watching her. His grin might have been acknowledgment of her victory. But he knew her, Asher reflected, knew her inside as no one else did.

"No thanks, I'll manage." Effortfully she rose to zip the cover around her racket. "I'll see you after you beat Fortini."

"Asher—"

"No, really, I'm fine now." Head high, muscles screaming, she walked toward the tunnel that led to the locker rooms.

Alone in the steam of the showers, Asher let herself empty, weeping bitterly for no reason she could name.

CHAPTER 3

It was the night after her victory in the semi-finals that Asher confronted Ty again. She had kept herself to a rigorous schedule of practice, exercise, press, and play. Her pacing purposely left her little time for recreation. Practice was a religion. Morning hours were spent in the peaceful tree-shaded court five, grooving in, polishing her footwork, honing her reflexes.

Exercise was a law. Push-ups and weight lifting, stretching and hardening the muscles. Good press was more than a balm for the ego. Press was important to the game as a whole as well as the individual player. And the press loved a winner.

Play was what the athlete lived for. Pure competition—the testing of the skills of the body, the use of the skills of the mind. The best played as the best dancers danced—for the love of it. During the days of her second debut, Asher rediscovered love.

In her one brief morning meeting with Ty she had rediscovered passion. Only her fierce concentration on her profession kept her from dwelling on a need that had never died. Rome was a city for lovers—it had been once for her. Asher knew that this time she must think of it only as a city for competition if she was to survive the first hurdle of regaining her identity. Lady Wickerton was a woman she hardly recognized. She had nearly lost Asher Wolfe trying to fit an image. How could she recapture herself if she once again became Starbuck's lady?

In a small club in the Via Sistina where the music was loud and the wine was abundant, Asher sat at a table crowded with bodies. Elbows nudged as glasses were reached for. Liquor spilled and was cheerfully cursed. In the second and final week of the Italian Open, the tension grew, but the pace mercifully slowed.

Rome was noise, fruit stands, traffic, outdoor cafés. Rome was serenity, cathedrals, antiquity. For the athletes it was days of grueling competition and nights of celebration or commiseration. The next match was a persistent shadow over the thoughts of the winners and the losers. As the music blared and the drinks were poured, they discussed every serve, every smash and error and every bad call. Rome was blissfully indolent over its reputation for bad calls.

"Long!" A dark, lanky Australian brooded into his wine. "That ball was inside by two inches. Two bloody inches."

"You won the game, Michael," Madge reminded him philosophically. "And in the second game of the fifth set, you had a wide ball that wasn't called."

The Australian grinned and shrugged. "It was only a little wide." He brought his thumb and forefinger close together at the good-natured razzing of his peers. "What about this one?" His gesture was necessarily shortened by the close quarters as he lifted a drink toward Asher. "She beats an Italian in the Foro Italico, and the crowd still cheers her."

"Breeding," Asher returned with a mild smile. "The fans always recognize good breeding."

Michael snorted before he swallowed the heavy red wine. "Since when does a bloody steamroller need breeding?" he countered. "You flattened her." To emphasize his point he slammed a palm down on the table and ground it in.

"Yeah." Her smile widened in reminiscent pleasure. "I did, didn't I?" She sipped her dry, cool wine. The match had been longer and more demanding than her first with Kingston, but her body had rebelled a bit less afterward. Asher considered it a double victory.

"Tia Conway will go for your jugular," he said pleasantly, then called to his countrywoman at a nearby table. "Hey, Tia, you gonna beat this nasty American?"

A dark, compact woman with striking black eyes glanced over. The two women measured each other slowly before Tia lifted her glass in salute. Asher responded in kind before the group fell back to its individual conversations. With the music at high volume, they shouted to be heard, but words carried only a foot.

"A nice woman," Michael began, "off the court. On it, she's a devil. Off, she grows petunias and rosemary. Her husband sells swimming pools."

Madge chuckled. "You make that sound like a misdemeanor."

"I bought one," he said ruefully, then looked back at Asher. She was listening with half an ear to the differing opinions on either side of her of a match by two players. "Still, if I played mixed doubles, I'd want Face for a partner." Asher acknowledged this with a curious lift of a brow. "Tia plays like a demon, but you have better court sense. And," he added as he downed more wine, "better legs."

For this Madge punched him in the shoulder. "What about me?"

"You have perhaps the best court sense of any female world-class player," Michael decided slowly. "But," he continued as Madge accepted her due with a regal nod, "you have legs like a shotputter."

A roar of laughter rose up over Madge's indignation. Asher leaned back in her chair, enjoying the loosening freedom of mirth as Madge challenged Michael to show his own and be judged. At that moment Asher's eyes locked with Ty's. Her laughter died unnoticed by her companions.

He'd come in late and alone. His hair was unruly, as though he had ridden in a fast car with the top down. Even completely relaxed, dressed in jeans, his hands in his pockets, some aura of excitement swirled around him. In the dim light his face was shadowed, all hollows and planes, with his eyes dark and knowing. No woman could be immune to him. A former lover was helpless not to remember what magic his mouth could perform.

Asher sat still as a stone—marble, pale and elegant in the rowdy, smoke-curtained bar. She couldn't forget any more than she could stop wanting. All she could do was refuse, as she had three years before.

Without taking his eyes from hers Ty crossed the room, skirted crowded tables. He had Asher by the arm, drawing her to her feet before the rest of the group had greeted him.

"We'll dance." It was a command formed in the most casual tones. As on court, Asher's decision had to be made in a tenth of a second. To refuse would have incited speculative gossip. To agree meant she had her own demons to deal with.

"I'd love to," she said coolly, and went with him.

The band played a slow ballad at ear-splitting volume. The vocalist was flat, and tried to make up for it by being loud. Someone knocked a glass off a table with a splintering crash. There was a pungent scent of spilled wine. A bricklayer argued with a Mexican tennis champion on the proper way to handle a topspin lob. Someone was smoking a pipe filled with richly sweet cherry tobacco. The floorboards were slightly warped.

Ty gathered her into his arms as though she had never been

away. "The last time we were here," he murmured in her ear, "we sat at that corner table and drank a bottle of Valpolicella."

"I remember."

"You wore the same perfume you're wearing now." His lips grazed her temple as he drew her closer. Asher felt the bones in her legs liquefy, the muscles in her thighs loosen. "Like sun-warmed petals." Her heartbeat was a light, uncertain flutter against his. "Do you remember what we did afterward?"

"We walked."

The two hoarsely spoken words seemed to shiver along his skin. It was impossible to keep his mouth from seeking small tastes of her. "Until sunrise." His breath feathered intimately at her ear. "The city was all rose and gold, and I wanted you so badly, I nearly exploded. You wouldn't let me love you then."

"I don't want to go back." Asher tried to push away, but his arms kept her pressed tight against him. It seemed every line of his body knew every curve of hers.

"Why? Because you might remember how good we were together?"

"Ty, stop it." She jerked her head back—a mistake as his lips cruised lazily over hers.

"We'll be together again, Asher." He spoke quietly. The words seemed to sear into the tender flesh of her lips. "Even if it's only once…for old times' sake."

"It's over, Ty." The claim was a whisper, the whisper unsteady.

"Is it?" His eyes darkened as he pressed her against him almost painfully. "Remember, Asher, I know you, inside out. Did your husband ever find out who you really are? Did he know how to make you laugh? How," he added in a low murmur, "to make you moan?"

She stiffened. The music whirled around them, fast now with an insistent bass beat. Ty held her firmly against him, barely swaying at all. "I won't discuss my marriage with you."

"I damn well don't want to know about your *marriage.*" He said the word as if it were an obscenity as his fingers dug into the small of her back. Fury was taking over though he'd sworn he wouldn't let it. He could still get to her. Yes, yes, that was a fact, he knew, but no more than she could still get to him. "Why did you come back?" he demanded. "Why the hell did you come back?"

"To play tennis." Her fingers tightened on his shoulder. "To win." Anger was growing in her as well. It appeared he was the only man who could make her forget herself enough to relinquish control. "I have every right to be here, every right to do what I was trained to do. I don't owe you explanations."

"You owe me a hell of a lot more." It gave him a certain grim satisfaction to see the fury in her eyes. He wanted to push. Wanted to see her anger. "You're going to pay for the three years you played lady of the manor."

"You don't know anything about it." Her breath came short and fast. Her eyes were nearly cobalt. "I paid, Starbuck, I paid more than you can imagine. Now I've finished, do you understand?" To his surprise, her voice broke on a sob. Quickly she shook her head and fought back tears. "I've finished paying for my mistakes."

"What mistakes?" he demanded. Frustrated, he took her by the shoulders. "What mistakes, Asher?"

"You." She drew in her breath sharply, as if stepping back from a steep edge. "Oh, God, you."

Turning, she fought her way through the swarm of enthusiastic dancers. Even as she sprang out into the sultry night Ty whirled her around. "Let me go!" She struck out blindly, but he grabbed her wrist.

"You're not going to walk out on me again." His voice was dangerously low. "Not ever again."

"Did it hurt your pride, Ty?" Emotion erupted from her,

blazing as it could only from one who constantly denied it. "Did it hurt your ego that a woman could turn her back on you and choose someone else?"

Pain ripped through him and took over. "I never had your kind of pride, Asher." He dragged her against him, needing to prove he had some kind of power over her, even if it was only physical. "The kind you wear so that no one can see you're human. Did you run because I knew you? Because in bed I could make you forget to be the perfect lady?"

"I left because I didn't want you!" Completely unstrung, she shouted, pounding with her free hand. "I didn't want—"

He cut her off with a furious kiss. Their tempers soared with vivid passion. Anger sizzled in two pairs of lips that clung because they were helpless to do otherwise. There was never any choice when they were together. It had been so almost from the first, and the years had changed nothing. She could resist him, resist herself, for only so long. The outcome was inevitable.

Suddenly greedy, Asher pressed against him. Here was the sound and the speed. Here was the storm. Here was home. His hair was thick and soft between her questing fingers, his body rock-hard against the firmness of hers. His scent was his "off-court" fragrance—something sharp and bracing that she'd always liked.

The first taste was never enough to satisfy her, so she probed deeper into his mouth, tongue demanding, teeth nipping in the way he himself had taught her. A loud crash of brass from the band rattled the windows behind them. Asher heard only Ty's moan of quiet desperation. Between the shadows and the moonlight they clung, passion building, old needs merging with new.

Her breath trembled into the night as he took a crazed journey of her face. His hands slid up until his thumbs hooked gently under her chin. It was a familiar habit, one of his more disarming. Asher whispered his name half in plea, half in acceptance before his mouth found hers again. He drew her into him, slowly, inevitably, while his fingers skimmed along her cheekbones. The more tempestuous the kiss, the more tender his touch. Asher fretted for the strong, sure stroke of his hands on her body.

Full circle, she thought dizzily. She had come full circle. But if once before in Rome she had been frightened when his kisses had drained and exhilarated her, now she was terrified.

"Please, Ty." Asher turned her head until her brow rested on his shoulder. "Please, don't do this."

"I didn't do it alone," he muttered.

Slowly she lifted her head. "I know."

It was the vulnerability in her eyes that kept him from dragging her back to him. Just as it had been her vulnerability all those years before that had prevented him taking her. He had waited for her to come to him. The same would hold true this time, he realized. Cursing potently under his breath, Ty released her.

"You've always known how to hold me off, haven't you, Asher?"

Knowing the danger had passed, she let out an unsteady breath. "Self-preservation."

Ty gave an unexpected laugh as his hands dove for his pockets. "It might have been easier if you'd managed to get fat and ugly over the last three years. I wanted to think you had."

A hint of a smile played on her mouth. So his moods could change, she thought, just as quickly as ever. "Should I apologize for not accommodating you?"

"Probably wouldn't have made any difference if you had." His eyes met hers again, then roamed her face. "Just looking at you—it still takes my breath away." His hands itched to touch. He balled them into fists inside his pockets. "You haven't even changed your hair."

This time the smile bloomed. "Neither have you. You still need a trim."

He grinned. "You were always conservative."

"You were always unconventional."

He gave a low appreciative laugh, one she hadn't heard in much too long. "You've mellowed," he decided. "You used to say radical."

"*You've* mellowed," Asher corrected him. "It used to be true."

With a shrug he glanced off into the night. "I used to be twenty."

"Age, Starbuck?" Sensing a disturbance, Asher automatically sought to soothe it.

"Inevitably." He brought his eyes back to hers. "It's a young game."

"Ready for your rocking chair?" Asher laughed, forgetting caution as she reached up to touch his cheek. Though she snatched her hand away instantly, his eyes had darkened. "I—" She searched for a way to ease the fresh tension. "You didn't seem to have any problem smashing Bigelow in the semi-finals. He's what, twenty-four?"

"It went to seven sets." His hand came out of his pocket. Casually he ran the back of it up her throat.

"You like it best that way."

He felt her swallow quickly, nervously, though her eyes remained level. "Come back with me, Asher," he murmured. "Come with me now." It cost him to ask, but only he was aware of how much.

"I can't."

"Won't," he countered.

From down the street came a high-pitched stream of Italian followed by a bellow of laughter. Inside the club the band murdered a popular American tune. She could smell the heat-soaked fragrance of the window-box geraniums above their heads. And she could remember, remember too well, the sweetness that could be hers if she crossed the line. And the pain.

"Ty." Asher hesitated, then reached up to grasp the hand that lingered at her throat. "A truce, please. For our mutual benefit," she added when his fingers interlaced possessively with hers. "With us both going into the finals, we don't need this kind of tension right now."

"Save it for later?" He brought her reluctant hand to his lips, watching her over it. "Then we pick this up in Paris."

"I didn't mean—"

"We deal now or later, Face, but we deal." He grinned again, tasting challenge, tasting victory. "Take it or leave it."

"You're just as infuriating as ever."

"Yeah." The grin only widened. "That's what keeps me number one."

On an exasperated laugh, Asher let her hand relax in his. "Truce, Starbuck?"

He let his thumb glide back and forth over her knuckles. "Agreed, on one condition." Sensing her withdrawal, he continued. "One question, Asher. Answer one question."

She tried to wrest her hand away and failed. "What question?" she demanded impatiently.

"Were you happy?"

She became very still as quick flashes of the past raced through her head. "You have no right—"

"I have every right," he interrupted. "I'm going to know that, Asher. The truth."

She stared at him, wanting to pit her will against his. Abruptly she found she had no energy for it. "No," she said wearily. "No."

He should have felt triumph, and instead felt misery. Releasing her hand, he stared out at the street. "I'll get you a cab."

"No. No, I'll walk. I want to walk."

Ty watched her move into the flood of a streetlight and back into the dark. Then she was a shadow, disappearing.

The streets were far from empty. Traffic whizzed by at the pace that seemed the pride of European cities. Small, fast cars and daredevil taxis. People scattered on the sidewalks, rushing toward some oasis of nightlife. Still, Ty thought he could hear the echo of his own footsteps.

Perhaps it was because so many feet had walked the Roman streets for so many centuries. Ty didn't care much for history or tradition. Tennis history perhaps—Gonzales, Gibson, Perry, these names meant more to him than Caesar, Cicero or Caligula. He rarely thought of his own past, much less of antiquity. Ty was a man who focused on the present. Until Asher had come back into his life, he had thought little about tomorrow.

In his youth he had concentrated fiercely on the future, and what he would do if… Now that he had done it, Ty had come to savor each day at a time. Still, the future was closing in on him, and the past was never far behind.

At ten he had been a hustler. Skinny and streetwise, he had talked his way out of trouble when it was possible, and slugged his way out when it wasn't. Growing up in the tough South Side of Chicago, Ty had been introduced to the seamier side of life early. He'd tasted his first beer when he should have been studying rudimentary math. What had saved him from succumbing to the streets was his dislike and distrust of organized groups. Gangs had held no appeal for Ty. He had no desire to lead or to follow. Still, he might have chosen a less honorable road had it not been for his unquestioning love for his family.

His mother, a quiet, determined woman who worked nights cleaning office buildings, was precious to him. His sister, four years his junior, was his pride and self-assumed responsibility. There was no father, and even the memory of him had faded before Ty reached mid-childhood. Always, he had considered himself the head of the family, with all the duties and rights that it entailed. No one corrected him. It was for his family that he studied and kept on the right side of the law—though he brushed the line occasionally. It was for them that he promised himself, when he was still too young to realize the full extent of his vow, to succeed. One day he would move them out, buy them a house, bring his mother up off her knees. The picture of how hadn't been clear, only the final result. The answer had been a ball and racket.

Ada Starbuck had given her son a cheap, nylon-stringed racket for his tenth birthday. The gift had been an impulse. She had been determined to give the boy something other than the necessary socks and underwear. The racket, such as it was, had been a gesture of hope. She could see too many of her neighbors' children fall into packs. Ty, she knew, was different. A loner. With the racket he could entertain himself. A baseball or football required someone to catch or pass. Now Ty could use a concrete wall as his partner. And so he did—at first for lack of something better to do. In the alley between apartment buildings he would smash the ball against a wall scrawled with spray paint. DIDI LOVES FRANK and other less romantic statements littered his playing field.

He enjoyed setting his own rhythm, enjoyed the steady thud, thump, smash he could make. When he became bored with the wall, he began haunting the neighborhood playground courts. There, he could watch teenagers or middle-aged weekenders scramble around the courts. He hustled pennies retrieving balls. Deciding he could do better than the people he watched, Ty badgered an older boy into a game.

His first experience on a court was a revelation. A human forced you to run, sent balls over your head or lined them at you with a speed a stationary wall couldn't match. Though he lost handily, Ty had discovered the challenge of competition. And the thirst to win.

He continued to haunt the courts, paying more attention to details. He began to select the players who took the game seriously. Possessing quite a bit of charm even at that age, Ty talked himself into more games. If someone took the time to teach, he listened and adjusted the advice to suit his own style. And he was developing a style. It was rough and untutored, with the flash the sportwriters would later rave about just a spark. His serve was a far cry from a grown Starbuck's, but it was strong and uncannily accurate. He was still awkward, as growing boys are, but his speed was excellent. More than anything else, his fierce desire to win had his game progressing.

When the cheap racket simply disintegrated under constant use, Ada raided the household budget and bought Ty another. Of the hundreds of rackets he had used in his career, some costing more than his mother had made in a week, Ty had never forgotten that first one. He had kept it, initially from childhood sentiment, then as a symbol.

He carved out a name for himself in the neighborhood. By the time he was thirteen it was a rare thing for anyone, child or adult, to beat Ty Starbuck on the courts. He knew his game. He had read everything he could get his hands on—tennis as a sport, its history, its great players. When his contemporaries were immersed in the progress of the White Sox or the Cubs, Ty watched the Wimbledon matches on the flickering black-and-white TV in his apartment. He had already made up his mind to be there one day. And to win. Again, it was Ada who helped the hand of fate.

One of the offices she cleaned belonged to Martin Derick, a lawyer and tennis enthusiast who patronized a local country club. He was an offhandedly friendly man whose late hours brought him in contact with the woman who scrubbed the hall outside his door. He called her Mrs. Starbuck because her dignity demanded it, and would exchange a word of greeting on his way in or out. Ada was careful to mention her son and his tennis abilities often enough to intrigue and not often enough to bore. Ty had come by his shrewdness naturally.

When Martin casually mentioned he would be interested in seeing the boy play, Ada told him there was an informal tournament set for that Saturday. Then she hurriedly arranged one. Whether curiosity or interest prompted Martin to drive to the battered South Side court, the results were exactly as Ada hoped.

Ty's style was still rough, but it was aggressive. His temper added to the spark, and his speed was phenomenal. At the end of a set, Martin was leaning against the chain-link fence. At the end of the match, he was openly cheering. Two hours on the manicured courts of his club had never brought him quite this degree of excitement. Ideas humming in his brain, he walked over to the sweaty, gangly teenager.

"You want to play tennis, kid?"

Ty spun the racket as he eyed the lawyer's pricey suit. "You ain't dressed for it." He gave the smooth leather shoes a mild sneer.

Martin caught the insolent grin, but focused on the intensity of the boy's eyes. Some instinct told him they were champion's eyes. The ideas solidified into a goal. "You want to play for pay?"

Ty kept spinning the racket, wary of a hustle, but the question had his pulse leaping. "Yeah. So?"

This time Martin smiled at the deliberate rudeness. He was going to like this kid, God knew why. "So, you need lessons and a decent court." He glanced at Ty's worn racket. "And equipment. What kind of power can you get out of plastic strings?"

Defensive, Ty tossed up a ball and smashed it into the opposing service court.

"Not bad," Martin decided mildly. "You'd do better with sheep gut."

"Tell me something I don't know."

Martin drew out a pack of cigarettes and offered one to Ty. He refused with a shake of his head. Taking his time, Martin lit one, then took a long drag.

"Those things'll mess up your lungs," Ty stated idly.

"Tell me something I don't know," the lawyer countered. "Think you can play on grass?"

Ty answered with a quick, crude expletive, then sliced another ball over the net.

"Pretty sure of yourself."

"I'm going to play Wimbledon," Ty told him matter-of-factly. "And I'm going to win."

Martin didn't smile, but reached into his pocket. He held out a discreet, expensively printed business card. "Call me Monday," he said simply, and walked away.

Ty had a patron.

The marriage wasn't made in heaven. Over the next seven years there were bitter arguments, bursts of temper and dashes of love. Ty worked hard because he understood that work and discipline were the means to the end. He remained in school and studied only because his mother and Martin had a conspiracy against him. Unless he completed high school with decent grades, the patronage would be removed. As to the patronage itself, Ty accepted it only because his needs demanded it. But he was never comfortable with it. The lessons polished his craft. Good equipment tightened his game. He played on manicured grass, well-tended clay and wood, learning the idiosyncrasies of each surface.

Every morning before school he practiced. Afternoons

and weekends were dedicated to tennis. Summers, he worked part-time in the pro shop at Martin's club, then used the courts to hone his skill. By the time he was sixteen the club's tennis pro could beat him only if Ty had an off day.

His temper was accepted. It was a game of histrionics. Women found a certain appeal in his lawlessness. Ty learned of female pleasures young, and molded his talent there as carefully as he did his game.

The only break in his routine came when he injured his hand coming to the defense of his sister. Ty considered the two-week enforced vacation worth it, as the boy Jess had been struggling with had a broken nose.

He traveled to his first tournament unknown and un-seeded. In a lengthy, gritty match heralded in the sports pages, he found his first professional victory. When he lost, Ty was rude, argumentative and brooding. When he won, he was precisely the same. The press tolerated him because he was young, brilliant and colorful. His rise from obscurity was appreciated in a world where champions were bred in the affluent, select atmosphere of country clubs.

Before his nineteenth birthday Ty put a down payment on a three-bedroom house in a Chicago suburb. He moved his family out. When he was twenty he won his first Wimbledon title. The dream was realized, but his intensity never slackened.

Now, walking along the dark streets of Rome, he thought of his roots. Asher made him think of them, perhaps because hers were so markedly different. There had been no back alleys or street gangs in her life. Her childhood had been sheltered, privileged and rich. With James Wolfe as a father, her introduction to tennis had come much earlier and much easier than Ty's. At four she had a custom-made racket and had hit balls on her father's private courts. Her mother had hired maids to scrub floors, not been hired out to scrub them.

At times Ty wondered if it was that very difference that had attracted him to her. Then he would remember the way she felt in his arms. Backgrounds were blown to hell. Yet there was something about her reserve that had drawn him. That and the passion he had sensed lay beneath.

The challenge. Yes, Ty admitted with a frown, he was a man who couldn't resist a challenge. Something about the cool, distant Asher Wolfe had stirred his blood even when she had been little more than a child. He'd waited for her to grow up. And to thaw out, he reminded himself ruefully. Turning a corner without direction, Ty found himself approaching one of Rome's many fountains. The water twinkled with light gaiety while he watched, wishing his blood were as cool.

God, how he wanted her still. The need grated against pride, infuriating and arousing him. He would have taken her back that night even knowing she had been another man's wife, shared another man's bed. It would have been less difficult to have thought about her with many lovers than with one husband—that damn titled Englishman whose arms she had run to straight from his own. *Why?* The question pounded at him.

How many times in those first few months had he relived their last few days together, looking for the key? Then he'd layered over the hurt and the fury. The wound had healed jaggedly, then callused. Ty had gone on because he was a survivor. He'd survived poverty, and the streets, and the odds. With an unsteady laugh he raked a hand through his thick mop of hair. But had he really survived Asher?

He knew he had taken more than one woman to bed because her hair was nearly the same shade, her voice nearly the same tone. Nearly, always nearly. Now, when he had all but convinced himself that what he remembered was an illusion, she was back. And free. Again, Ty laughed. Her divorce meant nothing to him. If she had still been legally tied to another man, it would have made no difference. He would still have taken her.

This time, he determined, he'd call the shots. He was out of patience. He would have her again, until he decided to walk away. Challenge, strategy, action. It was a course he had followed for half his life. Taking out a coin, he flipped it insolently into the rippling waters of a fountain, as if daring luck to evade him. It drifted down slowly until it nestled with a hundred other wishes.

His eyes skimmed the streets until he found the neon lights of a tiny bar. He wanted a drink.

CHAPTER 4

Asher had time to savor her title as Italian Woman's Champion on the flight between Rome and Paris. After the match she had been too exhausted from nearly two hours of unrelenting competition to react. She could remember Madge hugging her, the crowd cheering for her. She could remember the glare of flashbulbs in her face and the barrage of questions she had forced herself to answer before she all but collapsed on the massage table. Then the celebrations had run together in a blur of color and sound, interviews and champagne. Too many faces and handshakes and hugs. Too many reporters. Now, as the plane leveled, reaction set in. She'd done it.

For all of her professional career, the Italian clay had beaten her. Now—now her comeback was viable. She had proven herself. Every hour of strain, every moment of physical pain during the last six months of training had been worth it. At last Asher could rid herself of all the lingering doubts that she had made the right decision.

Though there had been no doubts about her choice to leave Eric, she mused, feeling little emotion at the dissolution of her marriage—a marriage, Asher remembered, that had been no more than a polite play after the first two months. If she had ever made a truly unforgivable mistake, it had been in marrying Lord Eric Wickerton.

All the wrong reasons, Asher reflected as she leaned back in her seat with her eyes closed. Even with her bitter thoughts of Eric, she could never remove the feeling of responsibility for taking the step that had legally bound them. He had known she hadn't loved him. It hadn't mattered to him. She had known he wanted her to fit the title of Lady. She hadn't cared. At the time the need to escape had been too overpowering. Asher had given Eric what he had wanted—a groomed, attractive wife and hostess. She had thought he would give her what she needed in return. Love and understanding. The reality had been much, much different, and almost as painful as what she had sought to escape. Arguments were more difficult, she had discovered, when two people had no mutual ground. And when one felt the other had sinned...

She wouldn't think of it, wouldn't think of the time in her life that had brought such pain and disillusionment. Instead, she would think of victory.

Michael had been right in his assessment of Tia on the court. She was a small, vibrant demon who played hard and never seemed to tire. Her skill was in picking holes in her opponent's game, then ruthlessly exploiting them. On court she wore gold—a thin chain around her neck, swinging hoops at her ears and a thick clip to tame her raven hair. Her dress was pastel and frilled. She played like an enraged tigress. Both women had run miles during the match, taking it to a full five sets. The last one had consisted of ten long, volatile games with the lead shooting back and forth as quickly as the ball. Never had it been more true that the match wasn't over until it was over.

And when it was over, both women had limped off the court, sweaty, aching and exhausted. But Asher had limped off with a title. Nothing else mattered.

Looking back at it, Asher found herself pleased that the match had been hard won. She wanted something the press would chatter about, something they would remember for more than a day or two. It was always news when an unseeded player won a world title—even considering Asher's record. As it was, her past only made her hotter copy. She needed that now to help keep the momentum going.

With Italy behind her, Paris was next. The first leg of the Grand Slam. She had won there before, on clay, the year she had been Starbuck's lady. As she had with Eric, Asher tried to block Ty out of her mind. Characteristically he wasn't cooperative.

We pick this up in Paris.

The words echoed softly in her head, part threat, part promise. Asher knew him too well to believe either was idle. She would have to deal with him when the time came. But she wasn't naïve or innocent any longer. Life had taught her there weren't any easy answers or fairy-tale endings. She'd lost too much to believe happy-ever-after waited at the end of every love affair—as she had once believed it had waited for her and Ty. They were no longer the prince and princess of the courts, but older, and, Asher fervently hoped, wiser.

She was certain he would seek to soothe his ego by trying to win her again—her body if not her heart. Remembering the verve and depth of his lovemaking, Asher knew it wouldn't be easy to resist him. If she could have done so without risking her emotions, Asher would have given Ty what he wanted. For three colorless years she had endured without the passion he had brought to her life. For three empty years she had wondered and wanted and denied.

But her emotions weren't safe. On a sigh, Asher allowed herself to feel. She still cared. Not a woman to lie to herself, Asher admitted she loved Ty, had never once stopped loving him. It had never been over for her, and deep within she carried the memory of that love. It brought guilt.

What if he had known? she thought with the familiar stir of panic. How could she have told him? Asher opened her eyes and stared blindly through the sunlight. It was as harsh and unforgiving as the emotions that raged through her. Would he have believed? Would he have accepted? Before the questions were fully formed, Asher shook her head in denial. He could never know that she had unwittingly married another man while she carried Ty's child. Or that through her own grief and despair she had lost that precious reminder of her love for him.

Closing her eyes, Asher willed herself to sleep. Paris was much too close.

"Ty! Ty!"

Pausing in the act of zipping the cover on his racket, Ty turned. Pleasure shot into his eyes. In a quick move he dropped his racket and grabbed the woman who had run to him. Holding her up, he whirled her in three dizzying circles before he crushed her against him. Her laughter bounced off the air in breathless gasps.

"You're breaking me!" she cried, but hugged him tighter.

Ty cut off her protest with a resounding kiss, then held her at arm's length. She was a small woman, nearly a foot shorter than he, nicely rounded without being plump. Her gray-green eyes were sparkling, her generous mouth curved in a dazzling smile. She was a beauty, he thought—had always been a beauty. Love surrounded him. He tousled her hair, dark as his own, but cut in a loose swinging style that brushed her shoulders. "Jess, what are you doing here?"

Grinning, she gave his ear a sisterly tug. "Being mauled by the world's top tennis player."

Ty slipped an arm around her shoulders, only then noticing the man who stood back watching them. "Mac." Keeping his arm around Jess, Ty extended a hand.

"Ty, how are you?"

"Fine. Just fine."

Mac accepted the handshake and careful greeting with light amusement. He knew how Ty felt about his little sister—the little sister who was now twenty-seven and the mother of his child. When he had married Jess, over two years before, Mac had understood that there was a bond between brother and sister that would not be severed. An only child, he both respected and envied it. Two years of being in-laws had lessened Ty's caution with him but hadn't alleviated it. Of course, Mac mused ruefully, it hadn't helped that he was fifteen years Jess's senior, or that he had moved her across the country to California, where he headed a successful research and development firm. And then, he preferred chess to tennis. He'd never have gotten within ten yards of Jessica Starbuck if he hadn't been Martin Derick's nephew.

Bless Uncle Martin, Mac thought with a glance at his lovely, adored wife. Ty caught the look and relaxed his grip on his sister. "Where's Pete?" he asked, making the overture by addressing Mac rather than his sister.

Mac acknowledged the gesture with a smile. "With Grandma. They're both pretty pleased with themselves."

Jess gave the bubbling laugh that both men loved. "Hardly more than a year old and he can move like lightning. Mom's thrilled to chase him around for a few weeks. She sends her love," she told Ty. "You know how she feels about long plane flights."

"Yeah." He released his sister to retrieve his bag and racket. "I talked to her just last night; she didn't say anything about your coming."

"We wanted to surprise you." Smug, Jess hooked her hand into Mac's. "Mac thought Paris was the perfect place for a second honeymoon." She sent her husband a brief but intimate look. Their fingers tightened.

"The trick was getting her away from Pete for two weeks." He gave Ty a grin. "You were a bigger incentive than Paris." Bending, he kissed the top of his wife's head. "She dotes on Pete."

"No, I don't," Jess disagreed, then grinned. "Well, I wouldn't if Pete weren't such a smart baby."

Mac began to unpack an old, favored pipe. "She's ready to enroll him in Harvard."

"Next year," Jess responded dryly. "So, you're going in as top seed," she continued, giving her full attention to her brother. Was there some strain around his eyes? she wondered, then quickly discounted it. "Martin's proud enough to bust."

"I was hoping he might make it out for the tournament." Ty glanced toward the empty stands. "Funny, I still have a habit of looking for him before a match."

"He wanted to be here. If there had been any way for him to postpone this trial, but…" Jess trailed off and smiled. "Mac and I will have to represent the family."

Ty slung the bag over his shoulder. "You'll do fine. Where are you staying?"

"At the—" Jess's words came to a stop as she spotted a slender blonde crossing an empty court a short distance away. Reaching up, she brushed at her brow as if pushing aside an errant strand of hair. "Asher," she murmured.

Ty twisted his head. Asher wasn't aware of them, as Chuck was keeping her involved in what appeared to be a long, detailed description of a match. "Yes," Ty said softly. "Asher." He kept his eyes on her, watching the movements of her body beneath the loosely fitting jogging suit. "Didn't you know she was here?"

"Yes, I—" Jess broke off helplessly. How could she explain the flurry of feelings that she experienced in seeing Asher

Wolfe again. The years were winked away in an instant. Jess could see the cool blue eyes, hear the firmly controlled voice. At the time there'd been no doubt in her mind about right and wrong. Even the chain reaction that had begun on a hazy September afternoon had only served to cement Jess's certainty. Now there'd been a divorce, and Asher was back. She felt her husband's warm palm against hers. Right and wrong weren't so clearly defined any longer.

A bubble of nausea rose as she turned to her brother. He was still watching Asher. Had he loved her? Did he still? What would he do if he ever learned of his sister's part in what had happened three years before? Jess found the questions trembling on her tongue and was afraid of the answers. "Ty…"

His eyes were dark and stormy, a barometer of emotion. Something in them warned Jess to keep her questions to herself. Surely there would be a better time to bring up the past. She had both a sense of reprieve and a feeling of guilt.

"Beautiful, isn't she?" he asked lightly. "Where did you say you were staying?"

"And because he's eighteen and played like a rocket in the qualifying rounds, they're muttering about an upset." Chuck tossed a tennis ball idly, squeezing it when it returned to his palm. "I wouldn't mind if he weren't such a little twerp."

Asher laughed and snatched the ball as Chuck tossed it again. "And eighteen," she added.

He gave a snort. "He wears designer underwear, for God's sake. His mother has them dry cleaned."

"Down boy," Asher warned good-naturedly. "You'll feel better once you wipe him out in the quarter-finals. Youth versus experience," she added because she couldn't resist. Chuck twisted a lock of her hair around his finger and pulled.

"You meet Rayski," he commented. "I guess we could call that two old pros."

Asher winced. "Your point," she conceded. "So, what's your strategy for this afternoon?"

"To beat the tar out of him," Chuck responded instantly, then grinned as he flexed his racket arm. "But if he gets lucky, I'll leave it up to Ty to smash him in the semis or the finals."

Asher bounced the ball on the clay. Her fingers closed over it, then released it again. "You're so sure Ty will get to the finals?"

"Money in the bank," he claimed. "This is his year. I swear, I've never seen him play better." Pleasure for his friend with the light lacing of envy gave the statement more impact. "He's going to be piling up titles like dominoes."

Asher said nothing, not even nodding in agreement as Chuck sought to prove his point by giving her a replay of Ty's qualifying match. A breeze stirred, sending blossoms drifting to the court at her feet. It was early morning, and the Stade Roland Garros was still drowsily charming and quiet. The thump of balls was hardy noticeable. In a few hours the fourteen thousand seats around the single center court would be jammed with enthusiasts. The noise would be human and emotional, accented by the sounds of traffic and squealing brakes on the highway that separated the stadium from the Bois de Boulogne.

Asher watched the breeze tickle a weeping willow as Chuck continued his rundown. In this first week of the games, tennis would be played for perhaps eleven hours a day so that even the first-round losers used the courts enough to make the trip worthwhile. It was considered by most pros the toughest championship to win. Like Ty, Asher was after her second victory.

Paris. Ty. Was there nowhere she could go that wasn't so firmly tied in with memories of him? In Paris they'd sat in the back of a darkened theater, necking like teenagers while an Ingmar Bergman film had flickered on the screen unnoticed. In Paris he had doctored a strained muscle in her calf, pampering and bullying so that she had won despite the pain. In Paris they had made love, and made love, and made love until they were both weak and exhausted. In Paris Asher had still believed in happy endings.

Fighting off memories, Asher glanced around the stadium. Her eyes locked with Jess's. Separated by a hundred yards, both women endured a jolt of shock and distress. They stared, unable to communicate, unable to look away.

"Hey, it's Jess!" Chuck interrupted himself to make the announcement. He waved, then grabbed Asher's hand to drag her with him. "Let's go say hi."

Panicked, Asher dug in her heels. "No, I—I have to meet…" Her mind was devoid of excuses, but she snatched her hand from Chuck's. "You go ahead, I'll see you later." Over Chuck's protest, she dashed in the opposite direction.

Breathless, Asher found herself in the Jardin des Plantes with its sweet, mingling scents, little plaques and poetry. It seemed an odd setting for jangled nerves. Making an effort to calm herself, she slowed her pace.

Silly to run, she told herself. No, she corrected herself, stupid. But she hadn't been prepared to see Ty's sister, the one person who knew all the reasons. To have confronted Jess then, when her mind was already so crowded with Ty, would have been disastrous. Steadying, Asher told herself she just needed a little time to prepare. And it had been obvious Jess had been just as stunned as she. At the moment, Asher was too busy calming herself to wonder why.

She wouldn't, couldn't, think about the last time she'd seen Jessica Starbuck—that hot, close Indian summer afternoon. It would be too easy to remember each word spoken in the careless disorder of the hotel room Asher had shared with Ty. She would remember the hurt, the frantic packing, then her irrevocable decision to go to Eric.

Oh, Ty had been right, she had run away—but she hadn't escaped. So little had changed in three years, and so much. Her heart had remained constant. With a sigh Asher admitted it had been foolish to believe she could take back what she had given so long ago. Ty Starbuck was her first lover, and the only man she had ever loved.

A child had been conceived, then lost before it could be born. She'd never forgiven herself for the accident that had taken that precious, fragile life from her. Perhaps more than a lack of love and understanding, it had been the loss of Ty's child that had destroyed any hope for her marriage.

And if the child had lived? she asked herself wearily. What then? Could she have kept it from him? Could she have remained the wife of one man while bearing the child of another? Asher shook her head. No, she would no longer dwell on possibilities. She'd lost Ty, his child, and the support of her own father. There could be no greater punishments to face. She would make her own future.

The touch of a hand on her shoulder had her whirling around. Asher stared up at Ty, her mind a blank, her emotions in turmoil. A hush seemed to spread over the garden, so she could hear the whisper of air over leaves and blossoms. The scent that reached her was sweet and heady—like a first kiss. He said nothing, nor did she until his hand slid down her arm to link with hers.

"Worried about the match?"

Almost afraid he would sense them, Asher struggled to push all thoughts of the past aside. "Concerned," she amended, nearly managing a smile. "Rayski's top seed."

"You've beaten her before."

"And she's beaten me." It didn't occur to her to remove her hand from his or to mask her doubts. Slowly the tension seeped out of her. Through the link of hands Ty felt it. They had stood here before, and the memory was sweet.

"Play her like you played Conway," he advised. "Their styles are basically the same."

With a laugh Asher ran her free hand through her hair. "That's supposed to be a comfort?"

"You're better than she is," he said simply, and earned an astonished stare. Smiling, he brushed his fingers carelessly over her cheek. "More consistent," he explained. "She's faster, but you're stronger. That gives you an advantage on clay even though it isn't your best surface."

At a loss, Asher managed a surprised, "Well."

"You've improved," Ty stated as they began to walk. "Your backhand doesn't have the power it should have, but—"

"It worked pretty well on Conway," Asher interrupted testily.

"Could be better."

"It's perfect," she disagreed, rising to the bait before she caught his grin. Her lips curved before she could stop them. "You always knew how to get a rise out of me. You're playing Kilroy," she went on, "I've never heard of him."

"He's been around only two years. Surprised everyone in Melbourne last season." He slipped an arm around her shoulders in a gesture so familiar, neither of them noticed. "What's that flower?"

Asher glanced down. "Lady's slipper."

"Silly name."

"Cynic."

He shrugged. "I like roses."

"That's because it's the only flower you can identify." Without thinking, she leaned her head on his shoulder. "I remember going in to take a bath one night and finding you'd filled the tub with roses. Dozens of them."

The scent of her hair reminded him of much more. "By the time we got around to clearing them out, it took over an hour."

Her sigh was wistful. "It was wonderful. You could always surprise me by doing something absurd."

"A tub of lady's slippers is absurd," he corrected. "A tub of roses is classy."

Her laughter was quick and appreciative. Her head still rested on his shoulders. "We filled everything in the room that could pass for a vase, including a bottle of ginger ale. Sometimes when I—" She cut herself off, abruptly realizing she would say too much.

"When you what?" Ty demanded as he turned her to face him. When she only shook her head, he tightened his grip. "Would you remember sometimes, in the middle of the night? Would you wake up and hurt because you couldn't forget?"

Truth brought tension to the base of her neck. In defense, Asher pressed her palms against his chest. "Ty, please."

"I did." He gave her a frustrated shake that knocked her head back. "Oh, God, I did. I've never stopped wanting you. Even hating you I wanted you. Do you know what it's like to be awake at three o'clock in the morning and need someone, and know she's in another man's bed."

"No, no, don't." She was clinging to him, her cheek pressed against his, her eyes tightly shut. "Ty, don't."

"Don't what?" he demanded as he drew her head back. "Don't hate you? Don't want you? Hell, I can't do anything else."

His eyes blazed into her, dark with fury, hot with passion. She could feel the race of his heart compete with hers. Abandoning pride, she pressed her lips to his.

At the instant of contact he stood still, neither giving nor taking. On a moan she drew him closer, letting her lips have their way. A shudder coursed through him, an oath ripped out, then he was responding, demanding, exciting. Why had he tried to resist? Nothing was clear to him as her lips raced crazily over his face. Wasn't this what he wanted? To have her again, to prove he could, to purge his system of her once and for all. Motives dimmed in desire. There was only Asher—the sweet taste of her, her scent more heady, more seductive than the garden of flowers. He couldn't breathe and not fill himself on her. So he surrendered to the persuading lips and soft body that had haunted his dreams.

Dragging his lips from hers only a moment, Ty pulled her through the fragile branches of a willow. The sun filtered through the curtain of leaves, giving intermittent light. In the cool dimness his mouth sought hers again and found it yielding. The blood pounded in his veins.

He had to know if her body was the same, unchanged during the years he'd been denied her. As his hand took her breast he groaned. She was small and firm and familiar. Through the material of her jacket he felt the nipple harden in quick response. Impatient, he tugged the zipper down, then dove under her shirt until he found the smooth tender flesh that had always made him feel his hands were too rough. Yet she didn't draw away as his calluses met her. She pressed against him. Her moan was not one of discomfort, but of unmistakable pleasure.

Trembling, her fingers reached for his hair. He could feel the urgency in them just as he could taste it on her heated lips. He broke his kiss only to change angles, then deepened it, allowing his tongue to drink up all the dark flavors of her mouth. Against his palm her heart thudded wildly, but only his fingers moved to arouse her.

Slowly his other hand journeyed to her hip to mold the long, slender bone. He was lost somewhere between yesterday and today. The heavy fragrance of flowers still wet with morning dew was more seductive than perfume. Half dreaming, Ty took his mouth to her throat. He heard her sigh float off on the scented air. Was she dreaming too? Was the past overlapping this moment for her as well as for him? The thoughts drifted into his mind, then out again before they could be answered. Nothing mattered but that he was holding her again.

From far off came a ripple of laughter. Ty brought his mouth back to Asher's. A rapid smattering of French drifted to him. Ty drew her closer until their bodies seemed fused. Footsteps and a giggle. Like a dreamer, he sensed the intrusion and swore against it. For another moment he clung, drawing on her lingering passion.

When he released her, Asher was breathless and swaying. Wordlessly he stared down at her with eyes nearly black with emotion. Her lips were parted, swollen from his, and he gave in to need and kissed her one long last time. Gently now, slowly, to store up every dram of sweetness. This time she trembled, her breath coming harsh and fast like a diver's who breaks surface after a long submersion. Disoriented, she gripped his arms.

How long had they been there? she wondered. It could have been seconds or days. All she was sure of was that the longing had intensified almost beyond control. Her blood was racing in her veins, her heart pounding desperately. She was alive. So alive. And no longer certain which path she would take.

"Tonight," Ty murmured, bringing her palm to his lips.

The vibration shot up her arm and into her core. "Ty…" Asher shook her head as she tried to draw her hand away. His fingers tightened.

"Tonight," he repeated.

"I can't." Seeing the temper shoot into his eyes, Asher covered their joined hands with her free one. "Ty, I'm frightened."

The quiet admission killed his anger. He let out a weary sigh. "Damn you, Asher."

Saying nothing, she wrapped her arms around his waist, pressing her cheek to his chest. Automatically Ty reached to smooth her hair. His eyes closed. "I'm sorry," she whispered. "I was frightened of you once before. It seems to be happening again." And I love you, she told him silently. As much as ever. More, she realized. More, because of the years of famine.

"Asher." He held her away from him. She felt the passion swirling around him. "I won't promise to wait for you to come to me this time. I won't promise to be gentle and patient. Things aren't the same."

She shook her head, but in agreement. "No, things aren't the same. It might be better, much better for both of us if we just stayed away from each other."

Ty laughed shortly. "We won't."

"If we tried," Asher began.

"*I* won't."

She let out a breath of exasperation. "You're pressuring me."

"Damn right." Before she could decide whether to laugh or to scream, she was in his arms again. "Do you think I don't feel pressured too?" he demanded with a sudden intensity that kept Asher from answering. "Every time I look at you I remember the way things were for us and drive myself crazy trying to figure out why you left me. Do you know what that does to me?"

She gripped his upper arms with strong hands. "You have to understand, I won't go back. Whatever happens to us now begins now. No questions, no whys." She saw the anger boiling in his eyes, but kept hers level. "I mean that, Ty. I can't give you explanations. I won't dig up the past."

"You expect me to live with that?"

"I expect nothing," she said quietly. The tone caused him to look deeper for the answers she refused to give. "And I've agreed to nothing. Not yet."

"You ask for too much," he bit off as he released her. "Too damn much."

She wanted to go to him, go back to his arms and beg him to forget the past. Perhaps it was possible to live for the moment if one wanted to badly enough. It might have been pride that stopped her, or the deeply ingrained survival instinct she had developed since that long-ago September afternoon when she had fled from him and the prospect of pain. Asher laced her fingers together and stared down at them. "Yes, I know. I'm sorry, Ty, we'll only hurt each other."

Tense and tormented, he turned back. "I've never wanted to hurt you, Asher. Not even when I thought I did."

The ache spread so quickly, she almost gasped from it. Isn't that what Jess had said that day? *He'd never want to hurt you...never want to hurt you.* Asher could hear the words echoing inside her head. "Neither of us wanted to," she murmured. "Both of us did. Isn't it foolish to do it again?"

"Look at me." The command was quiet and firm. Bracing herself, Asher obeyed. His eyes were locked on hers—those dark, penetrating eyes that conveyed such raw feeling. Gently he touched her cheek. Without hesitation her hand rose to cover his. "Now," he whispered, "ask me again."

A long, shuddering breath escaped. "Oh, Ty, I was so sure I could prevent this. So sure I could resist you this time."

"And now?"

"Now I'm not sure of anything." She shook her head before he could speak again. "Don't ask now. Give us both some time."

He started to protest, then managed to restrain it. He'd waited three years, a bit longer wouldn't matter. "Some time," he agreed, lowering his hand. But as she started to relax, he took her wrist. The grip was neither gentle nor patient. "The next time, Asher, I won't ask."

She nodded, accepting. "Then we understand each other."

His smile was a trifle grim. "That we do. I'll walk you back." He drew her through the curtain of leaves.

CHAPTER 5

Fifth set. Seventh game. At the baseline Ty crouched, ready to spring for Michael's serve. The air was heavy, the sky thick with rain-threatening clouds so that the light was dreary. Ty didn't notice. He didn't notice the stadium full of people, some dangling through the railing, some hanging from the scoreboard. He didn't notice the shouts and whistles that were either for or against him.

Tennis was a game of the individual. That was what had drawn him to it. There was no one to blame for a loss, no one to praise for a win but yourself. It was a game of motion and emotion, both of which he excelled in.

He had looked forward to meeting Michael in the semis. The Australian played a hot, passionate game full of dramatic gestures, furious mutters and pizzazz. There were perhaps five competitors Ty fully respected, Michael being one of them. Wanting to win was only a step below wanting a challenge. A fight. He'd grown up scrapping. Now the racket was merely an extension of his arm. The match was a bout. The bout was one on one. It had never—would never—be only a game.

The Australian was a set up, with his momentum still flowing. Ty's only thought at the moment was to break his serve and even the match. Thus far he had spotted no weak-nesses in his opponent's game. Like a boxer, he watched for the opening.

He heard the sound of the ball hitting the sweet spot of the racket before it rocketed toward him. It landed deep in the corner of the service court, beautifully placed. Ty's mind and body moved as one as he sprang for the return. Defense, offense, strategy all had to be formulated in a fraction of a second. Strength had to be balanced with form. Both men sprinted over the court for the rally, faces glowing with con-centration and sweat. The roar of the crowd rose to meet the distant thunder.

Thus far, the ratio had been nearly ten to one in favor of ground strokes. Ty decided to alter the pace and go with power. Using a vicious left-to-right slice, he shook Michael's balance. Ty blasted away at the attempted passing shot, barely shortening his backswing. Michael couldn't reach the back-hand volley, let alone return it. Love-fifteen.

Shaking the damp hair back from his face, Ty returned to the baseline. A woman in the crowd called out what could have been a congratulations or a proposition. Ty's French wasn't strong enough to decipher the phrase. Michael's serve sent up a puff of smoke. Before his return was over the net, Ty was at mid-court and waiting. A test-ing ground stroke, a sharp return. A tricky topspin, a slice. Michael's decision to try to lob over Ty was a mistake. The smoking smash careened off the court and into the grand-stands. Love-thirty.

Michael walked a complete circle, cursing himself before he took his position again. Casting off impatience, Ty waited. Crouched, swaying side to side, unblinking, he was ready. Both players exploited angles and depths with ground strokes. There was a long, patient rally as each watched for the chance to smash a winner. It might have been pure showmanship if it hadn't been for the sounds of exertion coming from the two players.

A UPI photographer had his motor drive humming as he recorded the game. He framed Ty, arms extended for balance, legs spread for the stretch, face fierce. It crossed his mind as he continued to snap that he wouldn't want to face that American on any playing field.

Gracefully, with an elegance belied by his expression, Ty executed a backhand with a touch of underspin. Michael's return thudded against the net. Love-forty.

Angry and shaken, Michael punched his first serve into the net. Having no choice at game point, he placed his next serve carefully. Ty went straight for the volley and took the net. The exchange was fast and furious, the players moving on instinct, the crowd screaming in a mixture of languages. Ty's wrist was locked. The ball whipped from racket to racket at terrifying speed. There were bare seconds between contact, making both men anticipate flight rather than see it. Changing tactics in the wink of an instant, Ty brought the racket face under at the moment of impact. With a flick of a wrist he dropped a dump shot over the net. Risky, experts would say. Gutsy, fans would claim. Ty would ignore both. Game and set.

"Oh, Mac!" Jess leaned back and expelled a long breath. "I'd nearly forgotten what it was like to watch Ty play."

"You watched him just a few weeks ago," he pointed out, using a damp handkerchief to wipe his neck. The wish for his air-conditioned office flitted only briefly into his mind.

"On television," Jess returned. "That's different. Being here…can't you feel it?"

"I thought it was the humidity."

Laughing, Jess shook her head. "Always down to earth, Mac. That's why I love you."

Her smile seemed to open just for him. It could still make his blood sing. "Then I intend to stay there," he murmured, kissing her knuckles. Feeling her hand tense, he looked up, puzzled. Her eyes were aimed over his shoulder. Curious, he turned, spotting a few tennis faces he recognized. Among them was Asher Wolfe. It was on her that his wife's gaze was locked.

"That's the former Lady Wickerton, isn't it?" he asked casually. "She's stunning."

"Yes." Jess tore her eyes away, but the tension in her fingers remained. "Yes, she is."

"She won her match this morning. We'll have an American going into the women's finals." Jess said nothing as Mac stuffed the handkerchief back into his pocket. "She was away from the game for a while, wasn't she?"

"Yes."

Intrigued by his wife's flat answer, Mac probed. "Didn't she and Ty have something going a few years back?"

"It was nothing." With a nervous swallow Jess prayed she spoke the truth. "Just a passing thing. She's not Ty's type. Asher's very cool, much more suited to Wickerton than to Ty. He was attracted to that for a while, that's all." She moistened her lips. "And it was obvious she wasn't serious about him, otherwise she'd never have married Wickerton so quickly. She was making Ty unhappy, very unhappy."

"I see," Mac murmured after a moment. Jess had spoken too quickly and too defensively. Studying his wife's profile, he wondered. "I suppose Ty's too involved in his career to be serious about a woman?"

"Yes." The look Jess gave him was almost pleading. "Yes, he'd never have let her go if he'd been in love with her. Ty's too possessive."

"And proud," he reminded her quietly. "I don't think he'd run after any woman, no matter how he felt about her."

Feeling her stomach roll, Jess said nothing. She turned to watch her brother take the position for his first serve.

Instead of the hazy afternoon she saw a brilliant morning. Instead of the clay of Roland Garros she saw the newly empty grass courts of Forest Hills. Ty was leaning over the rail, staring out at center court. She had a fanciful thought that he looked like the captain of a ship with his eyes on the open, endless sea. In her world she loved no one more than him, could conceive of loving no one more. He was brother and father and hero. He'd provided her with a home, clothes and an education, asking nothing in return. As a result, she would have given him anything.

Crossing to him, she slipped her arm around him, nestling her head in the crook of his shoulder.

"Thinking about this afternoon?" she murmured. He was slated to face Chuck Prince in the finals of the U.S. Open.

"Hmm?" Distracted, Ty shrugged. "No, not really."

"It must feel odd to compete against your closest friend."

"You must forget you're friends for a couple hours," Ty returned.

He was brooding; she sensed it. And unhappy. There was no one, including her mother, Jess felt more loyalty to. Her grip around him tightened. "Ty, what is it?"

"Just restless."

"Have you fought with Asher?"

Absently he tousled her hair. "No, I haven't fought with Asher."

He lapsed into silence for so long that Jess began to suspect he wasn't telling the entire truth. She was already worried about him and Asher. The relationship had lasted longer than was habitual for Ty. Jess saw Asher's reserve as coldness, her independence as indifference. She didn't hang on Ty as other women did. She didn't listen raptly to every word he spoke. She didn't adore him.

"Do you ever think back, Jess?" he asked suddenly.

"Think back?"

"To when we were kids." His eyes skimmed over the manicured courts, but didn't see them. "That crummy apartment with the paper walls. The DeMarcos next door screaming at each other in the middle of the night. The stairwell always smelled of old garbage and stale sweat."

The tone of his voice disturbed her. Seeking comfort as much as to comfort, she turned her face into his chest. "Not often. I guess I don't remember it as well as you. I hadn't turned fifteen when you got us out."

"I wonder sometimes if you can ever escape that, if you can ever really turn your back on it." His eyes were focused on something Jess couldn't see. She strained to share the vision. "Old garbage and stale sweat," he repeated quietly. "I can't forget that. I asked Asher once what smell she remembered most from her childhood. She said the wisteria that hung over her bedroom window."

"Ty, I don't understand."

He swore softly. "Neither do I."

"You left all that behind," she began.

"I left it," he corrected her. "That doesn't mean I left it behind. We were having dinner last night. Wickerton stopped by the table and started a conversation about French Impressionists. After five minutes I didn't know what the hell they were talking about."

Jess bristled. She knew because Ty had sent her to college. She knew because he had provided the opportunity. "You should have told him to get lost."

With a laugh Ty kissed her cheek. "That was my first thought." Abruptly he sobered. "Then I watched them. They understand each other, speak the same language. It made me realize there are some fences you just can't climb."

"You could if you wanted to."

"Maybe. I don't." He let out a long breath. "I don't really give a damn about French Impressionists. I don't give a damn about the mutual friends they have that are distant cousins of the Queen of England, or who won at Ascot last month." Storm warnings were in his eyes, but he shrugged. "Even if I did, I wouldn't fit into that kind of life because I'd always remember the garbage and sweat."

"Asher has no business encouraging that man," Jess stated heatedly. "He's been following her around since Paris."

Ty gave a grim laugh. "She doesn't encourage or discourage. Drawing room conversation," he murmured. "Ingrained manners. She's different from us, Jess, I've known that all along."

"If *she'd* tell him to get lost—"

"She couldn't tell anyone to get lost any more than she could sprout wings and fly."

"She's cold."

"She's different," Ty returned immediately but without heart. He cupped his sister's chin in his hand. "You and me, we're the same. Everything's up front. If we want to shout, we shout. If we want to throw something, we throw it. Some people can't."

"Then they're stupid."

This time his laugh was warm and genuine. "I love you, Jess."

Throwing her arms around him, she hugged him fiercely. "I can't bear to see you unhappy. Why do you let her do this to you?"

Frowning, Ty stroked her hair. "I've been trying to figure that out. Maybe…maybe I just need a shove in the right direction."

Jess held him tighter, searching her mind for the answer.

Seventh set. Tenth game. The crowd was as vocal, as enthusiastic and as hungry as it had been an hour before. Leaning forward in his seat, his eyes glued to the ball, Chuck sat between Asher and Madge.

"You've got something riding on this one, don't you, cowboy?" Madge commented dryly though her own heart was pumping. Chuck would face the winner in the finals.

"It's the best match I've seen in two years." His own face was damp, his own muscles tense. The ball traveled at such speeds, it was often only a white blur.

Asher spoke to neither of them. Her objectivity had been long since destroyed. Ty enthralled her. Both men possessed the raw athletic ability competitors admired and envied. Both were draining the other's resources without mercy. But it was Ty, always Ty, who ripped the emotion from her.

She could admire Michael, admit his brilliance, but he didn't cause that slow, churning ache in her stomach. Had she not once been Ty's lover, had she not even known him, would she still be so drawn? Controlled rage. How was it a woman raised in such an ordered, sheltered existence would be pulled irresistibly to a man with such turbulent passion? Opposites attract? she wondered. No, that was much too simple.

Sitting in the crowded stadium, Asher felt the thrill of desire as clearly as though she had been naked in his arms. She felt no shame. It was natural. She felt no fear. It was inevitable. Years made up of long, unending days vanished. What a waste of time, she thought suddenly. No, a loss, she corrected herself. A loss of time—nothing's ever wasted. *Tonight*. The decision came to her as effortlessly as it had the first time. Tonight they would be together. And if it was only once— if once was all he wanted—it would have to be enough. The long wait was over. She laughed out loud in relief and joy. Chuck sent her an odd look.

"He's going to win," Asher said on a second laugh. Leaning on the rail, she rested her chin on her folded hands. "Oh, yes, he's going to win."

There was a dull ache in his racket arm that Ty ignored. The muscles in his legs promised to cramp the moment he stopped moving. He wouldn't give in to them any more than he would give in to the man across the net. One thing hadn't changed in twenty years. He still hated to lose.

A point away from the match, he played no less tigerishly than he had in the first game. The rallies had been long and punishing. The ball whistled. Sweat dripped. For the last twenty minutes Ty had forsaken artistry for cunning. It was working.

Power for power, they were in a dead heat, so that Ty chose to outmaneuver the Australian. He worked him over the court, pacing him, some might say stalking him. The game went to deuce three times while the crowd grew frantic. An ace gave him advantage—a screeching bullet that brought Ty the final impetus he needed. Then Ty played him hot-blood-edly. The men drove from side to side, their faces masks of effort and fury. The shot came that he'd been waiting for. Michael's awesome backhand drove crosscourt to his south-paw forehand. The ball came to Ty at waist level. Michael didn't even have to see the return to know it was over.

Game, set and match.

The heat hit him then, and the fatigue. It took an effort not to stagger. Simply to have fallen to his knees would have been a relief. He walked to the net.

Michael took his hand, then draped his free arm around Ty's shoulder. "Damn you, Starbuck," he managed breath-lessly. "You nearly killed me."

Ty laughed, using his opponent for balance a moment. "You too."

"I need a bloody drink." Michael straightened, giving Ty a glazed grin. "Let's go get drunk."

"You're on."

Turning, they separated, victor and vanquished, to face the press, the showers and the massage tables. Ty grabbed the towel someone handed him, nodding at the questions and congratulations being hurled at him. Behind the cloth he could hear the click and whir of cameras. He was too weary to curse them. Someone was gathering his rackets. He could hear the clatter of wood on wood. The strength that had flowed freely through him only moments before drained. Exhausted, he let the drenched towel fall. His eyes met Asher's.

So blue, he thought. Her eyes are so blue. And cool, and deep. He could drown in them blissfully. The unbearable heat vanished, as though someone had opened a window to a fresh spring breeze.

"Congratulations." When she smiled, his fatigue slid away. Strangely it wasn't desire that replaced it, but comfort, sweet simple comfort.

"Thanks." He took the racket bag from her. Their hands barely brushed.

"I suppose the press is waiting for you inside."

The short retort Ty made was both agreement and opinion. On a low laugh she stepped closer.

"Can I buy you dinner?"

The quirk of his brow was the only indication of surprise. "Sure."

"I'll meet you at seven in the lobby of the hotel."

"All right."

"Starbuck, what do you feel was the turning point of the match?"

"What strategy will you use playing Prince in the finals?"

Ty didn't answer the reporters, didn't even hear them as he watched Asher weave her way through the crowd. From overhead Jess watched with a small, fluttering sensation of déjà vu.

Ty got under the stream of the shower fully dressed. He let the cool water sluice over him while he stripped. A reporter from *World of Sports* leaned against a tiled wall, scribbling notes and tossing questions. Naked, with his clothes in a soggy heap at his feet, Ty answered. Always, he handled the press naturally because he didn't give a damn what they printed. He knew his mother kept a scrapbook, but he never read the articles or interviews. Lathering the soap over his face with both hands, he washed the sticky sweat away. Someone passed him a plastic jug of fruit juice. With the water streaming over him, he guzzled it down, replacing lost fluid. The weakness was seeping back, and with it the pain. He made his way to the massage table by instinct, then collapsed onto it.

Strong fingers began to work on him. Questions still hammered in his ear, but now he ignored them. Ty simply closed his eyes and shut them out. A line of pain ran up his calf as the muscles were kneaded. He winced and held on, knowing relief would follow. For ten agonizing minutes he lay still while his body was rubbed and pounded. He began to drift. Like a mother's memory of the pain of childbirth, his memory of the pain began to dim. He could remember winning. And he could remember dark blue eyes. With those two visions tangling in his mind, he slept.

The floor of the lobby was marble. White marble veined with pink. Madge had commented that it would be the devil to keep clean. Her husband had dryly commented that she wouldn't know one end of the mop from the other. Asher sat, listening to their comfortable banter while she told herself she wasn't nervous. It was six-fifty.

She'd dressed carefully, choosing a simple crêpe de Chine as pale as the inside of a peach. Her hair fluffed back from her face, exposing the tiny pearl and coral drops at her ears. Her ringless fingers were interlaced.

"Where are you eating?"

Asher brought her attention back to Madge. "A little place on the Left Bank." There was an enthusiastic violinist, she remembered. Ty had once passed him twenty American dollars and cheerfully told him to get lost.

At the bellow of thunder Madge glanced toward the lobby doors. "You're going to play hell getting a cab tonight." She leaned back. "Have you seen Ty since the match?"

"No."

"Chuck said both he and Michael were sleeping on the tables like babies." A chuckle escaped as she crossed strong, short legs. "Some industrious stringer for a French paper got a couple of classic shots."

"Athletes in repose," her husband mused.

"It kind of blows the tough-guy image."

Asher smiled, thinking how young and vulnerable Ty looked in sleep. When the lids closed over those dramatic eyes, he reminded her of an exhausted little boy. It was the only time the frenetic energy stilled. Something stirred in her. If the child had lived… Hurriedly she censored the thought.

"Hey, isn't that Ty's sister?"

Asher turned her head to see Jess and Mac crossing the lobby. "Yes." Their eyes met, leaving no choice. Gripping her husband's hand, Jess walked across the white marble.

"Hello, Asher."

"Jess."

A quick moistening of lips betrayed nerves. "I don't think you know my husband. Mackenzie Derick, Lady Wickerton."

"Asher Wolfe," she replied smoothly, taking Mac's hand. "Are you related to Martin?"

"My uncle," Mac informed her. "Do you know him?"

The smile brought warmth to her eyes. "Very well." She made the rest of the introductions with a natural poise Mac approved of. Cool, yes, he mused, remembering his wife's description. But with an underlying vibrancy perhaps a man would discern more quickly than another woman. He began to wonder if Jess's opinion of Ty's feelings was accurate.

"Are you a tennis fan, Mr. Derick?" Asher asked him.

"Mac," he supplied. "Only by marriage. And no, I don't play, much to Uncle Martin's disgust."

Asher laughed, appreciating the humor in his eyes. A strong man, she thought instantly. His own man. He wouldn't take second place to Ty in his wife's life. "Martin should be satisfied having cultivated one champion." Her eyes drifted to Jess, who was sitting straight and tense beside Madge. "Is your mother well?"

"Yes, yes, Mom's fine." Though she met the cool, clear gaze, her fingers began to pleat the material of her skirt. "She's at home with Pete."

"Pete?"

"Our son."

Asher's throat constricted. Mac noticed with some surprise that her knuckles whitened briefly on the arm of her chair. "I didn't know you'd had a baby. Ada must be thrilled to have a grandchild." The pressure on her heart was unbearable. Her smile was casual. "How old is he?" she made herself ask.

"Fourteen months." As the tension built in one woman, it flowed out of the other. Jess was already reaching into her purse for her wallet. "I swear he never walked, he started out running. Mom says he's like Ty. He has his coloring too." She was offering a picture. Asher had no choice but to accept it.

There was some of his father in him—the shape of the face. But the Starbuck genes were strong. The baby's hair was dark and thick, like his mother's. Like Ty's. The eyes were large and gray. Asher wondered if she could actually feel the air of perpetual motion around the child, or if she imagined it. Another baby would have had dark hair and gray eyes. Hadn't she pictured the face countless times?

"He's beautiful," she heard herself say in a calm voice. "You must be very proud of him." When she handed the snapshot back her hands were perfectly steady.

"Jess thinks he should wait until he's twelve before he runs for president."

Asher smiled, but this time Mac didn't find the reflected warmth in her eyes. "Has Ty bought him a racket yet?"

"You know him very well," Mac observed.

"Yes." She looked back at Jess steadily. "Tennis and his family come first, always."

"I hate to admit it," Madge put in with a sigh, "but I can remember a dozen years ago when this one was a skinny teenager, chewing her fingernails at every one of Ty's matches. Now you're a mother."

Jess grinned, holding out her hands for inspection. "And I still bite my nails at Ty's matches."

It was Asher who saw him first. But then, her senses were tuned for him. Ty stepped off the elevator dressed in slim black slacks and a smoke-gray shirt. He wouldn't have chosen the shirt because it matched his eyes so perfectly. Asher knew he wore it because it would have been the first thing his hand had grabbed from the closet. He wore clothes with the casual style of one who gave no thought to them and still looked marvelous. A disciplined body and trained grace made it inevitable. His hair had been combed, but defied order. He paused briefly, even in stillness communicating motion. Asher's heartbeat was a dull, quick thud.

"Oh, there's Ty!" Jess sprang up, hurrying across the lobby to meet him. "I didn't get to congratulate you. You were absolutely wonderful."

Though his arm slipped around her, Jess saw that his eyes had drifted over her head. Without turning, she knew who they focused on.

Asher didn't see, nor did she speak.

"Well, Starbuck, you earned your pay today," Madge commented. "The Dean and I are going to the Lido to hold Michael's hand."

"Tell him I lost three pounds on the court today." He spoke to her, lightly enough, but his eyes never left Asher's.

"I don't think that's going to make him feel a hell of a lot better," she returned, giving her husband a nudge as she rose. "Well, we're off to fight for a taxi. Anyone going our way?"

"As a matter of fact," Mac began, picking up the hint easily, "Jess and I were on our way out too."

"Want a lift, Ty?" Madge's husband gave her an offended look as she ground her heel into his foot. But he shut his mouth firmly when Madge shot him a deadly glance.

Even to a man who rarely comprehended subtleties, it became obvious there were things being said without words. The little group had simply ceased to exist for Ty and Asher. After a hard look at the silent couple The Dean straightened his glasses and grinned at his wife.

"I guess not, huh?"

"You're so quick, babe." Madge began shepherding the rest toward the doors. "Anyone know some French obscenities? It's the best way to get a cab in the rain."

Asher rose slowly. From behind her she could hear the ding of a bell on the desk and the whoosh of the storm as the doors were opened then quickly closed. For a moment Ty thought she looked like something that should be enclosed in glass. Not to be touched, not to be soiled. She reached out her hand.

When he took it, it was warm. Flesh and blood.

In unspoken agreement they turned away from the doors and walked to the elevator.

CHAPTER 6

They didn't speak, but then they didn't need to. With one hand still holding hers, Ty pushed the button for his floor. The elevator began its silent rise. Once, the hand in his trembled lightly. He found it unbearably exciting. The numbers above their heads flashed ponderously until at last the car stopped. When the doors slid open they stepped into the carpeted hall together.

Asher heard the key jingle against loose change as Ty reached into his pocket. She heard the click of the lock before he released her hand. The choice was still hers. She stepped out of the light into the dimness of the room.

It smelled of him. That was her first thought. The air carried Ty's lingering fragrance. Something sharp, something vital. Something she had never forgotten. All at once her nerves began to jump. The poise that had carried her this far fell away. Searching for something to say, she wandered the room. It was untidy, with a shirt thrown here, shoes tossed there. She knew if she opened the closet, she would find a neat stack of rackets, the only semblance of order. Instead, she moved to the window. Rain ran like tears down the glass.

"It's going to storm all night."

As if to accent her words, lightning split the sky. Asher

counted to five, then heard the thunder answer. Hundreds of lights spread through the darkness. The city was there, crowded, moving—distant. Staring through the wet glass, she waited for Ty to speak.

Silence. The patter of rain on the window. The distant hum of traffic. Another moan of thunder. Unable to bear it, Asher turned.

He was watching her. The small bedside lamp threw both light and shadow into the room. His stance was neither relaxed nor threatening, and she understood. He had given her a choice before she entered. Now he wouldn't let her go. A bridge had been burned. Asher felt nothing but relief that the decision was already made. But her fingers were numb as she reached to loosen the thin belt at her waist.

Crossing to her, Ty laid his hands over hers, stopping the movement. Asher stared up at him, unsure, as nervous as the first time. Without speaking he took her face in his hands to study her. He wanted to remember her this way—in shadowed light with the fury of a storm at her back. Her eyes were dark with traces of fear, traces of desire. In a gesture of surrender her arms had dropped to her sides. But he didn't want surrender—perhaps she had forgotten.

As he lowered his head Ty watched her lids shut, her lips part in anticipation. Gently he kissed her temple, then the other, then the delicate curve of an eyebrow. Without haste, his eyes closed. He reacquainted himself with her face through taste and touch. Her lips beckoned, but he nibbled along the line of her jaw, on the hollow of her cheek.

His thumb brushed her bottom lip as he whispered kisses over her face. He remembered every curve. Her breath shuddered out as he kissed the corners of her mouth. He brushed his over it, retreating when Asher sought more pressure. There was only the fleeting promise of more. With a moan she gripped his forearms. He'd waited for the strength. He'd waited for the demands. Again he touched his lips to hers, allowing his tongue a brief taste. Now her arms wrapped possessively around him. Now passion exploded, mouth against mouth. Lightning flashed, illuminating them as one form in the ageless wonder of lovers.

"Undress me," she whispered breathlessly, hardly able to speak as her lips fused again and again with his. "I want you to undress me."

In answer, he lowered the zipper slowly, allowing his fingers to trail along her bare skin. He found more silk, something thin and fragile. The dress slithered down her body to lie at her feet. Growing impatient, Asher worked her hands between them to deal with the buttons of his shirt while her mouth continued to cling to his. She felt the hard muscle, the line of ribs, the mat of hair. A moan wrenched from her out of deep, desperate need.

The thigh-length chemise was too much of a barrier. Longing for the intimacy of flesh against flesh, Asher reached to draw down the strap. Again Ty stopped her.

"Don't rush," he murmured, then tore at her control with a deep, lingering kiss. The pressure was hard and demanding, the lips soft and heated. "Come to bed."

In a haze she let him lead her, felt the mattress give under her weight, then his. Anticipation shivered along her skin. "The light," she whispered.

As he circled her throat with his hand, Ty's eyes met hers. "I need to see you." Thunder exploded as his mouth crushed down on hers.

When she would have hurried, he set the pace. Languorous, sleepy, enervating. It seemed her lips alone would pleasure him enough for a lifetime. She was so soft, so moist. Far from pliant, Asher moved against him, inviting, insisting. Her urgency excited him, but Ty chose to savor. Over the silk his hands roamed to trace her shape from thigh to breast. The peaks strained against the sheer material.

He took his mouth to her shoulder, catching the narrow strap of the silk with his teeth. Inch by inch he lowered it until her flesh was exposed to him. She was firm and creamy-white in contrast to the tan of her arms and shoulders.

"So lovely," he whispered while his fingertip brought down the second strap.

When she was naked to the waist, his mouth ranged down slowly, though with her hands in his hair she urged him down. With lips parted, Ty sought the peak of her breast. Asher arched, pressing him down. She wanted him to be greedy, wanted to feel the rough scrape of his tongue. When she did she could no longer be still. Her body vibrated with the beat of a hundred tiny pulses. Desire, raw and primitive, tore through her with the power to obliterate all but one thought. She was woman; he was man. Seeking pleasure, Asher moved under him, letting her hands roam.

He abandoned gentleness because she wanted none. It had always driven him wild when her passion was unleashed. She had no inhibitions, no shame. When they came together like this she was all fire, and as dangerous as the lightning in the night sky. Ty wasn't even aware of his control slipping away. Hard-palmed hands ran bruisingly over tender skin. Short, manicured nails dug into strong shoulders.

His breathing was ragged when he tore the garment from her. She gave him no time to view her nakedness. Her fingers were busy, struggling to remove the last barrier of his clothing. Their frantic movements took them over the bed, tangling in the sheets. Her skin was damp and trembling, but her hands were so strong, and so certain. There could be no more waiting.

A pain stabbed into him as he entered her. It was sharp, then sweet. He thought he heard her cry out as she had that first night when he had taken her innocence. Then she was wrapped around him—legs, arms. Her mouth fastened on his. The storm crashed directly overhead. They rose with it.

His hand lay lightly on her breast. Asher sighed. Had she ever known such pure contentment? she wondered. No, not even when they had been together before. Then she hadn't known what it would be like to do without him. She shuddered, then moved closer.

"Cold?" Ty drew her to him until her head rested on the curve of his shoulder.

"A little. Where's my chemise?"

"Devoured."

She laughed, flinging her arms around him as though she would never let go. Free, she thought. How wonderful to be free—to love, to laugh. Supporting herself on his chest, she stared down into his face. For once his eyes were calm. A faint smile curved his lips. Beneath her his breathing was even and slow, to match hers. To match, her mind repeated. They had always been like two halves of the same whole.

"Oh, God, I missed you, Ty." On those words she buried her face against his throat. Empty, empty, she thought. It seemed like a lifetime of emptiness had been wiped away with an hour of fulfillment.

"Asher—"

"No, no questions. No questions." Wildly she rained kisses over his face. "Just feel, just be with me. I need to laugh tonight, the way we used to."

He stopped her hurried movements by taking her head in his hands. There was a plea in her eyes and a light trace of desperation. No, he didn't want to see that now. Pushing away the questions that drummed in his head, he smiled at her.

"I thought you were going to buy me dinner."

Relief washed over her before she grinned. "I have no idea what you're talking about."

"You asked me for a date."

Tossing her head back, she arched an elegant brow. "*I* asked you? You've been out in the heat too long, Starbuck."

"Dinner," he repeated, rolling her over until he loomed above her.

"As far as I can tell, you've already eaten a sixty-dollar silk chemise. Are you still hungry?"

For an answer, he lowered his mouth to her neck and bit, none too gently. Laughing, she tried to twist away. "Food," he muttered. "I have to eat."

Remembering a weakness, she found the spot on his ribs and squeezed. His body jerked, giving her the opportunity to slither away. She was giggling like a girl when he grabbed her and pulled her back. "How many people know the indomitable Starbuck is ticklish?" she demanded when he pinned her arms over her head. "What would the press pay to find out?"

"About the same as they'd pay to find out elegant Asher Wolfe has a heart-shaped birthmark on her very attractive bottom."

Asher considered this a moment. "Even," she decided. Her smile slanted seductively. "Do you really want to go out to eat?"

Desire fluttered lightly in the pit of his stomach as he looked down at her. The light angled across her face, accenting the smooth, glowing skin and darkened eyes. The thunder was a distant rumble now, but he felt it vibrate in his head.

"There's always room service," he murmured, tasting her lips. He kept her arms pinned as he dropped light, teasing kisses over her face. Nestling in the vulnerable curve of her neck, he used his tongue to stir and arouse.

"Ty," she moaned, unable to struggle against the captivity. "Make love to me."

His chuckle was low and he was pleased. "Oh, I am. This time," he whispered into her ear, "we won't hurry. Hours, love." His tongue darted to her ear, making her squirm in agonized delight. "Hours and hours." Then he shifted, bringing her close to his side. Cradling her, he felt her heart pounding against him. When he reached for the phone, Asher glanced up, puzzled. "Food," he reminded her.

She gave a weak laugh. "I should have remembered your stomach comes first."

His hand grazed over her breast. "Not necessarily." Her nipple was already taut. He flicked his thumb over it lazily.

"Ty—" With a kiss he silenced her.

"Champagne," he said into the phone while driving Asher mad with careless strokes and fondling. "Dom Pérignon. Caviar," he went on, sending her a questioning look that she was powerless to answer. "Beluga." He gave her a light kiss, running his hand down to the flat of her stomach. She quivered, turning into him. Legs tangled as he brushed his lips over her shoulder. "Cold shrimp." He bit her tender bottom lip. "Mmm, that'll do. Yes, for two." As he dropped the phone back on its cradle, Asher found his mouth in a desperate, yearning kiss. "Food excites you?" he mumbled against the hungry lips. Struggling not to take her instantly, he ran his hand to her hip, kneading warm flesh.

"I want you." Her voice was low and throaty, her hands questing. "I want you now."

"Shh." Slow, patient, his stroking aroused rather than subdued. "Relax. There's time. I want to see you again." He drew away from her. "Really see you."

She was burning for him. Now she lay naked and vulnerable under his gaze. As she watched, his eyes darkened, grew stormy. Her breathing quickened. When she reached out he took her hand, burying his lips in the palm.

"You're more beautiful than ever," he said huskily. "It

shouldn't be possible. I've looked at you so many times and have been afraid to touch."

"No." Asher pulled him to her until they were heart to heart. "I'm never more alive than when you touch me." With a sigh Ty nestled down until his head rested between her breasts. Asher combed her fingers through his hair as contentment layered over desire. "Today, when I watched you playing Michael, I wanted you. Sitting there, surrounded by thousands of people in the middle of the afternoon, all I could think about was being with you like this." She gave a gurgle of laughter. "Wicked thoughts, such wonderfully wicked thoughts."

"So your invitation to dinner carried an ulterior motive."

"In your weakened condition I knew you'd be a pushover, though I had thought I'd have to take you out and ply you with food and wine first."

"And if I'd refused?"

"I'd have come up with something else."

Grinning, he lifted his head. "What?"

Asher shrugged. "I could have come up here and seduced you before you'd gotten your strength back."

"Hmm...I almost wish I'd said no."

"Too late. I have you now."

"I could get stubborn."

Slowly she smiled. "I know your weaknesses," she whispered, running a fingertip up the nape of his neck. His shudder was quick and uncontrollable. Leaning up, she took his face in her hands. Lazily she rubbed her lips over his, then deepened the touch into a kiss—a long, draining taste that left him weak. Her tongue glided over his, then retreated.

"Asher." On an oath he crushed her beneath him, savaging her mouth with a need that had risen so quickly, it left him dazed. He didn't hear the discreet knock on the door, nor did he understand her murmurs.

"The door," she managed. "Ty, it's room service."

"What?"

"The door."

Laying his forehead on hers, he struggled to recapture his control. "They're awful damn quick," he muttered. He found he was trembling. How could he have forgotten that she could make him tremble? After letting out a long breath, he rose. Asher pulled the sheets up to her chin and watched him cross to the closet.

A beautiful body, she thought, both proud and admiring. Long and lean, with a network of muscle. She looked her fill as he rummaged through his closet for a robe. Strong shoulders, trim waist, narrow hips and long legs. An athlete's body, or a dancer's. He was made to compete.

He shrugged into the robe, belting it carelessly. Grinning, he turned to her. Asher's heart lodged in her throat. "Ty, you're so beautiful."

His eyes widened in astonishment. Torn between amusement and masculine discomfort, he headed for the door. "Good God," he said, making Asher smother a giggle. She brought her knees up to her chest as he signed the check at the door. In some ways, she mused, he was a little boy. To his way of thinking, the word *beautiful* applied only to a woman—or to an ace. He'd be more insulted than complimented having it applied to himself. Yet she saw him that way—not only physically. He was a man capable of lovely gestures, a man unashamed of his deep love for his mother, unafraid to show tenderness. He had no cruelty in him, though on the court he was unmerciful. His temper was explosive, but he was incapable of holding a grudge. Asher realized that it was his basic capacity for feeling that she had missed most of all. And still he had never, in all their closeness, in all the months of intimacy, told her that he loved her. If he had once said the words, she would never have left him.

"Where have you gone?"

Asher turned her head to see him standing beside a tray, a bottle of champagne in his hands. Quickly she shook her head and smiled again. "Nowhere." She cocked her head at the bottle. "All that just for us?"

He walked to the bed and sat on the edge. "Did you want some too?" The cork came off with a resounding pop as she cuffed his shoulder. With an easy stretch he rolled the tray toward them. "Here, hold the glasses." Without ceremony he poured champagne until it nearly ran over the rims.

"Ty, it'll spill on the bed."

"Better be careful then," he advised as he set the bottle back in the ice. He grinned as she sat cross-legged, balancing two glasses in her hands. The sheet was held in place over her breasts by arms pressed tightly to her sides.

She returned the grin with a glance of exasperation. "Aren't you going to take one?"

"Oh, I don't know." Hooking a finger under the sheet, he nudged it downward, exposing creamy flesh.

"Ty, cut it out, I'll spill it!"

"Better not, we have to sleep here." He urged the sheet a trifle lower. Frustrated, Asher looked from glass to glass. Wine swayed dangerously.

"This is a dirty trick, Starbuck."

"Yeah, I like it."

Asher narrowed her eyes. "I'm going to pour both glasses into your lap."

"Terrible waste," he decided, kissing her. "It's good stuff. I always found it strange," he began, lazily kissing her face as he spoke, "that I was bred for beer and you were bred for champagne, but you haven't any head for it."

"I have a perfectly good head for champagne."

Chuckling, he brushed his lips over her throat. "I remember one very memorable night when we shared a bottle. Three glasses make you crazy. I like you crazy."

"That's absurd." The lift of brow challenged him. Without hesitation Asher brought a glass to her lips, losing the sheet as she drank it. Ty watched the linen pool into her lap before she drained the last drop. "That's one," Asher announced, lifting the second glass. Ty plucked it from her fingers.

"Let's spread it out a little," he advised, amused. He drank, more conservatively, then reached for the tray of caviar. "You like this stuff."

"Mmm." Suddenly hungry, Asher spread a generous amount on a toast point. Ty settled down to the bowl of cold shrimp and spicy sauce. "Here, it's good." Though he allowed her to feed him a bite, he wrinkled his nose.

"Overrated," he stated. "This is better." He popped a shrimp into Asher's mouth.

"'S wonderful," she agreed with a full mouth, then chose another. "I didn't know I was so hungry."

Ty filled her glass again. Could anyone else imagine her, he wondered, sitting naked in bed, licking sauce from her finger? Did anyone else know how totally open she could be? She was talking now, in fits and starts as she ate, replaying her match. Ty let her ramble, pleased just to hear her voice, to see her animation. She was satisfied with her serve, worried about her backhand volley.

Publicly she chose her words with care, and made certain there were few of them. If a reporter could see her now, Ty mused, he'd wear a pencil down to the nub. She was full of joy and doubt, fear and self-congratulation. Words tumbled out without discretion. Her face was animated, her hands gestured. By the time she had slowed down, her second glass was empty. Perhaps she was completely happy, because she wasn't even aware of the sensation. She was simply at ease, completely herself. Comfortably full, she toyed with the last of the caviar.

"Are you worried about playing Chuck in the finals?"

Ty bit into a shrimp. "Why?"

"He was always good," Asher began, frowning a bit. "But he's developed over the past few years."

Grinning, Ty tilted more wine into her glass. "Don't you think I can beat him?"

She sent him a long, considering look. "You were always good too."

"Thanks." After setting the caviar on the tray, he stretched lengthwise on the bed.

"Chuck plays a bit like my father did," Asher mused. "Very clean, very precise. His talent's polished rather than raw."

"Like mine."

"Yes. That raw athletic ability is something every competitor envies. My father used to say that you had more natural talent than any player he'd seen in his career." Over the rim of her glass she smiled down at him. "Yet he always wanted to smooth out your form. Then there were your...antics on the court."

Ty laughed, kissing her knee through the sheet. "It used to drive him crazy."

"I imagine he'd be more pleased if he saw you play now."

"And you?" Ty countered. "How would he feel if he saw you play now?"

Asher shifted her eyes from his to stare into her glass. "He won't."

"Why?"

As if to erase the question, she lifted her hand. "Ty, please."

"Asher," he said quietly, grasping her fingers. "You're hurting."

If she could have held it back, she would have. But the words tumbled out. "I let him down. He won't forgive me."

"He's your father."

"And he was my coach."

Unable to comprehend, Ty shook his head. "What difference does that make?"

"All the difference." The pain slipped out. As if to numb it, she swallowed more wine. "Please, not tonight. I don't want anything to spoil tonight."

Her fingers had tightened on his. One by one Ty kissed them until he felt the tension relax. "Nothing could." Over their joined hands, dark, intense eyes met hers. Spontaneously her pulse began to race. "I never got you completely out of my mind," he confessed. "Too many things reminded me—a phrase, a song. Silence. There were times alone at night I would have sworn I heard you breathing in the quiet beside me."

The words moved her...hurt her. "Ty, those were yesterdays. We can start now."

"Now," he agreed. "But we'll have to deal with yesterday sooner or later."

Though she opened her mouth to disagree, she knew. "Later then. Right now I don't want to think about anything but being with you."

He grinned, brushing a stray curl from her cheek. "It's difficult to argue with that."

"Don't get cocky," she told him, then tossed off the rest of her champagne. "That was three," Asher said haughtily. "And I'm not the least affected."

Ty had no trouble recognizing the signs—the flushed cheeks, the glowing eyes and misty smile. Whatever she might say, he knew the champagne was swimming in her head. And when they loved again, she would be soft and strong and passionate. He found himself wanting to simply look at her for a few minutes more. Once they touched, the fire would take them.

"Want another?" he offered.

"Sure."

Wisely he filled her glass only halfway before he replaced the bottle. "I caught your interview today," Ty commented. "It was on while I was changing."

"Oh?" Asher shifted to lie on her stomach, propping herself on her elbows. "How'd I do?"

"Hard to say. It was all in French."

She laughed, adjusting her position so that she could take another sip. "I'd forgotten."

"How about a translation?"

"He asked things like—Mademoiselle Wolfe, do you find any changes in your style after your temporary retirement? And I said something like I feel I've tightened my serve." She chuckled into her wine. "I didn't mention that my muscles beg for me to give them a break after two sets. He asked how I felt about playing the *young* Miss Kingston in the finals and I refrained from punching him in the mouth."

"That was diplomatic," Ty answered, slipping the glass from her fingers.

"I'm a hell of a diplomat," Asher agreed. Rolling over on her back, she looked up at him. He lounged just behind her so that she had to tilt her head at an odd angle to make eye contact. "You stole my glass."

"Yes, I did." After setting it on the tray, Ty gave the wheeled table a slight shove.

"Did we finish dinner?" Reaching up and back, she locked her arms around his neck.

"We've definitely finished dinner." He allowed her to urge him down until his mouth hovered above hers.

"Got any suggestions about what we should do now?" She liked the strangeness of having his face upside down over hers. Playfully she nipped at his lip.

"No. Do you?"

"Got a deck of cards?"

"Uh-uh."

"Then I guess we'll have to make love." She gave a rich, low laugh before she kissed him again. "All night—just to pass the time."

"It's something to do. Rainy nights are so boring."

Eyes dancing, she nodded. "Mmm, yes. Let's make the best of it."

Her lips were curved in a smile as his met them, but they parted eagerly. She found it strangely seductive to have his tongue meet hers this way. On a gurgle of laughter, she closed her teeth gently, capturing him. In response, he trailed his fingers over her breast until her moan freed him.

"I get dizzy kissing you upside down," Asher murmured.

"I like you dizzy." Leaning forward, he trailed moist kisses over her throat. The tip of his tongue picked up her flavor, then lingered over it. He could feel pulse beats both with his hand and his lips. Finding the curve of his neck vulnerable, Asher began to give him the same pleasure he was bringing her.

"I want to touch you," she complained. "I can't touch you this way."

But he continued to explore from where he was, enjoying the freedom his hands had over her body. The scent of the rich sauce still lingering in the air, and the zing of champagne clung to two tongues as they joined. The mattress groaned quietly as she shifted. Then she was on her knees, pressed body to body. In a quick move she had stripped the robe from him so he was as naked as she. With a half laugh, half sigh, she ran her palms up his strong back.

Entwined, enchanted, neither noticed that the rain had ceased. Inside the quiet room, pleasure built. Strong thigh pressed against strong thigh, hungry lips sought hungry lips. Their passion was equal, their needs the same. Together, they lay down.

Soft sighs became moans. Before long, gentle caresses became demanding. Both seemed desperate to touch and be touched, to have their own weaknesses exploited. With instinctive understanding they held back the final gift. The inner fire built, dampening their flesh, but still they lingered over each other. There was so much to make up for, so much time to recapture. Though passion was flaring, this thought hovered in the back of both their minds. Tonight was a fresh beginning. They wanted all of it.

Asher thought her lungs would burst. The combination of wine and passion buzzed in her head. A laugh, smoky with desire, floated from her as he gasped her name. She wanted to tempt him, torment him, give to him. His stomach was hard and flat with muscle, yet the touch of her fingertip could make it quiver. Asher had forgotten this sense of power and exulted in it. Her small hands could make him weak. Her shapely, serious mouth could drive him wild.

The power shifted so abruptly, she was helpless. He found her greatest vulnerability and used his tongue to destroy her last vestige of control. Half wild, she called for him, struggling to have more, desperate to have all. Arching, she pressed him closer, cresting on a wave of delight that had no chance to recede. She thrashed as if in protest, yet arched again in invitation. As she built toward a higher peak, Ty slid up her body. Greedy, she drew him inside of her, hearing his gasp for breath before there was only feeling.

Later, they still clung together, damp, spent, fulfilled. He shifted only to turn out the light. In the midnight darkness they molded to each other, drifting toward sleep.

"You'll move in with me."

The murmur was a statement rather than a question. Asher opened her eyes before she answered. She could just see the outline of his face. "Yes, if you want me."

"I never stopped wanting you."

Without the light he didn't see the flicker of doubt in her eyes before he slept.

CHAPTER 7

She was afraid of London. Lady Wickerton had lived there—hostessing parties in the elegant three-story house in Grosvenor Square, attending the ballet at the Royal Opera House, the theater in Drury Lane, shopping in the West End. Lady Wickerton had played bridge with members of Parliament and had sipped tea at Buckingham Palace. Lady Wickerton had been a quiet, dutiful wife, a woman of intelligence, breeding and control. She had nearly suffocated in London.

Perhaps if Ty hadn't come between Jim Wolfe's daughter and Eric Wickerton's wife, Asher would have accepted her role with ease. She'd wanted to, had struggled to. Too much passion simmered inside her. It had been there all of her life, but the months with Ty had liberated it. Controlling something dormant was entirely different from harnessing something that pulsed with life. There had not even been her profession as an outlet for the energy that drove her.

Coming back to London was the most difficult step yet. There she would not only have to face memories of Ty, but the ghost of a woman she had pretended to be. It was all so familiar—Westminster Abbey, Trafalgar Square, the smells, the voices. Even the anticipation of Wimbledon couldn't block them out. There would be faces here that would remember the coolly elegant Lady Wickerton. And there would be questions.

Publicly she would remain aloof, distant and uninformative. Asher felt she owed Eric that much. She would simply refuse to discuss her marriage or its demise. Her early training, her years of following her father's rules, would serve her now more than ever.

She would give them tennis. With two straight championships now under her belt, Asher would have been spotlighted in any case. It was up to her to sway the press away from her personal life toward her professional resurgence. What was growing between her and Ty was still too fragile to be shared.

Happiness. She had nearly forgotten how simple and overwhelming the feeling was. Lazy midnight talks, crazy loving, quiet walks. They shared a hotel room and made it home for the days and nights they were there. She felt as much a gypsy as he, and was content to be so. Once she had looked for roots, stability, commitment. She'd learned that they meant nothing without the fullness of love. His spontaneity had always fascinated her. This time Asher would resolve the lingering fear of it and enjoy.

"Aren't you dressed yet?"

At the question Asher stopped tying her tennis shoe and glanced up. Ty stood in the doorway between the small parlor and bedroom. Fully dressed, impatient, he frowned at her. His hair fell over his forehead as unruly as ever and still slightly damp from the his shower. Waves of love radiated through her.

"Nearly," Asher tossed back. "Not everyone can move quickly in the morning, you know—especially on six hours sleep."

The frown became a grin. "Something keep you up?" He caught the shoe she hurled at him in one hand, his eyes never leaving her face. Apparently the late night hadn't affected him. He looked well rested and full of barely controlled energy. "You can always take a nap after morning practice."

"Awfully pleased with yourself this morning, aren't you?"

"Am I?" Still grinning, he came toward her, tossing her shoe lightly. "It probably has something to do with trouncing that British kid in the quarter-finals yesterday."

"Oh?" Lifting a brow, Asher looked up at him. "Is that all you're pleased about?"

"What else?"

"Let me have my shoe," she demanded. "So I can throw it at you again."

"Did you know you have a poor morning attitude?" he asked, holding the shoe out of reach.

"Did you know you've been insufferable ever since you won the French?" she countered sweetly. "Remember, it's only one quarter of the Grand Slam."

He moved the shoe farther out of reach as she made a grab for it. "For you too, Face," he reminded her.

"The rest's on grass." In an attempt to hold him still, Asher grabbed the waistband of his warm-up pants.

"The woman's insatiable," he sighed. Diving, he pinned her beneath him on the bed.

"Ty! Stop!" Laughing, Asher pushed against him as he nuzzled at her neck. "We'll be late for practice."

"Oh. You're right." Giving her a quick kiss, he rolled away from her.

"Well," Asher muttered as she sat up, "you didn't take much persuading." Even as she started to tidy her hair, she was spun back into his arms. Her startled exclamation was smothered by his lips.

Long, deep, infinitely tender, smolderingly passionate. His arms circled her. Asher felt her bones soften, then dissolve. Her head fell back, inviting him to take more. Cradling her,

Ty went on a slow exploration of her mouth. For the moment he enjoyed the sense of total domination. If they continued, he knew she would begin her own demands. Then it would be power for power. The knowledge excited him. Still, he laughed against her lips. There was time. A lifetime.

"You awake yet?" he asked her as he ran a hand lightly over her breast.

"Mmm-hmm."

"Good. Let's go." After setting her on her feet, he gave Asher's bottom a friendly pat.

"I'll get you for that," she promised. Needs stirred inside her, not quite under control.

"I certainly hope so." With an easy smile Ty slipped an arm around her shoulders. "You need to work on your backhand volley," he began as they walked from the room.

Insulted, Asher tossed her head back. "What are you talking about?"

"If you'd shorten your swing a bit more—"

"Shorten your own swing," she retorted. "And while you're at it," she continued, "you weren't exactly Mr. Speed yesterday."

"Gotta save something for the finals."

Asher snorted as she punched the elevator button. "Your conceit never wavers."

"Confidence," Ty contradicted. He liked seeing her this way—relaxed, but ready to laugh or to slap back. Briefly he wondered if she realized she was even more beautiful when she forgot caution. "What about breakfast?"

"What about it?"

"Want to grab some eggs after practice?"

She slid her eyes to his as the doors opened. "Is that your best offer?"

Ty lifted a brow as he followed her into the elevator. Asher exchanged a polite nod with a middle-aged couple in tweed.

"Maybe you'd like to take up where we left off last night?" Ty lounged against an elevator wall as Asher gaped at him. "What did you say your name was again?"

Asher could feel two pairs of shocked and interested eyes boring into her back. "Misty," she replied, allowing a trace of cockney to color her voice. "Will you spring for champagne again, Mr. Starbuck? It was ever so good."

He recognized the light of challenge in her eyes and grinned. "So were you, sweetie."

When the doors opened to the lobby, the older couple moved out reluctantly. Asher punched Ty in the arm before she followed.

In less than an hour they were both concentrating on form and speed and the capricious bounces a ball could take on grass. Was she playing better? Asher wondered as she sprang for Madge's slice. She felt looser, less encumbered. Indeed, she felt as though losing were not even a possibility. At Wimbledon she could forget the city of London.

Instead, she could remember the qualifying games at Roehampton, with their anything-goes attitude. Both bad language and rackets had flown. It was a contrast to the elegance and glamour of Wimbledon. Here both the players and the crowd were steeped in tradition. Hydrangeas against a backdrop of rich green grass, ivy-covered walls, limos and chauffeurs. Colors were soothing, mauve and green, as if time itself had sobered them.

Here spectators would be well-mannered, quiet between points, applauding after them. Even those in standing room would behave, or the chair judge would tell them politely to quiet down. No one hung from the scoreboards at Wimbledon. It was as revered as the changing of the guards, as English as double-decker buses.

There was no doubt, as one gazed around the immaculately tended velvet lawns, the pampered roses, the dollhouse kiosks and the stands that could accommodate more than twenty-five thousand, that Wimbledon *was* tennis. It was here former players migrated to. It was here future players aspired to. Asher remembered Ty telling her about watching the matches one long-ago July Fourth and making a vow. He had kept it, not once, but four times. More than anything she had wanted before, Asher wanted them to both walk away from Centre Court as champions.

Behind the baseline, Asher stood with a racket and a ball, staring off into space.

"Had enough?" Madge called out.

"Hmm…what?" Asher's head snapped around. Seeing Madge standing with her legs spread, hand on hips, had her laughing. "I suppose I have, I was daydreaming."

From opposite ends of the court, they walked toward their bags and jackets. "No sense asking if you're happy," Madge began conversationally. "You look absolutely miserable floating two inches off the ground."

"That obvious, huh?"

"I won't pretend not to be pleased," Madge added smugly. "I've always thought you two made a great team. Going to make it official?"

"I— No, we're just taking it one day at a time." Asher kept her eyes lowered as she packed her racket. "Marriage is just a formality, after all."

"And pigs fly," Madge countered calmly. When Asher glanced up with a cautious smile, she went on. "For some, yes, you're right. Not for you, Face. Why did you stay in an unhappy marriage for three years?" When Asher started to speak, Madge lifted a hand. "Because to you marriage is a promise, and you don't break promises."

"I failed once," she began.

"Oh, all by yourself? Isn't that being a bit self-absorbed?" Impatient, Madge settled her hands on her hips again. "Listen, you aren't going to let one mistake keep you from being happy, are you?"

"I am happy," Asher assured her, punctuating the statement by touching Madge's shoulder. "Ty's all I've ever wanted, Madge. I can't risk losing him again."

Her brow puckered in confusion. "But you left him, Asher, not the other way around."

"I'd already lost him," she said flatly.

"Asher, I don't—"

"It's a new day," she interrupted, then took a deep breath of scented morning air. "A fresh start. I know what mistakes I made and have no intention of repeating them. There was a time in my life that I thought I had to come first, before this." Holding up the small white ball, Asher examined it. "Before anything. I looked on tennis as a competitor, his family as a rival. That was stupid." Dropping the ball into a can, Asher closed it.

"That's funny," Madge mused. "There was a time in my life I thought The Dean's work came first. He thought the same about me. It wasn't true in either case."

With a smile Asher slung her bag over her shoulder. "Ty won't ever forget that tennis took him out of that tenement. Maybe he shouldn't. That's the thing that brings fire to his game."

She knows him so well in some ways, Madge thought, and not at all in others. "And what brings the ice to yours?"

"Fear," Asher answered before she thought. For a moment she gave Madge a blank look, then shrugged. Saying it aloud made it seem rather unimportant. "Fear of failure, or exposure." Laughing, she began to walk. "Thank God you're not a reporter."

The gravel crunched underfoot as they moved down the path. It was a sound Asher associated with the tidiness of English courts. "Remind me to tell you sometime what goes through my head five minutes before a match."

With a sigh Asher hooked her arm through her old partner's. "Let's hit the showers."

There was no dream. Asher slept as deeply as a child, with no worries, no nagging fears. The curtains were drawn closed so that the afternoon sun filtered through lazily. Traffic sounds muffled through it, coming as a quiet drone. She wore only a short terry robe and lay on top of the spread. Ty would come back to wake her so that they could spend some time sight-seeing before nightfall. Because they were both scheduled to play the following day, they would go to bed early.

The knock on the door wakened her. Sitting up, Asher ran a hand through her tousled hair. He'd forgotten his key, she thought groggily. She stepped from the dim bedroom into the brighter parlor, wincing against the change of light. Absently she wondered what time it was as she opened the door. Shock took a moment to penetrate.

"Eric," she whispered.

"Asher." He gave her what was nearly a bow before he elbowed his way into the room. "Did I wake you?"

"I was napping." She closed the door, trying to recover her scattered wits. He looked the same, she thought. Naturally he would. Eric would see no reason to change. He was tall, slim, with a military carriage. He had a sharp-featured European face, a bit haughty and remote. Dark blond hair was cut and groomed to indicate wealth and conservatism. Light eyes in a pale face—both romantic, yet intelligent and cold. Asher knew that his mouth could twist into a hard line when he was crossed. As a suitor he had been charming, as a lover, meticulous. As a husband he'd been unbearable. She drew herself straight. He was no longer her husband.

"I didn't expect to see you, Eric."

"No?" He smiled. "Did you think I wouldn't drop by while you were in town? Lost a bit of weight, Asher."

"Competition tends to do that." Years of training had her gesturing toward a chair. "Please, sit down. I'll get you a drink."

There was no reason to be upset by him now, she told herself. No need to feel fear or guilt. Divorced couples managed to be civilized more often than not. Eric, Asher thought with a grim smile, was a very civilized man.

"Have you been well?" She poured his scotch neat, then added ice to Perrier for herself.

"Quite well. And you?"

"Yes. Your family?"

"Doing wonderfully." Eric accepted the glass she offered, then eyed her over the rim. "And your father?" He watched for the flash of pain, and was satisfied.

"As far as I know, he's fine." Quite consciously Asher drew on the mask as she sat.

"Still hasn't forgiven you for giving up your career."

Her eyes were level now and expressionless. "I'm sure you're aware he hasn't."

Mindful of the crease in his pants, Eric crossed his legs. "I thought perhaps now that you're competing again…" He allowed the sentence to die.

Asher watched the bubbles rise in her glass, but left them untasted. "He no longer acknowledges me," she said flatly. "I'm still paying, Eric." She lifted her eyes again. "Does that satisfy you?"

He drank leisurely for a moment. "It was your choice, my dear. Your career for my name."

"For your silence," Asher corrected. "I already had your name."

"And another man's child in your belly."

Ice clinked against ice as her hands shook. Quickly she controlled the tremor. "One would have thought it would have been enough that I lost the child," she murmured. "Did you come all this way to remind me?"

"I came," Eric said as he leaned back, "to see how my ex-wife was adjusting. You're victorious on the courts, Asher, and as lovely as ever." She didn't speak as his eyes roamed the room. "Apparently you didn't waste too much time picking up with your old lover."

"My mistake was in leaving him, Eric. We both know that. I'm very, very sorry."

He sent her an icy look. "Your mistake was in trying to pass his bastard off on me."

Furious and trembling, Asher sprang to her feet. "I never lied to you. And by God, I'll never apologize again."

He remained seated, swirling liquor. "Does he know yet?"

Her color drained dramatically enough to make him smile genuinely. Hate ate at him. "No, I see he doesn't. How interesting."

"I kept my word, Eric." Though her hands were laced tightly together, Asher's voice was strong. "As long as I was your wife, I did everything you asked of me."

He acknowledged this with a slight nod. Her honesty hadn't been enough—nor had her three years of penance. "But you're not my wife any longer."

"We agreed. The marriage was intolerable for both of us."

"What are you afraid he'd do?" Eric mused, frowning up at the ceiling. "He's a very physical man as I remember, with a primitive sort of temper." Lowering his eyes, he smiled again. "Do you think he'd beat you?"

Asher gave a short laugh. "No."

"You're very confident," he murmured. "What exactly are you afraid of?"

Wearily she dropped her hands to her sides. "He wouldn't

forgive me, Eric, any more than you have. I lost the child, I lost my father. My self-esteem. I'll never lose the guilt. I hurt nothing but your pride, Eric, haven't I suffered enough for that?"

"Perhaps…perhaps not." Rising, he stepped toward her. She remembered the scent of his crisp, dignified cologne very well. "Perhaps the most perfect punishment might be in never knowing your secret is safe. I'll make you no promises, Asher."

"It astonishes me that I was ever naïve enough to think of you as a kind man, Eric," she said softly.

"Justice," he returned, toasting her.

"Revenge has little to do with justice."

He shrugged an elegant shoulder. "All in your viewpoint, my dear."

She wouldn't give him the satisfaction of breaking down— of weeping, of screaming or begging. Instead, Asher stood perfectly still. "If you've said all you've come to say, I'd like you to go."

"Of course." After finishing off the liquor, he set down the glass. "Sleep well, darling. Don't bother, I'll let myself out." Eric turned the doorknob and found himself face-to-face with Ty. Nothing could have pleased him more.

Ty noted his cold, satisfied smile before his gaze shifted to Asher. Standing in the center of the room, she seemed frozen. There was anguish, and, he thought, fear in her eyes. Her face was dead-white and still. Even as he wondered what it was she feared, Ty took in the rest of her appearance. The tousled hair, the brief robe and exposed skin had rage boiling in him. Asher could feel it from where she stood.

His eyes whipped back to Eric's. There was murder in them. "Get the hell out of here."

"Just on my way," Eric said equably, though he had inched back against the door in instinctive defense. His last thought as he shut it behind him was that Asher would bear the brunt of the fury in Ty's eyes. That alone had made it worth the trip.

The room vibrated with the silent storm. Asher didn't move. It seemed Ty would stare at her for eternity. The trembling was difficult to control, but she forced herself. If she made light of the incident, perhaps so would he.

"What the hell was he doing here?"

"He just dropped by…I suppose to wish me luck." The lie sliced at her.

"Cozy." Crossing to her, Ty caught the lapel of her robe in his hand. "Don't you usually dress for visitors, Asher? Then again, I suppose it isn't necessary for ex-husbands."

"Ty, don't."

"Don't what?" he demanded. Though he struggled against the words, the accusations, the feelings, he knew it was a losing battle. Against the unknown he would always attack. "Wouldn't it be better form to meet him somewhere else? It's a little sticky here, isn't it?"

The cold sarcasm hurt more than his fury would have. With so much to hide, she could only shake her head. "Ty, you know there's nothing between us. You know—"

"What the hell do I know?" he shouted, grasping the other lapel. "Don't ask, don't question. Then I walk in and find you entertaining the bastard you left me for."

"I didn't know he was coming." She gripped his arms for balance as he nearly lifted her off her feet. "If he had called, I would have told him to stay away."

"You let him in." Enraged, he shook her. "Why?"

Despair rather than fear clutched at her. "Would you be happier if I had slammed the door in his face?"

"Yes, damn it."

"I didn't." She pushed at him now, as furious as he. "I let him in, I gave him a drink. Make what you like of it. I can't stop you."

"Did he want you back?" he demanded, ignoring her struggles. "Is that why he came?"

"What does it matter?" Impotently she slammed her fists into his chest. "It's not what *I* want." She threw back her head, her eyes burning.

"Then tell me, tell me now why you married him." When she tried to pull away, he dragged her back. "I'll have that much, Asher, and I'll have it now."

"Because I thought he was what I needed," she cried out. Roaring in her ears was the anger, the fear she had felt for Eric.

"And was he?" To prevent her from striking out, Ty grasped her wrist.

"No!" She jerked but couldn't free herself. Frustration added to an almost unreasonable fury. "No, I was miserable. I was trapped." Her voice was both strong and harsh. "I paid in ways you can't imagine. There wasn't a day I was happy. Does that satisfy you?"

She did something he had never seen her do before. She wept. His grip on her wrists loosened as he watched tears flood her eyes and spill onto her cheeks. Never in all the years he'd known her had he seen that kind of torment on her face. Tearing herself from his grip, Asher fled into the bedroom, slamming the door at her back.

She wanted peace. She wanted privacy. The grief had hit her unexpectedly. If the tears hadn't clogged her throat, she would have told him about the baby. The words had been there, ready to spill out in anger. Then speech had been impossible. Now she needed to weep it out.

Ty stared at the closed door for a long time. The wrenching sound of sobbing came to him. It was a reaction he hadn't expected. His anger was justified, as were his questions. Anger for anger he could have comprehended, but the pain he heard was altogether different. Having come from a family of women, he understood a woman's tears. Over the years he'd done his share of comforting and soothing. But these sobs were hot and bitter—and Asher never wept.

Jess cried easily, quiet, feminine tears. His mother wept with joy or silent sadness. These he could handle. A shoulder could be offered, a few sympathetic words, a teasing comment. Instinctively he knew none of those were the prescription for raw grief.

He still had questions. He still had anger. But the sounds from the bedroom forced him to put them aside. Ty recognized when tears were used as a weapon or a defense. These were being torn from her unwillingly. Dragging a hand through his hair, he wondered if it was Eric or himself who was responsible for them. Or something he knew nothing about. Cursing softly, he went to the door and opened it.

She lay curled on the bed in a ball of misery. Her body shook. When he touched her she jerked away. Saying nothing, Ty lay down beside her, gathering her close. For another moment she fought him. *Alone.* Her tears were not to be observed, not to be shared. *Private.* Ty dealt with her struggles by merely holding her tighter in arms that were both strong and gentle.

"I'm not going anywhere," he murmured.

With no more protest, Asher clung to his comfort and let her grief run its course.

It had grown dark and her body was weak. There were no more tears left in her. Ty's arms were strong around her. Beneath her damp cheek she could hear the steady beat of his heart. Gently, almost absently, his fingers stroked the base of her neck.

She'd nearly told him. Asher closed her eyes, too weary to feel fear or regret. If she could have summoned up the energy, she would have been grateful for the tears that had prevented her confession.

I lost your baby. Would he be holding her now if those

words had spilled out? What good would it do to tell him? she asked herself. Why make him grieve for something he had never known? And grieve he would, she knew, after the anger passed. It came to her suddenly that it wasn't only fear that kept the secret locked inside her. She couldn't bear to see Ty hurt as she had hurt.

How could she explain to him about Eric without dragging up old bitterness, opening old wounds? Ty hadn't wanted her any longer—Jess had made that abundantly clear. But Eric had. It had been her pride that had turned to Eric, then her sense of duty that had kept her with him. Perhaps if she had been stronger after the accident she would never have made those promises to him....

Asher had floated to consciousness on a wave of pain. What reason was there to wake up and hurt? she thought groggily. Sleep, sleep was so peaceful.

She remembered the shouting, the fall, the swimming darkness. The baby...Ty's baby. Panic—the panic pierced by lethargy. Her eyelids seemed weighted with lead, but she forced them open even as she reached a protective hand to her stomach. Stern and cold, Eric's face floated in front of her eyes.

"The baby," she managed through dry lips.

"Dead."

Tearing, burning grief replaced the pain. "No." Moaning, she closed her eyes again. "Oh, God, no. My baby, not my baby. Ty—"

"Listen to me, Asher." Eric spoke briskly. For three days he had waited while Asher drifted in and out of consciousness. She had lost the baby and a great deal of blood. Once she had nearly slipped away, but he had willed her to live. The love he had once felt had turned to resentment that bordered on hate. She had deceived him, made a fool of him. Now he would have his payment.

"My baby…"

"The baby's dead," he said flatly, then gripped her hand. "Look at me." She obeyed with eyes glazed with sorrow. "You're in a private clinic. The reason for your being here will never be known beyond the front doors. If you do what I say."

"Eric…" A spark of hope flickered. With what strength she had, Asher tightened her fingers on his. "Are they sure? Couldn't there be a mistake? Please—"

"You miscarried. The servants will be discreet. As far as anyone knows, we've slipped away for a few days."

"I don't understand." She pressed her hand against her stomach as if to make the truth a lie. "The fall…I fell down the stairs. But—"

"An accident," he stated, making the loss of the child sound like a broken glass.

Insidiously the pain slipped through. "Ty," Asher moaned, shutting her eyes.

"You're my wife, and will remain so until I say differently." Eric waited until her eyes focused on him again. "Would you have me call your lover and tell him you married me while carrying his child?"

"No." She could only whisper the word. *Ty.* She ached for him. He was lost to her—as lost as the child they'd made together.

"Then you'll do as I say. You'll retire from professional tennis. I won't have the press speculating about the two of you and dragging my name through the mud. You'll behave as I expect Lady Wickerton to behave. I will not touch you," he continued with a trace of disgust. "Any physical desire I felt for you is gone. We will live in the manner I designate or your lover will hear from me about this game you played. Is this understood?"

What did it matter how she lived? Asher asked herself. She

was already dead. "Yes. I'll do whatever you want. Please, leave me alone now."

"As you wish." He rose. "When you're stronger, you'll give an official press release on your retirement. Your reason will be that you have no more time for tennis or any desire for a career that would take you away from your husband and your adopted country."

"Do you think it matters to me?" she whispered. "Just let me alone, let me sleep."

"Your word, Asher."

She gave him a long last look before she wearily closed her eyes. "My word, Eric."

And she had kept it. She had tolerated Eric's pleasure when her father had turned away from her. She had ignored his discreet but frequent affairs. For months she had lived like a zombie, doing as she was bid. When the layers of grief began to peel away, his hold remained through guilt and threats. When she had begun to come to life again, Asher had bargained for her freedom. Nothing was more important to Eric than his reputation. She held his many women in one hand, he held the knowledge of Ty's child in the other. They'd made an uneasy agreement.

Now he was back, Asher mused. Perhaps because she was making a success of her life again. Still, she felt he would keep his silence, if only to ensure a hold over her. Once he spoke, all ties were severed. Or if she spoke…

She remembered the look on Ty's face when he had seen her with Eric. Explanations would never be accepted now. Perhaps the day would come when they fully trusted each other, when the memory of betrayal would be dimmed.

She'd been silent for some time. By the steadiness of her breathing she might have been sleeping. Ty knew she was awake and thinking. What secrets was she holding from him? he wondered. And how long would it be before the air between them was finally cleared? He wanted to demand, but her vulnerability prevented him. More than anything else, he didn't want to risk her slipping behind the wall she could so easily erect.

"Better?" he murmured.

She sighed before he felt the faint movement of her head as she nodded. There was one thing she could settle between them, one thing she could make him understand. "Ty, he means nothing to me. Do you believe that?"

"I want to."

"Believe it." Suddenly intense, she sat up and leaned against his chest. If she could give him nothing else, she could give him this. "I feel nothing for Eric, not even hate. The marriage was a mistake. From the start it was nothing more than a façade."

"Then why—"

"It's always been you," she said before she crushed her mouth to his. "Always you." She pressed her lips to his throat, passion erupting in her as swiftly as the tears. "I stopped living for so long and now…" Her mouth ran wildly over his face. "I need you now, only you."

Her mouth met his fervently, saying more than words. Her ardor touched off his own. There was no need for questions now, or for answers. She pulled the shirt from him, eager to touch. Pressing her lips to heated flesh, she heard him groan. Though her hands moved swiftly to undress him, her lips loitered, lingering to arouse. With her tongue she left a moist trail of fire.

His body was a pleasure to her—hard muscle, long bones, taut flesh. Delighting in him, she sought new secrets. If she nibbled at his waist, his breathing grew shallow, his fingers gripped her hair. If she moved her palm along his thigh, his moan vibrated with need. Giddy with power, she ran a crazed trail from stomach to chest, her lips hungry and seeking.

He struggled to pull the robe from her as she caught his earlobe between her teeth. Low, sultry laughter drove him wild. Neither heard the seam rip as he tugged the terry cloth from her. Limber and quick, she made it impossible for him to grant them both the final relief. Her lovemaking tormented and thrilled him while her agility held him off.

"Now," he demanded, grasping her hips. "Asher, for God's sake."

"No, no, no," she murmured, then cut off his oath with a searing kiss. She found the torture exquisite. Though her own body begged for fulfillment, she wanted to prolong it. As his hands slid over her damp skin, she arched back, reveling in his touch. She belonged, and always would, to the man who could release her fires.

Neither was in control, each a slave to the other. She wanted nothing more than to be bound to him—here, in a dark room with the sound of her own breathing raging in her ears, in the sunlight with the secrets of the night still humming between them. For always.

Beneath her, his body was hot and moist and moving. The rhythm seduced her. Everything warm, everything giving, flowed through her. Thoughts vanished, memories dimmed. Now—there was only now—the all-powerful, greedy present.

This time when he gripped her hips she made no attempt to stop him. Her head fell back in complete abandonment as they joined. The moan was rich and deep, and from both of them. As one, they were catapulted up, beyond pleasure, into ecstasy.

CHAPTER 8

Asher had driven in limousines all her life. As a child she'd ridden behind a chauffeur named George in a shiny maroon car with smoked glass and a built-in bar. George had remained the family driver though the cars had changed—an elegant white Rolls, a sturdy blue Mercedes.

Lady Wickerton's driver had been Peter and the car had been an old discreet gray Daimler. Peter had been as silent and as efficient as the car. Asher felt no thrill at being driven in the long black limo toward Wimbledon.

As they passed through Roehampton, she watched the scenery. Tidy, healthy trees, trimmed shrubs, orderly flowers. In a few hours, she would be in Centre Court. Aching, sweating…and winning. This was the big prize. Credibility, prestige, press. They were all at Wimbledon.

Once before she and Ty had taken the championships and led the dancing at the Wimbledon Ball—in that year of her life that had brought complete joy and complete misery. Now she would play her old foe Maria Rayski with all the verve and all the cunning she had at her disposal.

Though she'd thought her life had begun to come to order with her first win, Asher now realized she'd been wrong. The turning point was today, here in the arena that was synonymous with her profession. She would play her best here, on the surface she knew best, in the country in which she had lived like a prisoner. Perhaps true confidence would begin after this match was over.

She thought of Ty, the young boy who had once vowed to play and win. Now, in the lush interior of the limo, Asher made a similar vow. She would have a championship season. Reestablish Asher Wolfe *for* Asher Wolfe. Then she would be ready to face the woman. The woman would face the only man who mattered.

The crowds waited for her and other arriving players. The greetings were enthusiastic. Roaming spectators sipped champagne and nibbled on strawberries and cream. Signing autographs, Asher felt light, confident, ready. Nothing, she thought, could mar such a day. The Fourth of July, the brilliant sunshine, the scent of garden flowers.

She remembered other Wimbledons. So little had changed. Fans mingled with players, chatting, laughing. The atmosphere was one of an informal tea party with the promise of a spectacle. But she could feel the nerves. They were there, just under the bonhomie, in the young players, the veterans, doubles and singles finalists. Mixing among them were rock stars and celebrities, millionaires and landed gentry.

Asher saw faces from the past, players from her father's generation. For them it was a reunion, nostalgia, tradition. There were people she had entertained in Grosvenor Square. For them it was a social event. The dress was summer-garden-party chic—picture hats and pastels. Because yesterdays had to be faced, Asher greeted former acquaintances.

"Asher, how lovely to see you again…." "What a sweet little outfit…." "How strange it is not to see you at the club anymore…." There was speculation, thinly veiled by stretched manners. She dealt with it calmly, as she had during her three years of marriage.

"Where's that old man of yours?"

Turning, Asher clasped two large hands warmly. "Stretch McBride, you haven't changed a bit."

Of course he had. When he'd first tickled Asher's chin, he'd been thirty. His face had been unlined, his hair untouched with gray. He'd won nearly every major championship there was to win twice around. Though he was still tall, and nearly as lean as he had been in his prime, the twenty years showed on his face.

"You always told a lie beautifully." Grinning, he kissed her cheek. "Where's Jim?"

"In the States," she answered, keeping her smile bright. "How have you been, Stretch?"

"Just fine. Got five grandchildren and a nice string of sporting goods stores on the East Coast." He patted her hand. "Don't tell me Jim isn't going to be here? He hasn't missed it in forty years."

It was a struggle not to show the pain, much less not to feel it. "As far as I know, he won't be. I'm awfully glad to see you again. I haven't forgotten that you taught me the dump shot."

Pleased, he laughed. "Use it on Maria today," he advised. "I love to see Americans win at Wimbledon. Tell your old man hello for me."

"Take care, Stretch." Her smile evaded the promise she couldn't give. With a parting kiss, he moved away.

Turning, Asher found herself face-to-face with Lady Daphne Evans. The striking brunette had been one of Eric's more discreet dalliances, and one of Asher's more difficult trials. Her eyes automatically cooled, though her voice was scrupulously polite.

"Daphne, you look exquisite."

"Asher." Daphne skimmed cool eyes over Asher's brief

tennis dress, down long bare legs to her court shoes. "You look different. How odd to find you an athlete."

"Odd?" Asher countered. "I've always been an athlete. Tell me, how is your husband?"

The thrust was parried with a quick laugh. "Miles is in Spain on business. As it happens, Eric escorted me today."

Though her stomach churned, her face remained composed. "Eric's here?"

"Yes, of course." Meticulously Daphne adjusted the brim of her rose-pink hat. "You don't think he'd miss this Wimbledon, do you?" Long mink lashes swept down, then up again. "We're all very interested in the results. Will we see you at the ball, darling?"

"Naturally."

"Well, I must let you mingle, mustn't I? That's traditional. Best of luck." With a flash of a smile Daphne swirled her skirts and was gone.

Asher fought the nausea, but began to nudge her way through the crowd. All she wanted was the comparative peace of the A locker rooms. The day ahead promised to be enough of a fight without contending with ghosts. With a few smiles and mechanically gracious greetings, she made her way out of the main throng. A few moments to herself— that was what she needed before the stands began to fill, before her strength and abilities were put to the test.

She knew Eric well enough to be certain he had asked Daphne to seek her out. Yes, he would want to be sure she knew he was there—before the match. As she slipped into the locker room, Asher noticed her hands were shaking. She couldn't allow it. In thirty minutes she would have to be in complete control.

When she walked onto the court Asher was careful not to look into the crowd. It would be easier on her nerves if the people who watched and cheered remained anonymous.

As she attempted to empty her mind of all but the first game, Asher watched Maria Rayski.

On her own side of the court, Rayski paced, gesturing occasionally to the crowd, tossing comments. Her nerves were undisguised. It was always so, Asher mused. Rayski chewed her nails, cracked her knuckles and said the first thing that came into her mind. In a wary sort of fashion Asher had always liked her. At five foot ten, she was tall for a woman and rangy, with a deadly stretch. Fatalistically Asher recalled she had a habit of badgering her opponent.

Well, she decided as she chose her game racket, Rayski's histrionics might just keep her mind off who was, and who was not, in the stands. She eyed the television camera dispassionately. With the wonder of technology, the match would be relayed to the States with only a brief delay. Would her father even bother to watch? she wondered. Silently she walked to the baseline for the first serve.

There was no cautious testing in the first games. Rayski went straight for the jugular. Both were fast players, and while Rayski was more aggressive, Asher was a better strategist. A ball could take ungodly bounces on grass, particularly the lush grass of Wimbledon's Centre Court. To defend, to attack, required instinct and timing. It also required complete concentration.

The lead jockeyed back and forth during the first set as the players gave the fourteen thousand spectators the show they'd come to see. Over the elegant, century-old court, they sweated, gritted their teeth and scrambled, not for the enjoyment of those who paid to see, but for the game. Rayski tossed an occasional taunt over the net between rallies. Asher might have been deaf for all the response she gave. She had her rhythm—nothing was going to interfere with it. She placed her ground strokes with deadly precision, charged the net for short angling volleys. Both her form and her energy seemed at perfect peak.

Everything changed when the women took their seats for the towel-off before the third set.

Because she had forgotten about everything but the game, Asher's defenses were lowered. An inadvertent glance up in the stands had her eyes locking with Eric's. A slow, icy smile spread over his face as he lifted a hand in salute—or reminder.

What the devil's wrong with her? Ty asked himself. He shifted closer to the edge of his seat and studied Asher with narrowed eyes. She'd just dropped two games straight, the second one on a double fault. True, Rayski was playing superbly, but so had Asher—until the third set. She was playing mechanically now, as if the life had gone out of her. Too often she was missing basic shots or failing to put anything extra on a return. Rayski's serve was not her strongest weapon, yet she was repeatedly breezing service winners past Asher.

If he didn't know her better, he would have sworn Asher was tanking the match. But Asher wasn't capable of deliberately losing.

Carefully Ty watched for signs of an injury. A strained muscle or twisted ankle would explain the change in her. She gave no sign of favoring a leg. The composure on her face was as perfect as a mask. Too perfect, Ty reflected as the third game went to fifteen-love. Something was definitely wrong, but it wasn't physical. Disturbed, he quickly scanned the crowd.

There were dozens of faces he knew, some by name, some by reputation. There was an award-winning actor he'd once played a celebrity tourney with. Ty had found him an earthy man with a credible forehand. He recognized the ballet star because Asher had once dragged him to see *The Firebird*. Beside the ballerina was a country-western singer with a cross-over hit. Ty passed over them, looking for an answer. He found it sitting near the Royal Box.

There was a cool, satisfied smile on Eric's face as he watched his ex-wife. Beside him, a thin, flashy woman in a rose-colored hat looked bored. Rage rose in Ty instantly. His first instinct was to yank Eric up by his five-hundred-dollar lapels and rearrange the expression on his face with his fists.

"Son of a bitch," he muttered, already rising. The hand that grasped his wrist was strong.

"Where are you going?" Madge demanded.

"To do something I should've done three years ago."

Still clinging to his arm, Madge twisted her head to follow the direction of his eyes. "Oh, boy," she said under her breath. Through her fingertips she could feel Ty's temper. Only briefly did she consider the personal satisfaction she would gain from letting Ty do what he wanted. "Hold on," she snapped between her teeth. "Listen to me. Punching him out isn't going to do anything for Asher."

"The hell it won't," he retorted. "You know why he's here."

"To upset her," Madge managed calmly enough. "Obviously he's succeeding. Go talk to her." A strong man might have cringed from the blazing look Ty turned on her. Madge merely arched a brow. "You want to start a fight, Starbuck, do it after the match. I'll referee. Right now, use your head."

His control didn't come easily. Madge watched him struggle for it, lose it, then finally win. Though his eyes were still stormy, the hand under hers relaxed. "If talking doesn't work," he said flatly, "I'm going to break him in half."

"I'll hold your coat," she promised before Ty slipped away.

Knowing he'd have only a moment, Ty decided to use words sparingly—and make them count. After losing the game without making a point, Asher slumped into her chair. She didn't see Ty waiting for her.

"What the hell's wrong with you?"

Her head jerked up at the harsh tone. "Nothing." She was tired, already defeated as she mopped at the sweat on her face.

"You're handing the match to Rayski on a platter."

"Leave me alone, Ty."

"Going to give him the satisfaction of watching you fall apart in front of fourteen thousand people, Face?" There was sarcasm without a trace of sympathy in his voice. He noted the quick, almost indiscernible flash in her eyes. He'd wanted to see it. Always, she played better if there was anger beneath the ice.

"I never thought I'd see you tank a match."

"Go to hell." Whirling, she stalked back to the baseline. Nobody, she thought as she waited for Rayski to take position, nobody accused Asher Wolfe of tanking. Rayski crouched in her pendulum receiving stance while Asher gave the ball a few testing bounces. Tossing it, she drew back her racket and lunged. The effort of the serve came out in a force of breath. The finely pulverized chalk at the baseline rose on contact. Without giving the ace a thought, Asher took her stance for the next serve.

Her anger had teeth. She could feel it gnawing at her. A photographer zoomed in on her face and captured the contradictory placid expression and frosted eyes. Temper was energy. Asher flew across the court, striking the ball as if it were the enemy. Yet her battle was sternly controlled. No one watching her would realize that she cursed Ty with each stroke. No one but Ty himself. Satisfied, he watched her turn her fury on her opponent.

Oh, she was fabulous to see, he thought. Those long, slim legs, the strong shoulders. Her form was so smooth, so precise, yet beneath was that excitement, that smoldering passion. She was as she played, he mused, and wanted her. No one but he knew just how reckless she could be, just how abandoned. The thought had desire moving through him.

She was the woman all men fantasized about—part lady, part wanton. And his, Ty told himself fiercely. Only his.

After watching Asher fire a backhand volley past Rayski, he glanced up. Eric's smile was gone. As if sensing the scrutiny, the Englishman looked down. The two men studied each other as the crowd applauded Asher's game. Ty laughed, softly, insolently, then walked away.

Though the match held close to the last point, the impetus Ty had instilled in her carried Asher to the win. She was polite, even charming as she accepted the Wimbledon plate. Inside she was raging. The joy of victory couldn't penetrate the fury and resentment she was feeling. Ty had turned the tide of her emotions away from Eric and onto himself.

She wanted to shout. She smiled and raised her trophy for the crowd to see. She wanted to scream. Politely she allowed the army of cameras to snap her. Fatigue didn't touch her. The ache in her arm might not have existed.

At last freeing herself from the press and well-wishers, she simmered under the shower and changed. Determination made her remain at Wimbledon to watch Ty's match. Stubbornness made her refuse to admire his game. Eric was forgotten. Asher's only thought was to vent her fury at the first possible moment. It took five hard sets and two and a half hours before Ty could claim his own trophy.

Asher left the stadium before the cheers had died.

He knew she'd be waiting for him. Even before Ty slipped the key in the lock, he knew what to expect. He looked forward to it. His adrenaline was still flowing. Neither the shower nor the massage had taken it from him. Wimbledon always affected him this way. As long as he played, winning there would be his first goal.

Now, the demanding games behind him, the win still sweet, he felt like a knight returning home victorious from the wars. His woman waited. But she wouldn't throw herself into his arms. She was going to scratch at him. Oh, yes, he was looking forward to it.

Grinning, Ty turned the knob. He had no more than shut the door behind him than Asher stormed out of the bedroom.

"Congratulations, Face," he said amiably. "Looks like I get first dance at the ball."

"How dare you say those things to me in the middle of the match?" she demanded. Eyes glittering, she advanced on him. "How dare you accuse me of tanking?"

Ty set his bag and rackets on a chair. "What do you call what you were doing?"

"Losing."

"Quitting," he corrected her. "You might as well have put up a sign."

"I've never quit!"

He lifted a brow. "Only for three years."

"Don't you dare throw that in my face." Raising both hands, she shoved him. Instead of being offended, he laughed. It pleased him enormously that he could rattle her control.

"You did good," he reminded her. "I couldn't take a chance on your losing." He gave her cheek an affectionate pinch. "I didn't want to open the ball with Maria."

"You conceited, overconfident louse!" She shoved him again. "Gramaldi almost took you. I wish he had." She shouted the lie at him. "You could use a good kick in the ego." With the intention of storming back into the bedroom, she whirled. Catching her wrist, Ty spun her back around.

"Aren't you going to congratulate me?"

"No."

"Aw, come on, Face." He grinned appealingly. "Give us a kiss."

For an answer Asher balled her hand into a fist. Ducking the blow, Ty gripped her waist and slung her over his shoulder. "I love it when you're violent," he said huskily as she pulled his hair.

To her own surprise—and annoyance—she had to choke back a laugh. "Then you're going to get a real charge out of this," she promised, kicking wildly as he threw her on the bed. Even though her reflexes were quick, Ty had her pinned beneath him in seconds. Breathless, she struggled to bring her knee up to his weakest point.

"Not that violent." Wisely he shifted to safety.

She twisted, squirmed and struggled. "You take your hands off me."

"Soon as I'm finished," he agreed, slipping a hand under the blouse that had come loose from her waistband.

Refusing to acknowledge the sensation of pleasure, Asher glared at him. "Don't you touch me."

"I have to touch you to make love to you." His smile was reasonable and friendly. "It's the only way I know how."

I will not laugh, she ordered herself as the gurgle rose in her throat. She was angry, furious, she reminded herself.

Ty recognized the weakening and capitalized on it. "Your eyes get purple when you're mad. I like it." He kissed her firmly shut mouth. "Why don't you yell at me some more?"

"I have nothing more to say to you," Asher claimed haughtily. "Please go away."

"But we haven't made love yet." Lightly he rubbed his nose against hers.

Refusing to be charmed, she turned her head away. "We aren't going to."

"Wanna bet?" With one swift move he ripped her blouse from neck to waist.

"Ty!" Shocked, Asher gaped at him, her mouth open.

"I nearly did that when you were on Centre Court today.

You should be glad I waited." Before she could react he tore her shorts into ragged pieces. Thinking he might have gone mad, Asher stayed perfectly still. "Something wrong?" he asked as his hand moved to cup her breast.

"Ty, you can't tear my clothes."

"I already did." Soft as a feather, his hand roamed down to her stomach. "Want to tear mine?"

"No." Her skin was beginning to quiver. She tried to shift away and found herself held prisoner.

"I made you angry."

Her head cleared long enough for her to glare at him. "Yes, and—"

"Angry enough to win," he murmured, trailing his lips along her throat. "And when I watched you I nearly exploded from wanting you. All that passion simmering just under the surface. And only I know what it's like when it escapes."

She gave a little moan as his fingers stroked the point of her breast but tried to cling to reality. "You had no business saying I was tanking."

"I didn't say that, I only planted the idea." When he lifted his head, the look in his eyes had her drawing in a quick breath. "Did you think I'd stand by and watch him get to you like that? No man gets to you, Asher, no man but me."

With a savage kiss he cut off all words, all thoughts.

It always surprised Asher that Ty could project such raw sexuality in black tie. Conservative, formal dress could do nothing to alter his air of primitive masculinity. The material could cover the muscles, but it couldn't disguise the strength. There had been times Asher had wondered if it was his earthiness that had drawn her to him. Glimpsing him in a room filled with elegantly attired men and women, she knew it was more than that. It was all of him, every aspect, from temper to humor, that had made her his.

The Wimbledon Ball was as traditional as the tournament. The music, the lights, the people. It was always an evening to remember for its beauty and tastefulness. Asher counted the hours until it would be over. Scolding herself, she tuned back into the conversation of her dance partner. She'd always enjoyed a party, always found pleasure in quiet well-run affairs. But now she wished she and Ty could have shared a bottle of wine in their room.

She didn't want the spotlight this evening, but candlelight. Over the heads of the other dancers her eyes met Ty's. It took only one brief glance to know that his thoughts mirrored hers. Love threatened to drown her.

"You're a lovely dancer, Miss Wolfe."

As the music ended, Asher smiled at her partner. "Thank you." Her smile never wavered as it ran through her head that she had completely forgotten the man's name.

"I was a great fan of your father's, you know." The man cupped a hand under her elbow to lead her from the dance floor. "The Golden Boy of Tennis." With a sigh he patted Asher's hand. "Of course, I remember his early days, before you were born."

"Wimbledon has always been his favorite. Dad loved the tradition…and the pomp," Asher added with a smile.

"Seeing the second generation here is good for the soul." In a courtly gesture he lifted her hand to his lips. "My best to you, Miss Wolfe."

"Jerry, how are you?"

A stately woman in silk brocade swept up to them. Lady Mallow, Eric Wickerton's sister, was, as always, elegant. Asher's spine stiffened.

"Lucy, what a pleasure!"

She offered her fingers to be kissed, sending Asher a brief

glance as she did so. "Jerry, Brian's been searching for you to say hello. He's just over there."

"Well then, if you ladies will excuse me."

Having dispatched him, Lucy turned to her former sister-in-law. "Asher, you're looking well."

"Thank you, Lucy."

She gave Asher's simple ivory sheath a brief survey, thinking that if she had worn something so basic, she would have blended in with the wallpaper. On Asher, the muted color and simple lines were stunning. Lucy gave her a candid stare. "And are you well?"

A bit surprised, Asher lifted a brow. "Yes, quite well. And you?"

"I meant that as more than small talk." Lucy's hesitation was brief, as was her glance to determine if they could be overheard. "There's something I've wanted to say to you for a long time." Stiffening, Asher waited. "I love my brother," Lucy began. "I know you didn't. I also know that throughout your marriage you did nothing to disgrace him, though he didn't return the favor."

The unexpected words had Asher staring. "Lucy—"

"Loving him doesn't blind me, Asher," she continued briskly. "My loyalty is with Eric, and always will be."

"Yes, I understand that."

Lucy studied Asher's face a moment, then she seemed to sigh. "I gave you no support when you were my brother's wife and I wanted to offer my apologies."

Touched, Asher took her hand. "There's no need. Eric and I were simply wrong for each other."

"I often wondered why you married him," Lucy mused, still searching Asher's face. "At first I thought it was the title, but that had nothing to do with it. Something seemed to change between you so soon after you were married, hardly two months." Asher's eyes clouded for only a moment under

Lucy's direct gaze. "I wondered if you'd taken a lover. But it became very obvious in a short time that it was Eric, not you, who was…dallying. Just as it's become obvious that there's been only one man in your life." Her gaze shifted. Asher didn't have to follow it to know it rested on Ty.

"Knowing that hurt Eric."

"Knowing that, Eric should never have married you." Lucy sighed again, a bit indulgently. "But then, he's always wanted what belonged to someone else. I won't speak of that, but I'll tell you now what I should have told you long before—I wish you happiness."

On impulse, Asher kissed her cheek. "Thank you, Lucy."

Smiling, she glanced over at Ty again. "Your taste, Asher, has always been exquisite. I've envied it, though it's never been right for me. It's time I joined Brian."

As she turned away, Asher touched her hand. "If I wrote you, would you be uncomfortable?"

"I'd be very pleased." Lucy moved away, silks rustling.

Smiling, Asher realized she had been right. Wimbledon was her turning point. Another layer of guilt had been lifted. She was coming closer to discovering who she was, and what she needed. Feeling a hand on her arm, she turned to smile at Ty.

"Who was that?"

"An old friend." Asher lifted a hand to his cheek. "Dance with me? There's no other way I can hold you until we can be alone."

CHAPTER 9

Asher knew she had made great strides when pressure from the press no longer tightened her nerves. Her habitual terror of saying the wrong thing, or saying too much, faded. She still had secrets. Before coming to Australia she'd promised herself a moratorium. Whatever decisions had to be made would wait. For the moment she wanted to concentrate on happiness. Happiness was Ty—and tennis.

There were good memories in Australia—wins, losses. Good tennis. The people were relaxed, casual. The friendliness was exactly what Asher needed after the tension of England. Aussies remembered The Face, and welcomed her. For the first time since her comeback Asher found the winning taking second place to the enjoying.

The change in her was noticeable even during the early rounds. Her smiles came more frequently. Though her play was no less intense and concentrated, the air of being driven was fading.

From the first row of the stands Ty watched her in early morning practice. He'd just completed two hours of his own. Now, his legs stretched out, he studied her from behind the protection of tinted glasses. She'd improved, he mused...not only as an athlete. He remembered how important athletic ability was to her. The fact that she was a strategist and a craftsman had never been enough. Always, she had striven to be recognized as a good athlete. And so she would be, he thought, as she raced to the net to slap a return with her two-fisted backhand. Perhaps in some ways the years of retirement had toughened her.

His face clouded a moment. Consciously he smoothed the frown away. This wasn't the time to think of that or to dwell on the questions that still plagued him. Whys—so many whys hammered at him. Yet he recognized that she was grabbing this time to be carefree. He'd give her that. He would wait. But when the season was over, he'd have his answers.

When her laughter floated to him he forgot the doubts. It was a rich, warm sound, heard all too rarely. Leaning back, Ty chugged down cold fruit juice and looked around him.

If Wimbledon was his favorite stadium, the grass of Kooyong was his favorite surface. It was as hard as a roadbed and fast. A ball bounced true here, unlike other grass courts. Even at the end of the season, when the courts were worn and soiled, the surface remained even. Even after a deluge of rain, the Australian grass was resilient. Kooyong was a treasure for the fast, for the aggressive. Ty was ready for just such a match. Through half-closed eyes he watched Asher. She was ready, too, he decided. And ever more ready to enjoy it. A smile touched his mouth. Whatever questions there were, whatever answers, nothing could harm what was between them now.

Noting the practice session was winding up, Ty jumped lightly down to the court. "How about a quick game?"

Madge shot him a look and continued to pack up her rackets. "Forget it, hotshot."

He grabbed a racket from her, bouncing a ball lightly on the strings. "Spot you two points."

With a snort Madge snatched the ball, dropping it into

the can. "Take him on, Asher," she suggested. "He needs a lesson."

Catching her tongue between her teeth, Asher studied him. "Head to head," she decided.

"You serve."

Asher waited until he had taken his receiving position. Cupping two balls in her hand, she sent him a smile. "Been a while, hasn't it, Starbuck?"

"Last time we played you never got to game point." He gave Madge a wink. "Sure you don't want that handicap?"

Her ace answered for her. As pleased as he was surprised, Ty sent her a long look. Removing the tinted glasses, he tossed them to Madge. "Not bad, Face." His eyes followed the trail of the next serve. He sent it to the far corner to brush the service line. Ty liked nothing better than to watch Asher run. The range of her backhand was limited, but perfectly placed. He was on it in a flash. The last time they had played he had beaten her handily even while holding back. Now he scented challenge.

Asher lined the ball straight at him, hard and fast. Pivoting, Ty slammed it back. The ball whistled on her return. With a powerful swing Ty sent her to the baseline, then nipped her return so that the ball brushed the net and died in the forecourt.

"Fifteen-all." Ty feigned a yawn as he went back to position.

Narrowing her eyes, Asher served. The rally was a study in speed and footwork. She knew he was playing with her, moving her all over the court. Aware that she was no match for his power, she chose to catch him off guard. The ball thudded. She raced. It soared. She followed. The sounds of rackets cutting air had a steady, almost musical sound. A rhythm was set. Patiently she adhered to it until she sensed Ty relaxing. Abruptly she altered the pacing and slapped the ball past him.

"Getting crafty," he muttered.

"Getting slow, old timer," she retorted sweetly.

Ty slammed her next serve crosscourt. After the bounce, it landed somewhere in the grandstands. Under her breath Asher swore pungently.

"Did you say something?"

"Not a thing." Disgusted, Asher shook her hair back. As she readied to serve, she caught the look in Ty's eyes. They rested not on her ball or racket, but on her mouth.

All's fair, she mused with a secret smile. Slowly and deliberately she moistened her lips with the tip of her tongue. Taking a long, preliminary stretch, she served. Distracted, Ty was slow to meet the ball. Asher had little trouble blowing the return past him.

"Game point," she said softly, sending him an intimate smile. Keeping her back to him, she bent to pick up a fresh ball, taking her time about it. She could almost feel Ty's eyes run up the long length of her legs. Smoothing a hand down her hip, she walked back to the baseline. "Ready?"

He nodded, dragging his eyes away from the subtle sweep of her breasts. When his eyes met hers, he read an invitation that had his pulse racing. His concentration broken, he barely returned her serve. The rally was very short.

Victorious, Asher let out a hoot of laughter before she walked to the net. "Your game seemed to be a bit off, Starbuck."

The gibe and the laughter in her eyes had him wanting to strangle her…and devour her. "Cheat," he murmured as he walked to meet her at the net.

Asher's look was guileless and she was faintly shocked. "I have no idea what you're talking about." The words were hardly out of her mouth when she was pulled against him, her lips crushed under his. Laughter and desire seemed to bubble in her simultaneously. Without being aware of it, she dropped her racket and clung to him.

"You're lucky I don't toss you on the ground here and now," he mumbled against her mouth.

"What's lucky about that?" Enchanted, Asher strained against him. How was it possible for one kiss to make her head swim?

Ty drew back, inches only. His whole body was throbbing for her. "Don't tempt me."

"Do I?" she asked huskily.

"Damn you, Asher. You know just how much."

His voice shook, delighting her. She found she needed him to be as vulnerable as she. "I'm never sure," she whispered, dropping her head to his chest.

His heart was beating too rapidly. Ty tried to fight down the impossible surge of need. Not the time, not the place, his sanity stated. Control was necessary. "You were sure enough to use a few tricks to distract me."

Lifting her head, Asher smiled at him. "Distract you? How?"

"Took your time picking up that ball, didn't you?"

She seemed to consider a moment. "Why, I've seen Chuck do the same thing playing against you. It never seemed to make any difference." She let out a whoop of surprise as he lifted her up and over the net.

"Next time I'll be ready for you, Face." After giving her a brief, bruising kiss, he dropped her to her feet. "You could play naked and I wouldn't blink an eye."

Catching her lip between her teeth, she sent him a teasing glance. "Wanna bet?" Before he could connect his racket with her bottom, she dashed away.

The locker room wasn't empty as Asher walked in, but the crowd was thinning. With the fifth rounds completed, there were fewer contenders, and therefore fewer bodies. She was looking forward to her match that afternoon with a hot newcomer who had hopped up in the rankings from one hundred and twentieth to forty-third in one year. Asher had no intention of strolling into the finals. Even the pressure of Grand Slam potential couldn't mar her mood. If ever there was a year she could win it, Asher felt it was this one.

She greeted a towel-clad Tia Conway as the Australian emerged from the showers. Both women knew they would face each other before the tournament was over. Asher could hear a laughing argument taking place over the sound of running water. As she started to remove her warm-up jacket, she spotted Madge in a corner.

The brunette sat with her head leaning back against the wall, her eyes shut. She was pale despite her tan, and there were beads of perspiration on her brow. Asher rushed over to kneel at her feet.

"Madge."

Opening her eyes slowly, Madge sighed. "Who won?"

For a moment Asher went blank. "Oh, I did. I cheated."

"Smart girl."

"Madge, what's wrong? God, your hands are like ice."

"No, it's nothing." She let out a breath as she leaned forward.

"You're sick, let me—"

"No, I've finished being sick." After a weak smile Madge swiped the sweat from her brow. "I'll be fine in a minute."

"You look terrible. You need a doctor." Asher sprang to her feet. "I'll call someone." Before she could move, Madge had her hand.

"I've seen a doctor."

Every sort of nightmare went through Asher's head. In stark terror she stared at her friend. "Oh, God, Madge, how bad?"

"I've got seven months." As Asher swayed, Madge caught her arm tightly. "Good grief, Asher, I'm pregnant, not dying."

Stunned, Asher sank to the bench. *"Pregnant!"*

"Shh." Quickly Madge glanced around. "I'd like to keep

this quiet for a while. Damn morning sickness catches me off guard at the worst times." Letting out a shaky breath, she relaxed against the wall again. "The good news is it's not supposed to last long."

"I don't—Madge, I don't know what to say."

"How about congratulations?"

Shaking her head, Asher gripped both of Madge's hands in hers. "Is this what you want?"

"Are you kidding?" On a half laugh, Madge leaned against Asher's shoulder. "I might not look too happy at the moment, but inside I'm doing cartwheels. I've never wanted anything so badly in my life." She sat silently for a moment, her hand still in Asher's. "You know, during my twenties all I could think about was being number one. It was great being there. The Wrightman Cup, Wimbledon, Dallas—all of it. I was twenty-eight when I met The Dean, and still ambitious as hell. I didn't want to get married, but I couldn't live without him. As for kids, I thought, hell, there's plenty of time for that. Later, always later. Well, I woke up one morning in the hospital with my leg screaming at me and I realized I was thirty-two years old. I'd won just about everything I thought I had to win, and yet something was missing. For the better part of my life I've floated around this old world from court to court. Team tennis, pro-am tourneys, celebrity exhibitions, you name it. Until The Dean there was nothing but tennis for me. Even after him, it was the biggest slice of the pie."

"You're a champion," Asher said softly.

"Yeah." Madge laughed again. "Yeah, by God, I am, and I like it. But you know what? When I looked at the snapshot of Ty's nephew I realized that I wanted a baby, The Dean's baby, more than I'd ever wanted a Wimbledon plate. Isn't that wild?"

She let the statement hang in silence a moment as both women absorbed it. "This is going to be my last tournament, and even while that's hurting, I keep wishing it was over so I could go home and start knitting booties."

"You don't know how to knit," Asher murmured.

"Well, The Dean can knit them then. I'll just sit around and get fat." Twisting her head to grin at Asher, Madge saw the tears. "Hey, what's this?"

"I'm happy for you," Asher muttered. She could remember her own feelings on learning of her pregnancy—the fear, the joy, the nausea and elation. She'd wanted to learn to sew. Then it had been over so quickly.

"You look overjoyed," Madge commented, brushing a tear away.

"I am really." She caught Madge to her in a viselike hug. "You'll take care of yourself, won't you? Don't overdo or take any chances?"

"Sure." Something in the tone had the seed of a thought germinating. "Asher, did you… Did something happen when you were married to Eric?"

Asher held her tighter for a moment, then released her. "Not now. Maybe someday we'll talk about it. How does The Dean feel about all this?"

Madge gave her a long, measuring look. The non-answer was answer enough, so she let it lay. "He was all set to take out a full-page ad in *World of Sports,*" she stated. "I've made him wait until I officially retire."

"There's no need to retire, Madge. You can take a year or two off, lots of women do."

"Not this one." Stretching her arms to the ceiling, Madge grinned. "I'm going out a winner, ranked fifth. When I get home, I'm going to learn how to use a vacuum cleaner."

"I'll believe that when I see it."

"You and Ty are invited to my first home-cooked dinner."

"Great." Asher kissed her cheek. "We'll bring the antacid."

"Not nice," Madge mused. "But wise. Hey, Face," she continued before Asher could rise. "I wouldn't want this to get around but—" her eyes were suddenly very young, and she looked very vulnerable "—I'm scared right out of my socks. I'll be almost thirty-four by the time this kid makes an appearance. I've never even changed a diaper."

Firmly Asher took Madge's shoulders and kissed both of her cheeks. "You're a champion, remember?"

"Yeah, but what do I know about chicken pox?" Madge demanded. "Kids get chicken pox, don't they? And braces, and corrective shoes, and—"

"And mothers who worry before there's anything to worry about," Asher finished. "You're already slipping right into the slot."

"Hey, you're right." Rather pleased with herself, Madge rose. "I'm going to be great."

"You're going to be terrific. Let's get a shower. You've got a doubles match this afternoon."

With feelings mixed and uncertain, Asher rode the elevator to her hotel room late that afternoon. She had won her round with the young upstart from Canada in straight sets. Six-two, six-love. There was little doubt that Asher had played some of the finest tennis in her career in court one. But she didn't think of that now. Her mind kept drifting back to her interlude with Madge, and from there back to her thoughts on learning of her own pregnancy.

Would Ty have wanted to take out full-page ads, or would he have cursed her? Like Eric, would he have accused her of deceit, of trickery? Now that they were being given a second chance, would he want marriage and children? What was it Jess had said that day? she wondered. *Ty will always be a gypsy, and no woman should ever expect to hold him.*

Yet Asher had expected to hold him, and, despite all her vows, was beginning to expect it again. Her love was so huge, so consuming, that when she was with him, it was simply impossible to conceive of doing without him. And perhaps because she had once, briefly, carried his child inside her, the need to do so again was overwhelming.

Could a woman tame a comet? she asked herself. Should she? For that's what he was—a star that flew, full of speed and light. He wasn't the prince at the end of the fairy tale who would calmly take up his kingdom and sit on a throne. Ty would always search for the next quest. And the next woman? Asher wondered, recalling Jess's words again.

Shaking her head, she told herself to think of today. Today they were together. Only a woman who had lived through change after change, hurt after hurt, could fully appreciate the perfection of a moment. Others might not recognize it, but Asher did. And the moment was hers.

She unlocked the door to their suite and was immediately disappointed. He wasn't there. Even had he been sleeping in the other room, she would have sensed him. The air was never still when Ty was around. Tossing her bag aside, she wandered to the window. The light was still full as the sun had only just began to set. Perhaps they would go out and explore Melbourne, find one of the tiny little clubs with loud music and laughter. She'd like to dance.

Twirling in a circle, Asher laughed. Yes, she would like to dance, to celebrate for Madge…and for herself. She was with the man she loved. A bath, she decided. A long, luxurious bath before she changed into something cool and sexy. When she opened the door to the bedroom, Asher stopped and stared in astonishment.

Balloons. Red, yellow, blue, pink and white. They floated throughout the room in a jamboree of color. Helium-filled, they rose to the ceiling, trailing long ribbons. There were dozens of them—round, oval, thin and fat. It was as if a circus had passed hurriedly through, leaving a few souvenirs.

Grasping a ribbon, Asher drew one down to her while she continued to stare.

They were three layers deep, she saw in astonishment—at least a hundred of them bumping against one another. Her laughter came out in a quick burst that went on and on.

Who else would think of it? Who else would take the time? Not flowers or jewelry for Ty Starbuck. At that moment she could have floated to the ceiling to join the gift he had given her.

"Hi."

She turned to see him lounging in the doorway. In a flash Asher had launched herself into his arms, the single balloon still grasped in her hand. "Oh, you're crazy!" she cried before she found his lips with hers. With her arms wrapped around his neck, her legs around his waist, she kissed him again and again. "Absolutely insane."

"Me?" he countered. "You're the one standing here surrounded by balloons."

"It's the best surprise I've ever had."

"Better than roses in the bathtub?"

Tossing her head back, she laughed. "Even better than that."

"I thought about diamonds, but they didn't seem like as much fun." As he spoke he moved toward the bed.

"And they don't float," Asher put in, looking up at the ceiling of colorful shapes.

"Good point," Ty conceded as they fell together onto the bed. "Got any ideas how we should spend the evening?"

"One or two," Asher murmured. The balloon she held drifted up to join the others.

"Let's do both." He stopped her laugh with a soft kiss that became hungry quickly. "Oh, God, I've waited all day to be alone with you. When the season's over we'll find someplace—an island, another planet—anyplace where there's no one but us."

"Anyplace," she whispered in agreement while her hands tugged at his shirt.

Passion soared swiftly. Ty's needs doubled as he sensed hers. She was always soft, always eager for him. If the pounding of his blood would have allowed, he would have revered her. But the force of their joined desire wouldn't permit reverence. Clothes were hastily peeled away—a blouse flung aside, a shirt cast to the floor. Overhead, the balloons danced while they savored each other. The scent of victory seemed to cling to both of them, mixed with the faint fragrance of soap and shampoo from the post-game showers. Her lips tasted warm and moist, and somehow of himself as much as of her.

When there was nothing to separate them, they tangled together, their bodies hot and throbbing. With questing hands he moved over territory only more exciting in its familiarity. He could feel reason spin away into pure sensation. Soft here, firm there, her body was endless delight. The warmth of her breath along his skin could make him tremble. Her moan, as he slipped his fingers into her, made him ache. With open-mouthed kisses he trailed over her, seeking the hot heady flavor of her flesh. It seemed to melt into him, filling him to bursting.

When she arched, offering everything, Ty felt a surge of power so awesome he almost feared to take her. Too strong, he thought hazily. He was too strong and was bound to hurt her. He felt he could have lifted the world without effort. Yet she was drawing him to her with murmuring pleas.

There was no control in madness. She stole his sanity with her smooth skin and soft lips. There were no more pastel colors from frivolous balloons. Now there was gleaming silver and molten reds and pulsing blacks whirling and churning into a wild kaleidoscope that seemed to pull him into its vortex. Gasping her name, Ty thrust into her. The colors shattered, seeming to pierce his skin with a multitude of shards. And in the pain was indescribable pleasure.

When he was spent, nestled between her breasts, Asher gazed up at the darkening ceiling. How could it be, she wondered, that each time they were together it was different? Sometimes they loved in laughter, sometimes in tenderness. At other times with a smoldering passion. This time there had been a taste of madness in their loving. Did other lovers find this infinite variety, this insatiable delight in each other? Perhaps the two of them were unique. The thought was almost frightening.

"What are you thinking?" Ty asked. He knew he should shift his weight from her, but found no energy to do so.

"I was wondering if it should be so special each time I'm with you."

He laughed, kissing the side of her breast. "Of course it should, I'm a special person. Don't you read the sports section?"

She tugged his hair, but tenderly. "Don't let your press go to your head, Starbuck. You have to win a few more matches before you wrap up the Grand Slam."

He massaged the muscles of her thigh. "So do you, Face."

"I'm only thinking as far ahead as the next game," she said. She didn't want to think of Forest Hills, or the States—or the end of the season. "Madge is pregnant," she said half to herself.

"What!" Like a shot, Ty's head came up.

"Madge is pregnant," Asher repeated. "She wants to keep it quiet until the Australian Open is over."

"I'll be damned," he exclaimed. "Old Madge."

"She's only a year older than you," Asher stated defensively, causing him to laugh again.

"It's an expression, love." Absently he twined one of Asher's curls around a finger. "How does she feel about it?"

"She's thrilled—and scared." Her lashes lowered, shielding her expression a moment. "She's going to retire."

"We're going to have to throw her one hell of a party." Rolling onto his back, he drew Asher close to his side.

After a moment she moistened her lips and spoke casually. "Do you ever think about children? I mean, it would be difficult, wouldn't it, combining a family with a profession like this?"

"It's done all the time, depends on how you go about it."

"Yes, but all the traveling, the pressure."

He started to pass it off, then remembered how she had lived her childhood. Though he had never sensed any resentment in her, he wondered if she felt a family would be a hindrance to her career. Physically a baby would prevent her from playing for some time. And she'd already lost three years, he reflected with an inner sigh. Ty pushed the idea of their children out of his mind. There was time, after all.

"I imagine it's a hassle to worry about kids when you've got a tournament to think of," he said lightly. "A player's got enough trouble keeping track of his rackets."

With a murmured agreement, Asher stared into space.

In the thin light of dawn she shifted, brushing at a tickle on her arm. Something brushed over her cheek. Annoyed, Asher lifted her hand to knock it away. It came back. With a softly uttered complaint she opened her eyes.

In the gray light she could see dozens of shapes. Some hung halfway to the ceiling, others littered the bed and floor. Sleepy, she stared at them without comprehension. Irritated at having been disturbed, she knocked at the shape that rested on her hip. It floated lazily away.

Balloons, she realized. Turning her head, she saw that Ty was all but buried under them. She chuckled, muffling the sound with her hand as she sat up. He lay flat on his stomach, facedown in the pillow. She plucked a red balloon from the back of his head. He didn't budge. Leaning over, she outlined his ear with kisses. He muttered and stirred and shifted away. Asher lifted a brow. A challenge, she decided.

After brushing the hair from the nape of his neck, she began to nibble on the exposed flesh. "Ty," she whispered. "We have company."

Feeling a prickle of drowsy pleasure, Ty rolled to his side, reaching for her. Asher placed a balloon in his hand. Unfocused, his eyes opened.

"What the hell is this?"

"We're surrounded," Asher told him in a whisper. "They're everywhere."

A half dozen balloons tipped to the floor as he shifted to his back. After rubbing his face with his hands, he stared. "Good God." With that he shut his eyes again.

Not to be discouraged, Asher straddled him. "Ty, it's morning."

"Uh-uh."

"I have that talk show to do at nine."

He yawned and patted her bottom. "Good luck."

She planted a soft, nibbling kiss on his lips. "I have two hours before I have to leave."

"'S okay, you won't bother me."

Wanna bet? she asked silently. Reaching out, she trailed her fingers up his thigh. "Maybe I'll sleep a bit longer."

"Mmm-hmm."

Slowly she lay on top of him, nuzzling her lips at her throat. "I'm not bothering you, am I?"

"Hmm?"

She snuggled closer, feeling her breasts rub against his soft mat of hair. "Cold," she mumbled, and moved her thigh against his.

"Turn down the air-conditioning," Ty suggested.

Brows lowered, Asher lifted her head. Ty's eyes met hers, laughing, and not a bit sleepy. With a toss of her head Asher rolled from him and tugged on the blanket. Though her back was to him, she could all but see his grin.

"How's this?" Wrapping an arm around her waist, he fit his body to hers. She gave him a shrug as an answer. "Warmer?" he asked as he slid his hand up to cup her breast. The point was already taut, her pulse already racing. Ty moved sinuously against her.

"The air-conditioning's too high," she said plaintively. "I'm freezing."

Ty dropped a kiss at the base of her neck. "I'll get it." He rose, moving to the unit. It shut off with a dull mechanical thud. With a teasing remark on the tip of his tongue, he turned.

In the fragile morning light she lay naked in the tumbled bed, surrounded by gay balloons. Her hair rioted around a face dominated by dark, sleepy eyes. The faintest of smiles touched her lips, knowing, inviting, challenging. All thoughts of joking left him. Her skin was so smooth and touched with gold. Like a fist in the solar plexus, desire struck him and stole his breath.

As he went to her, Asher lifted her arms to welcome him.

CHAPTER 10

"Asher, how does it feel being only three matches away from the Grand Slam?"

"I'm trying not to think about it."

"You've drawn Stacie Kingston in the quarter-finals. She's got an oh-for-five record against you. Does that boost your confidence?"

"Stacie's a strong player, and very tough. I'd never go into a match with her overconfident."

Her hands folded loosely, Asher sat behind the table facing the lights and reporters. The microphone in front of her picked up her calm, steady voice and carried it to the rear of the room. She wore her old team tennis jacket with loose warm-up pants and court shoes. Around her face her hair curled damply. They'd barely given her time to shower after her most recent win at Forest Hills before scheduling the impromptu press conference. The cameras were rolling, taping her every movement, recording every expression. One of the print reporters quickly scribbled down that she wore no jewelry or lipstick.

"Did you expect your comeback to be this successful?"

Asher gave a lightning-fast grin—here then gone—something she would never have done for the press even two months before. "I trained hard," she said simply.

"Do you still lift weights?"

"Every day."

"Have you changed your style this time around?"

"I think I've tightened a few things up." She relaxed, considering. Of all the people in the room, only Asher was aware that her outlook toward the press had changed. There was no tightness in her throat as she spoke. No warning signals to take care flashing in her brain. "Improved my serve particularly," she continued. "My percentage of aces and service winners is much higher than it was three or four years ago."

"How often did you play during your retirement?"

"Not often enough."

"Will your father be coaching you again?"

Her hesitation was almost too brief to be measured. "Not officially," she replied evasively.

"Have you decided to accept the offer of a layout in *Elegance* magazine?"

Asher tucked a lock of hair behind her ear. "News travels fast." Laughter scattered around the room. "I haven't really decided," she continued. "At the moment I'm more concerned with the U.S. Open."

"Who do you pick to be your opponent in the finals?"

"I'd like to get through the quarters and semis first."

"Let's say, who do you think will be your strongest competition?"

"Tia Conway," Asher answered immediately. Their duel in Kooyong was still fresh in her mind. Three exhausting sets—three tie breakers—in two grueling hours. "She's the best all-around woman player today."

"What makes you say that?"

"Tia has court sense, speed, strength and a big serve."

"Yet you've beaten her consistently this season."

"But not easily."

"What about the men's competition? Would you predict the U.S. will have two Grand Slam winners this year?"

Asher fielded the question first with a smile. "I think someone mentioned that there were still three matches to go, but I believe it's safe to say that if Starbuck continues to play as he's played all season, no one will beat him, particularly on grass, as it's his best surface."

"Is your opinion influenced by personal feelings?"

"Statistics don't have any feelings," she countered. "Personal or otherwise." Asher rose, effectively curtailing further questioning. A few more were tossed out at random, but she merely leaned toward the mike and apologized for having to end the meeting. As she started to slip through a rear door, she spotted Chuck.

"Nicely done, Face."

"And over," she breathed. "What are you doing here?"

"Keeping an eye on my best friend's lady," he said glibly as he slipped an arm around her shoulders. "Ty thought it would be less confusing if he kept out of the way during your little tête-à-tête with the members of the working press."

"For heaven's sake," Asher mumbled, "I don't need a keeper."

"Don't tell me." Chuck flashed his boy-next-door smile. "Ty had it in his head the press might badger you."

Tilting her head, Asher studied his deceptively sweet face. "And what were you going to do if they had?"

"Strong-arm 'em," he claimed while flexing his muscle. "Though I might have been tempted to let them take a few bites out of you after that comment about nobody beating Ty. Didn't you hear they were naming a racket after me?"

Asher circled his waist with her arm. "Sorry, friend, I call 'em like I see 'em."

Stopping, he put both hands on Asher's shoulders and

studied her. His look remained serious even when she gave him a quizzical smile. "You know, Face, you really look good."

She laughed. "Well, thanks…I think. Did I look bad before?"

"I don't mean you look beautiful, that never changes. I mean you look happy."

Lifting a hand to the one on her shoulder, Asher squeezed. "I am happy."

"It shows. In Ty too." Briefly he hesitated, then plunged ahead. "Listen, I don't know what happened between you two before, but—"

"Chuck…" Asher shook her head to ward off questions.

"But," he continued, "I want you to know I hope you make it this time."

"Oh, Chuck." Shutting her eyes, she went into his arms. "So do I," she sighed. "So do I."

"I asked you to keep an eye on her," Ty said from behind them. "I didn't say anything about touching."

"Oh, hell." Chuck tightened his hold. "Don't be so selfish. Second-seeds need love too." Glancing down at Asher, he grinned. "Can I interest you in lobster tails and champagne?"

"Sorry." She kissed his nose. "Somebody already offered me pizza and cheap wine."

"Outclassed again." With a sigh Chuck released her. "I need somebody to hit with tomorrow," he told Ty.

"Okay."

"Six o'clock, court three."

"You buy the coffee."

"We'll flip for it," Chuck countered before he sauntered away.

Alone, Asher and Ty stood for a moment in awkward silence while an airplane droned by overhead. The awkwardness had cropped up occasionally on their return to the

States. It was always brief and never commented on. In the few seconds without words, each of them admitted that full truths would soon be necessary. Neither of them knew how to approach it.

"So," Ty began as the moment passed, "how did it go?"

"Easily," Asher returned, smiling as she stood on tiptoe to kiss him. "I didn't need the bodyguard."

"I know how you feel about press conferences."

"How?"

"Oh…" He combed her hair with his fingers. "*Terrified*'s a good word."

With a laugh she held out her hand as they started to walk. "*Was* a good word," Asher corrected him. "I'm amazed I ever let it get to me. There was one problem though."

"What?"

"I was afraid I'd faint from starvation." She sent him a pitiful look from under her lashes. "Someone did mention pizza, didn't they?"

"Yeah." He grinned, catching her close. "And cheap wine."

"You really know how to treat a woman, Starbuck," Asher told him in a breathless whisper.

"We'll go Dutch," he added before he pulled her toward the car.

Twenty minutes later they sat together at a tiny round table. There was the scent of rich sauce, spice and melted candles. From the jukebox in the corner poured an endless succession of popular rock tunes at a volume just below blaring. The waitresses wore bib aprons sporting pictures of grinning pizzas. Leaning her elbows on the scarred wooden table, Asher stared soulfully into Ty's eyes.

"You know how to pick a class joint, don't you?"

"Stick with me, Face," he advised. "I've got a hamburger palace picked out for tomorrow. You get your own individual plastic packs of ketchup." Her lips curved up, making him want to taste them. Leaning forward, he did. The table tilted dangerously.

"You two ready to order?" Snapping her wad of gum, the waitress shifted her weight to one hip.

"Pizza and a bottle of Chianti," Ty told her, kissing Asher again.

"Small, medium or large?"

"Small, medium or large what?"

"Pizza," the waitress said with exaggerated patience.

"Medium ought to do it." Twisting his head, Ty sent the waitress a smile that had her pulling back her shoulders. "Thanks."

"Well, that should improve the service," Asher considered as she watched the woman saunter away.

"What's that?"

Asher studied his laughing eyes. "Never mind," she decided. "Your ego doesn't need any oiling."

Ty bent his head closer to hers as a defense against the jukebox. "So what kind of questions did they toss at you?"

"The usual. They mentioned the business from *Elegance.*"

"Are you going to do it?"

She moved her shoulders. "I don't know. It might be fun. And I don't suppose it would hurt the image of women's tennis for one of the players to be in a national fashion magazine."

"It's been done before."

Asher conquered a grin and arched her brows instead. "Do you read fashion magazines, Starbuck?"

"Sure. I like to look at pretty women."

"I always thought jocks tended to favor other sorts of magazines for that."

He gave her an innocent look. "What sorts of magazines?"

Ignoring him, Asher went back to his original question. "They're playing up this Grand Slam business for all it's worth."

"Bother you?" As he laced their fingers together, he studied them. There was an almost stunning difference in size and texture. Often he'd wondered how such an elegant little hand could be so strong…and why it should fit so perfectly with his.

"A bit," Asher admitted, enjoying the rough feel of his skin against hers. "It makes it difficult to go into a match thinking of just that match. What about you? I know you're getting the same kind of pressure."

The waitress brought the wine, giving Ty a slow smile as she set down the glasses. To Asher's amusement, he returned it. He's a devil, she thought. And he knows it.

"I always look at playing a game at a time, one point at a time." He poured a generous amount of wine in both glasses. "Three matches is a hell of a lot of points."

"But you'd like to win the Grand Slam?"

Raising his glass, he grinned. "Damn right." He laughed into her eyes as he drank. "Of course, Martin's already making book on it."

"I'm surprised he's not here," Asher commented, "analyzing every volley."

"He's coming in tomorrow with the rest of the family."

Asher's fingers tightened on the stem of her glass. "The rest of the family?"

"Yeah, Mom and Jess for sure. Mac and Pete if it can be arranged." The Chianti was heavy and mellow. Ty relaxed with it. "You'll like Pete; he's a cute kid."

She mumbled something into her wine before she swallowed. Martin had been there three years ago, along with Ty's mother and sister. Both she and Ty had gone into the U.S. Open as top seeds; both had been hounded by the press. The two of them had shared meals then, too, and a bed. So much was the same—terrifyingly so. But there had been so much in between.

There'd been no small boy with Ty's coloring then. No

small boy with that air of perpetual energy to remind her of what was lost. Asher felt the emptiness inside her, then the ache, as she did each time she thought of the child.

Misinterpreting her silence, Ty reached over to take her hand. "Asher, you still haven't spoken to your father?"

"What?" Disoriented, she stared at him a moment. "No, no, not since… Not since I retired."

"Why don't you call him?"

"I can't."

"That's ridiculous. He's your father."

She sighed, wishing it were so simple. "Ty, you know him. He's a very stringent man, very certain of what's right and what's wrong. When I left tennis I did more than disappoint him, I…wasted what he'd given me."

Ty answered with a short, explicit word that made her smile. "From his viewpoint that's the way it was," she went on. "As Jim Wolfe's daughter I had certain responsibilities. In marrying Eric and giving up my career I shirked them. He hasn't forgiven me."

"How do you know that?" he demanded. His voice was low under the insistent music, but rich with annoyance. "If you haven't spoken to him, how can you be sure how he feels now?"

"Ty, if his feelings had changed, wouldn't he be here?" She shrugged, wishing they could have avoided the subject for a while longer. "I thought, at first, that when I started playing again it might make the difference. It hasn't."

"But you miss him."

Even that wasn't so simple. To Ty, family meant something warm and loving and eternal. He'd never understand that Asher looked not so much now for her father's presence or even his love, but simply his forgiveness. "I'd like him to be here," she said finally. "But I understand his reasons for not coming." Her brow clouded for a moment with a realization that had just come to her. "Before, I played for him, to please him, to justify the time and effort he put into my career. Now I play for myself."

"And you play better," Ty put in. "Perhaps that's one of the reasons."

With a smile she lifted his hand to her lips. "Perhaps that's one of them."

"Here's your pizza." The waitress plopped the steaming pan between them.

They ate amid noise and their own casual chatter. Even the pressure of the upcoming matches had no effect on Asher's mood. The cheese was hot and stringy, making Ty laugh as she struggled against it. The contents of the squat bottle of Chianti lowered as they drank leisurely, content to let the meal drag on. Tennis was forgotten while they spoke of everything and nothing at all. A group of teenagers poured in, laughing and rowdy, to feed another succession of quarters into the jukebox.

Why am I so happy to be in this loud, crowded room? she wondered. The cooling pizza and lukewarm wine were as appealing as the champagne and caviar they had shared in Paris. It was Ty. The place never mattered when she was with him. Abruptly it occurred to Asher that it was herself as well. She was being herself. There weren't any guards, or the need for any. Ty was the only man she'd ever been close to who required none from her.

Her father had wanted her to be perfect—his glass princess. All through her youth she had done everything in her power to please him. With Eric, she had been expected to be the cool, well-mannered Lady Wickerton, a woman who could discuss art and politics intelligently. She was to have been like crystal, many-faceted, elegant and cold.

All Ty had ever expected her to be was Asher. He accepted her flaws, even admired them. Because he had wanted her to be herself, she'd been able to be just that. Not once in all the time she had known him had he ever demanded that she fit a pattern or requested that she conform to any standards but her own. Impulsively she reached over to take his hand, then pressed it to her cheek. There was warmth against warmth, flesh against flesh.

"What's this for?" he asked, allowing his fingers to spread.

"For not wanting glass."

His brows drew together in confusion. "Am I supposed to know what that means?"

"No." Laughing, Asher leaned closer. "Have you drunk enough wine that your resistance is down and you'll be easily seduced?"

A slow smile spread. "More than enough."

"Then come with me," Asher ordered.

It was late when Ty lay sleepless beside Asher. Curled close, her hand caught loosely in his, she slept deeply, drugged with loving and fatigue. Her scent hung in the air so that even in the dark Ty could visualize her. A small alarm clock ticked monotonously at his left, its luminous dial glowing. Twelve twenty-seven.

His mind was far too active for sleep. He sensed, as he knew Asher did, that the idyll was nearly over. They were back where they had once ended, and questions would not be put off too much longer. Impatience gnawed at him. Unlike Asher, Ty looked for the end of the season. Only then would the time be right for answers and explanations. He was not used to biding his time, and the strain was beginning to tell. Even tonight under the laughter he had understood her wordless request that he not probe.

The question of her father, Ty mused, shifting the pillow to brace his back. She was more unhappy about the estrangement than she admitted. It showed in her eyes. It was incomprehensible to him that members of a family could turn away from one another. His thoughts drifted to his mother, to Jess. There was nothing either of them could do he wouldn't forgive. He'd never be able to bear the thought of being responsible for their unhappiness. Could a father feel any different about a daughter? An only daughter, a much-loved daughter, Ty reflected.

He could remember Jim Wolfe's pride in Asher. Ty had often sat beside him during one of Asher's matches in her early days as a pro, then consistently during her last year. Even in such a private man the adoration had showed. It wasn't possible to believe it had been only for the athlete and not for the woman.

Surprisingly Jim had accepted Ty's relationship with his daughter. No, Ty corrected, approved. He'd seemed to enjoy seeing them together. Once, Ty recalled, he had gone as far as outlining his expectations to Ty of their future. At the time Ty had been both amused and annoyed at the fatherly interference. What plans he had had for a future with Asher had still been vague. Then, when they had crystalized in his mind, it had been too late. Frowning, Ty glanced down at her.

In the pale shaft of moonlight her face seemed very fragile. Her hair was a silvery, insubstantial cloud around it. A wave of longing swamped him so that he had to fight the need to wake her and satisfy himself that she was there for him. His feelings for her had always been mixed—wild desire, unbearable tenderness, traces of fear. There had been no other woman who had ever brought him such sharp and conflicting emotions. Watching her sleep, he felt the need to protect. There should be no shadow of unhappiness in her eyes when they opened.

How many obstacles would they have to overcome before they were really together? he wondered. There was one he might remove himself. Perhaps the time had come to take the first step. On impulse, Ty slipped from the bed and into the sitting room.

It took only moments by phone to travel from coast to coast. Dropping into a chair, Ty listened to the faint crackling on the wire before it began to ring.

"Wolfe residence."

In the two words, Ty recognized the trained voice of a servant. "Jim Wolfe please. It's Ty Starbuck."

"One moment please."

Ty sat back, keeping one ear trained on the adjoining bedroom. He heard two distinct clicks as one extension was lifted and the other replaced.

"Starbuck."

The quiet, cautious voice was instantly recognizable. "Jim. How are you?"

"Well." A bit surprised by the late night call, Jim Wolfe settled behind his desk. "I've been reading quite a bit about you."

"It's been a good year. You were missed at Wimbledon."

"That makes five for you there."

"And three for Asher," he returned pointedly.

There was a moment of complete silence. "Your slice volley's cleaner than it once was."

"Jim, I called to talk about Asher."

"Then we have nothing to say."

For a moment the cool, calm statement left Ty speechless. In a flood, fury took over. "Just a damn minute. I have plenty to say. Your daughter's battled her way back to the top. She's done it without you."

"I'm aware of that. Do you have a point?"

"Yes, I have a point," Ty retorted. "I've never seen anyone work as hard as she has these past few months. And it hasn't been easy, dealing with the pressure, the press, the constant questions on why her father isn't in the stands while she wins championship after championship."

"Asher knows my feelings," Jim said flatly. "They're no concern of yours."

"Whatever concerns Asher concerns me."

"So…" Jim picked up a slim gold pen from the desk and carefully examined it. "We're back to that."

"Yes, we are."

"If you've decided to resume your relationship with Asher, it's your business, Ty." He flung the pen back onto the desk. "And it's my business if I don't."

"For God's sake, Jim," Ty began heatedly, "she's your daughter. You can't turn your back on your own child."

"Like father, like daughter," Jim murmured.

"What the hell does that mean?" Frustrated, Ty rose to pace, dragging the phone with him.

"Asher wiped her child out of existence. I've done the same."

All movement stopped. Ty felt something freeze in him as his knuckles turned white on the receiver. "What child?"

"She turned her back on everything I taught her," Jim went on, not hearing Ty's harshly whispered question. "The daughter I knew couldn't have done it." The words, and the anger that accompanied them, had been held in for years. Now they came bursting out. "I tried to understand why she married that pale excuse for a man, even tried to resign myself to her throwing away her career. But some things I won't forgive. If the life she chose to live was worth the price of my grandchild, she's welcome to it."

Enraged at letting his feelings pour out so openly, Jim slammed down the receiver.

Three thousand miles away Ty stood, staring at nothing. With infinite care he placed the phone back on the table.

Too many thoughts were whirling in his head, too many questions and half-answers. He had to think, to take his time. Silently he walked back into the bedroom and dressed.

He wanted to shake her awake and demand an explanation; he wanted to wait until he had a grip on himself. Torn, Ty sat on a chair and stared at the still form in the bed. Asher slept so peacefully, her quiet breathing hardly stirred the air.

A child? Asher's child? But there was no child, Ty reasoned. If Lord and Lady Wickerton had produced an offspring, there would have been some mention of it in the press. An heir was never kept secret. Dragging a hand through his hair, Ty shifted. Besides, he reasoned, if Asher had had a child, where was it? Struggling to overcome the jealousy at imagining Asher's bearing another man's child, Ty went over his conversation with Jim Wolfe again.

Asher wiped her child out of existence....

His fingers tightened on the arms of the chair as he stared at her sleeping form. Abortion? Without warning, a storm of emotion took over that he had to systematically fight back until his pulse leveled. All attempts to think of the word with an open mind were futile. He couldn't rationalize it, not when it was Asher, not when the child was part of her. Could the woman he thought he knew have made that kind of choice? For what purpose? Was it possible that the social life she had sought had been more important than...

As bitterness filled him, Ty shook his head. He wouldn't believe it of her. Controlled, yes. There were times Asher could be infuriatingly controlled. But never calculating. Jim had been talking in riddles, he decided. There'd never been a child. There couldn't have been.

He watched Asher stir. With a soft murmur she shifted toward the emptiness beside her where Ty should have been. He sensed the moment she woke.

The moonlight gleamed on her arm as she lifted it, brushing her fingers at the hair that curled around her face. She placed her hand on his pillow, as if testing it for warmth.

"Ty?"

Not trusting himself, he said nothing. If only she would go back to sleep until he had resolved his feelings. He could still taste the bitterness at the back of his throat.

But she wouldn't sleep. Although groggy, Asher sensed tension in the air. Ty's emotions were always volatile enough to be felt tangibly. *Something's wrong, something's wrong,* hammered in her brain.

"Ty?" she called again, and a hint of fear touched the word. Asher had struggled to a sitting position before she saw him. The moonlight was enough to allow her to see that his eyes were dark and fixed on her face. It was also enough to let her see that they were cold. Her pulse began to race. "Couldn't you sleep?" she asked, struggling to convince herself it was all her imagination.

"No."

Asher laced her fingers together as she swallowed. "You should have woke me."

"Why?"

"We—we could have talked."

"Could we?" Cold anger filled him. "We can talk as long as I don't ask any questions you don't want to answer."

She'd been expecting the showdown, but not like this. His resentment was already wrapping around her. Still, he had a right, and she'd put him off too long. "Ty, if it's answers you want, I'll give them to you."

"Just like that?" he snapped, rising. "Just ask and you'll answer. Nothing more to hide, Asher?"

Stung by his tone, she stared up at him. "It wasn't a matter of hiding, Ty, not really. I needed time—we needed time."

"Why was that, Asher?" he asked in a tone that was uncharacteristically cool. She felt a shudder zip down her spine. "Why was time so important?"

"There were things I wasn't sure you'd understand."

"Like the baby?"

If he had slapped her, Asher couldn't have been more stunned. Even in the moonlight he could see her face go white. Her eyes grew huge and dark and desperate. "How…" The words wouldn't form. Though they raced around in her mind, Asher seemed incapable of forcing any through her lips. How had he found out? Who had told him? How long had he known?

"Eric," she managed, though the name threatened to strangle her. "Eric told you."

Sharp disappointment cut through him. Somehow he had hoped it hadn't been true that she had conceived and rejected another man's child. "So it's true," he exclaimed. Turning from her, Ty stared through the window at the darkness. He found he couldn't be logical or objective. It was one thing to understand the concept of freedom of choice, and another to apply it to Asher.

"Ty, I…" She tried to speak. All of her worst fears were hurtling down on her. The gulf between them was already tangible and threatening to widen. If only she had been able to tell him in her own way, in her own time. "Ty, I wanted to tell you myself. There were reasons why I didn't at first, and then…" Asher shut her eyes. "Then I made excuses."

"I suppose you thought it was none of my business."

Her eyes flew open again. "How can you say that?"

"What you do with your life when you're married to one man isn't the concern of another, even when he loves you."

Simultaneous flashes of pain and joy rushed through her. "You didn't," she whispered.

"Didn't what?"

"You didn't love me."

He gave a brief laugh, but didn't turn back to her. "No, of course I didn't. That's why I couldn't stay away from you. That's why I thought of you every moment."

Asher pressed the heel of her hand between her eyes. Why now? she thought wildly. Why is it all happening now? "You never told me."

This time he turned. "Yes, I did."

Furiously she shook her head. "You never said it. Not once. Even once would have been enough."

In concentration, his brows drew together. She was right, he decided. He'd never said the words. He'd shown her in every way he knew how, but he'd never said the words. "Neither did you," he blurted, speaking his thoughts.

She let out a breath that was perilously close to a sob. "I was afraid to."

"Damn it, Asher, so was I."

For a long, tense moment they stared at each other. Had she been that blind? Had she needed words so badly that she hadn't seen what he'd been giving her? The words would never have come easily to him because they meant everything. For Ty, a declaration of love wasn't a casual phrase but a declaration of self.

Asher swallowed a tremor, wanting her voice to be strong. "I love you, Ty. I've always loved you. And I'm still afraid." As she held out a hand he glanced down at it, but made no move to accept it. "Don't turn away from me now." She thought of the child she had lost. "Please, don't hate me for what I did."

He couldn't understand, but he could feel. It seemed love for her justified anything. Crossing to her, Ty took the offered hand and brought it to his lips. "It'll be better when we've talked this out. We need to start clean, Asher."

"Yes." She closed her hand over their joined ones. "I want that too. Oh, Ty, I'm so sorry about the baby." Her free arm wrapped around his waist as she dropped her head on his chest. The relief, she thought. The relief of at last being able to share it with him. "I couldn't tell you before, when it happened. I didn't know what to do. I didn't know how you'd feel."

"I don't know either," he answered.

"I felt so guilty." She shut her eyes tight. "When Jess showed me that picture of your nephew, I could almost see how the baby would have looked. I always knew he would have had your hair, your eyes."

"Mine?" For a moment nothing seemed to function. His mind, his heart, his lungs. Then, in a torrent, everything came together. *"Mine?"* Asher gave an involuntary cry as he crushed her fingers in his. Before she could speak he had her by the shoulders, digging into her flesh. His eyes alone brought her ice-cold terror. "The baby was mine?"

Her mouth moved to form words, but nothing came out. Confusion and fear overtook her. But he'd already known, she thought desperately. No, no, he hadn't. Eric's baby, her mind flashed. He'd thought it was Eric's baby.

"Answer me, damn you!" He was shaking her now, violently. Limp as a rag doll, Asher made no protest and sought no defense. Both would have been futile. "Was it my baby? Was it mine?"

She nodded, too numb to feel the pain.

He wanted to strike her. Looking at her face, Ty could almost feel the sensation of his hand stinging against it. And he'd want to keep striking her until rage and grief could no longer be felt. Reading his thoughts in his eyes, Asher made no move to protect herself. For an instant his fingers tightened on her arms. With a violent oath he hurled her away. Hardly daring to breathe, she lay on the bed and waited.

"You bitch. You had my child in you when you married him." He flung the words at her, struggling not to use his fists. "Did he make you get rid of it when he found out? Or did you take care of it so you could play the lady without encumbrances?"

She wasn't aware that her breathing was ragged, or that she was trembling. Her mind was too numb to take in more than half of his words. All she understood was the fury of his feelings. "I didn't know. I didn't know I was pregnant when I married Eric."

"You had no right to keep this from me." Towering over her, he reached down to yank her to her knees. "You had no right to make a decision like that when the child was mine!"

"Ty—"

"Shut up. Damn you!" He shoved her away, knowing neither of them was safe if they remained together. "There's nothing you can say, nothing that could make me even want to look at you again."

He strode from the room without a second glance. The sound of the slamming door echoed over and over in Asher's mind.

CHAPTER 11

Ty took the quarter-finals in straight sets. Most said he played the finest tennis in his career on that hazy September afternoon. Ty knew he wasn't playing tennis. He was waging war. He'd gone onto the court full of vengeance and fury, almost pummeling his opponent with the ball. His swing was vicious, his aim deadly.

The violence showed in his face, in the grim set of his mouth, in the eyes that were nearly black with emotion. It wasn't the winning or losing that mattered to him, but the release of the physical aspect of the temper that he'd barely controlled the night before. When he struck, he struck brutally, always moving. The motion itself was a threat. He'd often been called a warrior, but the description had never been more true. As if scenting blood, he hounded his opponent, then ground him mercilessly into the ground.

Ty's only disappointment was that the match didn't last longer. There hadn't been enough time to sweat out all of his fury. He wondered if there would ever be enough time.

In the stands there were differing reactions as he stalked off the courts.

"Name of God, Ada, I've never seen the boy play better." Martin Derick beamed like a new father. His voice was hoarse from cheering and cigarettes. A pile of butts lay crushed at his feet. "Did you see how he massacred that Italian?"

"Yes."

"Oh-ho, two matches more and our boy's going to have a Grand Slam." Martin squeezed Ada's workworn hands between his two smooth ones. "Nothing's going to stop him now!"

In her quiet, steady way, Ada stared down at the court. She'd seen more than Ty's victory. There'd been fury in her son's eyes. Outrage, hurt. She recognized the combination too well. She'd seen it in a little boy who'd been teased because his father had deserted him. Then, he'd used his fists to compensate. Today, Ada mused, he'd used a racket. As Martin recounted every serve and smash, Ada sat silently and wondered what had put that look back in her son's eyes.

"Mom." Jess leaned close so that her voice wouldn't carry. "Something's wrong with Ty, isn't it?"

"I'd say something's very wrong with Ty."

Jess rubbed her cheek against Pete's, wishing his powdery scent would calm her. Giggling, he squirmed out of her arms and dove toward his father. "Asher wasn't in the stands today."

Ada lifted her eyes to her daughter's. Jess had mentioned, perhaps too casually, that Ty was seeing Asher Wolfe again. Ada had hardly needed the information. Once she had heard Asher was competing again, she'd known what the results would be.

The only time she had ever seen Ty truly devastated had been when Asher had married the polished British lord. His rage and threats had been expected. But they turned to a brooding that had concerned her a great deal more.

"Yes, I noticed," Ada replied. "Then, she's got a match of her own."

"On the next court, and not for a half hour." Jess cast another worried glance around at the people who filled the stands. "She should have been here."

"Since she wasn't, there must be a reason."

A fresh tremor of unease ran up Jess's back. "Mom, I've got to talk to you—alone. Can we go get a cup of coffee?"

Without question, Ada rose. "You fellas keep Pete entertained," she ordered, tousling her grandson's hair. "Jess and I'll be back in a few minutes."

"You're going to tell her?" Mac spoke softly as he touched his wife's hand.

"Yes. Yes, I need to."

Bouncing his son on his knee, he watched them melt into the crowd.

After they had settled at a table, Ada waited for her daughter to begin. She knew Jess was marking time, ordering coffee, speculating on the chances of rain. Ada let her ramble. An orderly, even-tempered woman, she had learned the best way to deal with her emotional offspring was to ride out the storm. Eventually Jess stopped stirring her coffee and lifted her eyes to her mother's.

"Mom, do you remember when we were here three years ago?"

How could she forget? Ada thought with a sigh. That was the year Ty had won the U.S. Open, then barely had time to savor it before the world had crumbled around his ears. "Yes, I remember."

"Asher left Ty and married Eric Wickerton." When Ada remained silent, Jess lifted her coffee cup and drank as if to fortify herself. "It was my fault," she blurted out.

Ada took the time to taste her own coffee, deciding it wasn't half bad for restaurant brew. "Your fault, Jess? How?"

"I went to see her." In quick jerks Jess began to shred her napkin. She'd thought it would be easier now that she had told Mac everything, but with her mother's gaze steady and patient on hers, she felt like a child again. "I went to her hotel room when I knew Ty wouldn't be there." After pressing her lips together, she let the confession come out in a burst. "I told her Ty was tired of her. I told her he—he was bored."

"I'm surprised she didn't laugh in your face," Ada commented.

Quickly Jess shook her head. "I was convincing," she went on. "Maybe because I was convinced it was the truth. And I—I was sympathetic." Remembering how well she had played the role of reluctant messenger tore at her. "Oh, God, Mom, when I look back and remember the things I told her, how I said them…" Anguished, her eyes met her mother's. "I told her Ty thought she and Eric were suited to each other. There was enough truth in that, but I turned it around to give her the impression that Ty was hoping Eric would take her off his hands. And I defended Ty, telling Asher he'd never want to hurt her, that he was really very concerned that she'd gotten in over her head. I—I made it seem as though Ty had asked my opinion on the best way to untangle himself from an affair he had no more interest in."

"Jess." Ada stopped the movement of her nervous daughter's hands with her own. "Why did you do such a thing?"

"Ty wasn't happy. I'd talked to him just the night before, and he was so down, so unsure of himself. I'd never seen Ty unsure of himself." Her fingers began to move restlessly under her mother's. "It seemed so clear to me that Asher was wrong for him, hurting him. I was convinced I had to save him from being hurt more."

Leaning back, Ada let her gaze drift. The West Side Tennis Club was respectfully dingy, very American. Perhaps that was why she'd always liked it. It was noisy. The Long Island Railroad ran alongside, competing with helicopters, planes and road traffic. Ada had never completely gotten used to the relative quiet of suburbia after a lifetime in the inner city.

Now she sat back, absorbing the noise, trying to think of the right words. It occurred to her that parenting didn't stop when children became adults. Perhaps it never stopped at all.

"Ty loved Asher, Jess."

"I know." Jess stared down at the shredded paper napkin. "I didn't think he did. I thought if he'd loved her, he would have been happy. And if she had loved him, she would have…well, she would have acted like all the other women who hung around him."

"Do you think Ty would have loved her if she had been like all the other women?"

Jess flushed, amazing herself and amusing her mother. It was a bit disconcerting to think of the tiny, white-haired Ada Starbuck, mother, grandmother, knowing about passion. "It wasn't until after I met Mac that I realized love doesn't always make you smile and glow," Jess went on, keeping her eyes lowered. "There are times when I was miserable and confused over my feelings for Mac and I began to remember that last talk I had with Ty before I went to see Asher. I realized how alike Ty and I are, how the stronger our feelings are, the more moody we can become."

On a deep breath she met her mother's gaze levelly. "I tried to rationalize that Asher wouldn't have left Ty, that she wouldn't have married Eric if she had really cared. And that if he had, Ty wouldn't have let her go."

"Pride can be just as strong as love. The things you said to Asher made her feel unwanted, and betrayed, I imagine, that Ty would have spoken to you about it."

"If the situation had been reversed, I would have scratched her eyes out and told her to go to hell."

Ada's laugh was a warm, young sound. "Yes, you would. Then you'd have gone to the man you loved and used your claws on him. Asher's different."

"Yes." Miserable, Jess pushed her untouched coffee aside.

"Ty always said so. Mom, when they got back together, I was so guilty and frightened. Then I was relieved. And now, I can tell something's gone wrong again." As she had as a child, Jess gave her mother a long, pleading look. "What should I do?"

Strange, Ada mused, that her children wanted to pamper her on one hand, thrusting dishwashers and fancy jewelry on her, while on the other, they still looked to her for all the answers. "You'll have to talk to both of them," Ada said briskly. "Then you'll have to back off and let the two of them work it out. You might be able to heal what you did three years ago, but you can do nothing about what's between them now."

"If they love each other—"

"You made a decision for them once," Ada pointed out. "Don't make the same mistake again."

She hadn't been able to sleep. She hadn't been able to eat. Only the promise she had made to herself never to quit again forced Asher onto the court. Purposely she remained in the dressing room until the last moment to avoid the fans who wandered the walkways and mingled with players. It would take more effort than she could have summoned to smile and make small talk.

When she came outside the humidity hit her like a fist. Shaking off the weakness, Asher went directly to her chair. She heard the applause, but didn't acknowledge it. She couldn't afford to. Even before she began, Asher knew her biggest problem would be concentration.

Her arms ached, her whole body ached and she felt bone-deep exhausted. Pain was something she could ignore once the match was under way, but she wasn't sure she could ignore the jellied weakness inside her, the feeling that someone had punched a yawning hole in the center of her life. Still wearing her warm-up jacket, she took a few experimental swings.

"Asher." Cursing the interruption, she glanced over at Chuck. Concern touched his eyes as he stepped toward her. "Hey, you don't look good. Are you sick?"

"I'm fine."

He studied the shadowed eyes and pale cheeks. "Like hell."

"If I come out on the court, I'm well enough to play," she returned, exchanging one racket for another. "I've got to warm up."

Baffled, Chuck watched her stalk onto the court. It took only a moment of study to see that she wasn't in top form. Chuck moved away to find Ty.

He was in the showers, his eyes closed under the spray. He'd been curt and brief with the press and even briefer with his colleagues. He wasn't in the mood for congratulations. Anger lay curled inside him, undiminished by the physical demands he had placed on himself. He needed more—a sparring match, a marathon run—anything to pump the poison out of his system. Though he heard Chuck call him, Ty remained silent and kept his eyes shut.

"Ty, will you listen to me? Something's wrong with Asher."

Taking his time, Ty stepped back so that the water beat on his chest. Slowly he opened his eyes. "So?"

"So?" Astonished, Chuck gaped at him. "I said something's wrong with Asher."

"I heard you."

"She looks sick," Chuck continued, certain that Ty didn't comprehend. "I just saw her. She shouldn't be playing today. She looks awful."

Ty fought the instinctive need to go to her. He could remember vividly the scene the night before. With a flick of the wrist he shut off the shower. "Asher knows what she's doing. She makes her own decisions."

Too stunned to be angry, Chuck stared at him. He'd never seen Ty look cold any more than he'd ever seen Asher look furious. Until today. "What the devil's going on here?" he demanded. "I just told you your woman's sick."

Ty felt the tightening in his belly and ignored it. "She's not my woman." Grabbing a towel, he secured it lightly around his waist.

After dragging a hand through his hair, Chuck followed Ty into the locker room. He'd known since that morning when he and Ty had practiced together that something was wrong. Accustomed to his friend's mercurial moods, he had dismissed it, assuming Ty and Asher had had a lover's quarrel. But no lover's quarrel would make Ty indifferent to Asher's health.

"Look, if you two have had a fight, that's no reason—"

"I said she's not my woman." Ty's voice was deadly calm as he pulled on jeans.

"Fine," Chuck snapped. "Then if the field's clear, I might just try my luck." He was slammed back against the lockers, feet dangling as Ty grabbed his shirt in both hands, jerking him up. Coolly, Chuck looked into the stormy eyes. "Not your woman, friend?" he said softly. "Tell that to somebody who doesn't know you."

Breathing hard, Ty struggled against the need to strike back. The hours of violent tennis hadn't drained the anger or the grief. Without a word he dropped Chuck to his feet, then snatched a shirt from his locker.

"Are you going out there?" Chuck demanded. "Somebody should stop her before she makes whatever's wrong with her worse. You know damn well she isn't going to listen to me."

"Don't push me." Ty dragged the shirt over his head before he slammed the locker door. This time Chuck kept his silence. He heard the tremor in Ty's voice and recognized that the emotion wasn't anger. Only once before had he seen his friend this torn apart. It had been Asher then, as it was obviously Asher now. With warring loyalties, he reached out.

"Okay, you want to talk about it?"

"No." Clenching his fists, Ty fought to regain his control. "No, just go on out…keep an eye on her."

She was fighting, and losing. Asher had used almost all her reserve of energy to take the first set to a tie breaker. The ultimate loss had taken its emotional toll. Kingston was a crafty enough player to sense her opponent's flagging stamina and capitalized on it. Precision was nothing without strength. Asher's strength was ebbing quickly.

The noise played havoc with her concentration. Already playing below par, she needed the sound of the ball hitting the racket. Engines drowned it out, denying her the sense of hearing. On the brittle grass the ball jumped, skidded and stopped. Top speed was necessary, and she didn't have it.

Unable to prevent himself, Ty came to the edge of the tunnel to watch. Immediately he could see that Chuck hadn't exaggerated. She was too pale, too slow. Instinctively he took a step forward. Restraining himself was more difficult than going on, but he stopped, cursing her even as he cursed himself. She'd made her own choice. She herself had cut off any right he had to influence her. From where he stood he could hear her labored breathing, see the strain she fought to keep from her face. At the twinge of fresh pain he turned away from the court.

With a blind determination that was more nerves than power, Asher had taken the second set to three-all. Her face shone with sweat. Weakened, Asher knew that she would have to find a hole in Kingston's game soon, and have the wit and stamina to exploit it. Grit was a weapon, but not weapon enough against power, precision and cunning.

At double break point Asher prepared to serve again. If she could pull this one out, she'd have a chance. If Kingston broke her serve, the match was as good as over. *Concentrate, concentrate,* she ordered herself as she gave the ball a few testing bounces. She counted each one, trying to calm herself. Ty's furious, accusing words hammered in her brain. His face, enraged and stricken, floated in front of her eyes. Tossing the ball, Asher drove at it with her racket.

"Fault."

She shut her eyes and cursed. Control, she ordered herself. If she lost control now, she lost everything. As she took an extra moment, the crowd began to hum in speculation.

"Come on, Face, let's see what you're made of!"

Gritting her teeth, Asher put everything she had left into the serve. The ace brought a roar of approval. She wasn't beaten yet.

But her next serve was soft. Slapping it back to her, Kingston incited a hard, punishing rally. Asher battled by instinct, all reserve depleted. Her eyes, her mind, were fixed on the ball and the ball only. Dodging after a slice, she skidded, barely meeting it with her racket as she stumbled. She went down to her knees, crumbling into a ball of exhaustion and pain.

Someone's hands hooked under her armpits, pulling her to her feet. Asher pushed them away blindly to stagger to her chair.

"Come on, Asher." Chuck toweled off her streaming face, talking to her as she drew in ragged, straining breaths. "Come on, babe, you're not in any shape to be out here today. I'll help you inside."

"No." She shook off his hand. "No, I won't forfeit." Rising, she dropped the towel to the ground. "I'm going to finish."

Helpless, Chuck watched her fight a losing battle.

Asher slept for almost twenty-four hours straight. Her body recharged as she lay motionless in the bed she had shared so recently with Ty. The loss of the match—and the Grand Slam—meant little. She'd finished. Her pride was whole because she had refused to give up, because she had managed to face the reporters after the match and give them a calm accounting. When they had speculated on the state of her health, she'd told them she'd been fit to play. She would give no excuses for losing. If there was blame, it lay within herself. That was the primary rule of the game.

On returning to her room, Asher only took time to strip to her underwear before falling exhausted onto the bed. Sleep came immediately. Hours later she didn't hear the door open or Ty's footsteps as he crossed to the bedroom to look at her.

Asher lay flat on her stomach across the spread—something he knew she did only when absolutely depleted. Her breathing was deep, a heavy sound of fatigue. The hands he had thrust in his pockets balled into fists.

His emotions were pulling in too many directions. She shouldn't be allowed to do this to him, he thought furiously. She shouldn't make him want to hurt and protect at the same time. Walking to the window, he remained silent for a quarter of an hour, listening to her breathe. Before he left her, Ty drew the drapes closed so that the sunlight wouldn't disturb her.

When Asher awoke, a full day had passed. The aches made themselves known.

Keeping her mind a blank, she ran a hot bath. As the water lapped over her, she slipped into a half doze. Asher heard the knock on the door, and ignored it. The phone rang, but she didn't open her eyes.

Disturbed, Jess replaced the receiver after ten full rings. Where could Asher be? she wondered. She knew Asher was still registered at the hotel, but she hadn't answered the phone or the door in more than a day. She'd tried to tell Ty, but he simply wouldn't listen. Any more than he'd listened to her attempts at confession.

Her conscience plagued her. She hadn't tried hard enough, Jess berated herself. She'd been so afraid of losing Ty's love, she had allowed him to brush her off when she tried to talk to him. Well, no more, she determined.

Checking her watch, Jess calculated that Ty would be preparing for the day's match. She cursed, then fretted, then made herself a promise. When it was over, win or lose, she was going to corner her brother and make him listen until she'd told him everything.

Now that the vow had been made, Jess discovered that the waiting wasn't easy. In the stands she marked time. Ty played with the same fierce anger she had observed in his quarterfinal match. It was just as effective.

Beneath her pride in him was the constant thought that her brother might turn away from her after he'd heard her out. But Jess sat patiently through the match and through the press conference. She'd left it to her mother to persuade Martin to go back to the hotel instead of dragging Ty off for a replay of the match. Like a tennis groupie, Jess waited for Ty to emerge from the locker room, then pounced.

"Ty, I need to talk to you."

"I'm talked out, Jess." He patted her hand, then removed it from his arm. "I want to get out of here before the next sportswriter latches onto me."

"Fine, I'll drive. You'll listen."

"Look, Jess—"

"Now, Ty."

Annoyed, Ty stalked to the car. For the first time in his life he wished his family hadn't come. He'd managed to avoid them for the most part, using fatigue or practice as excuses. His mother knew him too well, and her silence questioned him constantly. Martin was ecstatic, wanting to analyze every volley and shower praise. And the hardest of all was watching Pete, darting here and there, babbling, laughing, reminding Ty of something that might have been.

"Look, Jess, I'm tired—"

"Just get in," she interrupted tersely. "I've already put this off for too long."

They slammed their doors simultaneously. Not a very auspicious start, she mused as she merged with traffic, but she'd never finish if she didn't begin. "Okay, I've got some things to tell you, and I'd like you to hear me out before you say anything."

"Unless I want to hitch a damn ride back, I don't have much choice, do I?"

She sent him a worried look. "Don't hate me, Ty."

"Oh, come on, Jess." Ashamed of wishing her away, he gave her hair a quick tousle. "I might be mad at being shanghaied, but I'm not going to hate you."

"Just listen," she started. Staring straight ahead, she began.

At first, Ty paid little attention. She was hopping back to the summer he had first been with Asher. He started once to interrupt, not wanting to be reminded. Jess shook her head fiercely and silenced him. With strained patience Ty sat back and watched the passing scenery.

When Jess told him that she had gone to see Asher, his brows lowered. His concentration focused. Listening to her pouring out the things she had said—*Ty's tired of you.... He doesn't know exactly how to end things without hurting you*—his rage built swiftly. Jess felt the fury swirling, and barely paused for breath.

"She seemed to have no reaction to anything I said. She was very cool, totally in control of herself. It just seemed to reinforce what I thought of her." Stopping for a light, Jess swallowed quickly. "I didn't understand how anyone could have strong feelings and not express them, not then. After I met Mac I realized…" When the light changed she gunned the motor with a jerk of her foot, then stalled the engine. On a frustrated oath she started the car again as Ty remained silent.

"When I look back on it," Jess continued after a shaky breath, "I remember how pale she got, how quiet. It wasn't indifference, but shock. She listened to everything I said, never raising her voice or shedding a tear. I must have hurt her terribly."

Her voice broke and she waited for him to speak, but there was nothing but thick, vibrant silence. "I had no right, Ty," Jess continued quickly. "I know that. I wanted—I wanted to help, to pay you back somehow for everything you'd done for me. At the time, I thought I was telling her the things you couldn't bring yourself to. I'd convinced myself… Oh, I don't know." Jess made a quick gesture with her hand before she gripped the gear shift. "Maybe I was even jealous, but I didn't think you loved her and I was so sure she didn't love you. Especially when she married so quickly."

Because tears were forming, she pulled over to the side of the road. "Ty, to tell you I'm sorry isn't enough, but I don't have anything else."

The silence in the car vibrated for the space of three heartbeats. "What made you think you could play God with my life?" Ty demanded in a sudden burst that had her jolting. "Who the hell put you in charge?"

Forcing herself to meet his eyes, Jess spoke quietly. "There's nothing you can say to me I haven't said to myself, but you're entitled."

"Do you have any idea what you did to my life?"

She shuddered involuntarily. "Yes."

"I was going to ask Asher to marry me that night, the night

I got back and found you in our room. The night you told me she'd gone off with Wickerton."

"Oh, God, Ty." Choking back a sob, Jess laid her head on the steering wheel. "I never thought…I never realized she meant that much to you."

"She was everything I wanted, don't you understand? Everything! I was half crazy because I wasn't sure she'd say yes." He drummed his fist against the dash. "And, God, I'm still not sure. I'll never be sure." The anguish in his voice made Jess straighten.

"Ty, if you'd go see her. If you'd—"

"No." He thought again of the child. His child. "There are other reasons now."

"I'll go," Jess began. "I can—"

"No!" The word whipped out at her, causing Jess to swallow the rest of the sentence. "Stay away from her."

"All right," she agreed unsteadily. "If that's the way you want it."

"That's the way I want it."

"You still love her," Jess asked.

Ty turned his head so that his eyes met his sister's. "Yes, I love her. That isn't always enough, Jess. I don't think I'd ever be able to forget…"

"Forget?" she prompted when he trailed off. "Forget what?"

"Something she took from me…" Angry energy built up again, grinding at his nerves. "I've got to walk."

"Ty." Jess stopped him with a tentative hand on the arm as he jerked open the door of the car. "Do you want me to go away—back to California? I can make up an excuse, even leave Pete and Mac here for the rest of the tournament. I won't stay for the finals if it upsets you."

"Do what you want," he told her shortly. He started to

slam the door of the car when he caught the look in her eyes. He'd protected her all of his life, too long to change now. Love was rooted in him. "It's history, Jess," he said in calmer tones. "Past history. Forget it."

Turning, Ty walked away, hoping he'd be able to believe his own words.

CHAPTER 12

Asher sat on the bed to watch the men's singles championship. The television commentary barely penetrated as she judged and dissected each stroke and volley for herself. She couldn't go to the stadium, but nothing would prevent her from watching Ty compete.

On the close-ups, she studied his face carefully. Yes, some strain showed, she noted, but his concentration was complete. His energy was as volatile as ever, perhaps more so. For that she could be grateful.

Each time they replayed a shot in slow motion, Asher could fully appreciate the beauty of his form. Muscles rippled as he stretched; feet left the turf in a leap for more power. He was a raw athlete with anger simmering just under the discipline. The graphite racket was no more than an extension of the arm that was whipping the ball harder and harder. As always, his hair flew around the sweatband, dramatic and unruly. His eyes were dark with a rage barely contained. Was it the game that drove him? she wondered. The insatiable thirst to win? Or were there other emotions pushing him this time?

If there were, it was easy to see that they added to the impetus. He was an explosion heating up, a storm rumbling just overhead. Asher knew him well enough to recognize that his control balanced on a very thin edge, but it made his game all the more exciting.

His topspin drove to Chuck's backhand and was returned, power for power. A slice, a lob, an overhead. Turned the wrong way, Chuck pivoted, sprinted, but had no chance to return. The call was late, judging Ty's ball long.

His head whipped around to the judge, his eyes deadly. Asher shuddered when the camera zoomed in so that the undisguised fury seemed aimed directly at her. For a moment they seemed to stare into each other's eyes. Disgust warred with temper before he turned to resume his receiving stance. Crouched like a cat, his eyes intense, he waited. Asher let out an unsteady breath.

Ty was judging the bounce with uncanny accuracy. If it threatened to die, he was under it. When it chose to soar, he got behind it. With unrelenting challenge he charged the net. He baited Chuck, dared him, and, time after time, outwitted him. His game was all aggression and power—Starbuck at his best, she thought with undiminished pride. He could demoralize even a seasoned pro like Chuck with a lightning-fast return that lifted chalk from the service line. With each swing she could hear the grunt of exertion and the swish of air. How she wanted to be there.

He wouldn't want her. She wouldn't soon forget that look of rage and disgust he had turned on her—too much like the one his video image had projected. A man like Starbuck had no ambivalent emotions. It was love or hate; she'd felt them both.

She'd been cut out of his life. She had to accept that. She had to…quit? Asher asked herself. Suddenly her chin rose. Was that what she was doing again? She looked back at the screen as the camera zoomed in on Ty's face. His eyes were opaque and dangerous before he went into a full stretch for his serve. The force of her feelings attacked her. She loved and wanted and needed.

No, damn it! Rising, Asher cursed him. No, if she was going to lose, she was going down fighting, just as she had on the courts. He wouldn't brush her out of his life so easily this time. Briefly she'd forgotten that she no longer aimed her actions at pleasing those around her. Perhaps he didn't want to see her, but that was just too bad. He would see her…and he would listen.

Just as she snapped off the set, a knock sounded on her door. Battling impatience, Asher went to answer. Her expression changed from grim determination to wonder.

"Dad!"

"Asher." Jim met her stunned expression with an unsmiling nod. "May I come in?"

He hadn't changed, she thought wildly. He hadn't changed at all. He was still tall and tanned and silvery-blond. He was still her father. Her eyes filled with love and tears. "Oh, Dad, I'm so glad to see you." Grasping his hand, she drew him into the room. Then the awkwardness set in. "Sit down, please." While gesturing to a chair, Asher sought something to fill the gap. "Shall I order up something to drink? Some coffee?"

"No." He sat as she suggested and looked at his daughter. She was thinner, he noted. And nervous, as nervous as he was himself. Since Ty's phone call, he'd done little but think of her. "Asher," he began, then sighed. "Please sit down." He waited until she settled across from him. "I want to tell you I'm proud of the way you've played this season."

His voice was stiff, but she expected little else. "Thank you."

"I'm most proud of the last match you played."

Asher gave him a small smile. How typical that it was tennis he spoke of first. "I lost."

"You played," he countered. "Right down to the last point,

you played. I wonder how many people who watched knew that you were ill."

"I wasn't ill," Asher corrected him automatically. "If I came on court—"

"Then you were fit," he finished, before he shook his head. "I drummed that into you well, didn't I?"

"A matter of pride and sportsmanship," she said quietly, giving him back the words he had given her again and again during her training.

Jim lapsed into silence, frowning at the elegant hands that lay folded in her lap. She'd always been his princess, he thought, his beautiful, golden princess. He'd wanted to give her the world, and he'd wanted her to deserve it.

"I didn't intend to come here to see you."

If the statement hurt, she gave no sign. "What changed your mind?"

"A couple of things, most particularly, your last match."

Rising, Asher walked to the window. "So, I had to lose to have you speak to me again." The words came easily, as did the light trace of bitterness. Though love had remained constant, she found no need to give him unvarnished adulation any longer. "All those years I needed you so badly, I waited, hoping you'd forgive me."

"It was a hard thing to forgive, Asher."

He rose, too, realizing his daughter had grown stronger. He wasn't sure how to approach the woman she had become.

"It was a hard thing to accept," she countered in the calm voice he remembered. "That my father looked at me as athlete first and child second."

"That's not true."

"Isn't it?" Turning, she fixed him with a level stare. "You turned your back on me because I gave up my career. Not once when I was suffering did you hold out a hand to me.

I had no one to go to but you, and because you said no, I had no one at all."

"I tried to deal with it. I tried to accept your decision to marry that man, though you knew how I felt about him." The unexpected guilt angered him and chilled his voice. "I tried to understand how you could give up what you were to play at being something else."

"I had no choice," she began furiously.

"No choice?" His derision was sharp as a blade. "You made your own decision, Asher—your career for a title— just as you made it about the child. My grandchild."

"Please." She lifted both hands to her temples as she turned away. "Please don't. Have you any idea how much and how often I've paid for that moment of carelessness?"

"Carelessness?" Stunned into disbelief, Jim stared at the back of her head. "You call the conception of a child carelessness?"

"No, *no!*" Her voice trembled as it rose. "The loss. If I hadn't let myself get upset, if I had looked where I was going, I never would have fallen. I never would have lost Ty's child."

"What!" As the pain slammed into his stomach, Jim sank into the chair. "Fallen? Ty's child? *Ty's?*" He ran a hand over his eyes as he tried to sort it out. Suddenly he felt old and frail and frightened. "Asher, are you telling me you miscarried Ty's child?"

"Yes." Wearily she turned back to face him. "I wrote you, I told you."

"If you wrote, I never received the letter." Shaken, Jim held out a hand, waiting until she grasped it. "Asher, Eric told me you aborted his child." For an instant, the words, their meaning, failed to penetrate. Her look was blank and vulnerable enough to make him feel every year of his age. "A calculated abortion of your husband's child," he said deliberately. When she swayed he gripped her other hand. "He told me you'd done so without his knowledge or permission. He seemed devastated. I believed him, Asher." As she went limp, he drew her down to her knees in front of him. "I believed him."

"Oh, God." Her eyes were huge and dark with shock.

Her father's fingers trembled in hers. "He phoned me from London. He sounded half mad—I thought with grief. He said that you hadn't told him until after it was done. That you had told him you wanted no children to interfere with the life you intended to build as Lady Wickerton."

Too numb for anger, Asher shook her head. "I didn't know even Eric could be so vindictive, so cruel."

It all began to make horrid sense. Her letters to her father hadn't been answered. Eric had seen that they were never mailed. Then, when she had phoned him, Jim had been cold and brief. He'd told her that he could never resolve himself to her choice. Asher had assumed he meant her rejection of her career.

"He wanted me to pay," she explained as she dropped her head on her father's lap. "He never wanted me to stop paying."

Gently Jim cupped her face in his hands. "Tell me everything. I'll listen, as I should have a long time ago."

She started with Jess, leaving nothing out including her final stormy estrangement from Ty. Jim's mouth tightened at her recounting of the accident and the hospital scene with Eric. Listening, he cursed himself for being a fool.

"And now, Ty…" As realization struck her, she paled. "Ty thinks—Eric must have told him I'd had an abortion."

"No, I told him."

"You?" Confused, Asher pressed her fingers to the headache in her temple. "But how—"

"He called me a few nights ago. He wanted to convince me to see you. I told him enough to make him believe the lie just as I'd believed it."

"That night when I woke up," Asher remembered. "Oh, my God, when he realized it had been his baby… The things he was saying! I couldn't think at the time." She shut her eyes. "No wonder he hates me."

Color flooded back into her face. "I have to tell him the truth and make him believe it." Scrambling up, she dashed for the door. "I'll go to the club. I have to make him listen. I have to make him understand."

"The match must be nearly over." Jim rose on unsteady legs. His daughter had been through hell, and he had done nothing but add to it. "You'll never catch him there."

Frustrated, Asher looked at her watch. "I don't know where he's staying." Releasing the doorknob, she went to the phone. "I'll just have to find out."

"Asher…" Awkward, unsure, Jim held out his hand. "Forgive me."

Asher stared into his face as she replaced the receiver. Ignoring the hand, she went into his arms.

It was nearly midnight when Ty reached the door of his room. For the past two hours he'd been drinking steadily. Celebrating. It wasn't every day you won the Grand Slam, he reminded himself as he searched for his keys. And it wasn't every day a man had a half dozen women offering to share their beds with him. He gave a snort of laughter as he slid the key into the lock. And why the hell hadn't he taken one of them up on it?

None of them was Asher. He shook away the thought as he struggled to make the doorknob function. No, he simply hadn't wanted a woman, Ty told himself. It was because he was tired and had had too much to drink. Asher was yesterday.

The hotel room was dark as he stumbled inside. If he was right about nothing else, he was right about having too much to drink. Through glass after glass Ty had told himself the liquor was for celebrating, not for forgetting. The kid from the Chicago slum had made it to the top, in spades.

The hell with it, he decided, tossing his keys into the room. With a thud they landed on the carpet. Swaying a bit, he stripped off his shirt and threw it in the same direction. Now if he could just find his way to the bed without turning on a light, he'd sleep. Tonight he'd sleep—with enough liquor in his system to anesthetize him. There'd be no dreams of soft skin or dark blue eyes tonight.

As he fumbled toward the bedroom, a light switched on, blinding him. With a pungent curse Ty covered his eyes, balancing himself with one hand on the wall.

"Turn that damn thing off," he muttered.

"Well, the victor returns triumphant."

The quiet voice had him lowering the hand from his eyes. Asher sat primly in a chair, looking unruffled, soft and utterly tempting. Ty felt desire work its way through the alcohol.

"What the hell are you doing here?"

"And very drunk," she said as if he hadn't spoken. Rising, she went to him. "I suppose you deserve it after the way you played today. Should I add my congratulations to the host of others?"

"Get out." He pushed away from the wall. "I don't want you."

"I'll order up some coffee," she said calmly. "We'll talk."

"I said get out!" Catching her wrist, he whirled her around. "Before I lose my temper and hurt you."

Though her pulse jumped under his fingers, she stood firm. "I'll leave after we talk."

"Do you know what I want to do to you?" he demanded, shoving her back against the wall. "Do you know that I want to beat you senseless?"

"Yes." She didn't cringe as his fury raged down on her. "Ty, if you'll listen—"

"I don't want to listen to you." The image of her lying exhausted on the bed raced through his mind. "Get out while I can still stop myself from hurting you."

"I can't." She lifted a hand to his cheek. "Ty—"

Her words were cut off as he pressed her back into the wall. For an instant she thought he would strike her, then his mouth came down on hers, bruising, savage. He forced her lips apart, thrusting his tongue deep as she struggled. His teeth ground against hers as though to punish them both. There was the faint taste of liquor, reminding her he had drink as well as anger in his system. When she tried to turn her head, he caught her face in his hand—not gently, in the touch she remembered, but viselike.

He could smell her—the soft talc, the lightly sexy perfume. And the fear. She made a small, pleading sound before she stopped fighting him. Without being aware of what he did, he lightened the grip to a caress. His lips gentled on hers, tasting, savoring. Mumbling her name, he trailed kisses over her skin until he felt the essence of her flowing back into him. God, how he'd missed her.

"I can't do without you," he whispered. "I can't." He sank to the floor, drawing her down with him.

He was lost in her—the feel, the taste, the fragrance. His mind was too full of Asher to allow him to think. Sensation ruled him, trembling along his skin to follow the path of her fingers. It was as if she sought to soothe and arouse him at once. He was helpless to resist her—or his need for her. As if in a trance, he took his lips over her, missing nothing as his hunger seemed insatiable. Her quickening breaths were like music, setting his rhythm.

The air grew steamier as his hands homed in on secrets that made her moan. Her body shuddered into life. No longer gentle, but demanding, she tangled her fingers in his hair and guided him to sweet spaces he'd neglected. Then ever greedy, ever giving, she drew him back to her mouth. Her tongue toyed with his lips, then slid inside to drink up all the flavors. His head swimming, he answered the kiss.

The need for her was unreasonable, but Ty was beyond reason. Without her there'd been an emptiness that even his fury couldn't fill. Now the void was closing. She was in his blood, in his bone, so essential a part of him he had been able to find no place of separation. Now there was no will to do so.

Under him, she was moving, inviting, entreating. He whispered a denial against her mouth, but his pounding blood took control. He was inside her without being aware of it. Then all sensations spiraled together in an intensity that made him cry out. And it was her name he spoke, in both ecstasy and in despair.

Drained, Ty rolled from her to stare at the ceiling. How could he have let that happen? he demanded. How could he have felt such love, found such pleasure in a woman he had vowed to amputate from his life? He wondered now if he'd ever find the strength to stay away from her. Life with her, and life without her, would be two kinds of hell.

"Ty." Reaching over, Asher touched his shoulder.

"Don't." Without looking at her he rose. "Get dressed, for God's sake," he muttered as he tugged on his own jeans with trembling hands. Who had used whom? he wondered. "Do you have a car?"

Sitting up, Asher pushed her hair out of her face. Hair, she remembered, that only moments before he had been kissing. "No."

"I'll call you a cab."

"That won't be necessary." In silence she began to dress. "I realize you're sorry that this happened."

"I'm damned if I'll apologize," he snapped.

"I wasn't asking you to," she told him quietly. "I was going to say that I'm not sorry. I love you, and making love with you is only one way to show it." She managed, after three attempts, to button her blouse. When she looked up, he was at the window, his back to her. "Ty, I came here to tell you some things you must know. When I'm finished, I'll go and give you time to think about them."

"Can't you understand I don't want to think anymore?"

"It's the last thing I'll ask of you."

"All right." In a gesture of fatigue she rarely saw in him, he rubbed both hands over his face. The liquor had burned out of his system—by the anger or the passion, he wasn't sure. But he was cold sober. "Maybe I should tell you first that what Jess said to you three years ago was her own fabrication. I didn't know anything about it until the other day when she told me what she'd done. In her own way, she was trying to protect me."

"I don't understand what you're talking about."

Turning, he gave her a grim smile. "Did you really think I was tired of you? Looking for a way out? Wondering how I could ditch you without raising too much fuss or interfering with my career?"

Asher opened her mouth to speak, then shut it again. How strange that the words still hurt and made her defensive.

"Obviously you did."

"And if I did?" she countered. "Everything she said fit. You'd never made a commitment to me. There'd never been any talk about the future."

"On either side," he reminded her.

Asher pushed away the logic. "If you'd once told me—"

"Or perhaps you were uncertain enough of your own feelings that when Jess dumped that on you, you ran right to Wickerton. Even though you were carrying my baby."

"I didn't know I was pregnant when I married Eric." She saw him shrug her words away. In fury she grabbed both of his arms. "I tell you I didn't know! Perhaps if I had known before I would have simply gone away. I don't know what I would have done. I was already terrified you were growing tired of me before Jess confirmed it."

"And where the hell did you get a stupid idea like that?"

"You'd been so moody, so withdrawn. Everything she said made sense."

"If I was moody and withdrawn, it was because I was trying to work out the best way to ask Asher Wolfe, Miss Society Tennis, to marry Starbuck, from the wrong side of the tracks."

Asher took an uncertain step toward him. "You would have married me?"

"I still have the ring I bought you," he answered.

"A ring?" she repeated stupidly. "You'd bought me a ring?" For some inexplicable reason the thought of it stunned her more than anything else.

"I'd planned to try a very conventional proposal. And if that didn't work, maybe a kidnapping."

She tried to laugh because tears were entirely too close. "It would have worked."

"If you'd told me you were pregnant—"

"Ty, I didn't know! Damn it!" She pounded once against his chest. "Do you think I would have married Eric if I had known? It was weeks afterward that I found out."

"Why the hell didn't you tell me then?"

"Do you think I wanted to get you back that way?" The old pride lifted her chin. "And I was married to another man. I'd made him a promise."

"A promise that meant more than the life of the child we'd made together," he retorted bitterly. "A promise that let you walk into one of those antiseptic clinics and destroy something innocent and beautiful. And mine."

The image was too ugly, the truth too painful. Flying at

him, Asher struck him again and again until he pinned her hands behind her back. *"And mine!"* she shouted at him. "And mine, or doesn't my part matter?"

"You didn't want it." His fingers closed like steel as she tried to pull away. "But you didn't have the decency to ask me if I did. Couldn't you bear the thought of carrying part of me inside you for nine months?"

"Don't ask me what I could bear." She wasn't pale now, but vivid with fury. "I didn't have an abortion," she spat at him. "I miscarried. I miscarried and nearly died in the process. Would you feel better if I had? God knows I tried to."

"Miscarried?" His grip shifted from her wrists to her shoulders. "What are you talking about?"

"Eric hated me too!" she shouted. "When I learned I was pregnant and told him, all he could say was that I'd deceived him. I'd tried to trick him into claiming the baby after you'd refused me. Nothing I said got through to him. We argued and argued. We were near the steps and he was shouting. All I wanted to do was get away." Her hands flew up to cover her face as she remembered again, all too clearly. "I didn't look, I only ran. Then I was falling. I tried to stop, but my head hit the railing, I think. Then I don't remember anything until I woke up and the baby was gone."

Somehow he could see it as vividly as though it were being played on film in front of his eyes. "Oh, God, Asher." When he tried to take her in his arms, she pulled away.

"I wanted you, but I knew you'd never forgive me. It didn't seem to matter anymore, so I did what Eric wanted." To force back the tears, she pressed her fingers to her eyes. "I didn't want you to know, I couldn't have stood it if you had known when you didn't want me." Lowering her hands, she looked at him, dry-eyed. "I paid for losing your baby, Ty. For three years I did without everything that mattered to me, and I grieved alone. I can't mourn any longer."

"No." Going to the window, he flung it up as if he needed air. There was no breeze, nothing to relieve the burning that he felt. "You've had years to deal with it. I've had days." And she'd had no one, he thought. Years with no one. Ty took several long breaths. "How badly were you hurt?"

Puzzled by the question, she shook her head. "What?"

"Were you badly hurt?" The question was rough and turbulent. When she remained silent he turned. "When you fell, how bad was it?"

"I—I lost the baby."

"I asked about you."

She stared without comprehension. No one had asked her that, not even her father. Looking into Ty's ravaged face, she could only shake her head again.

"Damn it, Asher, did you have a concussion, did you break any bones? You said you almost died."

"The baby died," she repeated numbly.

Crossing to her, he grabbed her shoulders. *"You!"* he shouted. "Don't you know that you're the most important thing to me? We can have a dozen babies if you want. I need to know what happened to you."

"I don't remember very much. I was sedated. There were transfusions…" The full impact of his words penetrated slowly. The anguish in his eyes was for her. "Ty." Burying her face against his chest, she clung. "All that's over."

"I should have been with you." He drew her closer. "We should have gone through that together."

"Just tell me you love me. Say the words."

"You know that I do." He cupped her chin to force her head back. "I love you." He saw the first tear fall and kissed it away. "Don't," he pleaded. "No more tears, Face. No more grieving."

She held him close again until the fullness left her chest. "No more grieving," she repeated, and lifted her face.

He touched it gently, fingertips only. "I hurt you."

"We let other people hurt us," she contradicted. "Never again."

"How could we be stupid enough to almost lose it all twice?" he wondered aloud. "No more secrets, Asher."

She shook her head. "No more secrets. A third chance, Ty?"

"I work best under pressure." He brushed his lips over her temple. "Double break point, Face, I'm on a winning streak."

"You should be celebrating."

"I did my share."

"Not with me." She gave him a light kiss full of promise. "We could go to my place. Pick up a bottle of champagne on the way."

"We could stay here," he countered. "And worry about the champagne tomorrow."

"It is tomorrow," she reminded him.

"Then we've got all day." He began to pull her toward the bedroom.

"Wait a minute." Snatching her hand away, she stepped back. "I'd like to hear that conventional proposal now."

"Come on, Asher." He made another grab for her hand, but she eluded him.

"I mean it."

Flustered, he stuck his hands into his pockets. "You know I want you to marry me."

"That's not a conventional proposal." She folded her arms and waited. "Well," she began when he remained silent, "should I write you a cheat sheet? You say something like, Asher—"

"I know what I'm supposed to say," he muttered. "I'd rather try the kidnapping."

Laughing, she walked over and twined her arms around his neck. "Ask me," she whispered, letting her lips hover an inch from his.

"Will you marry me, Asher?" The lips held tantalizingly near his curved, but she remained silent. His eyes dropped to them, lingered, then rose to hers. "Well?"

"I'm thinking it over," she told him. "I was hoping for something a bit more flowery, maybe some poetry or—" The wind was knocked out of her as he hefted her over his shoulder. "Yes, that's good too," she decided. "I should be able to let you know in a few days."

From the height he dropped her, she bounced twice before she settled on the bed.

"Or sooner," she decided as he began unbuttoning her blouse.

"Shut up."

She cocked a brow. "Don't you want to hear my answer?"

"We'll get the license tomorrow."

"I haven't said—"

"And the blood tests."

"I haven't agreed—"

His mouth silenced her in a long, lingering kiss as his body fit unerringly to hers.

"Of course," Asher sighed, "I could probably be persuaded."

THE HEART'S VICTORY

CHAPTER 1

Foxy stared at the underbelly of the MG. The scent of oil surrounded her as she tightened bolts. "You know, Kirk, I can't tell you how much I appreciate your lending me these coveralls." Her smooth contralto voice was touched with sarcasm.

"What are brothers for?" Foxy heard the grin in his voice though all she could see were the bottoms of his frayed jeans and his grimy sneakers.

"It's wonderful you're so broad-minded." She gritted her teeth on the words as she worked with the ratchet. "Some brothers might have insisted on fixing the transmission themselves."

"I'm no chauvinist," Kirk returned. Foxy watched Kirk's sneakers as he walked across the concrete floor of the garage. She heard the click and clatter of tools being replaced. "If you hadn't decided to be a photographer, I'd have put you on my pit crew."

"Fortunately for me, I prefer developing fluid to motor oil." She wiped the back of her hand over her cheek. "And to think if I hadn't been hired to shoot the photos for Pam Anderson's book, I wouldn't be here right now up to my elbows in car parts."

When Foxy heard his quick, warm laugh, it struck her how much she had missed him. Perhaps it was because their two-year separation had worked no change on him. He was precisely the same, as if she had closed the door and opened it again only minutes later. His face was still weathered and bronzed with creases and dents that promised to grow only deeper and more attractive with age. His hair was still as thickly curled as her own, though his was a dark gold and hers a rich russet. The familiar mustache twitched above his mouth when he smiled. Foxy couldn't remember him ever being without it. She had been six and he sixteen when it had first appeared, and seventeen years later it was a permanent fixture on his face. Foxy had seen, too, that the recklessness was still there. It was in his smile, in his eyes, in his movements.

As a child, she had worshiped him. He had been a tall, golden hero who allowed her to tag behind and pay homage. It had been Kirk who had absently dubbed her Foxy, and the ten-year-old Cynthia Fox had clung to the name as if it were a gift. When Kirk left home to pursue a career in professional racing, Foxy had lived for his occasional visits and short, sporadic letters. In his absence, he grew more golden, more indestructible. He was twenty-three when he won his first major race. Foxy had been thirteen.

This tender, testing, learning year of her life had been one of indescribable pain. It had been late when Foxy had driven home from town with her parents. The road was slick with snow. Foxy watched it hurl itself against the windows of the car while the radio played a Gershwin tune she was too young to either recognize or appreciate. She had stretched out on the back seat, closed her eyes, and begun to hum a tune popular with her own generation. She wished briefly that she was home so that she could put on her records and call her best friend to talk about things that were important—*boys*.

There had been no warning as the car began its skid. It circled wildly, gaining speed as the tires found no grip on the slick, wet snow. There was a blur of white outside the car windows and she heard her father swear as he fought to regain control of the wheel, but her fear never had the chance to materialize. Foxy heard the crunching impact as the car slammed into the telephone pole, felt the jerk and the quick pain. She felt the cold as she was tossed from the car, then the wet swish of snow against her face. Then she felt nothing.

It had been Kirk's face that Foxy saw upon awakening from the two-day coma. Her first wave of joy froze as she remembered the accident. She saw it in his eyes—the weariness, the grief, the acceptance. She shook her head to deny what he had not yet told her. Gently, he bent down to rest his cheek on hers. "We've got each other now, Foxy. I'm going to take care of you."

And so he had, in his fashion. For the next four years, Foxy followed the circuit. She received her education from a series of tutors with varying degrees of success. But during her teenage years, Cynthia Fox learned more than American history or algebra. She learned about piston displacement and turbo engines; she learned how to take an engine apart and how to put it back together; she learned the rules of pit lane. She grew up in what was predominantly a man's world, with the smell of gasoline and the roar of engines. Supervision at times had been lax, at others, nonexistent.

Kirk Fox was a man with one consuming passion: the race. Foxy knew there were times he forgot her existence completely, and she accepted it. Seeing the dents in his perfection only caused her to love him more. She grew up wild and free and, inconsistently, sheltered.

College had been a shock. Over the next four years, Foxy's world had expanded. She discovered the eccentricities of living in a dormitory with females. She began to learn more about Cynthia Fox. Having a discerning eye for color, cut, and line, she had developed her own distinctive taste in clothes. She found that clubs and sororities were not for her; her childhood had been too freewheeling to allow her to accept rules and regimentation. It had been easy for Foxy to resist college men because they seemed to her to be foolish, immature boys. She had entered college a gangling, awkward girl and graduated a willow-slim woman with her own innate grace and a passion for photography. For the two years following college, Foxy poured every ounce of her talent and effort into building her career. The assignment with Pam Anderson was a two-fold gift. It allowed her to spend time with her brother while nudging the crack in the door of opportunity yet wider. Foxy knew the first part of the gift was still more important to her than the second.

"I suppose you'd be shocked to learn I haven't seen the underside of a car in over two years." Foxy made the admission as she tightened the last of the bolts.

"What do you do when your transmission needs work?" Kirk demanded as he took a final look under the MG's hood.

"I send it to a mechanic," Foxy muttered.

"With your training?" Kirk was appalled enough to bend down and glare at the top of her head. "You can get twenty years to life for a crime like that."

"I don't have time." Foxy sighed, then continued, as if to make amends, "I did change the points and plugs last month."

"This car is a classic." Kirk closed the hood gently, then wiped the surface with a clean rag. "You're crazy if you let just anybody get their hands on it."

"Well, I can't send it out to Charlie every time it gets the sniffles, and besides…" Foxy stopped her justifications at the sound of a car pulling up outside.

"Hey, this ain't no place for a businessman." Foxy heard the smile in her brother's words as she set down the ratchet.

"Just checking on my investment."

Lance Matthews. She recognized the low, drawling voice instantly. Just as instantly her hands clenched into tight balls. Heat bubbled in her throat. Slowly, Foxy forced herself to remain calm. *Ridiculous,* she thought as she flexed her fingers; *resentments shouldn't survive a six-year separation.*

She saw from her vantage point that he, too, wore jeans and sneakers. While his showed no streaks of grease, they were frayed and worn. *He's just slumming,* she thought and suppressed an indignant sniff. Six years is a long time, she reminded herself. He might be almost tolerable by now. But she doubted it.

"I couldn't get here for the practice run this morning. How'd she do?"

"200.558." She heard the click and fizz of a beer being opened. "Charlie wants to give her a last going over, but she's prime, absolutely prime." From the tone of her brother's voice, Foxy knew he had forgotten she was there, forgotten everything but the car and the race.

"He's got his mind fixed on setting a pit record Sunday." There was a faint snap and a pungent aroma drifted to Foxy. It annoyed her that she recognized it as the scent of the slender cigars Lance habitually smoked. She rubbed her nose with the back of her hand as if to erase the fragrance from her senses. "New toy?" Lance asked, walking over to the MG. Foxy heard the hood lift. "Looks like the little number you bought your sister after she got her license. She still playing with cameras?"

Incensed, Foxy gave a push and rolled out from under the car. For the instant she lay on the creeper, she saw a look of surprise cross Lance's face. "It's the same little number," she said coldly as she struggled to her feet. "And I don't play with cameras, I work with them."

Her hair was pulled in a ponytail back from her grease-smeared face. The coveralls left her shapeless and sloppy. In one oil-splattered hand, she held the ratchet. Through her indignation, Foxy noted that Lance Matthews was more attractive than ever. Six years had deepened the creases in his rawboned face, which, by some odd miracle, just escaped being handsome. Handsome was too tame a word for Lance Matthews. His hair was richly black, curling into the collar of his shirt and tossed carelessly around his face. His brows were slightly arched over eyes that could go from stone-gray to smoke depending on his mood. The classic, aristocratic features were offset by a small white scar above his left brow. He was taller than Kirk with a rangier build, and there was an ease in his manner that Kirk lacked. Foxy knew the indolent exterior covered a keen awareness. Through his twenties he had been one of the top drivers in the racing world. She had heard it said that Lance Matthews had the hands of a surgeon, the instinct of a wolf, and the nerve of the devil. At thirty, he had won the world championship and abruptly retired. From her brother's less than informative letters, Foxy knew that for the past three years Lance had successfully sponsored drivers and cars. She watched as his mouth formed the half-tilted smile that had always been his trademark.

"Well, if it isn't the Fox." His eyes ran down the coveralls and back to her face. "Six years hasn't changed you a bit."

"Nor you," she retorted, furious that their first meeting would find her so attired. She felt like a foolish, gangling teenager again. "What a pity."

"Tongue's as sharp as ever." His teeth flashed in a grin. Apparently the fact that she was still a rude, bad-tempered urchin appealed to him. "Have you missed me?"

"As long as I possibly could," she replied and held the ratchet out to her brother.

"Still hasn't any respect for her elders," Lance told Kirk while his eyes lingered on Foxy's mutinous face. "I'd kiss you hello, but I never cared for the taste of motor oil."

He was teasing her as he had always done and Foxy's chin shot up as it always had. "Fortunately for both of us, Kirk has an unlimited supply."

"If you walk around like that for the rest of the season," Kirk warned as he replaced his tool, "you might as well work in the pits."

"The season?" Lance's look sharpened as he drew on his cigar. "You going to be around for the season? That's some vacation."

"Hardly." Foxy wiped her palms on the legs of the coveralls and tried to look dignified. "I'm here as a photographer, not as a spectator."

"Foxy is working with that writer, Pam Anderson," Kirk put in as he picked up his beer again. "Didn't I tell you?"

"You mentioned something about the writer," Lance murmured. He was studying Foxy's face as if to see beneath the smears of grease. "So, you'll be traveling the circuit again?"

Foxy remembered the intensity of his eyes. There were times when they could stop your breath. There was something raw and deep about the man. Even as an adolescent, Foxy had been aware of his basic sensuality. Then she had found it fascinating, now she knew its dangers. Willpower kept her eyes level with his. "That's right. A pity you won't be along."

"Not a pity," he countered. The intensity disappeared from his eyes and Foxy watched them grow light again. "Kirk's driving my car. I intend to tag along and watch him win." He saw Foxy frown before he turned to her brother.

"I suppose I'll meet Pam Anderson at the party you're having tonight. Don't wash the grease off, Foxy." He patted a clean spot on her chin before he walked to the door. "I might not recognize you. We should have a dance for old times' sake."

"Stuff it in your manifold," Foxy called after him, then cursed herself for trading dignity for childish taunts. After shooting Kirk a glare, she stepped out of the coveralls. "Your taste in friends eludes me."

Kirk shrugged, glancing out the window as Lance drove away. "You'd better test-drive the car before you drive to the house. It might need some adjustments."

Foxy sighed and shook her head. "Sure."

The dress Foxy chose for the evening was made of paper-thin crepe de chine. The muted pastels of lavender and green clung and floated around her slender, curved figure. With a draping skirt and strapless bodice covered by the sheerest of short jackets, it was a romantic dress. It was also very alluring. Foxy thought with grim satisfaction that Lance Matthews was in for a surprise. Cynthia Fox was not a teenager any longer. After placing small gold hoops in her ears, she stood back to judge the results.

Her hair was loose, left to fall below her shoulders in a thick mane of gleaming russet curls. Her face was now clear of black smudges. Her prominent cheekbones added both elegance and delicacy to the piquant quality of her triangular face. Her eyes were almond-shaped, not quite gray, not quite green. Her nose was sharp and aristocratic, her mouth full and just short of being too wide. There was a hint of her brother's recklessness in her eyes, but it was banked and smoldering. There was something reminiscent of the wilds in her, part deer, part tigress. Much more than beauty, she possessed an earthy, untapped sensuality. She was made of contradictions. Her willowy figure and ivory complexion made her appear fragile while the fire in her hair and boldness of her eyes sent out a challenge. Foxy felt the night was ripe for challenge.

Just as she was slipping into her shoes, a knock sounded at her door. "Foxy, can I come in?" Pam Anderson peeked through a crack in the door, then pushed it wider. "Oh, you look marvelous."

Foxy turned with a smile. "So do you."

The dreamy pale blue chiffon suited Pam's china-doll looks perfectly. Studying the petite blond beauty, Foxy wondered again how she had the stamina for as demanding a career as that of a freelance journalist. How does she manage to get such in-depth interviews when she speaks like a magnolia blossom and looks like a hothouse orchid? They had known each other for six months, and though Pam was five years Foxy's senior, the younger woman was developing maternal instincts toward the older.

"Isn't it nice to start off a job with a party?" Pam moved to the bed and sat as Foxy ran a comb through her hair. "Your brother's home is lovely, Foxy. My room's perfect."

"It was our house when we were kids," Foxy told her, frowning over her perfume bottle. "Kirk kept it as sort of a base camp since it's so close to Indianapolis." Her frown turned upward into a smile. "Kirk's always liked to camp near a track."

"He's charming." Pam ran her fingers over her short, smooth page boy. "And very generous to put me up until we start on the circuit."

"Charming he is." Foxy laughed and leaned closer to the mirror as she added color to her lips. "Unless he's plotting track strategy. You'll notice, sometimes he leaves the rest of the world." Foxy stared down at the lipstick tube, then carefully closed it. "Pam…" Taking a quick breath, she glanced up and met Pam's eyes in the mirror. "Since we'll be traveling so closely, I think you should understand Kirk a bit. He's…" She sighed and moved her shoulders. "He's not always charming. Sometimes he's curt, and short-tempered, and downright unkind. He's very restless, very competitive. Racing is his life, and at times he forgets people aren't as insensitive as cars."

"You love him a lot, don't you?" The clear insight and hint of compassion in the quiet blue eyes were a part of the reason for Pam's success in her field. She was not only able to read people, but to care.

"More than anything." Foxy turned until she met the woman's face rather than the reflection. "More still since I grew up and discovered he was human. Kirk didn't have to take on the responsibility of raising me. I don't think it occurred to me until I was in college that he'd had a choice. He could have put me in a foster home; no one would have criticized him. In fact—" she tossed her head to free her shoulders of her hair, then leaned back against the dresser "—I'm sure he was criticized by some for not doing so. He kept me with him, and that's what I needed. I'll never forget him for that. One day perhaps I'll pay him back." Smiling, Foxy straightened. "I suppose I'd better go down and make sure the caterer has everything set. The guests will be arriving soon."

"I'll come with you." Pam rose and moved to the door. "Now, what about this Lance Matthews you were grumbling about earlier? If I did my homework properly, he's a former driver, a very successful driver, now head of Matthews Corporation which among other things designs racing cars. He's designed and owns several Formula One cars, including the ones your brother will be driving this season. And yes…the Indy car too. Isn't he…?" She made a small cluck of frustration as her inventory of facts grew sketchy. "He's from a very old, wealthy family, isn't he? Boston or New Haven, shipping or import-export. Disgustingly rich."

"Boston, shipping, and disgusting," Foxy affirmed as they moved down to the first floor. "Don't get me started on him tonight or you'll have nightmares."

"Do I detect a smidgeon of dislike?"

"You detect a ton of dislike," Foxy countered. "I've had to rent a room to hold my extra dislike of Lance Matthews."

"Mmm, and rent prices are soaring."

"Which only makes me dislike him more." Foxy moved directly to the dining room and examined the table.

Lacquered wooden dishes were set on an indigo tablecloth. The centerpiece was an earthenware jug filled with sprays of dogwood and daffodils. One look at the setting, at the chunky yellow candles in wooden holders, assured Foxy that the caterer knew his business. "Relaxed informality" was the obvious theme.

"Looks nice." Foxy resisted dipping a finger into a bowl of iced caviar as the caterer bustled in from the kitchen.

He was a small, fussy man, bald but for a thin ring of hair he had dyed a deep black. He walked in quick, shuffling steps. "You're too early." He stood protectively between Foxy and the caviar. "Guests won't be arriving for another fifteen minutes."

"I'm Cynthia Fox, Mr. Fox's sister." She offered a smile as a flag of truce. "I thought perhaps I could help."

"Help? Oh no, good heavens, no." To prove his words, he brushed at her with the back of his hand as though she were an annoying fly threatening his pâté. "You mustn't touch anything. It's all balanced."

"And beautifully, too," Pam soothed as she gave Foxy's arm a warning squeeze. "Let's go have a drink, Foxy, and wait for the others to arrive."

"Silly, pompous man," Foxy mumbled as Pam urged her into the living room.

"Do you let anyone else set your f-stops?" Pam asked with bland curiosity as she sank into a chair.

Foxy laughed as she surveyed the portable bar. "Point taken. Well, there seems to be enough liquor here to keep an army reeling for a year. Trouble is, I don't know how to fix anything more complicated than the gin and tonic Kirk drinks."

"If there's a bottle of dry sherry, pour some in a very small glass. That shouldn't tax your ingenuity too far. Going to join me?"

"No." Foxy scouted through the bottles. "Drinking makes me just a little too honest. I forget the basic rules of survival—tact and diplomacy. You know the managing editor of *Wedding Day* magazine, Joyce Canfield?" Pam gave an affirmative response as Foxy located and poured sherry. "I ran into her at this cocktail party a few months back. I'd done several layouts for *Wedding Day*. Anyway, she asked me what I thought of her dress. I looked at her over the rim of my second spritzer and told her she should avoid yellow, it made her look sallow." Foxy crossed the room and handed Pam her glass. "Honest but dumb. I haven't taken a picture of a wilted bouquet for *Wedding Day* since."

Pam laughed her quiet, floating laugh and sipped her sherry. "I'll remember not to ask you any dangerous questions when you have a glass in your hand." She watched Foxy run a finger over a high, piecrust table. "Does it feel strange being home?"

Foxy's eyes were dark, the green merely sprinkled over the

gray. "It brings back memories. Strange, I really haven't thought of my life here in years, but now…" Walking to the window, she pulled back the sheer ivory curtain. Outside, the sun was dipping low in the sky, shooting out sprays of red and gold light. "Do you know, this is really the only place I could define as home. New York doesn't count. Ever since my parents died, I've moved around so much, first with Kirk, then with my career. It's only now that I'm here that it occurs to me how rootless my life has been."

"Do you want roots, Foxy?"

"I don't know." When Foxy turned back to Pam, her face was puzzled. "I don't know," she repeated. "Maybe. But I want something. It's out there." She narrowed her eyes and stared at something she could not yet see.

"What is?"

Foxy jolted as the voice shattered her thoughts. Kirk stood in the doorway studying her with his easy smile, his hands thrust into the pockets of dun-colored slacks. As always, there was an aura of excitement around him.

"Well." Giving him a considering look, Foxy crossed to him. "Silk, huh?" With sisterly prerogative, she fingered the collar of his shirt. "Guess you don't change too many engines in this." Kirk tugged on her hair and kissed her simultaneously.

In her heels, she was nearly as tall as he, and their eyes were level with each other's. As Pam watched she noticed how little family resemblance they shared; only the curling heaviness of their hair was similar. Kirk's eyes were a dark true green, and his face was long and narrow. There was nothing of his sister's elegance or her delicacy about him. Studying his profile, Pam felt a tiny quiver chase up her spine. Quickly she glanced down at her drink. Long-term assignments and quivering spines didn't mix.

"I'll fix you a drink," Foxy offered, drawing away from her

brother and moving to the bar. "We don't dare go into the other room for another two and a half minutes. Oops, no ice." She closed the lid on the ice bucket and shrugged. "I'll be heroic and challenge the caterer. Pam's drinking sherry," she called over her shoulder as she left the room.

"Want a refill?" Kirk asked, turning his attention to Pam for the first time.

"No, thanks." She smiled and lifted her glass to her lips. "I haven't had a chance to thank you yet for putting me up. I can't tell you how nice it is not to be sleeping in a hotel."

"I know all about hotels." Kirk grinned and sat across from her. For the first time since they had met the day before, they were alone. Pam felt the quiver again and ignored it. Kirk took a cigarette from the holder on the table and lit it. For those few seconds, he studied her.

Class, he thought. *And brains.* This was no racing groupie. His eyes lingered an instant on the soft pink mouth. *She looks like something in a store window. Beautiful, desirable, and behind a wall of glass.*

"Foxy's spoken of you so often, I feel I know you." Pam immediately cursed herself for the inanity and took another sip of sherry. "I'm looking forward to the race."

"So am I," Kirk answered, then leaned back in his chair and studied her more openly. "You don't look the type to be interested in pit stops and lap speeds."

"No?" Pam countered as she collected her poise. "What type do I look like?"

Kirk smoked in long, deep drags. "The type who likes Chopin and champagne."

Pam swirled the remaining sherry in her glass and held his gaze. "I do," she answered, then relaxed against the cushions of her chair. "But as a journalist, I'm interested in all kinds of things. I hope you'll be generous with your thoughts and feelings and your knowledge."

A smile lifted the corners of his mustache. "I've been known to be generous with all manners of things," he mocked, wondering if the dewy texture of her skin was as soft as it looked. The doorbell broke the silence. Kirk rose, took the drink from Pam's hand, and pulled her to her feet. Though she told herself it was a foolish reaction, her heart thundered. "Are you married?" he asked.

"Why…no." She frowned, confused.

"Good. I never like sleeping with married women."

He spoke so matter-of-factly, it took Pam a moment to react. Angry color flooded her porcelain cheeks. "Of all the presumptuous—"

"Listen," Kirk interrupted. "We're bound to sleep together before the season's finished. I'm not much on games, so I don't play."

"And would it shock you very deeply," Pam returned with the coldness only a southern-bred voice can achieve, "if I decline your generous invitation?"

"Seems like a waste," Kirk concluded with a careless shrug. He took Pam's hand as the doorbell pealed a second time. "We'd better answer it."

CHAPTER 2

Over the next hour, the house filled with people and grew noisy. As the room filled, the patio doors opened to allow guests to spill outside. The night was warm and still.

For Foxy, there were both new faces and old friends. She wandered from group to group, assuming the role of unofficial hostess. The caterer's proud balance had been long since shattered as trays and bowls were scattered throughout the house. People milled in every corner. Still, the breezy informality of the party was linked with a common bond. These were racing people, whether they were drivers, wives, or privileged fans.

Flushed and laughing, Foxy answered the door to admit a late arrival. Her smile of greeting faded instantly. There was some satisfaction to be gained from seeing a look of surprise in Lance's gray eyes. It came and went with the lift and fall of his brow. Slowly he took his gaze over the length of her. There was a look of consideration on his face, which Foxy equated with a man about to purchase a piece of sculpture for his den. Instantly the ease fled from her stance as her chin lifted and her shoulders straightened. Annoyed, she gave him the same casual appraisal he gave her.

Both his turtleneck and slacks were black. The night apparel lent him a mysterious, dangerous look only accentuated by his leanness and reckless looks. About him was the odd air of calm Foxy remembered. It was an ability to remain absolutely motionless and absorb everything. The true hunter possesses it, and the bullfighter who survives. Now, as she knew he was absorbing her, Foxy challenged him with her eyes though her heart beat erratically. *Anger,* she told herself. *He always makes me so angry.*

"Well, well, well." Lance's voice was quiet and oddly intimate over the hum of the party. He met her eyes, then smiled at her sulky pout. "It seems I was wrong."

"Wrong?" she repeated and reluctantly shut the door behind him rather than in his face.

"You have changed." He took both her hands, ignoring her sharp jerk of protest. Holding her away from him, he let his eyes roam down the length of her again. "You're still ridiculously thin, but you've managed to fill out a bit in a few interesting places."

Her skin trembled as if a cool breeze had caressed it. Furious with the sensation, Foxy tried to snatch her hands away. She failed. "If that's a compliment, you can keep it. I'd like my hands back, Lance."

"Sure, in a minute." Her anger and indignation rolled off him as he continued to study her. "You know," he said conversationally, "I always wondered how that funny little face of yours would turn out. It had an odd appeal, even when it was splattered with transmission fluid."

"I'm surprised you remember how I looked." Resigned that he would not let her go until he was ready, Foxy stopped struggling. She took a long, hard look at him, searching his face for any flaws that might have developed during the past six years. She found none. "You haven't changed a bit."

"Thanks." With a grin, he transferred his hold to her waist and led her toward the sounds of the party.

"That wasn't intended as a compliment." Foxy had a strange reaction to his quick grin and intimate touch. The wariness remained with her, but it was tempered with amusement. Foxy drew firmly away from him as they entered the main room. It was, she reminded herself, always so simple for him to charm her. "I imagine you know just about everyone." She made a quick sweep of the room with the back of her hand. "And I'm certain you can find your way to the bar."

"Gracious to the last," Lance murmured, then gave her another measuring stare. "As I recall, you didn't always dislike me so intensely."

"I was a slow learner."

"Lance, darling!" Honey Blackwell bore down on them. Her hair was short and fluffed and silver blond, her face pretty and painted, her body all curves and dips. She had money and an unquenchable thirst for excitement. She was, in Foxy's opinion, the classic racing leech. As her arms circled Lance's neck he rested his hands on her generous hips. She kissed Lance with single-minded enthusiasm as he watched Foxy's disdainful smirk over Honey's bare shoulder.

"Apparently, you two have met." Inclining her head, she turned and moved to the center of the party. *And apparently,* she added to herself, *you can manage to amuse yourselves without me.* Feeling a hand on her arm, Foxy glanced up.

"Hi. I knew you'd stand still long enough eventually for me to introduce myself. I'm Scott Newman."

"Hello. Cynthia Fox." Her hand was taken in a very proper shake.

"Yes, I know. You're Kirk's sister."

Foxy smiled at him as she completed her study of his features. His face was well formed, just escaping fullness. His eyes were deep brown, his nose straight, his mouth long and curved. He wore his brown hair at a conservative length, neither long nor short. They stood eye to eye, as he was a few inches short of six feet. He was handsomely tanned and trim without being lean. His three-piece suit was well cut, but the jacket had been casually left unbuttoned. He was, Foxy decided, the perfect model for a study of up-and-coming young executives. She thought briefly that it was a pity he hadn't dressed up the beige suit with a deep-toned shirt.

"We'll be seeing a lot of each other over the next few months," he told her, unaware of the trend of her thoughts.

"Oh?" She gave him her full attention as she eased out of the way of someone bearing a tray of crackers and Gouda cheese.

"I'm Kirk's road manager. I see to all the traveling arrangements, accommodations for him and the crew, and so forth." His eyes smiled over to hers while he lifted his glass to his lips.

"I see." Foxy tilted her head, then tossed back her hair. "I haven't been around for a few years." Catching a glimpse of her brother out of the corner of her eye, Foxy focused on him, then smiled. He had the animated look of a knight-on-quest as a brunette hung on his arm and a small tangle of people hung on his words. "We didn't use a road manager when I was on the team," she murmured. Foxy remembered more than once falling asleep in the back seat of a car in a garage that smelled of gasoline and stale cigarettes. Or camping on the infield grass, waiting for the morning and the race. *He's a comet,* she thought, watching her brother. *A brilliant, flaming comet.*

"There've been a number of changes in the past few years," Scott commented. "Kirk began winning more important races. And of course, with Lance Matthews' sponsorship, his career has come more into focus."

"Yes." She gave a quick laugh and shook her head. "Money talks after all, doesn't it?"

"You haven't got a drink." Scott noticed the lack of glass, but not the sarcasm in her voice. "We'd better fix that."

"Sure." Foxy linked her arm in his and allowed him to lead her to the bar. *I don't care one way or the other about Lance Matthews' money.*

"What would you like?" Scott asked.

Foxy glanced at him, then at the short, graying professional bartender. "A spritzer," she told him.

Moonlight shone through the young leaves. The flowers in the garden were still new with spring, their colors were muted with night. Their fragrance was light and tender, only whispering of the promise of summer.

With a mighty sigh, Foxy dropped on one seat of a white glider and propped her feet up on the other. Dimly over the stretch of lawn, she could hear the sounds of the party ebb and flow. By slipping into the kitchen and out the back door, she had escaped to steal a few moments of quiet and solitude. Inside, the air was thick with smoke and clashing perfumes. Foxy took a long, greedy breath of spring air and pushed with her feet to set the glider into motion.

Scott Newman, she decided, was handsome, polite, intelligent, and interested. And, she admitted, ordinary. Rolling her eyes on a sigh, Foxy stared up at the sky. Wisps of dark clouds were edged in gray. As they passed lazily across the moon the light shifted and swayed. *There I go,* she mused, *being critical again. Does a man have to stand on one foot and juggle for me to consider him entertaining? What am I looking for? A knight?* Foxy frowned and rejected the choice. *No, knights are all pol-*

ished and shiny and pure. I think my taste runs to something with a bit of tarnish and maybe a few scratches. Someone who can make me laugh and cry and make me angry and make my knees tremble when he touches me. She laughed quietly, wondering how many men she was looking for. Leaning her head back, she crossed her ankles. The hem of her dress lifted to tickle her knee. Tossing up her arms, she gripped the slender poles on either side of the glider. *I want someone dangerous, someone wild and gentle and strong and smart and foolish.* With another laugh for her own specifications, she stared up at the stars. With a hazy blue light, they peeked and glimmered through the shifting clouds.

"Which star do I wish on?"

"The brightest is usually the best."

With a quick gasp, Foxy dropped her hands and searched for the owner of the voice. He was only a dark shadow, tall and lean. As it moved she thought of the steady stalking grace of a panther. Lance's black attire blended with the night, but his eyes caught the luminescence of the moon. For a moment, Foxy felt an eeriness, a displacement of the quiet suburban garden into a primitive, isolated jungle. Like a large cat of prey, his eyes glowed with their own light and conquered the dark. Shadows fell over his face and deepened its chiseled lines. She thought Lucifer must have looked equally dark and compelling as he fell from heaven into the flames.

"What are you wishing for?" His voice was so quiet, it shook the air.

Suddenly Foxy became aware that she was holding her breath. Carefully she released it. It was only the surprise, she insisted, that had made her skin quiver. "Oh, all I can get," she returned flippantly. "What are you doing out here? I thought you'd be knee-deep in blondes."

Lance swung onto the glider. "I wanted some air," he told her as he stood staring down at her, "and some quiet."

Disturbed that his motives mirrored hers, Foxy shrugged and closed her eyes as if to ignore him. "How did you manage to tear yourself away from Miss Lush Bust?"

The sounds of the party penetrated the quiet of the night. Foxy felt his eyes on her face but stubbornly kept hers closed. "So," he murmured, "you've grown claws. You shouldn't sharpen them on someone's back, Foxy. The face is cleaner."

She opened her eyes and met his. Reluctantly she admitted that she had been nasty from the moment she had seen him again. Unprovoked nastiness was out of character for her. Foxy sighed and shrugged. "I'm sorry. I don't usually make a habit of snarling and spitting. Sit down, Lance, I'll try to behave." A small smile accompanied the invitation. He did not, as she had expected, sit across from her. Instead, he dropped down beside her. Foxy stiffened. Either unaware of or unconcerned by her reaction, Lance propped his feet next to hers on the opposite bench.

"I don't mind sparring, Fox, but a rest between rounds is always refreshing." Pulling out his lighter, he flicked it at the end of a long, thin cigar. The flame licked and flared. Strange, she thought as she relaxed her muscles, how clearly I remember that scent.

"Let's see if we can manage to be civilized for a few minutes," Foxy suggested and twisted slightly to face him. A smile hovered on her lips. She was an adult now, she reminded herself, and could meet him on his own terms. "Shall we discuss the weather, the latest best-seller, the political structure of Romania? I know—" she propped her cheek on her palm "—the race. How does it feel to be designing cars instead of racing them? Are you more hopeful for the Indy car you designed, or the Formula One for the Grand Prix races? Kirk's done very well on the GP circuit since the season opened. The car's supposed to be very fast and very reliable."

Lance saw the mischief in her eyes and lifted a brow. "Still reading racing magazines, Foxy?"

"If I didn't keep up to date, Kirk would never forgive me." She laughed, a low, heavy sound.

"I see that hasn't changed," Lance commented. She gave him a puzzled smile. "Even at fifteen, you had the sexiest laugh I'd ever heard. Like something stealing through the fog." He blew out a stream of smoke as she shifted in her seat. Moonlight showered on her hair, shooting out hundreds of tiny flames. She felt just the smallest hint of his power tempting her.

"The main branch of your company is in Boston," Foxy began, navigating to safer ground. "I suppose you live there now."

Lance smiled at her maneuver and tipped off the ash at the end of his cigar. "Most of the time. Ever been there?" He tossed his arm over the back of the seat. The gesture was so casual Foxy was barely aware of it.

"No." The glider's motion continued, slow and soothing. "I'd like to. I know there are fabulous contrasts. Brownstones and ivy, and steel and glass. I've seen some very effective pictures."

"I saw one of yours not too long ago."

"Oh?" Curious, she turned her head toward him and was surprised to find their faces nearly touching. His warm breath touched her lips. The power was stronger this time, and even more tempting. As she inched cautiously away his eyes never flickered from hers.

"It was taken in winter, but there was no snow, only a bit of frost on naked trees. There was a bench, and an old man was sleeping on it wrapped up in a gray and black topcoat. The sun came low through the trees and fell right across him. It was incredibly sad and quite beautiful."

Foxy was for the moment at a total loss. She had not expected Lance Matthews to possess any sensitivity or appreciation for the fine points of her craft. As they sat in silence something was happening between them, but she knew neither how to resist or encourage it. It was something as elemental as man and woman and as complex as emotion. His eyes continued to hold hers as his fingers tangled in the tips of her hair.

"I was very impressed," he went on as she remained silent and perplexed. "I noticed your name under it. I thought at first it couldn't be you. The Cynthia Fox I remembered didn't have the ability to take a picture with that much depth, that much feeling. I still knew you as a wide-eyed adolescent with a vile temper." When Lance broke the look to flick away the stub of his cigar, Foxy let out a quiet, shaky breath.

Relax, she ordered herself. *Stop being an idiot.*

"In any case, I was curious enough to do some checking. When I found it was you, I was doubly impressed." As he turned back to her one brow lifted and disappeared under the tousled front of his hair. "Obviously you're very good at what you do."

"What? Play with cameras?" But she smiled with the question. The evening air had mellowed her mood.

His grin was quick. "I've always thought a person should enjoy their work. I've been playing with cars for years."

"You can afford to play," she reminded him. Her voice cooled without her being aware of it.

"You've never forgiven me for having money, have you?" There was a light amusement in his voice that made her feel foolish.

"No." She shrugged. "I suppose not. Ten million always seemed so ostentatious."

He laughed, a low rumble, then tugged on her hair until she faced him again. "Only new money is ostentatious in Boston, Foxy. Old money is discreet."

"What constitutes 'old,' financially speaking?" Foxy found she enjoyed his laugh and the friendly hand on her hair.

"Oh, I'd say three generations would be the bare minimum. Anything less would be suspect. You know, Fox, I much prefer the lily of the valley to the gasoline you used to wear."

"Thanks. I do wear unleaded now and again, but only when I'm feeling reckless." She rose with a sigh. It surprised her that she would have preferred sitting with him to rejoining the party. "I'd better get back in. Are you coming?"

"Not yet." He took her hand and with a swift jerk spun her around until she tumbled into his lap.

"Lance!" With a surprised laugh, she pushed against his chest. "What are you doing?" Her struggles were halfhearted, though his hands were still firm on her waist. Foxy's mood was still mellow.

"I never kissed you hello."

Laughter died on her lips as she sensed danger. Quickly she jerked back, but he cupped his hand around the base of her neck. She managed a startled "no!" before his mouth closed over hers.

The kiss began light and teasing. Indeed, she could feel the curve of a small smile on the lips that touched hers. Perhaps if she had struggled, perhaps if her protest had continued, it would have stopped at a careless brush of lips. But as their mouths met, Foxy froze. It seemed her heart stopped pumping, her lungs stopped drawing and releasing air, her pulse stopped beating as her blood lay still. Then, in a sudden wild fury, her blood began to swim again.

Who deepened the kiss first she would never know. It seemed instantaneous. Hot and hungry, their mouths took from each other in a moist, depthless, endless kiss. The muffled groan that touched the air might have come from either of them or both. Her breasts were soft and yielding against his chest as she used tongue and teeth and lips to take the kiss still deeper. He explored all the intimate recesses of her mouth while she wallowed in his flavor, his scent, in the feel of his skin against hers. His hand moved once in a long, bruising stroke down her back and waist and over her hip and thigh. The thin material of her dress was little more than air between them. At the rough caress, Foxy strained closer, nipping his lip to provoke more heat. His answer was to crush her mouth savagely, desperately, until her senses tangled into ecstatic confusion. With a quiet sound of pleasure, she went limp in his arms. Their lips clung for an instant longer as he drew her away.

Her eyes seemed as gray as his as they watched each other in silence. Her arms were still locked around his neck. Foxy could no longer smell the flowers but only his warm, male aroma, she could no longer hear the laughter of the party for the quiet sound of his breathing, she could no longer feel the breeze, but only the spreading heat of his hands. Only he existed. An owl swooped from the tree behind them and hooted three times. Instantly the spell was shattered. Foxy shuddered, swallowed, and struggled to her feet.

"You shouldn't have done that." As tingles continued to race along her skin she avoided his eyes and brushed distractedly at the skirt of her dress.

"No? Why not?" Lance's voice was as calm as a shrug. "You're a big girl now." He stood, and she was forced to tilt her head to see his face. "You enjoyed that as much as I did. It's a little late to play the flustered maiden."

"I'm not playing the flustered maiden," Foxy denied hotly as her eyes shot back to his. "Whether I enjoyed it or not is beside the point." Realizing she was fitting his description precisely, she tossed her hair behind her back in annoyance. She planned to make a dignified exit as she stepped from the glider, but Lance stopped her with a hand on her arm before she had taken two steps across the grass.

"What is the point, Fox?" He no longer sounded amused or calm but irritated.

"The point is," she said between her teeth, "don't do it again."

"Orders?" he murmured softly. "I don't take orders very well."

"I'm not asking for a ham on rye," she countered. "I was off guard." Foxy tried to reason out her response to him while justifying it. "And—and tired and perhaps a bit curious. I overreacted."

"Curious?" His laugh was male and again amused. "Did I satisfy your curiosity, Foxy? Maybe like Alice, you'll find it 'curiouser and curiouser.'" He trailed his fingers lightly up her arm. Foxy shied away as her skin trembled.

"You're impossible!" She pushed the hair from her face in impatient fury. "You've always been impossible." With this, she whirled and ran toward the safety of the party. Lance watched her dress float and swirl around her.

CHAPTER 3

The Indianapolis 500 is an event that transforms Indianapolis from an ordinary midwestern city into the focus of the racing world. More people watch this one race than any other single sporting event in the country. It is for car racing what Wimbledon is for tennis, what the Kentucky Derby is for horse racing, what the World Series is for baseball—prestige, honor, excitement.

Foxy was relieved that the sky was empty of clouds. There was not even the smallest wisp to hint of rain. The mixture of rain and racing always made her uneasy. A breeze teased the ends of the ribbon that held her hair in a ponytail. Her jeans were old friends, nearly white with wear at the knees and snug at the hips. A baseball-style shirt in red and white pinstripes was tucked neatly into the waist. Around her neck hung the secondhand Nikon she had purchased while in college. Foxy would not have traded it for a chest of gold. From her vantage point in the pits, she could see that the grandstands were empty. Reporters, television crews, drivers, mechanics all milled about attending to business or drinking coffee from foam cups. The air was quiet enough to allow an occasional bird song to carry, but it was not calm. A current ran through the air, stirring up waves of tension and excitement. In less than two hours, the stands and infield would be swarming with people. When the green flag was waved, Indianapolis Motor Speedway would hold four hundred thousand people, a number that rivaled the population of some American cities. The noise would explode like one long roar of thunder.

During the hours that followed, there would be a continuous drone of engines. The pits would grow steamy with heat and thick with the smell of fuel and sweat. Eyes would be glued to the small, low-slung cars as they tore around the two-and-a-half-mile oval. Some would think only of the thrill of the race.

Foxy's feelings were more complicated. It had been two years since she had stood near a racetrack and six since she had been a part of the racing world. But it was, she discovered as she stared around her, like yesterday. The feelings, the emotions inside her, had not been altered by her absence. There was anticipation, excitement. She was almost lightheaded with it, and she knew it would grow only more intense after the race began. There was a wonder and pride at knowing her brother's skill, a talent which seemed more innate than learned. But underlying all was a deep-rooted fear, a terror so rich and sharp, it never dulled with the years. All the sensations scrambled inside of her, and she knew when the green flag was waved, they would all merge together into one heady, indescribable emotion. Nothing had changed.

Foxy knew the ropes. There were some drivers who would grant interviews and speak cheerfully, casually, about the race to come. Others would be technical or abstract, some belligerent. She knew Kirk would grant early interviews, answering questions with his patented brand of appealing arrogance. To Kirk each race was the same and each race was unique. It was the same because he drove each to win, unique because each race presented problems unlike any before or after. Foxy knew after the interviews that he would disappear and remain alone until it was time to be strapped into the cockpit. From long experience, she knew how to be unobtrusive. She moved among drivers and timers and mechanics and the dozens of other photographers, letting her camera record the prerace routine.

"What are you poking around here with that thing for?"

Foxy recognized the grumble but finished her shot before turning. "Hiya, Charlie." With a grin, she tossed her arms around his neck and nuzzled his grizzled cheek. She knew he would protest and grumble as well as she knew the hug pleased him.

"Just like a female," he muttered, but Foxy felt the slight squeeze of his hands on her back before he pulled away.

For the next few minutes, they studied each other openly. She saw little change. There was a bit more gray in his beard, a bit less hair on his head, but his eyes were the same clear blue she had first seen ten years before. He had been fifty then, and she had thought him ancient. As Lance Matthews' chief mechanic, Charlie Dunning had ruled the pits like a despot. He continued to do so now as the head of Kirk's team.

"Still skinny," he said in disgust. "I should've known a few years wouldn't put any weight on you. Don't you make enough money to eat by taking pictures?"

"No one's been leaving chocolate bars lying around for me lately." She pinched his cheek as she spoke, knowing he would suffer torture and death before admitting he had planted chocolate bars for a skinny kid to find. "I missed you at Kirk's party the other night," she added as he shuffled and grumbled.

"I don't go to kids' parties. So you and the fancy lady are

going to take in the Indy and the rest of the Grand Prix races this season." He sniffled and set his mouth in a disapproving line.

"If you mean Pam, then yes, we are." Foxy decided Charlie had nearly perfected irascibility. "And she's a journalist."

"You just mind that neither of you gets in the way."

"Yes, Charlie," Foxy said demurely, but his eyes narrowed at the gleam in hers.

"Still sassy, too. If you hadn't been so puny, I'd have taken a strap to you years ago."

Grinning, Foxy lifted the camera and shot a full-faced picture. "Smile," she suggested.

"Sassy," Charlie repeated. As his lips started to twitch he turned and lumbered away.

Foxy watched until he had disappeared into the crowd before she turned around. She gave a small gasp as she bumped into Lance. He rested his hands briefly on her shoulders as his eyes locked with hers. She had managed to completely block out the interlude on the glider, but now it all came flooding back in full force. The mouth, which had been hungry on hers, twitched in a half smile.

"He always did have a soft spot for you."

Foxy had forgotten everything but the dark gray eyes that watched her. As his smile grew, touched now with arrogance, she jerked out of his hold. He was dressed in much the same manner as she was, in jeans and a T-shirt. His hair danced on his forehead as the breeze caught it. Mentally she cursed him for being so wickedly attractive.

"Hello, Lance." Her voice was marginally friendly with overtones of aloofness. Foxy was pleased with it. "No reporters dogging your footsteps?"

"Hello, Foxy," he returned equally. "Taking a few snapshots?"

"Touché," Foxy muttered. Turning away, she lifted the Nikon to her face and became absorbed in setting the aperture. She thought she must have gained an extra sense where Lance Matthews was concerned. His presence could be felt on the surface of her skin. It was both uncomfortable and arousing.

"Looking forward to the race, Foxy, or has it lost its charm?" As he spoke Lance tangled his fingers in the thick softness of her ponytail. Foxy wasted four shots.

"I heard Kirk won the pole position in the time trials. He knows how to cash in on that kind of advantage." When she turned back to him, her face was calm, her eyes cool. One kiss, she told herself, was nothing to be concerned about. They were still the same people. "I imagine as the owner, you're pleased." His smile was not the answer Foxy was looking for. "I've seen the car. It's very impressive." When he still did not reply, Foxy let out a frustrated breath and squinted up at him. "This conversation is fascinating, Lance, but I really must get back to work."

His hand curled firmly around her upper arm as she turned to go. He watched her in silence, and she was forced to toss up a hand to shield her eyes from the sun. "I'm having a small party tonight." His voice was quiet. "In my suite at the hotel."

"Oh?" Foxy employed the arched-brow look she had perfected in college.

"Seven o'clock. We'll have dinner."

"How small a party?" Foxy met his eyes steadily, though hers were shadowed by her hand.

"Very small, as in you and me."

"Smaller," she corrected evenly, "as in just you." Two mechanics, clad in the vivid red shirts of Kirk's team, moved past them. Lance's gaze never wandered from hers. "I have a date with Scott Newman."

"Break it."

"No."

"Afraid?" he taunted, bringing her an inch closer with a slight movement of his hand.

"No, I'm not afraid," Foxy retorted. The green in her eyes shimmered against the gray in his. "But I'm not stupid either. Maybe you've forgotten, I'm not a newcomer where you're concerned. I've already seen your string of—ah—ladies," she said with a dash of scorn. "It was quite a boost to my education, watching you pick and shuffle and discard. I do my own picking," she added, growing angrier as he remained silent. "And I do my own discarding. Go find someone else to feed your voracious ego."

Abruptly Lance smiled. His voice was light and amused. "You still have a vile temper, Foxy. You've also got a bright, inquiring mind and energy in every cell. You'll outdistance Newman in an hour, and he'll bore you to distraction."

"That's my problem," Foxy snapped, then remembered to jerk her arm free.

"That it is," Lance agreed cheerfully. He deprived her of having the last word by walking away.

Infuriated, Foxy whirled around, prepared to stomp off in the opposite direction. With a small shock, she saw that the grandstands were filling with people. Time was moving quickly. Annoyed, she swiftly walked down into the pit area.

As she interviewed a rookie driver Pam watched the entire scene between Lance and Foxy. It wasn't possible for her to hear what passed between them, but she had clearly seen the variety of emotions take possession of Foxy's face. She watched them with the objectivity and curiosity peculiar to her trade. There was something physical between them, she had only to see them together to be certain. She was certain, too, that Foxy was kicking out against it like an ill-tempered mule and that she had come out second best in the battle that had just taken place.

Pam had liked Lance Matthews immediately. She was prone to judge people quickly, then calculate the most direct and productive approach to them. The consistent accuracy of her judgment had helped her climb to success in her profession. She had judged Lance Matthews as a man who did not so much shun convention as make his own. He would attract both men and women simply because he had so much to offer. He had strength and arrogance and a rich sensuality. Pam thought he would be indispensable as a friend and terrifying as a lover.

The rookie, blissfully unaware of her preoccupation, continued to answer her questions as she wound up the interview. With one eye cocked on Lance's back, Pam thanked him graciously, wished him luck, and hurried off.

"Mr. Matthews!"

Lance turned. He watched a small, delicate-faced blonde dressed impeccably in gray slacks and a blazer running toward him. A tape recorder was slung over one shoulder, a purse over the other. Curious, he waited until she caught up with him. Pam paused and offered Lance a breathless smile.

"Mr. Matthews, I'm Pam Anderson." She held out a hand whose nails were polished a baby-pink. "I'm doing a series of articles on racing. Perhaps Foxy mentioned me."

"Hello." Lance held her hand a moment as he studied her. He had expected someone sturdier. "I suppose we missed each other at Kirk's party the other night."

"You were pointed out to me," Pam told him, deciding to use flat-out honesty as her approach. "But you disappeared before I could wrangle my way over to you. Foxy disappeared, too."

"You're very observant." Though the annoyance in his

voice was only slight, Pam recognized it and was pleased. She knew she had his full attention.

"Our friendship is still at the apprentice stage, but I'm very fond of Foxy. I also know how to mind my own business." She brushed absently at her hair as the wind teased it into her eyes. "Professionally, I'm only interested in the race and any and all aspects thereof. I'm hoping you'll help me. Not only do you know what it's like to design and own a Formula One, you know what it's like to compete in one. You also know this track and the specifics of an Indy car. The fact that you're a well-known figure not only in racing circles but in society will add tremendous readability to the series."

Sometime during Pam's speech, Lance had stuck his hands in his pockets. He waited for a full ten seconds to see if she was finished before he started to chuckle. "A few minutes ago, I was trying to figure out how you could be the same Pam Anderson who wrote that blistering series on foul-ups in the penal system." He inclined his head in a gesture she took as a seal of approval. "Now I know. We'll have plenty of time to talk over the next few months." Pam watched his gaze shift and focus to where Foxy leaned against a fence and fiddled with lenses. She saw the birth of his patented smile. "Plenty of time." When his attention darted back to Pam, his grin widened and settled. "What do you know about the 500?"

"The first 500 was in 1911, and the winning car had an average speed of 74.59 miles per hour. The track was originally paved in brick, hence the nickname the Old Brickyard. It's a full-throttle race where a driver moves to high gear and stays there. It's not a Grand Prix race because no points are given, but there are many similarities between the Formula One car and the Indy car. There are also a number of drivers who have competed in both the 500 and the Grand Prix circuit…like Kirk Fox. The cars here are fueled by alcohol. An alcohol fire is particularly dangerous because there's no flame."

"You've done your homework." Lance grinned at the computerlike flow of information.

"Oh, I have the facts," she agreed, liking the directness of his gaze. "But they don't tell the whole story. Forty-six people have died at this race, but only three in the last ten years. Why?"

"Cars are safer," Lance answered. "They used to be built like battleships, and in a crash they stayed solid and the driver absorbed all the power. Now it's the fragility of the cars that saves lives. Cars self-destruct around a driver, diffusing the power away from him. The restraint systems have been improved, and the drivers wear fire-resistant clothes from the shoes up." Sensing that the starting time was drawing near, Lance led her back toward the start-finish line.

"So racing has become fairly safe?" Pam asked. Her look was as candid as her voice was soft.

Again Lance gave her his full attention. She was a very sharp lady. "I didn't say that. It's safer, but there will always be the element of risk. Without it, a race like the Indy would just be some cars going in a circle."

"But a crash doesn't bring the fear it once did?"

He grinned again and shook his head. "I doubt if many drivers think about crashing. If they did, they wouldn't get into a cockpit. It's never going to happen to you, always to someone else. When you do think about it, you accept it as part of the rules. A crash is never the worst fear in any case. It's fire. There isn't a driver alive who doesn't have a gut fear of fire."

"What about when you're driving and another driver crashes? What do you feel then?"

"You don't," he answered simply. "You can't. There isn't room in the cockpit for emotion."

"No." She nodded. "I can understand that. But there is one thing I don't understand. I don't understand why."

"Why?"

"Why do people strap themselves into a car and whirl around a circuit at earth-shattering speeds. Why do they risk injury or death? What's the motivation?"

Lance turned and frowned at the track. "It varies. I imagine there're as many motivations as there are drivers—the thrill, the competition, the challenge, the money, the prestige, the speed. Speed can be addictive. There's the need to prove your own capabilities, to test your own endurance. And, of course, there's the ego that goes with any sport." As he turned back to Pam he saw Kirk step out into the sunlight. "Drivers all have different degrees of need, but they all need to win."

Foxy moved around the car, crouching and snapping as Kirk was strapped into the cockpit. He pulled the balaclava over his head, and for the moments before he fixed the helmet over it, he looked like an Arthurian knight preparing to joust. He answered Charlie's questions with short words or moves of his head. Already, his concentration was consumed by the race. Beneath his helmet visor, his eyes were unfathomable, his expression neither relaxed nor tense. There was an air about him of being separate, not only from the people crowded around the car, but from himself. Foxy could sense his detachment, and her camera captured it. As she straightened she watched Lance walk over and bend close to her brother's head.

"I got a case of scotch says you won't break the track record."

She saw Kirk's imperceptible nod and knew he had accepted the challenge. He would thrive on it. From the opposite side of the car, Foxy studied Lance, realizing he knew Kirk better than she had imagined. His eyes lifted and met hers as the engine roared to life between them. As Kirk cruised onto the track to take his pole position Foxy disappeared inside the garage area.

As the last strands of "Back Home Again in Indiana" floated on the air, the crowd roared with approval at the release of the thousands of colored balloons. For miles, those who were not at the Motor Speedway would see the drifting orbs and know that the 500 was under way. The order was official, ringing out over the rumble of the crowd. "Gentlemen, start your engines." On the starting grid, tension revved as high as the engines.

The stands were a wave of color and noise as the cars began their pace lap. The speed seemed minimal. The cars themselves, low splashes of color and lettering, were in formation and well behaved. They shone clean and bright in the streaming light of the sun. No longer could bird songs be heard. Suddenly the pace car pulled away and sped off the track.

"This is it," Foxy murmured, and Pam jumped slightly.

"I thought I'd lost you." She pushed her sunglasses more firmly on her nose.

"You don't think I'd miss the start, do you?" There was a long sports lens on her camera now, and she had it trained on the track. "They'll get the green flag any second now." Pam noticed that she seemed a bit pale, but as she opened her mouth to comment, the air exploded with noise. With professional ease, Foxy drew a bead on the white flash of Kirk's racer.

"How can they do it?" Pam spoke to herself, but Foxy lowered her camera and turned to her. "How can they keep up that pace for five hundred miles?"

"To win," Foxy said simply.

The afternoon wore on. The noise never abated. The heat in the pits was layered with the smell of fuel, oil, and sweat. Out of a field of thirty, ten cars were already out of the running due to mechanical failure or minor crashes. A broken gearbox, a failed clutch, a split-second error in judgment brought the curtain down on hope. Pam had discarded her blazer, rolled up the sleeves of her white lawn blouse, and now stalked the pit area with her tape recorder. Trickles of dampness worked their way down Foxy's back. Her shirt clung to her skin, and her hair curled damply around her face. But there was another tickle between her shoulder blades, one that had her stiffening and turning away from the track. Lance stood directly behind her. He spoke first but looked beyond her. The track was a valley cupped inside the mountains of the grandstands.

"He's going into lap 85." He had a cold drink in his hand and held it out to her without shifting his gaze. Foxy took it and drank, though his thoughtfulness confused her. "Yes, I know. He's got nearly a full lap on Johnston. Have you timed his average speed?"

"Just over 190."

Foxy watched Kirk maneuver through a tight cluster of cars. She held her breath as he passed a racer in the short chute between turns three and four. She stared down into floating chunks of ice, then drank again. "You've set up a tremendous pit crew. I timed the last fuel stop at under twelve seconds. They've given Kirk an edge. And it's obvious the car's fast and handles magnificently."

Slowly Lance lowered his eyes and looked down at her. "We both know racing is a matter of teamwork."

"All but this part," Foxy countered. "Out there it's really up to Kirk, isn't it?"

"You've been standing a long time." The softness of Lance's voice brought Foxy's attention back to him. "Why don't you sit down for a while." He could nearly see the headache that was drumming inside her skull. Surprising them both, he lifted a hand to her cheek in a rare gesture of tenderness. "You look tired." He dropped his hand, then stuck it in his pocket.

"No, no, I can't." Foxy turned away, oddly moved by the lingering warmth on her cheek. "Not until it's over. You're going to lose that scotch, you know."

"I'm counting on it." He swore suddenly, causing her to turn back to him. "I don't like the way number 15 handles turn one. He gets closer to the wall every time."

"Fifteen?" Foxy narrowed her eyes as she searched the streaking stream of cars. "That's one of the rookies, isn't it? The kid from Long Beach."

"The *kid*'s a year older than you are," Lance muttered. "But he hasn't the experience to go that high in the groove. He's going to lose it."

Seconds later, number 15 approached turn one again, only to challenge the unforgiving wall too closely. Sparks flew as the rear wheels slammed into the solid force, then were sheared off and tossed into the air as the car began to spin out of control. Pieces of fiberglass began to spray the air as three cars swerved, maneuvering like snakes around the wounded racer. One nearly lost control, its wheels skidding wildly before gripping the asphalt. The yellow flag came down as number 15 flipped into the infield and lay still. Instantly it was surrounded by emergency crews and fire extinguishers.

As always when she witnessed a crash, a frozen calm descended over Foxy. She did not think or feel. From the instant the car connected with the wall, she had lifted her camera and recorded each step of the crash. Dispassionately she focused, set speed and depth of field. One of her shots would be a classic study of a car in distress. She felt only a shudder of relief when she saw the driver crawl from the wreckage and give the traditional wave to assure the crowd he was unharmed.

"My God. How can a man walk away from a wreck like that?" Foxy heard Pam's voice behind her but continued to shoot the routine of the emergency crew in the infield.

"As I told you before, the very fragility of the racer and the improved restraints have saved more than one life on the grid." Lance answered Pam but his attention was on Foxy. Her face was without color or expression as she lowered her camera.

"But not all of them," she stated as she caught the blur of Kirk's car as it whizzed by. "And not every time." She felt the cold passing as warmth seeped back under her skin. "You'd better go interview that driver. He'll be able to give you a firsthand report on what it's like to see your life pass before your eyes at two hundred miles an hour."

"Yes, I will." Pam gave her a searching look but said nothing more before she moved away.

Foxy pushed a stray hair from her face, allowing her camera to dangle by its strap. "I suppose number 15 will have more respect for turn one the next time."

"You're very professional and unflappable these days, aren't you, Fox?" Lance's eyes were cold as steel under his lowered brows. Foxy remembered the look and felt an inward tremor.

"Photographers have to have good nerves." She met his look of annoyance without flinching. She knew if annoyance turned to genuine anger, he could be brutal.

"But feelings aren't necessary," he countered. He gathered the strap of her camera in one hand and pulled her closer. "There was a man in number 15. You never missed a frame."

"What did you expect me to do?" she tossed back. "Get hysterical? Cover my eyes with my hands? I've seen crashes before. I've seen them when they haven't walked away, when there hasn't been anything to see but a sheet of fire. I've watched both you and Kirk being dragged out by the epaulettes. You want emotion?" Her voice rose in a sudden torrent of fury. "Go find someone who didn't grow up on the smell of death and gasoline!"

Lance studied her in silence. Color had shot back into her face. Her eyes were like a raging sea under a haze of clouds. "Tough lady, aren't you?" His tone was touched with amusement and scorn, a combination Foxy found intolerable.

"Damn right," she agreed and tossed her chin out further. "Now, take your hands off my camera."

At first, the only thing that moved was his left brow. It rose in an arch which might have indicated humor or acceptance. In an exaggerated gesture, he lifted both hands, holding them aloft, empty palms toward her. Still, he did not back off, and they stood toe to toe. "Sorry, Fox." She knew him well enough to detect the dregs of temper in his voice. Her own anger forced her to ignore it.

"Just leave me alone," she ordered and started to brush by him. To her fury, he stepped neatly in her path and blocked her exit.

"I'll just be another minute," he told her. Before she had grasped his motive, Lance had shifted the camera to her back and pulled her into his arms.

As she opened her mouth to protest he closed his over it and plundered its depths. She was caught fast. Instead of pushing against him, her hands gripped desperately on his upper arms. They would not obey the command her brain shot out to them. Her mouth answered his even as she ordered it to be cold and still. The flame sparked and burned just as quickly, just as intensely, as it had the night on the glider. She could not deny that even if her mind and her heart were her own, her body was his. Never had she known such perfection in a touch, such intimacy, such hunger. She lifted her arms to lock them around his neck as her body melted into his. The whine of finely tuned engines whirled in her brain, then was lost in a flood of need and desire. The people who milled around them faded, then disappeared from her world as she strained closer. She demanded more of him even as she gave all of herself. Ultimately it was Lance who drew away. They were still tangled in each other's arms, their faces close, their bodies molded. With his quiet, probing intensity, he stared down at her.

"I suppose you'll tell me I shouldn't have done that."

"Would it make any difference if I did?" Her knees wanted badly to tremble, but Foxy forced them to be still.

"No," he answered. "It wouldn't."

"Will you let me go now?" Foxy was pleased at the cool, impersonal timbre of her voice. Inside her stomach dozens of bats were waging war.

"For now," he agreed. Though he loosened his grip, he kept his hands light on her hips. "I can always pick up where I left off."

"Your conceit is threatening to outweigh your arrogance these days, Lance." Firmly Foxy drew his hands from her hips. "I don't know which is more unappealing."

Lance grinned at the insult and tweaked her nose in a brotherly fashion. "You're cute when you're dignified, Foxy." His glance wandered over her head as he saw Kirk veer off the track and onto the pit lane. "Kirk's coming in. With any luck, the second half of the race will run as smoothly as the first."

Refusing to dignify any of his comments with an answer, Foxy dragged her camera back in front of her and walked away. Tucking his hands in his pockets, Lance rocked gently on his heels and watched her.

Only half of the starters finished the race. Foxy had known Kirk would win. She had studied his face during his brief, final pit stop and had seen the confidence mixed with the strain and tension. Cars no longer looked shiny in the sun but were dull with grime. After the checkered flag came down, Foxy watched Kirk take his victory lap as the roars of the crowd and the crew washed over her. She knew he would come into the pits ready for adulation. His eyes would no longer be opaque. His mouth would be lifted in that easy boyish grin, and all the lines of strain would have magically vanished. Tirelessly he would grant interviews, sign autographs, accept congratulations. The layers of sweat and grime that covered him were his badge of success. He would take it all in, recharging his system. Then it would be over for him, a thing of the past. In two days, they would be on their way to Monaco for the qualifying races. The Indianapolis 500 would be to Kirk no more than a newspaper clipping. For him, it was always the next race.

CHAPTER 4

Monte Carlo is cupped between the high, forested peaks of the Maritime Alps and the brilliant blue waters of the Mediterranean Sea. Buildings are packed together, a dense pattern of skyscrapers and elegant old homes. It has the feel and look, if not the size, of a great city while maintaining a fairy-tale aura.

It was the colors that appealed to Foxy. The whites and pastels which dominated the buildings, the rich, ripe greens and browns of the mountains, and the perfect blue of the sea. Lush flowers and palms added a taste of the exotic. It was a country of culture and castles, warm sea breezes, and barren peaks. The romantic in Foxy instantly fell in love with it.

With Kirk immersed in qualifying races and practice sessions and Pam involved with interviews and local color, Foxy often found herself thrown together with Scott Newman. She found him kind, considerate, intelligent, and—though she detested Lance for being right—dull. He planned too thoroughly, considered too carefully, and followed through too accurately for Foxy's taste. Each of their dates, no matter how casual, was given an itinerary. He dressed perfectly, even elegantly, and his manners were identical. With Scott,

Foxy knew there would be no disasters, no dangers, no surprises. More than once, she felt a twinge of guilt, knowing her character would never be as untarnished as his. He was a knight on a white charger who rescued his quota of damsels in distress each day then polished his armor.

Restlessly Foxy wandered from window to window mulling over her analysis. There was a light staccato clicking from Pam's typewriter. She could see boats of all sizes and descriptions docked in the Bay of Monaco or moving out to sea. She recalled that during one of the qualifying races, a car had taken a turn badly and joined the boats in the water. Foxy turned from the window and watched Pam's fingers fly over the keys. The table where she worked was strewn with notes and paper and cassettes. There was a unique organization to it all, but only Pam had the solution.

"Are you going to the casino tonight?" Foxy asked. She felt restless and dissatisfied.

"Mmm, no…I want to finish this segment." Pam's rhythm never altered. "You going with Scott?"

Frowning, Foxy threw herself into a chair and draped her feet over the arm. "Yes, I suppose."

At the sulky tone, Pam sighed and stopped typing. Foxy's long mouth was pursed in a pout, and her brows were drawn together over moody eyes. Russet curls tumbled without design over her shoulders. All at once, Pam felt very old.

"All right." She propped her elbows on her table and laid her chin on her laced hands. "Tell Momma." Quite purposely, her tone was mild and patronizing. Foxy's chin shot out. Met with Pam's amused, affectionate smile, however, her defiance melted.

"I'm being an idiot," Foxy confessed with a self-deprecating laugh. "And I don't know why. I'm absolutely crazy about Monte Carlo. It has to be one of the most romantic, exotic, perfect spots in the universe. More, I'm getting paid to be here. I even have a terrific-looking man dancing attendance on me, and I'm…" She drew a deep breath and swept her arms in a huge circle.

"Bored," Pam supplied. She lifted her cup, sipped cold coffee, and grimaced. "You've been left almost entirely in Scott's company. Though he is nice, he isn't the most stimulating companion. Kirk's not available, I'm tied up, Lance is—"

"I don't need Lance's company," Foxy said too quickly. Her frown became more pronounced. Not having Lance Matthews to contend with was a blessing, not a problem.

Pam said nothing for a moment, recalling the tempestuous kiss she had seen them exchange at the Indianapolis Speedway. "In any case," she said carefully, "you've been deserted."

"Scott really is very nice." Somehow, Foxy felt the statement defended both Scott and herself. "And he's not pushy. I made it clear from the beginning that I wasn't interested in a serious relationship and he accepted it. He didn't argue." Foxy swung herself out of the chair and began to pace. "He hasn't tried to lure me into the bedroom, he doesn't lose his temper, he doesn't forget the time, he doesn't do anything outrageous." Foxy remembered that both times Lance had kissed her, it had been over her protests. "He makes me feel comfortable," she added tersely. She glared at Pam, daring her to comment.

"My fuzzy blue slippers do the same thing for me."

Foxy wanted badly to be angry, but a gurgle of laughter escaped. "That's terrible."

"You're not built to be satisfied with comfortable relationships." Pam twirled a pencil between her fingers and frowned at the eraser. "Like your brother, you thrive on challenges of one sort or another." Shaking off a quick moodiness, she lifted her eyes and smiled. "Now, Lance Matthews…"

"Oh no," Foxy interrupted, holding her hand up like a traffic cop. "Stop right there. I might not be looking for comfort, but I'm not looking for a bed of nails either."

"Just a thought," Pam said mildly. "I seriously doubt he would ever make you feel bored or comfortable."

"Comfortable boredom begins to sound more appealing," Foxy commented. "In fact," she added as she headed for the door, "I'm going to thoroughly enjoy myself tonight. In all probability I'll win a fortune at roulette. I'll buy you a hot dog out of my winnings at the race tomorrow." With a wink, she shut the door behind her.

Alone, Pam allowed her smile to dissolve. For the next few minutes, she stared down at the typewritten page in her machine. *Kirk Fox,* she decided, *is becoming a problem. Not that he has made even the slightest advance since his arrogant declaration the night of his party,* she mused. *He's been much too involved with the races to do any more than vaguely acknowledge my presence.* Pam ignored the annoyance the fact brought her and straightened a pile of blank typing paper. *And of course, he's had all those women hanging around him.* Pam sniffed and shrugged and went back to her typing. *With any luck,* she thought as she attacked the keys, *he'll be just as busy throughout the entire season.*

Feeling guilty over her discussion of Scott, Foxy dressed with special care for the evening. Her dress was a stretchy black jersey that clung to her curves and left her shoulders bare. The neckline was cut straight, secured with elastic just above the subtle swell of her breasts. She swept her hair off her neck into a chignon, letting loose tendrils fall over her brow and cheeks. With the addition of a thin silver chain around her neck and a quick spray of cologne, she felt ready for the elegance of the Monte Carlo casino.

Just as she was transferring the bare necessities into a

small silver evening bag, a knock sounded on her door. With one quick glance around the hotel room, Foxy went to admit Scott. She found herself face-to-face with Lance Matthews.

"Oh," she said foolishly as she recalled her success in avoiding him since Indiana. Abruptly it occurred to her that she had never seen him in evening dress before. His suit was impeccably cut, fitting over his broad shoulders without a wrinkle. He looked different, if no less dangerous. He was, for a moment, a stranger: the Harvard graduate, the longtime resident of Beacon Hill, the heir to the Matthews fortune.

"Hello, Fox, going to let me in or do I have to stand out in the hall?" The tone, and the ironic lift of his mouth made him Lance again. Foxy straightened her shoulders.

"Sorry, Lance, I'm practically on my way out."

"Prompt as well as beautiful?" There was an amused light in his eyes. "The two rarely go together." He stepped forward and cupped her chin in his hand before she had time to start evasive action. "We'll have to have a cocktail before dinner. The reservation isn't until eight."

Foxy backed up, then noted with disgust that the action only brought Lance further into the room. "You'll have to run that by me again." She lifted a hand to the one on her chin but found it unbudgeable.

"We've nearly an hour before dinner," Lance stated simply. His eyes roamed her face with a hint of a smile. "Perhaps you've an idea how we might pass the time."

"You might try a few hands of solitaire," Foxy suggested evenly. "In your *own* room. Now, I'd like my face back."

"Would you?" Amusement was smooth and male in his tone. "Pity. I'm quite taken with it." With the barest of pressure, he brought her an inch closer as his gaze dropped and lingered on her mouth. "Newman sends his regrets," Lance said softly as his eyes moved back to hers. "Something—ah—came up. Do you have a wrap?"

"Came up?" Foxy repeated. She found no relief when her chin was released as his hands moved to her bare shoulders. She felt the temperature of the room rise ten degrees. "What are you talking about?"

"Newman discovered he didn't have the evening free after all. It's a pity to cover up such elegant shoulders, but the nights here can be cool in June." They were closer than they had been a moment before, but Foxy didn't know how he had contrived it. His hands were still light on her shoulders.

"What do you mean, didn't have the evening free?" she demanded. She started to back away but his hands tightened on her shoulders slightly but meaningfully. The mockery in his smile caused her temper to soar along with her heart rate. "What did you do? What did you say to him? He's much too polite to break a date without telling me himself. You intimidated him," she finished hotly, glaring into Lance's smile.

"I certainly hope so since that was my intention." He confessed to the crime so easily, Foxy could only splutter. "Fetch your wrap."

"My—my…I certainly will not!" she managed in a choked voice.

"Suit yourself." Lance shrugged and took her hand.

"If you think I'm going out with you," Foxy began as she tugged furiously at her hand, "you're not running on all your cylinders. I'm not going anywhere."

"Fine." Lance's hands spanned her waist. "I find the idea of staying here very appealing." Before she could move away, he lowered his mouth to the gentle incline between her neck and shoulder. Her skin trembled.

"No." Hearing the waver in her voice, Foxy fought to steady it. The room was already swaying. "You can't stay."

"Room service is excellent here," Lance murmured as he caught the lobe of her ear between his teeth. "You smell like the woods in spring, fresh and full of secrets."

"Lance, please." It was becoming very difficult to think as his mouth roamed over her skin, leaving a soft trail of quick kisses.

"Please what?" he whispered. Lightly he rubbed his lips over hers. His tongue teased the tip of hers before she could answer. Foxy could feel the quicksand sucking and pulling at her legs. Desperately she pushed away from him and filled her lungs with air.

"I'm starving," she said abruptly. She considered the statement a tactical retreat. Hoping to hide her vulnerability, she brushed casually at the curls that rested on her flushed cheeks. "Since you frightened off my escort, I suppose I should make you pay for my dinner. At a restaurant," she added hastily as he cocked a brow. "Then you'll have to take me to the casino as Scott was going to do."

"My pleasure," Lance replied with a faint bow.

"And I," she said, feeling stronger with the distance between them, "shall take pains to lose as much of your money as possible." Lifting a thin silk shawl from the bed, Foxy tossed it over her shoulders and flounced from the room. She managed for nearly an hour to remain cool and aloof.

Moonlight spilled over the Bay of Monaco. A breeze that had been born far out to sea drifted easily into shore. It carried its own perfume. The terrace of the restaurant was canopied by stars and palm fronds. Music floated by the secluded table, but it was too soft for Foxy to distinguish any words. Only the melody flickered like the lights of the twin white candles on the tablecloth. Between these was a red rose in a slender vase. The murmur of other diners seemed more a backdrop than a reality. Foxy was finding it difficult to maintain an indifference to an ambience which called so strongly to her romantic soul. Above all else, she wanted Lance to see her as a mature sophisticated woman and not a silly child who melted at soft music and starlight. Still, she trod carefully with the iced champagne. So far she had managed to keep the conversation impersonal and safe.

"I noticed the car gave Kirk a bit of trouble yesterday." Foxy speared her steamed shrimp and dipped it absently in its sauce. "I hope it's been worked out."

"An engine ring; it's been replaced." As he spoke Lance watched her over the rim of his glass. There was a light in his eyes which had Foxy doubling her guard.

"It's amazing, isn't it? So often it's a tiny thing, a twenty-five-cent part or an overlooked screw that can be the deciding factor in a race where hundreds of thousands of dollars are at stake."

"Amazing," Lance agreed in a somber tone that was belied by his half smile.

"If you're going to laugh at me," Foxy said as her chin tilted, "I'll simply get up and leave."

"I'd just bring you back." With narrowed eyes, she studied Lance for a full minute. Her prolonged examination did not appear to disturb him as he kept his eyes steady on hers. His mouth was still curved in an annoying half smile.

"You would, too," Foxy conceded with grudging admiration. Chivalrousness was simply not one of Lance's qualities, and Foxy knew that she had had enough of chivalrousness for a while. "And if I kicked up a scene that landed us both in a cell, you wouldn't be a bit bothered…not as long as you had your way." She sighed and shook her head, then took a sip of wine. "It's hard to gain an edge on a man who's so utterly nerveless. You drove that way. I remember." Her mouth moved in a pout as she looked back in time. "You drove with the same single-minded intensity as Kirk, but there was a smoothness he still lacks. You stalked; he charges. He's all fire and thrust, you were precise and ruthlessly steady. There was an incredible ease in your driving; you made it look simple, so effortless. But then you raced because you enjoyed it." Foxy twirled the stem of her glass between her fingers and watched the starlight play on the swirling wine.

Intrigued, Lance studied her with more care. "And Kirk doesn't?"

"Enjoy it?" Her surprise was evident in both her eyes and her voice. "He lives for it, and that's entirely different. Enjoyment comes much lower on the list." She tilted her head, and her eyes caught the flicker of the candles. "You didn't live for it or you couldn't have given it up at thirty. If Kirk lives to be a hundred, they'll have to carry him to the cockpit, but he'll still race."

"It appears you had more perception as a teenager than I gave you credit for." Lance waited until their steak Diane was served, then thoughtfully broke a roll in half. "You've always hated it, haven't you?"

Foxy met his eyes levelly. "Yes," she agreed and accepted the offered roll. "Always." Her silence grew pensive as she spread butter on the roll. "Lance, how did your family feel about your racing?"

"Embarrassed," he said immediately. Foxy was forced to laugh as she met his eyes again.

"And you enjoyed their embarrassment as much as you enjoyed racing."

"As I said—" he lifted his glass in toast "—you are perceptive."

"Families of drivers all seem to have different ways of dealing with racing. It's more difficult standing in the pits than driving on the grid, you know," she said softly, then sighed and deliberately shook off the mood. "I suppose now that you're in the business end of it, your family's no longer embarrassed." Foxy bit into the crusty roll. "It's more acceptable, though you hardly need the money."

"You took an oath to see that I do after tonight," he reminded her. "You'd better eat all of your steak. Losing money takes more energy than winning it."

Sending him a disdainful smirk, Foxy picked up her knife and fork.

The evening was still young when they entered the casino. Foxy found her indifferent veneer dissolving. The combination of elegance and excitement was too potent.

"Oh!" She took in the room with a long, sweeping glance and squeezed Lance's arm for emphasis. "It's fabulous."

Clothes in a kaleidoscope of hues and the glitter and gleam of jewels caught her eye. There was a hum of voices in a hodgepodge of languages accented by the quick precise French of the croupiers. There was a mix of other sounds: the click and clatter of the roulette balls jingling in the wheels, the soft scrape of wood on baize as markers were drawn in, the flutter and whoosh of cards being shuffled, the crackle of new money and the jangle of coin.

With a laugh, Lance tossed an arm around her shoulders. "Foxy, my love, your eyes are enormous and shockingly naive. Haven't you ever been to a den of iniquity before?"

"Stop teasing," she demanded, too impressed to be properly insulted. "It's so beautiful."

"Ah, but gambling's gambling, Fox, whether you do it in a plush chair with a glass of champagne or in a garage with a bottle of beer."

"You should know." Tilting her head, she shifted her eyes

to his and smiled. "I remember the poker games. You would never let me play."

"You were a very precocious brat." He slid his hand up her neck and squeezed.

"You were just afraid that I'd beat you."

His grin was quick and powerful. Guiltily Foxy admitted that she was glad to be there with him instead of with Scott. Lance Matthews exuded an excitement Scott Newman would not even understand.

"What big eyes you have," Lance murmured as his fingers lingered on her skin. "What goes on behind them, Foxy?"

"I was thinking how furious I should be with you because of the maneuvering you did with Scott, and how guilty I am that I'm not."

He laughed, then gave her a hard, brief kiss. "Too guilty to enjoy yourself?"

"No," she said immediately, then shrugged. "I suppose I'm basically selfish and not very nice."

Lance's mouth twisted into a grin. "Then we should suit each other well enough." He laced his fingers with hers, then led her to a roulette table.

Seated, Foxy moved her attention instantly to the wheel as the tiny silver ball bounced and jumped. When it stilled, she watched the croupier scoop in the losing markers and add them to those of the winners. Foxy thought the table a Tower of Babel. As she glanced from face to face she heard lilting Italian, precise London-style English, low, guttural German, and other languages that she could not distinguish. Faces were varied as well; some old, some young, some bored, some animated, many carrying the unmistakable polish of wealth. But it was the face directly across from her that fascinated her.

The older woman was beautiful. Her hair was like white

silk swept around a fine-boned oval face. The lines in her skin were far too much a part of it to detract from the beauty. Rather, they matured and gave character to what had once been a delicate elegance. Her eyes were like sharp green emeralds, but it was diamonds she wore at her throat and ears. They seemed more fire than ice. She wore flaming red silk with absolute confidence. Foxy watched in fascination as she lifted a long, slender black cigarette and drew gently.

"Countess Francesca de Avalon of Venice," Lance whispered in Foxy's ear as he followed her gaze. "Exceptional, isn't she?"

"Fabulous." Turning to Lance, Foxy was vaguely surprised to see him offer her a glass of champagne. As the stem passed from his fingers to hers she noticed the tidy pile of markers in front of her. "Oh, are these the chips?" Tracing a fingernail down the edges, she looked back at Lance. "How much do you bet at a time?"

He shrugged and cupped his hands around the end of his cigarette as he lit it. "I'm just along for the ride."

With a laugh, Foxy shook her head. "I have a hard enough time with plain francs, Lance. I don't even know how much these little things are worth."

"An evening's entertainment," he said easily and lifted his glass.

Sighing, Foxy chose five chips and unwittingly bet five thousand francs on black. "I don't suppose I should lose all your money at once," she said confidentially.

"That's generous of you." Repressing a smile, Lance settled back and watched the wheel spin.

"Vingt-sept, noir."

"Oh!" Foxy said, surprised then pleased. "We've won." Looking up, she caught the blatant amusement on Lance's face. His eyes, she realized, were more silver than gray. "You needn't look so smug." She shook off her preoccupation and sipped the effervescent wine. "That was just beginner's luck. Besides—" she gave him a wicked grin "—it'll hurt more if I win a bit first." Her gaze shifted to the two stacks of five markers on black, but as she started to reach for them, Lance laid a hand on her arm.

"He's started the wheel, Fox. You've let it ride." Her face was so completely horrified, Lance dissolved into laughter.

"Oh, but I didn't mean…that must be over a hundred dollars." A glance at the spinning wheel made her giddy, and she swallowed more wine.

"Must be," Lance agreed gravely.

Foxy watched the ball bounce its capricious way around the wheel. She felt a mixture of fear, guilt, and excitement as the wheel began to slow.

"Cinq, noir."

She closed her eyes on a shudder of relief. Remembering herself, she quickly drew the four stacks of five in front of her. As Lance chuckled she turned and gave him a haughty glare. "It would have served you right if I *had* lost."

"Quite right." Lance signaled for more champagne. "Why don't you bet on one of the columns, Foxy," he suggested as he tapped the ash of his cigar into an ashtray. "You've got to take more than a fifty-fifty chance in life."

She grinned and tossed her head. "Your loss," she announced as she impulsively pushed five chips to the head of column one.

It was, as it turned out, his gain. With uncanny consistency, the stack of markers in front of Foxy grew. Once, she unknowingly lost twenty thousand francs, then cheerfully gained it back on the following spin. Perhaps it was her complete ignorance of the amounts she wagered, or her random betting pattern, or simply the generosity of Lady Luck, but she won, spin after spin after spin. And she found winning was much to her taste. It was a heady experience that left her nearly as giddy as the seemingly bottomless glass of champagne at her side. Lance sat calmly back and watched the flow and ebb and flow of her winnings. He enjoyed the way she used her eyes to speak to him, letting them widen and glisten on a win or roll and dance on a loss. Her laugh reminded him of the warm mists on Boston's Back Bay. Her pleasure in winning was engagingly simple, her nonchalance in losing charmingly innocent. She was a child and woman at perfect balance.

"Are you sure you wouldn't like to bet some of this?" Foxy asked generously, indicating the stacks of markers.

"You're doing fine." Lance twirled a stray curl of russet around his finger.

"That, young man, is a gross understatement."

Foxy twisted her head quickly and looked into sharp emerald eyes. The Countess de Avalon stood behind her, leaning on a smooth, ivory-handled cane. It shocked Foxy momentarily to see that she was so tiny, no more than five feet. Imperiously she waved Lance to sit as he started to get to his feet. Her English was quick and precise, with only a trace of accent. "You have won resoundingly, signorina, and cleverly."

"Resoundingly, Countess," Foxy returned with a wide smile, "but accidentally rather than cleverly. I came determined to lose."

"Perhaps I will change my strategy and come determined to lose," the countess commented. "Then I, too, might have such an accident." She gave Lance a slow, thorough, and entirely feminine appraisal. Foxy felt a tickle of jealousy and was completely astounded by it. "You appear to know me; might I return the pleasure?"

"Countess de Avalon." Lance gently inclined his head. "Cynthia Fox." Foxy took the extended hand in hers and found it small and fragile. But the quick study the green eyes made of her was full of power.

"You are very lovely," the countess said at length, "very strong." She smiled, showing perfect white teeth. "But even ten years ago, I would have lured him away from you. Never trust a woman of experience." Dismissing Foxy with a mere shifting of the eyes, the countess gave her attention to Lance. "And who are you?"

"Lance Matthews, Countess." He brought the offered hand to his lips with perfect charm. "It's an honor to meet you."

"Matthews," she murmured, and her eyes narrowed. "Of course, I should have seen from the eyes, the 'devil-take-it' look. I knew your grandfather quite well." She laughed. It was a young, sultry sound. "Quite well. You've the look of him, Lancelot Matthews…you're named for him. Very appropriate."

"Thank you, Countess." Lance's smile warmed. "He was one of my favorite people."

"And mine. I saw your Aunt Phoebe in Martinique two years ago. A singularly boring woman."

"Yes, Countess." The smile became grim. "I'm afraid so."

With a regal sniff, the countess turned to a fascinated Foxy. "Never relax for a moment with this one," she advised. "He is every bit the rake his grandfather was." She laid her hand briefly on Foxy's, and squeezed. "How I envy you." She turned and walked away in a flash of red silk.

"What a magnificent woman," Foxy murmured. Turning back to Lance, she gave him a wistful smile. "Do you suppose your grandfather was in love with her?"

"Yes." With a gesture of his finger, Lance signaled the croupier to cash in his markers. "He had a blistering affair with her, which the family continues to pretend never happened. It was also complicated because they were both married. He wanted her to leave her husband and live with him in the south of France."

"How do you know so much about it?" Intrigued, Foxy made no objection when he drew her to her feet.

"He told me." Lance set her shawl around her shoulders. "He told me once he'd never loved anyone else. He was over seventy when he died, and he would still have left everything to live with her if she had permitted it."

Foxy walked slowly through the casino with Lance unaware of how many pairs of eyes watched them; a russet-haired beauty and the man with the dark, brooding attraction. "It sounds so wonderfully sad," she said after a moment. "But I suppose it was dreadful for your grandmother, knowing he loved someone else all those years."

"My dear, innocent Fox," Lance said dryly. "My grandmother is a Winslow of Boston. She was quite content with the Matthews merger, their two offspring, and her bridge club. Love is untidy and plebeian."

"You're making that up."

"As you like," he said easily.

"Let's not take a cab," she said as they stepped outside. She tossed her head back to the stars. "It's so beautiful." Smiling into his eyes, she tucked her hand in his arm. "Let's walk, it isn't far."

They ignored the light stream of traffic and walked under the warm glow of street lamps. Champagne spun pleasantly in Foxy's head and lifted her feet just an inch from the sidewalk. The countess's warning was forgotten, and she was completely relaxed. The walk under the slice of moon and smattering of stars seemed to occur in a timeless realm, full of the scents and mysteries of night.

"Do you know," Foxy began and spun away from him, "I love palm trees." Giggling, she rested her back against one and smiled at Lance. "I always wanted one when I was little, but they don't do well in Indiana. I had to settle for a pine."

Moving closer, he brushed curls from cheeks flushed with wine and excitement. "I had no idea you were so interested in horticulture."

"I have my secrets." Swirling out of reach, she leaned over a sea wall. "I wanted to be a skin diver when I was eight," she told him as she peered out into the dark sea. "Or a heart surgeon, I could never make up my mind. What do you want to be when you grow up, Lance?" She turned back to him, and the wind caught and pulled at her free curls. Her eyes were speared with laughter.

"Starting pitcher for the Red Sox." His eyes dropped to the elegant curve of her neck as she threw back her head and laughed.

"I bet you've got a whole bagful of pitches." She sighed with the pleasure of laughter. "You never told me how much I won in there."

"Hmm?" Lost in the flicker of moonlight in her hair, he listened with half an ear.

"How much did I win in the casino?" she repeated, pushing dancing curls from her face.

"Oh." He shrugged. "Fifty, fifty-five thousand francs."

"What?" The one syllable was half laugh, half choke. "Fifty-five *thousand*? That's—that's more than ten thousand dollars!"

"At the current rate of exchange," Lance agreed carelessly.

"Oh, good grief!" Her hands flew up to cover her mouth as her eyes grew impossibly wide. "Lance, I might have lost!"

"You did remarkably well." Amusement was back in his

eyes and in his voice. "Or remarkably poorly considering your desire to lose."

"I had no idea I was gambling with that kind of money; I never would have tossed it around that way. Why…you're crazy!" Helplessly she began to laugh. "You're a lunatic. Certifiable." She dropped her head to his shoulder as her laughter floated warmly on the quiet night. When he brought his arms around her, she made no protest. "I might have lost, you know," she managed between giggles. "And I might easily have fainted cold if I'd have found out how much those chips were worth while the wheel was still spinning." Taking a deep breath, she lifted her brilliant eyes to his. "Now, it seems I've added to your already disgusting fortune."

"The winnings are rightfully yours," he corrected, but Foxy stepped back horrified.

"Oh no, it was your money. In any case…" She paused, distracted, and plucked a daisy from a clump of grass at the foot of the sea wall. The champagne was still flowing. "In any case," she repeated as she tucked the flower in her hair. "You wouldn't have expected me to make up your losses." With this logic, she began to walk again, holding out a hand for his. "Of course," she began on a new thought, moving away before Lance could take her hand. "You could buy me something extravagant." She whirled back to him with a smile. "That would be perfectly aboveboard, I believe."

"Is there anything particular you have in mind?"

Her footsteps clicked on the sidewalk as she continued to circle away from him. "Oh, perhaps a pack of Russian wolfhounds." Her laughter drifted. "Or a line of those marvelous horses with the sturdy legs…Clydesdales. Or a flock of Albanian goats. I'm almost certain they have goats in Albania."

"Wouldn't you rather have a sable?"

"Oh no," she answered. She wrinkled her nose and, either by accident or design, moved just out of his reach. "I don't care much for dead animals. I know! A pair of black Angus so I can start my own herd." The decision made, she stopped. Lance slipped his arms around her. "You will be sure to get one male and one female, won't you? It's very important if you want things to move along properly."

"Of course," he agreed as his lips traced her jawline.

"I shouldn't tell you this." Foxy sighed as her arms encircled his neck. "I'm terribly glad you intimidated Scott."

"Are you?" Lance murmured, gently nipping at the pulse in her throat.

"Oh yes," she whispered and drew him closer. "And I'd very much like it if you'd kiss me now. Right now." The last word was muffled as their lips found each other.

They seemed to fuse together in one instant of blinding heat. The instant was an eternity. She tangled her fingers in his hair as if she could bring him yet closer when now even the breeze from the sea could not come between them. Her body had molded to his as if it had no other purpose. She could feel his heart beat at the same speeding rhythm as her own. Unnoticed, her shawl slipped to the ground as he explored the smooth skin of her back. Together, they began to taste more of each other. His lips tarried on her throat, lingering and savoring the sweetness before moving to trace her cheekbone and whisper over her closed lids.

She discovered a dark, male flavor along the column of his neck. She wanted to go on tasting, go on learning, but his mouth demanded that hers return to his. The power of the new kiss pierced her like a spear of lightning, shooting a trembling heat through her every cell. With a moan, she swayed against him. Lance plundered her surrendering mouth, drawing more and more from her until she was limp in his arms.

When his lips parted from hers, she murmured his name and rested her head on his shoulder.

"I don't know if it's you or the champagne, but my head's spinning." Foxy shivered once, then snuggled closer. Lance moved his hand to the base of her neck and tilted her face back to his. Her eyes were dark and heavy, her cheeks flushed, her mouth soft and swollen from his.

"Does it matter?" His voice was rough as he tightened his grip to bring her closer. She did not resist, but stepped back into the fire. "Isn't it enough to know that I want you tonight?" he murmured against her ear before his tongue and teeth began to fill her senses again.

"I don't know. I can't think." Drawing away, Foxy took two steps back and shook her head. "Something happens to me when you kiss me. I lose control."

"If you're telling me that so I'll play fair, Foxy, you've miscalculated." In one quick motion, he closed the distance between them. "I play to win."

"I know," she replied and lifted a hand to his cheek. "I know that very well." Turning, she walked back to the sea wall and breathed deeply to clear her head. She leaned back and lifted her face to the moon. "I always admired your unswerving determination to come out on top." She lowered her face to look at him, but his was still shadowed by the palm. "I loved you quite desperately when I was fourteen."

He didn't speak for a moment but bent and picked up her wrap. "Did you?" he murmured as he stepped from the shadows.

Moonlight fluttered over her as she tossed windblown curls from her eyes. "Oh yes." Relaxed, Foxy continued with champagne-induced honesty. "It was a wonderfully painful crush, my very first. You were quite impressive and I was quite romantic." Lance was beside her now, and Foxy turned her head to smile at him. "You always looked so indestructible, and very often you brooded."

"Did I?" He answered her smile as he lay the wrap over her shoulders.

"Oh yes. You had this single-minded intensity about you…you still do a great deal of the time. It's terribly attractive, but it was more pronounced when you were racing. Then, there were your hands."

"My hands?" he repeated and paused in the act of reaching in his pocket for his lighter.

"Yes." Foxy surprised him by taking both his hands in hers and studying them. "They're quite the most beautiful hands I've ever seen. Very lean, very strong, very elegant. I always thought you should've been an artist or a musician. Sometimes I'd pretend you were. I'd set you up in a drafty old garret where I'd take care of you." She released his hands and pulled absently at her wrap as it slipped off her shoulders. "I wanted badly to take care of someone. I suppose I should've had a dog." She laughed lightly but was too involved with her memories to notice that Lance did not laugh with her. "I was snarling jealous of all those women you had. They were always beautiful. I remember Tracy McNeil especially. You probably don't remember her at all."

"No." Lance flicked on his lighter and frowned at the flame. "I don't."

"She had beautiful blond hair. It was clear down to her hips and straight as an arrow. I hated my hair as a child. It was all curly and unmanageable and such an awkward color. I was quite certain the only reason you kissed Tracy McNeil was because she had straight blond hair." The scent from Lance's cigar stung the air, and Foxy breathed it in. "It's amazing how naive I was for someone raised in a man's world.

Anyway, I languished over you for the better part of a year. I imagine I was a nuisance around the track, and you were very tolerant for the most part." A yawn escaped her as she grew sleepy in the sea air. "After I turned sixteen, I felt I was quite grown up and ready to be treated as a woman. The crush I'd had on you became very intense. I'd find every opportunity to be around you. Did you notice?"

"Yes." Lance blew out a thin stream of smoke, and it vanished instantly into the breeze. "I noticed."

Foxy gave a rueful laugh. "I thought I was being so clever in my pursuit. You were always so kind to me, I suppose that's why when you stopped being kind, it was all the more devastating. Do you remember that night? It was at Le Mans, the twenty-four-hour race," she went on before he could answer. "The night before the race I couldn't sleep so I walked down to the track. When I saw you going into the garage area, I was certain it was fate." With a sigh, Foxy absently fingered the flower in her hair. "I followed you in. My palms were sweating. I wanted you to notice me." Turning her head, Foxy met Lance's eyes with a gentle smile. "As a woman. A girl's right on the border at sixteen, and I wanted so desperately to get to the other side. And my feelings for you were very adult and very real, even though I had no idea how to handle them.

"I was very nonchalant when I came in, do you remember? 'Hello, how are you, couldn't you sleep?' You were wearing a black sweater; black always suited you. You were very remote, you'd been remote off and on for weeks. It only made you more romantic." With a soft, low laugh, she lifted her palm to his cheek. "Poor Lance. How uncomfortable my adulation must have made you."

"Uncomfortable is a mild word for what you were doing to me," he muttered. Turning away, he tossed his cigar over the wall and into the sea.

"I wanted to be sophisticated," she went on, not hearing the annoyance in his tone. "I had no idea how to make you want to kiss me. I tried to remember all the ploys I'd ever seen the heroine use in the movies. It was dark, we were alone. What next? The only thing I could come up with was to keep as close as possible. You were tinkering under the hood of the car, doing your best, I'm sure, to ignore me so that I'd go away and let you get on with it. There was just that one small light on, and the garage smelled of oil and gasoline. I thought it was as romantic as Manderley." Foxy turned and grinned cheerfully while the wine made her remember. "Romance has always been my big weakness. Anyway, I was standing behind you, trying to think of what to do next, and I began to wonder what in the world you were doing to the car. I started to peek over your shoulder just as you turned around, and we collided. I remember you grabbed my arms to steady me, and my knees turned to water instantly. The physical part of it was incredible, probably because I'd never experienced it before. My heart started pounding, and my skin went hot then cold. It seemed as though I'd be swallowed up by your eyes, they'd gotten so dark, so intense. I thought: *This is it.* I was positive you were going to pull me into your arms and kiss me. I *knew* you were. We were Clark Gable and Vivien Leigh and the garage was Tara. Then you were shouting at me, absolutely livid that I was continually in your way. You swore magnificently, giving me a good shake before you pushed me away. You said some really dreadful things; the worst, to me, was that you called me an annoying child. Anything else, I could have passed off, but that crushed my pride and my ego and my fantasies with one blow. I never gave a thought to the tension you must have been under with the race the next day, or to the simple fact that I *was* in your way. I only thought about what you were saying to me and how it hurt. But I've always been a survivor. As soon as it began to hurt too badly, my defenses came up. When I turned and ran out of that garage, I didn't love you anymore, but I hated you almost as obsessively."

"You were better off," Lance murmured. After a moment, he twisted his head and ran a fingertip down her cheek. "Have you forgiven me?"

Foxy gave him an easy smile. "I suppose. It's been years, and since it cured me of being in love with you, I should be grateful." With another yawn, she rested her head against his shoulder.

"Yes, I suppose you should," he agreed softly. "Come on, I'll get you back before you fall asleep on the sidewalk."

Drowsy but willing, Foxy went with him as he slipped an arm around her waist.

CHAPTER 5

Monaco's Grand Prix is a classic example of a round-the-houses circuit. The course is short, just under two miles, and in the heart of a crowded civic complex. No part of the circuit is straight for more than a few feet, and among its eleven curves are two hairpins. One lap includes seventeen corners. The course is anything but flat; its ups and downs range from sea level to one hundred and thirty-two feet above. Its hazards include curbs, sea walls, a three-hundred-foot tunnel, utility poles, and, of course, the sparkling Mediterranean. For the driver, there is not a second's rest in the hundred laps. It is short, slow, and unlike any other Formula One course in the world. It stands as a great test of man and machine as its constant demands make it more fatiguing than longer, faster circuits. Here was a course that tested a car's reliability and a man's endurance. Still, it remains romantic and somehow mystical, like a yearly joust before the prince and princess.

Through quick maneuvering, Pam had managed to corner Kirk for an interview. There were just over two hours before race time, and the pits were crowded and noisy. Monaco's pits stood exposed to the course at the head of the small, picturesque harbor. Behind them, the water was crowded with yachts and sailboats. Pam found herself glancing around for Foxy. Though it annoyed her, she knew she would be more comfortable if she did not interview Kirk alone. Pushing this thought aside, she looked directly into his eyes. This type of contact was as essential to her style as her clean-lined, elegant clothes and her calm, unruffled manner. The sharp, probing, tenacious mind was well camouflaged by the fragility of her appearance.

"I've heard a lot of differing opinions on this course," she began, adding her professional smile. "Some, especially the carmakers I've spoken to, consider Monaco a drawing-room circuit. How do you feel about it?"

Kirk was leaning back against a wall, sipping from a foam cup. Thin wisps of smoke rose from it. His eyes squinted against the sun, and he looked completely at ease. Pam felt stiff and formal. It annoyed her that Kirk Fox always caused her to feel stiff and formal and somehow out of place.

"It's a race," he answered simply as he watched her over the rim of his cup. "It's not fast. It's rare a driver goes over a hundred and forty and usual to go less than thirty on the hairpins. But then, it's more a test of stamina and ability than speed."

"The driver's or the car's?" Pam countered.

His eyes crinkled deeper at the corners as he grinned. To her fascination, they seemed to grow greener. "Both. Two thousand or more gear changes in two and a half hours is a strain on a man and a machine. And there's the tunnel. You go from daylight to dim and back to daylight. Do your batteries ever run down?" he asked, taking the tape recorder which hung at her side.

"No," she returned coolly. If he was going to laugh at her, she wasn't going to give him the satisfaction of reacting. She cleared her throat and straightened her shoulders. "You had a crash here two years ago that totaled your car and broke your left shoulder. Will that experience affect your driving today?"

"Why should it?" Kirk countered, then drained his coffee. He was watching her with complete concentration, oblivious to the milling crowds in the pit area.

"Don't you worry about crashing again?" Pam insisted. As the frisky breeze tugged at her hair she tucked it behind her ear with a quick, impatient gesture. There was a tiny turquoise stone on the lobe. "Don't you ever consider that the next time you crash, you might be killed? Doesn't that come home to you, particularly when you pass over the part of the course where you crashed before?"

"No." Kirk crushed the cup between his fingers, then tossed it carelessly aside. "I never think about the next crash, only about the next race."

"Isn't that foolhardy?" Knowing her tone had become argumentative did not prevent her from continuing. She was irritated with him without having a clear reason why. Pam always conducted her interviews craftily, charmingly. Now she knew she had lost the reins but felt no impulse to reach for them again. "Or are you just smug? One instant of miscalculation, one insignificant mechanical flaw, can result in disaster, yet you don't think about it? You've had your share of crashes, been yanked out of wrecks, had your bones broken, and been laid up in hospitals. Tell me," she demanded, "what goes through your mind as you're roasting in the cockpit, hurtling around a track at two hundred miles an hour? What do you think of when they're strapping you into that machine?"

"Winning," Kirk answered without hesitation. The sharpness of her tone apparently bounced off the smooth nonchalance of his. His eyes roamed calmly over her face. The faint pink tint that temper gave her skin emphasized its flawlessness. He wondered how it would feel under his hand. The gold of her hair grew more vibrant as the sun washed over it. Pam watched the journey of his eyes and frowned. His eyes dropped to her lips.

"Is winning really all that important?"

Kirk's gaze shifted from her mouth to her eyes. "Sure. It's all there is."

It was clear from his tone that he was completely sincere. Helplessly Pam shook her head. "I've never known anyone like you." It was unlike her to lose her temper on the job, and she took a long breath to steady it. "Even here among all these other drivers, I haven't met anyone who thinks along the same straight, unswerving line you do. I suppose if you had the choice, you'd like to die on the track in a blaze of glory."

Kirk's grin was quick. "That would suit me, but I'd like to put it off about fifty years, and I'd prefer it to be *after* I'd crossed the finish line."

Pam's lips curved of their own accord. He was outrageous, she thought, but honest. "Are all race-car drivers as mad as you are?"

"Probably." Before she realized his intent, Kirk tangled his fingers in her hair. "I wondered if it was as soft as it looked. It is." The back of his hand brushed her cheek. "Like your skin." Pam's usual aplomb deserted her, leaving her silent and staring. "Your voice is soft, too, and very appealing. I like the way you always look as though you've stepped out of a bandbox. It gives me the urge to muss you up a bit." His voice was as insolent and amused as his grin.

Pam felt her cheeks grow warm and was infuriated. She had thought she had left blushing behind years before. "Is this a pass?" she asked in a scathing voice.

Kirk laughed, and she heard a trace of Foxy in the sound. "No, it's just an observation. When I make a pass, you won't have a chance to ask." Still grinning, he pulled her close and planted a long, hard kiss on her mouth. He thought she tasted like some rich, dangerous dessert and lingered over her longer than he had intended. When he released her, he felt the small whisper of air escape her lips as if she had held it there in surprise. "That," he said easily, "was a pass."

As he turned and sauntered away Pam lifted a finger to trace the place where his mustache had brushed her skin. *A crazy man,* she decided, unwilling to admit how deeply shaken she was. *A truly crazy man.*

Nearly two hours later, Foxy stood in almost the precise spot where her brother had been. Her mood was just short of grim. All too clearly, she remembered every detail from the evening before. The wine had not been kind enough to dull her memory.

I told him to kiss me, she thought on a wave of self-disgust. *I practically ordered him to. It wasn't bad enough that I went out with him when I should've known better, but I made certain he knew I was enjoying myself every minute. Blasted champagne!* Letting out her breath in a huff, she crammed the straw hat she wore further down on her head. *Then I babble on about the silly crush I had on him when I was a teenager. Oh boy, when I go out to humiliate myself, I don't do it by halves. All that business about being in love with him and fantasizing about him.* Closing her eyes, Foxy made a strangled sound in her throat. The breeze blew from the harbor, cooling her skin under her white gauze blouse. She set her teeth and lifted her camera as the parade lap began. *I wonder if it's possible to avoid him for the rest of the season? Better,* she added as she worked systematically, *for the rest of my life.*

As the drivers lined up for the green flag Foxy scurried for a new angle. In a moment, the air thundered with engines, and utilizing the motor drive, she shot each row of cars as the flag set the start. Crouched on one knee, she caught the low, fragile sleekness so unique to the Formula One racer. Her movements were calm and professional, absorbing her concentration, lending her an air of efficiency at odds with the sassy straw hat and thin, faded jeans. The lead car was already rounding the first curve before she rose. As she turned back toward the pits she collided with Lance. His hands came out to steady her, bringing her an uncomfortable sensation of déjà vu. Hastily Foxy disentangled herself from his hold, then made a business of adjusting her camera.

"I'm sorry, I didn't know you were behind me." Realizing she would have to meet his eyes sooner or later, she tossed her hair behind her shoulder and boldly lifted her chin. The amusement she had expected to see on his face was absent. There was no mockery in the dark gray depths of his eyes. She recognized the long, thorough study he was making and backed away from it. "You're looking at me as though I were an engine that wasn't responding properly." Frowning, Foxy busied herself by dragging sunglasses out of her camera case. She felt more at ease once they were in place. A shield was a shield, however slight.

"You might say I found a few surprises when I opened the hood."

Foxy was not certain how to take the quiet quality of his voice. His continued unblinking study was unnerving. She knew he was capable of watching her endlessly without speaking. He could be incredibly, almost unnaturally patient when he chose to be. Knowing she would be outmatched in this sort of contest, Foxy took the initiative. "Lance, I'd like to speak with you about last night." Her sophisticated demeanor was hampered by rising color. The roar of engines cut her off, and she turned away to watch the cars hurtle by. The pack was still thick after the first lap. Cheeks cool, Foxy took a deep breath and turned back to Lance. His eyes left the track to meet hers, but he said nothing. He was waiting, composed and contained. Foxy could have cheerfully strangled him. "I wasn't really myself last night, you see," she began again. "Wine…liquor has a tendency to go straight to my head, that's why I usually avoid it altogether. I don't want you to think, that is, I wouldn't want you to feel…I didn't mean to be so…" Frustrated, she jammed her hands into her pockets and shut her eyes. "Oh help," she muttered and turned away again. Lance remained silent as she squirmed and struggled. She wondered how it was possible to cast the line and be the fish at the same time.

That was brilliant, Foxy, she berated herself. *Why don't you try again, maybe you can top your own incoherency record. Get it out quick and stop stammering like an idiot.* Setting her chin, she turned to face him again, meeting his eyes straight on. "I didn't mean to give you the impression I would sleep with you." Once it was said, Foxy let out a hasty breath and plunged ahead. "I realize I might have given that impression last night, and I don't want you to misunderstand."

Lance waited nearly a full minute before he spoke, all the while watching Foxy steadily. "I don't believe I misunderstood anything." His comment was ambiguous and left her floundering.

"Yes, well…I know when you took me back to my room you didn't, well, you didn't…"

"Make love to you?" he supplied. In a quick move, he stripped off her sunglasses, leaving her eyes vulnerable. Even as she blinked against the change in light, he closed the slight distance between them. His hand came to her arm, warning her not to back away. "No, I didn't, though we're both perfectly aware that I could have. Let's say I had a whim to play by the rules last night." His smile spread lazily, packed with confidence, while his voice became low and intimate. "I don't need champagne to seduce you, Foxy." His mouth lowered to brush lightly over hers before she could move. It was a kiss that promised more.

Infuriated by his calm arrogance, incensed that her pulses had responded instantly, Foxy snatched the glasses back from him and jerked away. "Stuff your seductions." Her suggestion was drowned out by the noise of the second lap. Foxy threw an annoyed glare over her shoulder at the line of cars. Temper sparked in her eyes when she turned back to face Lance. "Just remember that last night was a lapse of intelligence on my part, that's all. And all that—that stuff I talked about…" To her greater fury, she felt her cheeks grow warmer. What had possessed her to confess that foolish crush? "All that business about that night in the garage was just as ridiculous as it sounded."

"How ridiculous was that?" Lance asked with an ease in direct contrast to Foxy's agitation. She barely resisted stomping her foot.

"I was sixteen years old and very naive. I'm sure it's not necessary to go into it any further."

"You're not sixteen anymore," Lance commented with a slight inclination of his head that reminded her of the elegant man of the evening before. "But you're still naive."

"I am not," she blurted out indignantly, then saw his brow lift and disappear under his fall of hair. Knowing her dignity was threadbare, she drew herself straight. "That's hardly relevant and strictly a matter of your own opinion." He smiled at that with quick charm, and Foxy hurried on. "I've got work to do, and I imagine you can find something to keep you busy for the next ninety-eight laps."

"Ninety-seven," Lance corrected as the leaders sped by. "Kirk's in third position," he noted absently before he looked back down at Foxy. "My opinion, Fox, might be to your advantage as it should induce me to continue playing by the rules for a while longer. It makes an interesting change." He grinned, a crooked, challenging half grin, and she was instantly wary. "There's no telling when I'll stop being a nice guy, though."

"Nice guy!" Foxy repeated and rolled her eyes at the thought.

Still grinning, Lance took the sunglasses from her and perched them back on her nose before walking away.

Over the next three months, Foxy used all her skill to avoid Lance Matthews. From Monaco to Holland to France to England to Germany, she made certain to stay out of his way. Whenever possible, she coupled herself with Pam. She felt if she was not alone, Lance would not find the opportunity to approach her for a personal conversation. Her pleasure with her success was slightly marred by the fact that he did not appear to be fretting for lack of personal conversations. Their schedule since Monaco had been tight. For the racing team there had been little time for anything but work and travel, meals and sleep. It was a hard, demanding circuit, packed with qualifying heats and practice runs and races. Away from the track, the hotels all began to seem the same. But each grid had a separate identity. Each was different, with its own problems, its own dangers.

With the end of summer came Italy and the Monza circuit. The grueling months in Europe had taught Foxy an important lesson. When the season was over, she would never follow the circuit again. Her days of moving from town to town, from pit area to pit area, were over. With each race her nerves had become more highly strung, her composure more difficult to maintain. It became apparent to her that the two years she had spent away from racing had left their mark. She could never be a part of it again. She knew if she ever came back to Italy, it would be to visit Rome or Venice, not Monza.

With night came utter silence. All during the day, the track had vibrated with the practice runs. As Foxy sat alone in the deserted grandstands she thought she could hear ghost cars whiz past, feel their phantom breeze. Sixty years of speed. The sky was faultlessly clear with a white moon and gleaming blue stars. The musky scent of the forest drifted to her, almost crowding the air. Behind her came the quiet chirp of crickets and small insects. It was warm, without the burning heat of the long, sun-filled day. There were no harsh fumes, no screaming tires or thundering engines. It was a night for promises and secrets, a night for romance and soft words. With a sigh, Foxy closed her eyes on the thought of Lance. *More than anything else,* she realized wearily, *I need a little peace.*

A hand on her shoulder brought her quickly back to the present. "Oh, Kirk!" She placed a hand to her drumming heart and smiled up at him. "I didn't hear you."

"What are you doing out here all alone?"

"I wanted some quiet," she told him as he dropped down beside her. "There's too much going on back at the hotel. What are you doing here?"

He shrugged. "I like the track the night before a race." Carelessly he leaned back, then propped his feet on the seat in front of him. She saw he wore his old, reliable sneakers. "This is a fast track. We'll set a record tomorrow." He spoke with the absolute confidence of fact, not speculation.

"Did Charlie fix the exhaust problem?" Foxy studied his profile. Her mind was not on the car, not on the race, but on him. As in the past, she tried to draw on his confidence to soothe her own nerves.

"Yeah. Has Lance been bothering you?"

The question was so abrupt and so unexpected, Foxy took nearly a full minute to react. "What?" The one syllable was spoken with complete incredulity.

"You heard me." She heard the annoyance in Kirk's tone as he shifted in his seat to face her. His features were set and serious. "Is he bothering you?"

"Bothering me," Foxy repeated carefully. She ran the tip of her tongue between her teeth, then lifted her brows. "Maybe you should be more specific."

"Damn it, you know what I mean." Exasperated, Kirk rose and stared out at the track. His hands retreated into his pockets. Foxy could feel his discomfort and marveled at it. She understood Kirk well enough to know he rarely put himself into an uncomfortable position. "I've seen the way he's been looking at you," he muttered, and she heard the scowl in his voice. "If he's been doing more than looking, I want to know about it."

Though Foxy clasped both hands over her mouth, the giggle escaped. When Kirk whirled around, his face was a study in fury. Even in the dark, she could see his eyes glitter with temper. She pressed her lips together firmly, but her laughter burst out of its confines. She could only shake her head and struggle to compose herself as he glared at her.

"What the devil's so funny?" he demanded.

"Kirk, I…" She was forced to stop and cough, then take several deep breaths before she could trust herself to speak. "I'm sorry, I just didn't expect you to—to ask me something like that." She swallowed hard as another giggle threatened. "I'm twenty-three years old."

"What does that have to do with anything?" he tossed

back, watching her eyes shine with good humored affection. He felt like a total fool and scowled more deeply.

"Kirk, when I was sixteen, you never paid a bit of attention to any of the boys who hung around the track, and now you're—"

"Lance isn't a boy." Kirk cut her off furiously, then ran a hand through his hair. The thick locks sprang back in precisely the same manner Foxy's did. "And you're not sixteen anymore."

"So I've been told," she murmured.

Letting out a frustrated breath, Kirk jammed his hands farther into his pockets. "I should've paid more attention to you when you were."

"Kirk." The humor left her voice as she rose to stand beside him. "It's nice of you to be concerned, but it's unnecessary." Touched both by his caring and his discomposure, Foxy laid her head on his shoulder. *What an odd man he is,* she thought, *with such unexpected scraps of sweetness.*

"It is necessary," he muttered, wishing he didn't feel obligated to pursue the matter. He was closer to Lance than to any other person in his life other than his sister. With Lance, there was the added bond of manhood and shared adventures. It was some of these adventures which prodded Kirk on when he wanted nothing more than to drop the entire subject. "You're still my sister," he added, half to himself. "Even if you have grown up a bit."

"A bit?" Foxy grinned again. A reckless mischief gleamed in her eyes, reminding Kirk uncomfortably of himself. "Kirk, I passed 'a bit' at twenty."

"Look, Foxy," Kirk cut in impatiently. "I know Lance. I know how he…" He hesitated and swore.

"Operates?" Foxy supplied and earned a fierce glare. Her laughter was unavoidable, but she tempered it by kissing his cheek. "Stop worrying about me. I learned a little more than photography in college." When Kirk's expression failed to alter, she kissed his other cheek and continued. "If it makes you feel any better, Lance isn't bothering me. If he were, I could handle it quite nicely, I promise you, but he isn't. We hardly speak." She tried to be pleased by the statement, but found herself annoyed.

"He looks," Kirk mumbled. His sister's scent lifted on the faint breeze. Her hair had been soft and fragrant against his cheek. His frown deepened. "He looks a lot."

"You're imagining things," Foxy said firmly, then tried to draw Kirk away from the subject of Lance Matthews. She found speaking of him brought back disturbing memories. "Tell me, Mr. Fox," she began, mimicking the tone of a sports reporter, "are you always so introspective the night before a race?"

He did not answer at once, but simply stared out over the track. Foxy wondered what he saw there that she didn't. "It occurred to me recently that a woman's better off not getting involved with a man like me. She'll only get hurt." Restlessly he shifted, then turned to her. Foxy studied him curiously. There was something in his eyes she could not understand, and it puzzled her that he seemed tense. She sensed it was more than the race that was pulling at his nerves. "Lance is a lot like me," he continued. "I don't want you hurt. He could do that, maybe not meaning to, but he could do it."

"Kirk, I…"

"I know him, Foxy." He pushed away the beginnings of her objections and placed his hands on her shoulders. "No woman's ever been more important to him than cars. I don't think it's smart to get mixed up with men like us. There's always going to be another race, Foxy, another car, another track. It pushes everything and everyone else into the back seat. I don't want that for you. I know it's what you've always had. I've never done the things I should've done for you, and I…"

"No, Kirk." She stopped him by flinging her arms around his neck. "No, don't." Foxy buried her face in his shoulder the same way she had years before in her hospital bed. He had been her rock when her world had crumbled away from its foundations. "You did everything you could."

"Did I?" Kirk sighed and hugged her tighter. "If I had it to do again, I know I'd do exactly the same things. But that doesn't make them right."

"It was right for us." She lifted her face to look at him with glistening eyes. "It was right for me."

Letting out a long breath, he tousled her hair. "Maybe." After cupping her face in his hands, he kissed both her cheeks. His mustache whispered along her skin causing her to smile at the old familiarity. "I never expected you to grow up, I guess. And I never thought you'd be beautiful and that I'd have to worry about men. I should've paid more attention while it was happening. You never complained."

"What about? I was happy." When he dropped his hands from her face, she took them in hers. His palms were hard and she felt the faint line of a scar along the back. She remembered that he had gotten it in Belgium eight years before in a minor crash. "Kirk," she spoke quickly, wanting to put his mind at ease, "we were both where we needed to be. I don't regret anything, and I don't want you to. Okay?"

She stood still as he studied her face. His eyes had long since adjusted to the night, enabling him to see her features clearly. He realized she had grown up right under his eyes. Somehow the woman who looked back at him roused his protective instincts profoundly, while the girl had always seemed somehow indestructible. Perhaps he understood the pitfalls of womanhood, while those of childhood were a mystery to him. It was an uncharacteristic gesture when he lifted her fingers to his lips, yet it was a gesture that flooded Foxy's eyes with warm tears. "I love you," he said simply. "Don't do that," he warned as he brushed a tear from her lashes. "I don't have anything to mop them up with. Come on." He slipped an arm around her shoulders and began to walk with her from the grandstands. "I'll buy you a cup of coffee and a hamburger. I'm starved."

"Pizza," she countered. "This is Italy."

"Whatever," he said agreeably as they moved without haste through the moonlight.

"Kirk." Foxy tilted her face, and now her eyes shone with mischief. "If Lance does bother me, will you beat him up?"

"Sure." Kirk grinned and tugged on her hair. "As soon as the season's over."

Foxy laughed. "That's what I figured."

It was just after eleven when they walked down the hall of the hotel to their rooms. Pam heard Foxy's laugh and the low answering sound of her brother's. Nibbling on her lip, she waited for the sounds of their doors closing. She badly needed to talk to Foxy, to have someone laugh and joke and take her mind off Kirk Fox. For weeks Pam had been able to think of little but him. As they had moved from country to country, from race to race, he had grown remote. He spoke to her rarely, and when he did, he was unmistakably aloof. It became apparent that he had lost interest in the flirtation he had initiated. His coolness might have caused her some minor annoyance or even some amusement under normal circumstances. But Pam had discovered that the circumstances here were far from normal.

As Kirk had gradually grown more taciturn she had grown gradually more tense. Sleeping had become a major feat and eating a monumental task. Her tension had come to an unexpected climax when Kirk stepped from his car during the final laps of the race in France. Their eyes met for only one brief instant, but abruptly the realization had come to her that she was in love with him. The very thought had terrified her; he was so different from any of the men she had been attracted to in the past. But this was not mere attraction, and the old rules were insignificant. Briefly Pam had considered chucking the assignment and returning to the States. Professional pride refused to allow her this convenient escape. Personal pride kept her aloof from him. She did not want to be another of his trophies, another victory for Kirk Fox.

Hearing no sound in the hall, Pam drew a thin robe over her nightgown, deciding to slip down to Foxy's room. The instant she opened the door, she froze. Kirk walked silently down the hall. His head was bent but it snapped up immediately as she made a small sound of surprise. Stopping, he surveyed her carefully with eyes that held no expression. Framed in the doorway, Pam felt her breath backing up in her lungs. She seemed to have lost the power to force it out, just as she had lost the power to command her feet to move back into the room. His eyes held hers as he began to walk again, and though her fingers tightened on the knob, she did not retreat. Calm settled over her suddenly. This, she knew, was what she wanted, what she needed. When he stopped in front of her, they stood unsmiling, studying each other. The light from her room bathed them in a pale yellow glow.

"I've walked by your door a hundred times the last few months."

"I know."

"I'm not walking by tonight." There was a challenge in his voice, a hint of anger around his mouth. "I'm coming in."

"I know," Pam said again, then stepped back to allow him to enter. Her calm acceptance caused him to hesitate. She saw doubt flickering in his eyes.

"I'm going to make love to you," he told her in a statement that reflected a rising temper.

"Yes," she agreed with a nod. A smile touched her lips as she recognized the nervousness in his tone. *He's just as terrified as I am,* she realized when, after a brief hesitation, Kirk stalked into the room. Quietly Pam closed the door behind him. They turned to face each other.

"I don't make promises." His voice was rough as he studied her. His hands stayed firmly in his pockets.

"No." Her robe whispered gently as she moved to switch off the light. The room was softened by starlight and moonbeams. In the courtyard below her window someone spoke quickly in Italian, then laughed heartily.

"I'll probably hurt you," he warned in a lowered voice.

"Probably," Pam agreed. She walked to him until they were both silhouetted in the moonlight. He found her perfume quiet, understated, and unforgettable. "But I'm much sturdier than I look."

Unable to resist, he lifted a hand to her hair. It was as soft as a cloud under his palm. "You're making a mistake." In the dim light, he watched the sheen of her eyes.

"No." Pam lifted her arms until they circled his neck. "No, I'm not."

On a low groan, Kirk pulled her against him and took the offered mouth. As she felt him lift her Pam melted against him.

CHAPTER 6

There was the usual crush of people and noise as the starting time approached. The light, insistent drizzle did nothing to hamper attendance. The skies were lead-gray and uncompromising. Slicks were exchanged for rain tires.

Foxy stood before the basin in the empty ladies' room and rinsed the taste of sickness from her mouth. With the absent gestures of habit, she sponged her face and touched up her pallor with makeup. The palms of her hands were still hot and moist, and automatically she ran cool water over them. The drone of the loudspeaker penetrated the walls. Knowing she had only a few minutes until the start, she picked up her camera case and hurried out. The swarming crowd swallowed her instantly. Because she was preoccupied she didn't notice Lance until she was nearly upon him.

"Cutting it a bit closer than usual, Foxy?" She glanced up just as the thrust of the crowd pushed her against him. His grin faded as his hands touched the still clammy skin of her arms. "You're like ice," he muttered, then pulled her free of the throng and into a narrow hallway.

"For heaven's sake, let me go," she protested. Her legs were still a bit rubbery and nearly folded under her at the sudden movement. "They're going to start in a minute."

Ignoring her, Lance put a firm hand under her chin, then jerked her face to his. His eyes were narrowed and probing. Color had not yet returned to her cheeks, and the camouflage of makeup did not deceive him. "You're ill." The statement came partly as an accusation as he propped her against a wall. "You can't go out there while you're sick." Lance slipped an arm around her waist to lead her away, and she struggled against him. The sound of revving engines filled the air.

"For Lord's sake!" Foxy pushed unsuccessfully against him, frustrated by his interference. "I'm sick before every race, but I don't miss the start. Let me go, will you?"

His expression altered rapidly from surprise to disbelief to fury. Trapped between him and the wall, Foxy saw the changes and realized she had made a mistake. "You'll damn well miss this one," he grated, then half dragged, half carried her away from the pits. Feeling his grip, Foxy conceded and went peacefully. In silence, he led her to the restaurant under the main grandstand. "Coffee," he barked to the waiter as he pushed Foxy into a corner booth.

"Listen, Lance," she began, recovered enough to be indignant.

"Shut up." His voice was quiet, but so full of fury, she obeyed instantly. She had seen him angry before, but she decided she would have to go back some years to find a memory of an anger that sharp. His mouth was set in an uncompromising line, his voice vibrated with temper just under control. But it was his eyes, heated to a smoky gray, which kept her silent. Discretion, she reflected, sometimes is the better part of valor.

The restaurant was empty, silent save for the vibrations of

the cars outside on the grid. There was a gray wall of gloom beyond the window, broken only by thin, clear rivulets of rain on the glass. Foxy watched one wind its slow, erratic way down the pane. The waiter set a pot of coffee and two cups on the table between them, then disappeared. The look in Lance's eyes told him he wanted solitude not service. Picking up the angry vibes Lance transmitted, Foxy watched as he poured the coffee into each cup. Curiosity began to temper her annoyance. *What is he so worked up about?* she wondered.

"Drink your coffee," he ordered in clipped tones.

Her brows arched at the command. "Yes, sir," she said humbly and lifted her cup.

A flash of trembling fury sparked in his eyes. "Don't push me, Foxy."

"Lance." She set down her coffee untasted, then leaned toward him. "What's the matter with you?"

He studied the perplexity on her face before drinking half his coffee, hot and black. The pallor clung stubbornly to her cheeks, lending her a look of vulnerability. Her eyes were young and earnest as her own coffee sat cooling in front of her. "How do you feel?" he asked as he drew out a cigar and his lighter.

"I'm fine," she answered cautiously. She noted he didn't light the cigar but merely twirled it between his fingers. Silence spread again. *This is ridiculous,* Foxy decided, and opened her mouth to demand an explanation.

"You're sick before every race?" Lance demanded suddenly.

Foxy hesitated over the question and began to stir her coffee. "Listen, Lance—"

"Don't start with me." The sharp order startled her and she lifted her eyes and encountered dark fury in his. "I asked you a question." His voice was too controlled. Though never timid, Foxy respected a temper more volatile than her own. "Are you ill, physically ill," he repeated in slow, precise tones, "before every race?"

"Yes."

Though soft, his oath was so violent she shuddered. Her wary eyes settled on his face. "Have you told Kirk?" he demanded.

"No, of course not. Why should I?" His temper flared again at the incredulity in her voice. Sensing danger, Foxy quickly laid her hand on his. "Lance, wait a minute. In the first place, at this point in my life, it's certainly my problem. When I was a kid, if I had told Kirk how I reacted to the start of a race, he would have worried, he would have been concerned, he might even have banned me from the track. All of those things would have made me guilty and miserable." She paused a moment and shook her head. "But he wouldn't have stopped. He couldn't have stopped."

"You know him well." Lance drained his cup, then poured more from the pot. His movements were smooth but Foxy was aware that his temper was just below the surface.

"Yes, I do." Their eyes met again, his heated, hers calm. "Racing's first with Kirk, it always has been. But I've always been second." Foxy made an imploring gesture, wanting him to understand her as badly as she had wanted Kirk to understand the night before. "That was enough. If he had put me first, he would have been a different person altogether. I love Kirk just the way he is...maybe because of the way he is. I owe him everything." As Lance opened his mouth to speak Foxy rushed on. "No, please listen, you don't understand. He gave me a home, he gave me a life. I don't know what would have happened to me after the accident if I hadn't had Kirk. How many twenty-three-year-old men would choose to be saddled with a thirteen-year-old girl? He's been good to me.

He's given me everything he was capable of giving. I know he's not perfect. He's moody, he's self-absorbed. But, Lance, in all these years, he's never asked for anything except that I be there." She let out a long breath, then stared into her coffee. "It doesn't seem like much to ask."

"That all depends," Lance said quietly. "But in any case, you can't be there forever."

"No, I know that." Her shoulders moved with her sigh. Facing the window again, she watched the rain trickle down the glass without seeing her own ghostly reflection. "I realized this time around that I can't cope with it anymore, not in person anyway. I can't handle watching him get into a car and waiting for him to crash, knowing one day he might not walk away from it." She shifted her eyes back to Lance, and for a moment they were drenched in despair. "I won't watch him die."

"Foxy." Lance leaned over to take her hand. His voice was gentle now, without any sign of temper. "You know better than most that not every driver is killed on the track."

"I don't love every driver," she countered simply. "I've already lost two people in a car. No, no," she said quickly as he began to speak. She pressed her fingers to her eyes, simultaneously shaking her head as if to push the words away. "I don't dwell on it. I don't think about any of this often. You go crazy if you do." After taking a deep breath, Foxy felt more composed and met his eyes. "I'm not morbid about all of this, Lance. I just don't cope with it very well. And it gets harder all the time."

"I know the danger shouldn't be minimized, Foxy," Lance began, frowning at the weariness he saw in her eyes. "But you're aware of the improved safety features. A driver's much more protected than he used to be. Fatalities are the exception, not the rule."

"Statistics are just numbers on paper. They don't mean anything to me." She smiled as his brows drew together, then shook her head. "You can't understand because you're one of them. You're a unique breed. You all say you race for a variety of reasons, but there's really only one. You race because you love it. It's your mother and mistress and best friend. Drivers flirt with death, break their bones, singe their skins, and get back on the grid before the smoke's cleared. In the hospital one day, in the cockpit the next; I've seen you do it. It's like a religion, and I can't condemn it any more than I can comprehend it. Some people call it a science, but that's a lie. I've lived with it all my life, and it never makes any more sense. That's because it's emotional, and emotions rarely make sense." Foxy leaned her head against the cool glass of the window and stared into the rain. "I keep hoping one day he'll have had enough. Someday he'll find something else to take its place." When she looked back at Lance, her eyes were steady and studying. "I always wondered…why did you quit?"

"I didn't love it anymore." With a half smile, he reached over and tucked her hair behind her ear.

"I'm glad," she said simply, smiling back at him. Toying with her coffee, she lapsed into silence a moment. "Lance, you won't say anything about this to Kirk?" Foxy lifted her eyes and used them shamelessly.

"No, I won't say anything." He watched relief flutter over her face before she lifted her cup. "But, Fox." The cup paused at her lips. "I'd like you to skip the last races in the circuit."

"I can't do that." She shook her head as she tasted the coffee. It was strong and cold, causing her to wrinkle her nose and set it back down. "Not only because of Kirk, but because I have a commitment to Pam." Foxy leaned back and watched Lance frown at her through a haze of cheroot smoke. "It's my job to photograph these races, and my work is very important to me."

"And when the season's over?"

It was her turn to frown. Her eyes reflected the gray light coming through the window. "I have my own life, my own work. I have to resolve to myself that I can't be a part of Kirk's life. I'm not equipped for it. My emotions are too near the surface. And I'm a coward," she added briskly, then started to slide from the booth. "I have to get back."

Lance was out of the booth before her and blocking her way. Even as her eyes rose to his in question, his arms came around her. He drew her close, nestling her head against his chest. "Oh, don't," she murmured and shut her eyes. A treacherous warmth flooded through her. "I can't handle you when you're kind." She could feel his lips trail over her hair while his hand moved gently up and down her spine. "Lance, please, if you're not careful I'll start flooding the place with tears, and you've already terrified the waiter."

"Tears?" He spoke quietly, as if considering. "You know, Foxy, I don't believe I've ever seen you cry, not once in all the years I've known you."

"I have an aversion to humiliating myself in public." She felt cozy and pampered and entirely too right in his arms. "Lance, please don't be nice to me. I could get used to it." She lifted her face, but her smile never materialized. She could read his intent in his eyes. "Oh help," she murmured as his mouth touched hers.

There was no need to brace herself for the explosion because his lips were gentle. There was no demand, no fire, just a lingering tenderness. Even as she felt her bones melt into submission, she felt oddly protected. The slow, soft embrace confused her, disarmed her, seduced her more successfully than his most ardent demand. His lips were warm, tasting hers without pressure, giving only comfort and pleasure. She had not known he was capable of such poignant tenderness. Because he was not asking, she gave more freely. The kiss lengthened, but remained a quiet gift. Reality slipped away leisurely, leaving Foxy with only Lance inside her world. When her mouth was free, she could not speak. Her eyes asked him questions.

"I'm not quite sure what to do with you," he murmured. Taking a handful of her hair, he let it run through his fingers. "It was simpler before I found out you had a fragile side. I doubt that I deal very well with frailty."

Nonplussed, Foxy bent to lift her camera gear. She had not felt fragile until he had touched her so gently. Knowing there was no safety in the feeling, she tried to shake it off. "I'm not frail at all," she denied, then stood straight and faced him.

A smile flickered over his face, lifting his mouth and lighting up his eyes. "You don't like to be."

"I'm not," she countered with a quick shake of her head. No one had ever made her feel that way before, and Foxy was afraid he would touch her, making her feel that way again. She knew from experience that only the strong survived intact.

Lance studied her face before he took the camera case from her. "Humor me then," he suggested, then closed his hand over hers to lead her outside.

When the team returned to the States, Kirk led the competition for the world championship by five points. A win at Watkins Glen would give him the title. But through the high spirits and growing confusion, Foxy noticed subtle changes in the people closest to her. She herself had been preoccupied since the race in Italy. Something seemed to be nagging at the outside of her mind. The sensation did not make her uneasy as much as curious. She was accustomed to being in full control of her thoughts and feelings, but now it seemed part of her mind belonged to someone else. She found herself thinking more and more of Lance.

Since their talk over coffee, he had treated her with a strange gentleness. Oddly the gentleness was mixed with an aloofness that only added to Foxy's confusion. Since the kiss he had given her in the restaurant, Lance had not touched or indeed attempted to touch her again. Having never seen him be gentle or diffident before, Foxy began to wonder if she really knew him as well as she had assumed. Unwillingly she was drawn to him.

She noted a change in her brother. He grew more quiet and more withdrawn. Because she had seen him go inside himself before, Foxy accepted it. She attributed his mood to pressure over the championship. In Pam, she saw a growing serenity. Often during the qualifying races and long practice sessions, Foxy wished for a portion of Pam's absolute calm.

The two-point-three-mile course climbed and weaved through terrain that was alternately wooded and open. Trees were ablaze with autumn colors, which grew more vibrant with each passing day. Foxy had forgotten that New York possessed such rustic charm. October leaves stretched toward a hard blue sky and swirled and spun to the ground. There was the combination of biting air and heat from the sun so peculiar to fall. Of all the tracks she had seen in a decade of her life, Foxy favored Watkins Glen. There was something simple and basically American about it.

She watched the race begin through the lens of her camera. *The last one,* she thought, and let out a long breath as she straightened. Beside her, Charlie Dunning stared after the cars while he rolled the stub of a fat cigar around in his mouth.

"This'll do it, Charlie." Foxy smiled as he turned to her, squinting against the sun.

"Don't you get tired of taking pictures?" he demanded as he scowled at her camera.

"Don't you get tired of playing with cars and chasing women?" she countered sweetly.

"Those are both worthwhile occupations." He pinched her waist and snorted. "You're getting skinnier."

"You're getting cuter." Foxy rubbed his grizzled beard with her palm and winked. "Wanna get married?"

"You're still a smart-aleck brat," he grumbled as he turned a rosy pink under his whiskers.

Grinning, Foxy dipped in his shirt pocket and pulled out a candy bar. "Let me know if you change your mind," she told him as she unwrapped the chocolate and took a bite. "I'm not getting any younger, you know."

With grumbles and mutters, Charlie moved away to lecture his mechanics.

"That's the first time Charlie's blushed in his life," Lance commented.

Foxy twisted her head and watched him approach. An odd thrill sped up and down her spine before it spread out at the base of her neck. His dark gray turtleneck was snug, showing off his lean torso. His mouth was cocked in a half smile. Abruptly she felt the memory of its pressure on hers. The sensation was so genuine, so vital, she was certain he must feel it too. As she looked at him it was as though a thin veil lifted from her eyes, and she saw him clearly for the first time: the dark gray eyes that saw so much and told so little, the well-shaped mouth that could give such pleasure, the firm chin and rawboned features that were so much more interesting than clean good looks. This was why Scott Newman had seemed so dull, why no boy or man she had ever known had measured up in her eyes. There was only one, had always been only one man in her heart.

I've never stopped loving him, she realized on a wave of alarm. *I never will.*

"You all right?" He reached for her as the color drained from her face. The gesture, coupled with the concern in his voice, snapped her back to reality.

"No…yes, yes, I'm fine." Foxy brushed a hand over her eyes as if to clear the mists. "I—I was daydreaming, I suppose."

"About wedded bliss with Charlie?" The careless brush of his hand through her hair sent tremors speeding through her.

"Charlie?" Blankly she glanced down at the chocolate bar in her hand. It was softening in the sunlight. "Oh, yes, Charlie. I was—I was teasing him." She wished desperately for a moment alone to pull herself together. Her mind was whirling with new knowledge. All of her senses seemed to be competing with each other for dominance.

Lance studied her with growing interest. "Are you sure you're all right?" His brow lifted in that habitual gesture and disappeared under his hair. "You look rattled."

Rattled? she thought, nearly giggling at the understatement. I'm going under for the third time. "I'm fine," she lied, then forced herself to smile. "How are you?"

Cars wound around the "Ss" and zoomed past. Absently she wondered how many laps she had missed while she had been in her trance. "Just fine," Lance murmured. There was a faint smile on his lips as he watched her. "Your chocolate's melting."

Dutifully Foxy took a bite of the bar. "What will you do after the race is over?" she asked, hoping she sounded only mildly interested.

"Relax."

"Yes." A portion of the tension slid out of her shoulders

as she glanced around. It would be over in a matter of hours. "I guess we all will. It's been a long summer."

"Has it?" Lance retorted. Foxy wore a white Oxford shirt under a navy crew-neck sweater. Carelessly, Lance rubbed the collar between his thumb and forefinger while his eyes rested on hers. There was something proprietary in the casual gesture. "It doesn't seem very long ago that you popped out from under the MG in Kirk's garage."

"It seems like years to me," Foxy murmured as she turned back to the track. Cars hurtled by, and the noise was one continuous demand—roar and whine. She could smell oil and gas and heated rubber. "It doesn't seem to bother Pam at all," Foxy commented as she spotted the small blond figure near the edge of the pits. "I suppose it's easier if you're not personally involved with one of the drivers."

With a quick laugh, Lance took her chin and examined her face. "Do you need glasses or have you been off in space for the past few weeks?"

"What are you talking about?" Foxy was not ready to have him touch her and carefully backed away.

"Foxy, my love, Pam is very personally involved with one of the drivers. Take off your blinders."

Eyes narrowed against the sun, Foxy turned to study Pam's profile. She was watching the race steadily with her delicate hands tucked into the pockets of a spotless ivory blazer. Foxy turned back to Lance's amused face with a sharp glance. "You don't mean Kirk?" *Of course he means Kirk,* she realized even as she spoke. I'd have seen it myself if I hadn't been so tangled up with Lance. "Oh dear," she said on a sigh.

"Don't you approve, little sister?" Lance said dryly, then turned her back to face him. His hands remained light on her arms. "Kirk's a big boy now."

"Oh, don't be ridiculous." Foxy pushed her hair behind

her back in a quick gesture of annoyance. "It's not a matter of approving, and in any case, Pam's wonderful."

"Then what's the problem?"

Foxy turned and gestured to where Pam stood. Her hair was rolled neatly at the nape of her neck with only a few wisps dancing gently around her composed face. "Just look at her," Foxy ordered impatiently. "That's how Melanie Wilkes would look today. Lord, she even sounds like her, with that quiet, cultured voice. Pam's tiny and fragile and should be serving tea in a drawing room. Kirk will swallow her whole."

"You've forgotten what a strong lady Melanie Wilkes was, Foxy." His fingers trailed lightly over her cheek. "Think about it," he advised before he turned and walked away.

For some moments, Foxy stood still. Being in love with Lance was not a new sensation, but now she loved as a woman and not as a child. This was no fairy-tale crush but a real, encompassing need. She knew now the agonies and joys of being in his arms, knew the heat and pressure of his mouth. She could never, as she had at sixteen, be content with making him the hero of her dreams. And after tomorrow, she remembered and shut her eyes against the painful reality, *I'll very likely never see him again.* Unable to deal with her situation, Foxy pushed it from her mind.

And now, there's Pam and Kirk, she reminded herself. Her loyalties at war, she walked over to the blond woman and stood beside her as the grid vibrated with passing cars.

"He's taken the lead a bit sooner than usual," Pam commented as she followed the flash of Kirk's car. "He wants badly to win this one." With a light laugh, she turned to Foxy. "He wants badly to win every one."

"I know…he always has." The calm blue eyes caused Foxy to take a long breath. "Pam, I know it's none of my business, but I'd…" With a sound of frustration, she turned back to the track and stuck her hands in her pockets. "Oh, I'm going to make a terrible fool of myself."

"You think I'm wrong for Kirk," Pam supplied gently.

"No!" Foxy's eyes grew wide with distress. "I think Kirk's wrong for you."

"How strangely alike the two of you are," Pam murmured, studying Foxy's earnest face. "He thinks so, too. But it doesn't matter, I know he's exactly right for me."

"Pam…" Foxy shook her head as she searched for the right words. "Racing…"

"Will always come first," Pam finished, then shrugged her slim shoulders. "Of course I know that. I accept that. The fact is, as much as it surprises even me, it's partly that which attracted me to him—the racing, his absolute determination to come out on top, his almost negligent attitude about danger. It's as exciting as it is frustrating, and I'm hooked. I think I'm going to be terrified, and then when the race starts, I'm not. I want him to win." She turned to Foxy with a brilliant smile. "I think I'm almost as bad as he is. I love him, I love who he is and what he is. Being second in his life is enough for me." Hearing her own words echo back to her, Foxy could do no more than stare out at the track. "I'm not trying to usurp your place with him," Pam began, and Foxy turned back quickly.

"Oh, no. No, it's not that. It's nothing like that. I'm glad for Kirk, he needs someone…someone who understands him the way you do." She ran her fingers through her thick mane of hair. It glowed like the russet leaves on the surrounding trees. "But I care about you, too." She made a frustrated gesture with her hands as if that would help her express herself. "He can be cruel by just forgetting."

"I don't bruise easily." Pam laid a hand on Foxy's shoulder. "Not as easily, I think, as you do." At Foxy's confused expression, she smiled. "It's easy for one woman in love to recognize another. No, no, don't start babbling a denial." She laughed as Foxy's mouth opened then closed. "If you need to talk, we will. I feel quite an expert on the subject."

"It's academic," Foxy told her with a restless movement of her shoulders. "Tomorrow we'll go our separate ways."

"You still have today." Pam gave Foxy's shoulder a quick squeeze. "Isn't that really all there is?"

It happened so suddenly. At first Foxy's brain rejected it. Even as Pam spoke, Kirk rounded the turn in front of them. She saw him swerve to avoid the abrupt fishtailing of the racer to his right, then waited for him to regain control. She saw the skid begin, heard its squeal echo through her head as she watched it grow wider and more violent. Part of her brain screamed in panic while still another kept insisting he would pull out of it. He had to pull out of it. The sound of the blowout was like a gunshot and just as lethal. Then there were columns of smoke and shrieking metal as the car slammed into the wall and careened away. Wheels and pieces of fiberglass rained in the air as the racer continued to spin wildly.

"*No!*" The cry was wrenched from Foxy as she darted toward the track. With one quick jerk, she freed herself from Pam's restraining hand and ran.

Jagged pieces of fiberglass flew with deadly abandon. A fear greater than any she had ever known filled her, blacking out all thoughts, all feelings. Her only reality was the twisting hulk of machine that held her brother in its bowels. Inches from the grid, her breath was cut off by a vise around her waist. The force lifted her off the ground, and she kicked uselessly in the air to free herself. She shook the hair from her eyes in time to see Kirk's car topple into the infield.

"For God's sake, Foxy, you'll kill yourself." Lance's voice was harsh in her ear as she writhed and struggled for freedom. In terror, she waited for the belching smoke to burst into flame.

"Let me go!" she shouted as she realized the vise around her waist was his arm. "It's Kirk, can't you see? I've got to get to him." Her breathing was ragged as she clawed at the imprisoning arm. "Oh God, I've got to get to him!" she shouted again, desperately fighting to free herself.

"There's nothing you can do." Lance jerked her back against him, cutting off her wind for a moment. Over her head, he could see members of the emergency team spraying the wreck with extinguishers while others worked to free Kirk from the cockpit. "There's nothing you can do," he said again. Her struggles ceased abruptly. She went so completely limp, he thought she had fainted until he heard her speak.

"Let me go." Foxy spoke quietly now, so that he barely heard her. "I won't do anything stupid," she added when he did not lessen his grip. "I'm all right, Lance, let me go."

Slowly he lowered her back to the ground and released her. She neither turned to him nor spoke, but watched in silence as they pulled Kirk from the wreckage. She gave no sign that she knew Pam stood beside her. Behind them, the pits were like a tomb. The white flag fluttered in the autumn breeze.

CHAPTER 7

The walls in the hospital waiting room were pale green. The floor was uncarpeted; an inconspicuous beige tile with tiny brown flecks disguised a day's collection of dust and dirt. On the wall opposite Foxy was a print of a Van Gogh still life. It was the sole spot of color in the drab little room. Foxy knew she would never see the print again without remembering the hours of torment and ignorance. Pam sat near the window, framed by drapes just darker than the walls. Occasionally she took sips of cold coffee. Charlie sat on a vinyl sofa and gnawed at the stub of a long-dead cigar. Lance paced. Unceasingly he prowled the small room, sometimes with his hands in his pockets, sometimes smoking. Once or twice, Foxy heard Pam murmur something to him, then caught the low rumble of his response. She did not hear the words, nor did she attempt to. They did not interest her. She felt the same nameless, unspeakable fear she had known in the first moments of consciousness after her own accident. She had been helpless then, and she knew she was helpless now. Lance had been right when he told her there was nothing she could do. Now Foxy accepted it. Anger and panic were buried under the numbing terror of the unthinkable.

Her mind drifted and emptied as she stared at the Van Gogh print. Kirk's skid had begun more than three hours before.

"Miss Fox?"

With a jolt, Foxy was pulled back to the present. For a moment, she merely stared at the green-gowned figure in the doorway. "Yes?" she managed in a surprisingly strong voice as she rose to meet him. It floated through her mind that the doctor was very young. His mustache was dark but reminded Foxy of Kirk's. His surgical mask hung by its ties at his throat.

"Your brother's out of surgery." There was a quietness to his voice which, like his hands, he used for healing. "He's in recovery."

Cautiously Foxy held off relief and kept her gaze steady on his face. "How extensive are his injuries?"

The doctor heard and respected the control in her tone, but saw that her eyes were hurting and afraid. "He had five broken ribs. His lungs collapsed, but they've been reinflated and the concussion's mild. The ribs will be painful, but since there was no puncture, the danger's minimal. His leg…" He hesitated a moment, and Foxy felt a fresh thrill of fear.

"He didn't…" She swallowed, then forced herself to ask. "He didn't lose it?"

"No." He took her hand for reassurance and found it ice cold but without a tremor. "But it's a complicated injury, we've had to do some reconstructing. It's an open, comminuted fracture, and there's some artery damage. We've realigned the bones, and the outlook is good that he'll have full use of the leg in a few months. Meanwhile, there's a risk of infection." After releasing her hand, the doctor allowed his gaze to sweep the people behind her before returning to Foxy. "He's going to be here for some time."

"I see." Foxy let out a shaky breath. "Is there anything else?"

"Minor burns and abrasions. He's a very lucky man."

"Yes." Foxy's agreement was solemn as she stared down at her hands. She joined them together, not knowing what else to do with them. "Is he conscious?"

"Yes." The doctor grinned and looked younger yet. "He wanted to know who won the race." Foxy bit her bottom lip hard and continued to look straight ahead as he went on. "He'll be in a room in about an hour; you can see him then. Only one visitor tonight," he added firmly, again letting his eyes trail over the people behind Foxy. "The others can see him tomorrow. We're not giving him a phone for twenty-four hours."

Foxy nodded and spoke quickly. "Miss Anderson will stay to see him tonight then."

"Foxy," Pam began, shaking her head as she stepped forward.

"He'll want you," Foxy told her as their eyes met. "He'll be satisfied knowing I was here. You will stay, won't you?"

Feeling tears well up behind her eyes, Pam nodded quickly, then turned away. She had managed with a great deal of willpower to remain composed during the wait. Now, Foxy's simple generosity did what the hours of torture had not. Moving to the window, she stared out and let the tears have their freedom.

"The desk has my number," Foxy told the doctor. "Will you see that I'm called if there's any change before morning?"

"Certainly. Miss Fox," he added, recognizing the signs of shock and fatigue in her eyes. "He's going to be fine."

"Thank you."

"Charlie, wait around and take Pam back after she's seen Kirk," Lance ordered as he took Foxy's arm. "I'll take Foxy now." He turned to the doctor and spoke briskly. "There'll be reporters downstairs in the lobby. I don't want her to have to deal with them tonight."

"Take the service elevator down to the garage level. There's a cabstand near the entrance."

"Thanks." Without waiting for her assent, Lance began to lead Foxy down the corridor.

"You don't have to do this," she said. Her voice held no inflection at all as she allowed herself to be piloted.

"I know what I have to do," he tossed back and jammed the button on the service elevator. Behind them, the crepe soles of nurses' shoes made soft sounds against the tile.

"I didn't thank you before for stopping me from running out on the track." There was a quick ding of a bell before the doors slid open. Foxy made no protest as he pulled her into the empty car. "It was a stupid thing to do."

"Stop it, damn it! Just stop it." He whirled and took her by the shoulders. His fingers pressed tightly into her flesh. "Scream, cry, take a punch at me, but stop acting like this."

Foxy stared up into the furious heat of his eyes. Her emotions refused to surface. Her defenses remained sealed, as if they knew it was still too soon to allow anything to escape. She spoke quietly and her eyes were dry. "I already did all the screaming I'm going to do. I can't cry yet because I'm still numb, and I don't have any reason to take a punch at you."

"It was my car, isn't that enough?" he demanded. The doors opened, and he took her hand before he stalked out. Their footsteps echoed hollowly in the garage as he pulled her toward the entrance.

"Nobody forced Kirk into that car. I'm not blaming you, Lance. I'm not blaming anyone."

"I saw the way you looked at me when they pulled him out."

Fatigue was pouring over Foxy as Lance nudged her into a cab. Turning her head to face him, she made herself speak clearly. "I'm sorry. Maybe I did blame you for a minute.

Maybe I wanted to blame you or anyone else who was handy. I thought he was dead." Because her voice trembled slightly, she paused until she was certain she could continue. "I've tried to be prepared for something like this every day of my life. But I wasn't prepared at all. It doesn't seem to make any difference that I've seen him crash before." Foxy sighed and leaned back against the seat. The streetlights came through the cab window to dance on her closed lids. "I don't blame you for what happened, Lance, any more than I blame Kirk for being who he is. Maybe this time he'll have had enough."

No answer came from Lance but the click and hiss of his lighter. Not having the energy to open her eyes, Foxy kept them closed and took the rest of the brief journey in silence. When they arrived at the motel, they found Scott Newman pacing the corridor in front of Foxy's room. He wore the disheveled look of an executive who has just left a hassle-filled board meeting.

"Cynthia." Giving Lance a quick nod, he held out both hands to her. "The hospital said you were on your way back. How's Kirk? They tell you next to nothing over the phone."

"He's going to be fine," Foxy told him, letting him squeeze her hands. She gave him a shortened version of the doctor's report.

"Everybody's been worried; they'll be glad to hear he's going to be all right. How about you?" He gave her an encouraging smile. "I thought you might need me."

"What she needs is some rest," Lance said shortly.

"It was very considerate of you to wait." Foxy smoothed over Lance's rudeness and added a smile which cost her some concentrated effort. "I'm fine, really, just a bit tired. Pam stayed behind to keep Kirk company for a while."

"The press is itching for the full story," Scott commented

as he released her hands and straightened the knot in his tie. "We took a look at the replay. There's no doubt that Kirk had to swerve to avoid a crash with Martell, and that's when he lost it. Defective steering in Martell's racer is the verdict. A bad break for Kirk. Perhaps you'd like to give them a statement or pass one on through me."

"No," Lance answered before Foxy could respond. "Leave it. If you want to be useful, tell the switchboard not to pass any calls through to this room unless it's the hospital." His voice was curt and annoyed. "Give me the key, Foxy," he ordered.

"Of course." Scott nodded as he watched Foxy dig in her bag. "I'm sure I can hold them off at least until morning, but—"

"Come on to my room in a couple hours." Lance cut him off and snatched the key from Foxy's hand. "I'll give you enough for a press release. Just see that you keep her out of it. Understand?" Lance jerked open the door.

The fury registered. Scott agreed with another nod before turning to Foxy. "Let me know if there's anything I can do, Cynthia."

"Thank you, Scott. Good night," she managed before Lance shut the door in his face. Bone weary, she moved to a chair and sank into it. "You were very rude," she commented absently as she rubbed at a headache near her temple. "I don't recall that I've ever seen you be quite that rude before."

"Maybe if you took a look in the mirror, you'd understand why." The fury was still in his voice. Foxy watched him calmly from behind the numbing shield of shock and fatigue. "You're standing there getting paler by the minute. I swear the only color in your face right now is in your eyes. And he rambles on like an idiot about press releases." Lance made a gesture of disgust with his hand. "He's got the brains of a soft-boiled egg."

"He's a good manager," Foxy murmured, fighting against the building ache in her head.

"And a great human being," Lance added sarcastically.

"Lance," Foxy began with the first stirrings of curiosity, "were you protecting me?"

When he turned on her, she watched his temper boil in his eyes. Her curiosity increased as she watched him control it. "Maybe," he muttered, then turned to the phone. Foxy heard him mumble a series of instructions but paid no attention to the words.

Odd, she thought, *he seems to be making a habit of protecting me. First in Italy, and now here. It certainly doesn't seem to make him very comfortable, though.* She continued to study him after he had hung up the phone. Instantly he began to pace the room just as he had paced the waiting area in the hospital.

"Lance." He stopped when she quietly said his name. Foxy held out her hand, realizing suddenly how grateful she was that he was there. She wasn't ready to be alone yet. She wasn't feeling strong and capable and indestructible, but tired and vulnerable and afraid. Lance stared at her a moment without moving, then crossed to her to take the offered hand. "Thank you." Her eyes were dark and grave as they clung to his. "It's just occurred to me that I wouldn't have made it through all this without knowing you were there. I didn't even realize that I needed you, but you did. I want you to know how much it means to me."

Something flickered over his face before he raked his free hand through his hair. It was an uncharacteristic gesture of frustration, which reminded Foxy that he was as weary as she. "Fox," he began, but she continued quickly.

"You won't go away tomorrow, will you?" Knowing she was being weak did not prevent her from asking. She needed him, and her hand tightened on his. "If you could just stay for a couple of extra days, just until things settle. I can lie," she continued in a voice which was growing desperate. "I can walk right in that hospital room tomorrow and look at Kirk, look right in his eyes and lie. It's a trick I've learned over the years; and I'm good at it. He'll never have to know how much I hate him being in there. But if you could stay, if I could just know you were there. I know it's a lot to ask, but I…" She stopped, then pressed both hands to her eyes. "Oh, Lord, I think the numbness is wearing off." She heard the knock at the door, but took deep steadying breaths, leaving Lance to answer it. In a moment, she heard him move back to her.

"Foxy." He spoke her name gently and took her wrist until she had lowered her hands. Her eyes were young and devastated. "Drink this." He held out a glass filled with the brandy room service had delivered. Though she took it obediently, she only stared down into the amber liquid. Lance watched her for a moment, then crouched down until their eyes were level. "Fox." He waited until she had shifted her gaze from the brandy to him. "Marry me."

"What?" Foxy stared at him, saw the familiar intentness in his eyes, then squeezed her own shut. "What?" she said again, opening them.

Lance urged the brandy toward her lips. "I said, marry me."

Foxy drank the entire contents of the glass in one swallow. Her breath caught on the burn of the brandy, and the small sound thundered in the absolute silence of the room. For several long seconds, she stared into his eyes trying to penetrate the impenetrable. She sensed that under the calm lay a whirlpool of energy, a power that would escape at any instant. He held something, she was unsure what, on a very tight leash. Tension gripped tight in her throat. She tried to swallow it and failed. Her eyes remained steady on his, but her voice was only a whisper. She was afraid. "Why?"

"Why not?" he countered then took the empty glass from her nerveless fingers.

"Why not?" Foxy repeated. She lifted her hand to make some helpless gesture, but he caught it in his own. Her fingers trembled as he brought them to his lips. Steadily he watched her.

"Yes, why not?"

"I don't know, I…" He had succeeded in distracting her with the unconventional proposal. She ran her free hand through her hair and tried to think properly. "There must be a reason, I just can't think."

"Well, if you can't think of any substantial reason against it, marry me and come to Boston."

"Boston?" Foxy echoed him blankly.

"Boston," Lance agreed, and for the first time, a faint smile touched his lips. "I live there, remember?"

"Yes, of course." Foxy rubbed a line between her brows and struggled to concentrate. "Of course I remember."

"We could leave when you were confident that Kirk was settled. More than likely, he'll be staying here for the next couple of months, but there's no need for you to be here." Lance's voice was practical, his face absolutely calm. Frustrated and unsure, Foxy shook her head. *I'm hallucinating. Hallucinations don't hurt,* she reminded herself, then quickly shook off the argument. It was easier to believe it was an illusion than to believe Lance was asking her to marry him in the same tone he might ask her to fetch him a cup of coffee.

"Lance, I…" Foxy hesitated, then decided to evade the issue rather than face it head-on. "I don't think I'm taking all this in properly. I'm still a little fuzzy." She swallowed and tried to match his casual tone. "Let me think about it. Give me a day or two."

Lance inclined his head. "That sounds reasonable," he

agreed as she rose to move away from him. "No," he said, causing her to turn and gape at him.

"What did you say?"

"I said no, you can't think about it for a day or two." In one quick gesture, he had her firmly by the shoulders and had abolished the distance between them. Foxy saw that his eyes were no longer calm but turbulent. He had held her like this before, she remembered, and had looked at her in precisely the same way. Years ago, she reflected, confused and foolishly disoriented, in the empty garage at Le Mans. Was he going to shout at her again? she wondered. Her brows drew together as she tried to keep the past and present separate.

"What do you want?" she asked, struggling with her feelings for him.

"You." He pulled her yet closer as his eyes burned into hers. "I'm not about to let you walk out of my life, Fox, and I've waited for you long enough." His mouth lowered swiftly but was gentle on hers. Even so, she could feel the imprisoned passion in the grip of his hands. The kiss was thorough, possessive. "Did you really think I'd calmly walk out that door and give you a couple of days to think it over?" His mouth closed over hers again, preventing any response she might have made. Once again, he drew her away, this time to stare down into her bemused eyes. "Do you think I could want you the way that I do, then walk away after you've told me you need me?"

"Lance, I didn't mean to…" Foxy shook her head as she searched for some scraps of common sense. "You shouldn't feel obligated, I was grateful…."

"The hell with grateful," he declared, then grabbed her hair with both hands. "I'm not interested in some nice, patient emotion like gratitude. That's not what I want from you." Foxy saw the determination in his face, heard the fire in his voice. Her blood began to heat in response. "I don't give a damn if the timing's wrong, or that I'm pressing you when your defenses are down. I'm a selfish man, Foxy, and I've wanted you for longer than I care to think about. I'm going to have you."

Her pulse was beating so quickly, she was giddy. She steadied herself, placing her hands on his arms. "Lance…" Her voice would not behave but insisted on coming out in breathless whispers. "What you're talking about isn't what's necessary for marriage. That's a big step, a lifetime commitment, I don't know…"

"I love you," he said and stopped her speech cold. Her lips trembled open to form words which would not come. "I want to spend my life with you, and I'm not going back to Boston without you. I can't give you the candlelight and soft words that might smooth the road because I haven't the time or patience for them right now. I'll have to make it up to you later." His hands moved from her hair to her shoulders to her waist, but he brought her no closer. "Foxy, you drive me out of my mind." As she watched, she saw both demand and doubt flicker in his eyes. "You love me, too, I know you do."

"Yes." She rested her cheek against his chest and sighed. "Yes, I love you. Hold me," she murmured, finding again she fit perfectly into his arms. "I need you to hold me." For the next few moments, she allowed herself the incredible luxury of being held and cherished by the man she loved. It's all happening so fast, she thought, then pushed away the fears and listened to the steady drum of Lance's heart. *He loves me.* "Lance." Tilting her head, Foxy brought her lips to his. Instantly his mouth answered hers, passion for passion, wonder for wonder, until their bodies were heated and entwined. Lance loosened his hold as she shivered from spiraling emotions.

"We can be married in a couple of days." He spoke calmly again, but his hands wandered up and down her back before they rested on her hips. "The paperwork will take that long. Then we'll go to Boston." His eye grew serious on her face. "Pam will be here for Kirk, you understand that, don't you?"

"Yes." Foxy closed her eyes a moment and tried to block out the rushing image of the accident. "Yes, that's for the best. I want to go," she told him as she opened her eyes. "I want to be with you." Her nerves were jumping inside her stomach, refusing to grow steady, and she met his mouth desperately. Foxy felt his hunger and matched it. "Stay with me tonight," she whispered as she buried her face against his neck. "I don't want you to go."

Slowly Lance drew her away and scanned her face. Her cheeks were still pale, her eyes like smoke against her skin. Already there were faint shadows haunting them. "No." He shook his head as he brushed the back of his hand down her cheek. "You're too vulnerable tonight, I've already taken advantage of that. You need sleep." With this, he swept her up in his arms and carried her to the bed. Foxy's body responded to the weightlessness by floating with the fatigue. After he laid her on the mattress, he sat beside her. "Do you want anything?"

"Tell me again."

Lance lifted her hand and turned the palm to his lips. "I love you. Will you sleep?"

"Yes, yes, I'll sleep." Foxy could feel the weariness pressing down on her. She closed her eyes and immediately began to dream. Lance's lips were a soft promise on hers.

"I'll come for you in the morning," he murmured. Dimly she felt the bed shift as he stood. She was asleep before the door closed behind him.

CHAPTER 8

Sunlight fell fresh and brilliant over Foxy's face. She moaned as it began to penetrate her slumber. Her mind gently floated to the surface, noticing small, inconsequential things: the rapid ticking of her travel alarm on the stand beside the bed, the vague itch between her shoulder blades, the uncomfortable warmth of the spread that lay on top of her. She had huddled under it during the night when she awakened cold and frightened in the dark. She did not remember the nightmare yet, the vivid clarity in which she had relived Kirk's crash. She had awakened, panting for breath, cold as ice, with terror ripping away all thought of sleep. She did not remember yet that the tears had finally come in torrents until her eyes were raw and her ribs ached from the strain. She had wept herself numb, then had fallen into a fitful sleep, plagued with doubts about her unconventional engagement to Lance. Perhaps he had proposed out of a sense of duty. Foxy had tried to recapture the feeling she had experienced when he had told her he loved her, but she was cold and miserable. She had huddled under the blanket and wished for morning.

Now that it was here, she found the light annoying and the spread stifling. She shifted crossly, still half asleep, and wished the spread would disappear without her having to move. As her consciousness swam reluctantly closer to the surface her memory began to merge with it. Her mind clear, she sat up abruptly and rested her face on her knees.

Pull yourself together, Foxy, she ordered, drawing her breath slowly in and out of her lungs. *You had a bad night; now shake it off and get down to business. Lance will be here soon.* Lifting her head, Foxy narrowed her eyes and stared at her left hand, trying to imagine an engagement ring on the third finger.

"I'm going to marry him," she said aloud, just to hear how the words would sound. Her stomach shivered, announcing the state of her nerves. It came to her abruptly that she knew absolutely nothing about the man who lived in Boston and ran a multimillion-dollar business. The Lance Matthews she knew was a cocky ex-driver who played a mean hand of poker and knew how to tear down an engine. The only hint she had seen of the other side of him had been on their date in Monte Carlo. It was, she reflected, not enough. She was going to marry him without knowing the whole man. Did he belong to the country club? Did he play golf on Saturdays? Foxy tried to imagine Lance swinging a nine iron and got nowhere. Shutting her eyes, she let the reckless side of her push away the doubts. *This is no time to sit around thinking,* she told herself. *What does it matter if he plays golf or backgammon or if he's into yoga? What does it matter if he wears a three-piece suit and carries a briefcase or if he wears jeans and sneakers?* Biting down on her lips, Foxy wondered when she had sewn this particular patchwork of thought together. *I've got to get up and put myself together so that I don't look like a zombie when he gets here.*

Throwing off the spread, Foxy rose from the bed and discovered that every muscle in her body was taking revenge on her for the restless night. *A hot shower,* she reflected, and began to strip off the clothes she had slept in. *I'm not nervous, I'm just groggy.* When Lance knocked at her door thirty minutes later, Foxy was just completing her attempt to camouflage the results of the wakeful night.

She wore a plain yellow shift, with her hair neatly coiled at her neck. Lance studied her face carefully before speaking. Her eyes were freed now from shock but were still haunted by shadows. He took her chin in his hand and frowned. Her fragile looks were intensified by the violet smudges under her eyes. Weeping had left them faintly swollen and weary.

"You've been crying," he accused, making Foxy realize that all her attempts with base and blusher and mascara had been for nothing. His voice was taut, and she could feel the tension in his fingers. It added to her own. "Didn't you sleep?" he demanded.

"Not very well," she admitted and wondered why he seemed so angry. "I woke during the night. It all seemed to hit me at once."

Lance's frown deepened. "I should have stayed."

"No." She shook her head, searching his eyes for the reason for the roughness in his voice. "I needed to be alone to get it out of my system. I'm better now."

Something flickered in his eyes before they became unfathomable. "Have you changed your mind?"

Foxy knew he was speaking of their marriage and felt a quick thrill of alarm. She forced herself to speak calmly. "No."

Lance nodded and released her chin. "Fine. We'll take care of the paperwork before we go by the hospital. Ready?"

Foxy frowned but stepped into the corridor, closing the door at her back. "When we see Kirk," she began as they walked toward the steps, "I'd like to tell him about our plans myself…when the time's right."

Lance's brow lifted and fell. "Fine."

Miffed by his tone and by his cool self-possession, Foxy tilted her face to his and spoke coldly. "Maybe I should've asked if you'd changed your mind."

"I'd have let you know if I had," he returned as they stepped into the sunlight.

"Undoubtedly," she agreed. Saying nothing, Lance led her to the sleek blue Porsche he had rented that morning. For the first time since her screaming fear of the previous afternoon, Foxy began to feel the full emotion of anger. "Are you going to have your lawyers draw up a contract? I want to be certain to read the fine print."

"Save it, Foxy," Lance warned and opened the passenger door.

"No." She stood back and glared. "I don't know why you're acting like this. Maybe you're just a miserable human being in the mornings. I'll get used to it, I suppose. But you'd better get used to the fact that I say what I want when I want. If you don't like it, you can—"

Her tirade was cut off as he slammed the door shut and pulled her roughly into his arms. His mouth came down hard on hers. Angry and dominant, his lips bruised hers while she stood too surprised to protest or respond. He held her, ravishing her mouth until she was breathless. Then, with a suddenness that left her gasping, he set her aside. "And I know how to shut you up when I don't want to hear it."

Foxy managed one indignant huff. "You're a maniac," she told him as he opened her door again.

"All right," he agreed. Then, without giving her a chance for further comment, he nudged her into the car.

For the first time, Foxy noticed two young girls standing on the sidewalk giggling. Furious and embarrassed, she folded her arms and clamped her lips shut. She would not give him the satisfaction of either arguing or submitting herself to his idle conversation. In utter silence, they drove off to secure a marriage license.

A scant two hours later, after speaking only when unavoidable, they walked into Kirk's hospital room. Foxy did her best not to register any shock at the sight of the bandages and plaster. His leg was surrounded by an external fixture rather than a cast. To Foxy's eyes it looked like an erector set built by a clever teenager. Surrounded by white sheets and bandages, tubes and metal, Kirk lay propped up in bed. He was scowling at Pam with the look of a man who has just finished giving a heated speech. Instantly Foxy sensed the tension and glanced from one to the other. She thought it best to employ tact and make no comment. Because she had known Kirk would hate them, she hadn't brought any flowers. Empty-handed, she crossed to the bed and gravely studied him.

"You're a mess," she concluded, making her voice lightly scornful. Her stomach trembled at the amount of bandages and the terrifyingly foreign-looking apparatus around his leg. As she had hoped, the scowl faded and a grin took its place.

"You're cute, too. Hi, Lance. I think I might have dented a fender on your car."

"Scraped the paint, too," he said easily as his hands disappeared into his pockets. Watching him, Pam noted that he was uncomfortable in hospital rooms. Foxy, she mused, was putting up a front Kirk would see through if it occurred to him to look. But of course it wouldn't. "I'd keep clear of Charlie for a while," Lance advised as he glanced over to find Pam's eyes on him. Her face was composed, but he could detect the signs of a sleepless night. He had seen the expression she wore before, on wives, parents, and lovers of countless other drivers. A quick, silent understanding passed between them before he looked back at Kirk.

"I heard Betinni took first and hooked the championship." Hampered by the position, Kirk's shrug was awkward. "He's a good driver. We've been passing off the lead all season." He shifted a bit, and Foxy caught the brief wince of pain. Knowing sympathy would only earn her a growl, she turned to Pam.

"Well," she said with a smile a shade too bright, "I don't suppose he's been giving you any trouble."

"On the contrary." Pam glanced at Kirk, then back to his sister. "He's been giving me a great deal."

"Pam." Kirk's irritated tone held a warning. She ignored both.

"He's ordered me back to Manhattan. He's very annoyed because I'm not going."

Unsure what to say, Foxy looked from Pam to Kirk, then to Lance. "Well," she said and cleared her throat.

"He seems to think I'm being quite unreasonable," Pam added in the same mild tone.

"And stupid," Kirk tossed out. His scowl was back, deeper than before.

"Oh yes." Pam smiled gently. "And stupid. I'd forgotten that."

"Look," Kirk began, and Foxy recognized the dangerous pitch in his voice. "You've got no reason to hang around here."

"I've got a hospital fetish," Pam returned.

"Damn it, I don't want you!" Kirk shouted, then cursed at the pain that followed his outburst.

Firmly Lance took Foxy's arm as she started to move forward. "Keep out of it," he ordered quietly.

"Too bad," Pam retorted. Her voice was soft, but she stood like a general facing the enemy, her shoulders straight. The sun streamed through the window behind her, haloing her hair. "You're not getting rid of me. I love you."

"You're crazy," Kirk threw back, fidgeting in the bed.

"Very likely."

He narrowed his eyes at her careless response. In the strong sunlight, her skin looked like alabaster. He felt the need rise surprisingly fast. "I'm not letting you stay," he ground out in defense.

"What're you going to do?" Pam countered with a shrug. "Kick me back to Manhattan with your good leg?"

"I will as soon as I can get up," Kirk muttered, furious that he had to lay flat on his back to argue with a woman half his size.

"Yeah?" The slang came with elegant ease from Pam's delicately tinted lips. She walked over and gave his mustache a hard tug that brought out a sound of surprised protest. "Remind me to be scared later. Now as I see it I've got three choices. I can murder you, jump off a bridge, or I can cope. I come from a long line of copers. You, on the other hand," she added with a pat on his cheek, "simply have no choice at all. You're stuck with me."

"Think so, huh?" Kirk's mouth twisted into a reluctant grin. "Guess you're pretty tough."

"You guess right," she agreed, then bent to kiss him lightly. Kirk grabbed a handful of her hair and took the kiss deeper.

"We're going to settle this when I can stand up," he muttered, but pulled her back to kiss her again.

"I'm sure we will," Pam said with a smile as she sat on the edge of the bed. Foxy noted that his hand sought hers.

He loves her, she realized suddenly. *He really loves her.* Her eyes fastened on Pam with a look of respect and hope. *Maybe,* she thought rapidly, *maybe she's the answer. Maybe he's finally found an alternative.*

"Well." Pam smiled into Foxy's bemused face. "Is there any news from the outside world?"

"News?" Foxy repeated, trying to reorganize her thoughts.

"Earthquakes, floods, wars, famine," Pam prompted with a laugh. "I feel I've been neatly cut off for the past twenty-four hours."

"There hasn't been any of those that I know of," Foxy answered with a glance at Kirk. *This is the time,* she told herself. *This is the time to tell him.* Suddenly she felt ridiculously nervous and awkward. "Lance and I," she began, then her eyes sought his for reassurance. Taking a deep breath, she looked back at Kirk and spoke quickly. "Lance and I are going to be married." Instantly Foxy saw the surprise and puzzlement cover Kirk's face. His brows drew together as he stared at her.

"Well!" Pam rose quickly and hugged Foxy. "This is news. The best kind." Glancing over Foxy's head, she met Lance's eyes. "You're a very lucky man."

"Yes," he returned, unsmiling. "I know."

"Married?" Kirk interrupted. "What do you mean, married?"

"The usual definition," Foxy told him as she moved to his bedside. "You've heard it before, it's still quite popular."

"When?" he demanded shortly.

"As soon as the blood tests and paperwork are taken care of," Lance put in casually. After strolling over to the bed, he slipped an arm around Foxy's shoulders. Kirk watched the gesture, then lifted his eyes to Lance's face. "What's the matter?" Lance asked him with a grin. "Did you want us to get your permission?"

"No," Kirk mumbled uncomfortably. Looking up into Foxy's face, he remembered the little girl. "Yeah," he admitted with a sigh. "Maybe. I could have used a little warning, anyway."

"You're hardly in any shape to beat him up now," Foxy

pointed out. Lance's arm around her eased away her tension, and her eyes laughed down at Kirk.

Kirk studied his best friend and then his sister. When he held out his hand, Foxy slipped hers into it. "You sure?"

Foxy turned her head until she faced Lance. *He's the only man I've ever loved,* she mused. *It's not a fantasy anymore, but real. Am I sure?* she asked herself, keeping both her mind and heart open. She took her time studying his familiar face, then answered the question she thought she saw in his eyes. "Yes," she said and smiled. "I'm sure." Rising on her toes, she met his mouth and felt the morning's nerves drain away. "Very sure." Her hand was still warm in Kirk's. "Don't worry about me," she told Kirk as she turned back to him.

"It's a new habit I've gotten into, but be happy and I won't worry," he countered, foolishly feeling as if something precious was being stolen from him. "I guess you're all grown up."

"I guess so," she said softly and returned the pressure of his hand.

"Give me a kiss," he ordered. After Foxy raised her head again, Kirk fastened his eyes on Lance. An essential male understanding passed between them. They knew each other as well as brothers ever do, but now they were joined deeper by the woman between them. Perhaps if they had not been close, had not been intimate with each other's thoughts over the years, it would have been simpler. The very quality of their friendship made it complex. "Don't hurt her," Kirk warned as he kept possession of Foxy's hand. "Are you going to live in that house in Boston?"

"That's right," Lance answered. Foxy watched them, knowing they said more than she could translate.

Abruptly Kirk's expression softened and a smile appeared. "I'm not going to be in any shape to walk down an aisle to give her away." He squeezed the hand he held in his, lingering over it a moment before he offered it to Lance. "Keep her happy," he commanded as Foxy's hand passed from one man to the other.

CHAPTER 9

Three days later, Foxy sat in Lance's rented Porsche as it ate up the miles between New York and Massachusetts. Her hands lay in her lap but were rarely still. She continued to twist the plain gold band around and around the third finger of her left hand. *Married,* she thought yet again. *We're actually married.* It had been so quick, so lacking in emotion—a few moments in front of a blank-faced judge, a few words spoken. An unruffled fifteen minutes. It had been almost like a play until the ring had slipped onto her finger. That made it real. That made her Mrs. Lancelot Matthews.

Cynthia Matthews, she mused, trying out the sound in her mind. *Or perhaps,* she reflected, *I could try for more elegance with Cynthia Fox-Matthews.* She nearly laughed aloud. *Elegance needs more than a hyphen. Foxy Matthews,* she decided with a mental nod. *That'll just have to be good enough.*

"You're going to wear a ridge into your finger before we get to Rhode Island." Lance spoke quietly, but Foxy jumped in her seat as if he had shouted. "Nervous?" he asked with a laugh in his voice.

"No." Not wanting to confess what silliness her mind had been engaged in, she prevaricated. "I was just thinking…Kirk looked much better, didn't he?"

"Um-hum." Lance switched on the wipers as a light rain began to fall. "Pam's the best medicine he can get."

"Yes, she is." Foxy shifted in her seat so that she had a clear view of his profile. *My husband,* she thought and nearly lost the thread of the conversation. "I've never known anyone else who could handle Kirk so well. Except you."

"Kirk needs a co-driver who can't be intimidated into backing off," Lance told her, glancing toward her briefly. "You've always handled him in your own way. Even when you were thirteen, you could do it without letting him know he was being handled."

The faintest frown line appeared between Foxy's brows. "I never considered it handling exactly…. And I didn't realize anyone else noticed."

"There isn't anything about you I haven't noticed over the years." Lance turned to her again with a deep, quiet look. Foxy's pulse hammered erratically.

Will he always be able to do this to me? she wondered. *Even after the novelty of marriage wears off, will he be able just to look at me to turn me into jelly? It hasn't changed in ten years, will it change in ten more?* Lance's voice broke into her thoughts, and she twisted her head to look at him again. "I'm sorry, what?"

"I said it was a nice gesture for you to give Pam your bouquet. Of course, it's rather a shame you don't have some small remembrance."

Foxy started to speak, then flushed and fumbled in her bag for her brush. Buried at the bottom was the white velvet ribbon she had removed from the spray of orchids Lance had given her for a bridal bouquet. The thought that he might think her sentiment foolish held her tongue. She had the brush in her hand before she remembered her hair was pinned up. Hastily she stuffed the brush back in her bag. Rain pattered lightly on the windows and blurred the autumn landscape.

"I suppose it was a bit cut and dried, wasn't it?" Lance commented. "Ten minutes in front of a judge, no friends or traditional trappings, no tears or rice." He glanced at her again, his brow lifted under his hair. "I suppose you're feeling a bit cheated."

"No, of course not." Though her mind had wandered once or twice to the complicated beauty of a traditional wedding, she didn't feel cheated so much as curious. *Would she feel married if the wedding had included veils and organ music? Would she have this awkward sense of it not being quite real if there had been a ceremony ending with old shoes and rice?* "Besides," she said with a shake of her head. "I don't have any Great-aunt Sarah to weep softly in the back pew." The thought of family had her worrying her wedding band again.

"You did specify plain gold with no stones or markings?"

"What?" Foxy followed Lance's brief glance to her hands. "Oh, yes." Guiltily she dropped her right hand to her side. "Yes, it's exactly what I wanted."

"Does it fit?"

"Fit? Why yes, it fits."

"Then why the devil do you keep twisting it on your finger?" The annoyance in his tone was sharp.

Well aware it was justified, Foxy sighed. "I'm sorry, Lance. It all seems to be happening so fast, and going to Boston…" She bit her lip, then confessed. "I'm nervous about meeting your family. I haven't had a great deal of experience with families."

Lance lay his hand on hers a moment. "Don't judge the way of families by mine," he advised dryly. "They're not the type you see on a Christmas card."

"Of course," Foxy concluded with a wry grin, "that's supposed to reassure me."

"Just don't let them bother you," Lance advised with a careless shrug. "I don't."

"Easy for you to say," she retorted, wrinkling her nose at him. "You're one of them."

"So are you." Lifting her hand, Lance ran his thumb over her wedding band. "Remember it."

"Tell me about them."

"I suppose I'll have to sooner or later." With this, he drew out a cigar and punched in the car lighter. "My mother is a Bardett—that's an old Boston family. I believe they gave Paul Revere directions."

"How patriotic."

"The Bardetts are notoriously patriotic," he returned before he touched the glowing lighter to the tip of his cigar. "In any case, my mother enjoys being both a Bardett and a Matthews, but more than anything else, she enjoys committees."

"Committees?" Foxy repeated. "What sorts of committees?"

"All sorts of committees, as long as they're suitable for a Bardett-Matthews. She loves to organize them, attend them, complain about them. She's a snob from the top of her pure white coiffure to the tip of her Italian shoes."

"Lance, how dreadful of you."

"You said you wanted to hear about them," he countered easily. "Mother loves doing charitable work. It reads well in the society pages. She also feels anyone poor enough to require aid should have the good taste not to ask for it until she has a chance to organize the committee. But snob or not, she does a lot of good despite her motives, so it hardly matters."

"You're being very hard on her." Foxy frowned at the tone of his voice as she remembered her own mother: a happy, disorganized, loving woman with Kirk's penchant for ragged sneakers.

Lance gave Foxy a curious, sidelong glance. "Perhaps. She and I have never seen things the same way. My father used to find her committees amusing and harmless. I'm not as tolerant as he was." Foxy's frown deepened, and he gave her his crooked smile. "Don't worry, Fox, you won't see any blood spilled. We don't get along, but we're quite civilized about it. Bardetts, you see, are always civilized."

"And the Matthews?" Foxy asked, becoming intrigued.

"The Matthews have a tendency to produce a black sheep every generation or so. A couple of hundred years back, a Matthews ran off and married a serving wench from a local tavern. Spoiled the blood a bit." He grinned as if pleased with the flaw, then drew on his cigar. "But for the most part, the Matthews are every bit as…upstanding as the Bardetts. My grandmother is all dignity. According to the stories that drop from time to time, she never batted an eye when my grandfather had his affair with the countess. As far as she was concerned, it didn't happen. Her daughter, my aunt Phoebe, is exactly as the countess said: dull. She hasn't had an original thought in fifty years. There's an alarming amount of aunts, uncles, cousins, and in-laws."

"They don't all live in Boston, do they?"

"No, thank heaven. They're spread over the States and Europe, but a large clutch huddle in Boston and Martha's Vineyard and thereabouts."

"I suppose your mother was surprised when you told her about our getting married." Foxy caught herself before she twisted the ring again.

"I haven't told her."

"What?" Incredulous, she turned to stare at him. "You didn't tell her?"

"No."

Foxy started to demand why, then thought of the reason herself. *He's ashamed of me.* Swallowing, she twisted back to stare at the gray autumn rain. Cynthia Fox of Indiana doesn't measure up to the Bardetts and Matthews of Boston. "I suppose," she said in a tight voice, "you could keep me hidden in an attic room. Or we could forge a pedigree."

"Hmm?" Preoccupied, Lance glanced at her averted head, then back at the road. After passing a slow-moving truck, he tossed his cigar out the window.

For several moments, Foxy tried to hold her tongue and temper. She failed. "We could tell them I'm a deposed princess from some Third World country. I won't speak any English for the first six months." She rounded on him, hurt and furious. "Or I could be the daughter of some English baron who died and left me penniless. After all, it's the lineage that's important, not the money."

Her tone captured Lance's attention. Looking over, he caught the sheen of angry tears in her eyes. Instantly his brows drew together. "What are you babbling about?"

"If you don't think I'm good enough to pass as Mrs. Lancelot Matthews, then you can just…" Her suggestion was lost as he whipped the car to the shoulder of the road. Before she could catch her breath, he had her arms in a punishing grip.

"Don't you ever let me hear you say that again, do you understand?" His face was furious, but Foxy tilted her chin and met it levelly.

"No, no, I don't understand. I don't understand anything." To her humiliation, tears began to well up in her eyes and spill out onto her cheeks. The weeping surprised both of them; her because it began so suddenly, not giving her an opportunity to control it, and him because he had never seen her cry before.

"Don't," Lance ordered roughly, then gave her a brisk shake. "Don't do that."

"I will if I want to." Foxy swallowed and let the tears fall.

Lance swore before he let her go. "All right, go ahead. We'll swim back to Boston, but I want to know what brought on the flood."

Foxy fumbled in her purse for a tissue and found none. "I don't have a tissue," she said miserably, then wiped at the tears with the back of her hand. With another well-chosen oath, Lance pulled his handkerchief from his jacket pocket and stuffed it into her hand. "It's silk," she said and tried to give it back to him.

"I'll strangle you with it in a minute." As if to prevent himself from doing so, Lance gripped the steering wheel. "We're not moving," he said in a firm voice, "until you tell me what's gotten into you."

"It's nothing, nothing at all," she claimed as she dampened the white silk. Foxy was thoroughly disgusted with herself, but her temper forced her to continue. "Why should it bother me that you haven't even told your family we're married?"

For a few moments, there was only the sound of the drizzling rain and Foxy's sniffles. The car became still except for the monotonous back-and-forth movement of the windshield wipers. "Do you think," Lance began in even, precise tones, "that I didn't tell my family of our marriage because I'm ashamed of you?"

"What else should I think?" Foxy tossed back. "I don't suppose a Fox from Indiana is very impressive."

"Idiot!" The word vibrated in the small closed car. Foxy's sob was transformed into a gasp. Fascinated, she watched Lance struggle to control what appeared to be a violent surge of temper. When he spoke, it was too soft and too controlled. "I didn't tell my family because I wanted a couple of days of peace before they descend on us. As soon as they know we're married, the whole social merry-go-round gets started. A honeymoon would have been the ideal answer, but I explained to you it's impossible until I straightened out a few things. I've been away from the business for several months. I felt after the circuit and Kirk's accident, we both could use a few days of quiet. It never occurred to me you'd see it as anything else."

With a quick gesture of his hand, Lance put the car in first gear and merged back into the traffic. The silence was complete and unbearable. Foxy crumpled Lance's handkerchief into a tight ball and wished for a way to begin the conversation over again.

The days since Kirk's accident had been jumbled together into a mass of time rather than distinct minutes and hours. She knew she had slept and eaten, but could not have told how many hours her eyes had been closed or what food she had tasted. Her marriage seemed steeped in unreality. But it is real, she reminded herself. And Lance is right. I'm an idiot.

"I'm sorry, Lance," she murmured, lifting her eyes to his profile.

"Forget it." His answer was curt and unforgiving. Recognizing the dismissal in his tone, she turned back to the view of misty rain.

Are all brides so insecure? she wondered, closing her eyes. *This isn't like me. I'm acting like a different person, I'm thinking like a different person.* Weariness began to close over her, and she let her mind drift. *I'll feel better once we're settled in. A few days of quiet is exactly what I need.* She let the pattering rain lull her to sleep.

Foxy moaned and stirred. She no longer heard the steady hum of the Porsche beneath her but felt a quiet swaying. She felt a cool spray on her face and turned her head away from it. Her cheek brushed something warm and smooth. The scent that teased her nostrils was instantly familiar. Opening her eyes, she saw Lance's jawline. Gradually she realized she was being carried. She nuzzled her face into his shoulder as the rain continued to fall halfheartedly. A gloomy dusk was settling, bringing with it a thin fog.

Along with Lance's scent she could detect the fragrance of damp leaves and grass, an autumn smell she would soon begin to associate with New England. His footsteps were nearly soundless, swallowed by the mists swirling close to the ground. There was something eerie and surreal about the dimming light and silence. Disoriented, Foxy shifted in his arms.

"Decide to join the living again?" Lance asked. He stopped, heedless of the drizzle and looked down at her.

"Where are we?" Totally confused, Foxy twisted her head to peer around. Almost at once, she saw the house. A three-story brownstone rose in front of her. Its walls were cloaked in ivy, dark green and glistening in the rain. Wrought-iron balconies circled the second and third stories, and they, too, were tangled with clinging ivy. The windows were tall and narrow. Even in the gloom, the house had an ageless elegance and style. "Is that your house?" Foxy asked. As she spoke she let her head fall back in order to see the roof and chimney.

"It was my grandfather's," Lance answered, studying her reaction. "He left it to me. My grandmother always preferred their house in Martha's Vineyard."

"It's beautiful," Foxy murmured. The rain that washed her face and dampened her hair was forgotten. She felt an immediate affection for the aged brownstone and tenacious ivy. *He had roots in this house,* she thought, and fell in love. "It's really beautiful."

"Yes, it is," Lance agreed as his eyes roamed her face.

Foxy looked up to meet his gaze. She smiled, blinking raindrops from her lashes. "It's raining," she pointed out.

"So it is." He kissed her, lingering for a moment. "Your lips are wet. I like the way the rain clings to your hair. In this light you look very pale and ethereal." His eyes were the color of the mist that grew thicker and seemed to be spun into threads around them. "If I let you go, will you vanish?"

"No," she murmured, then combed her fingers through the damp hair that fell over his forehead. "I won't vanish." A quick surge of need for him throbbed through her, causing her to shiver.

"I suppose you're real enough to catch a chill from standing in the rain." He tightened his grip on her and began to walk again.

"You don't have to carry me," she began.

Lance climbed nimbly up the front steps. "Don't you think we should do something traditional?" he countered as he maneuvered a key into the lock of the door. Pushing it open with his shoulder, he carried Foxy over the threshold and into the darkened house. "Welcome home," he murmured, then captured her lips in a long, quiet kiss.

"Lance," she whispered, incredibly moved. "I love you."

Slowly he set her on her feet. For a moment, they stood close, their faces silhouetted by the darkening sky. Before they closed the door, Foxy decided, there should be nothing between them. "Lance, I'm sorry about making that scene in the car."

"You've already apologized."

"You were angry enough for two apologies."

He laughed and kissed her nose, changed his mind and took her mouth again. It seemed that he could draw from a kiss more than she had known she had to offer. "Anger is the handiest weapon against tears," he told her as he ran his hands up and down her arms. "You threw me, Fox. You always do when you forget to be invincible." He lifted his finger to run it along her jawline, and his eyes were dark as he watched the journey. "Perhaps I should have explained things to you, but I'm simply not used to explaining myself to anyone. We're both going to have some adjustments to make." He took both her hands in his, then lifted them to his lips. "Trust me for a while, will you?"

"All right." She nodded. "I'll try."

After releasing her hands, Lance closed the door, shutting out the damp chill. For an instant, the house was plunged into total darkness, then abruptly the entrance hall streamed with light. Foxy stood in its center and turned around in a slow circle. To her left was a staircase, gleaming and uncarpeted. Its oak banister looked smooth as silk. To her right was a mirrored clothes stand that had once reflected the face of Lance's great-great-grandmother. He watched as she made a study of Revere candlesticks and a gilt-framed Gainsborough. The light from the chandelier showered down on her, catching the glint of rain in her hair. She had a wraithlike quality in the simple green dress she had chosen to wear as a bride. It had long narrow sleeves and a high mandarin collar. Its skirt fell straight and unadorned from a snug waist. Her only jewelry was the plain gold band he had placed on her finger. She looked as untouched as springtime, but the sensuality of autumn was in her movements.

"I wouldn't have pictured you in a place like this," Foxy said after completing her circle.

"Oh?" Lance leaned against the wall and waited for her to elaborate.

"It's beautiful," she went on in a voice touched with wonder. "Really beautiful, but it's so…settled," she decided, then looked back at him. "I suppose that's it. I've never thought of you as settled."

"I enjoy being settled now and again," was his careless answer. Foxy thought that in the trim gray suit he looked at ease amid the ivy and brownstone. Yet there was something in his eyes, she realized, that would never quite be tamed. Expert tailoring and priceless antiques would never alter the man he was. Knowing she was mad to prefer the sinner to the saint, Foxy was nevertheless glad.

"But I should be prepared to pack at a moment's notice?" she asked, giving him a smile a great deal like her brother's.

"How fortunate I am to have married a woman who understands me." His grin was crooked and familiar and still managed to send her pulse racing. He moved toward her, then wound one of the curls that framed her face around his finger. "And an exceptional-looking creature as well; quite bright, quick with her tongue, impulsive enough to be fascinating, and with a voice that constantly sounds like she's just been aroused."

Foxy flushed with a mixture of amusement and embarrassment. "Sounds like you made quite a deal."

"Oh, I did," Lance agreed but his grin faded and he studied her with serious eyes. "A smart businessman knows when to make his pitch." As quickly as it had grown grave, his expression lightened. Bemused, Foxy watched the changes. "Hungry?" he asked suddenly.

Intrigued, Foxy shook her head. "No, not really." She remembered the long hours he had spent driving, "I suppose there must be a can or something around I could open."

"I think we might do better." Taking her hand, Lance led her down the hallway. The rooms to the right and left were dark and mysterious. "I called Mrs. Trilby yesterday. She does the housekeeping and so forth. I told her I was coming in and to have things ready. I'm not fond of dustcovers and empty pantries." He passed through a door at the end of the hall. As he turned the switch light spilled into the kitchen.

"Oh, it's wonderful!" Foxy cried as she moved into the room. "Does it work?" she demanded, going immediately to the small arched fireplace that was built into one wall.

"Yes, it works." Lance smiled as she bent closer to peer inside.

"I love it," she said with a laugh as she straightened. "I'll probably want a fire in it in August." She ran her finger over a pine trestle table, which stood in the bow of a bay window. "The only fire I have in my kitchen is when I burn the bacon."

"This is your kitchen," Lance reminded her. He watched her as he loosened the knot in his tie, then slipped it off. There was something intensely intimate in the casual gesture. Foxy felt a quick thrill and turned to walk the room.

"I'm not very domestic," she confessed. "I don't even know where I keep the coffee."

"Try the counter behind you," Lance suggested as he turned to find what Mrs. Trilby had tucked into the refrigerator. "Can you cook?"

"Name it," Foxy challenged, then located the coffee. "I can cook it."

"We'll skip the Beef Wellington due to lack of time and imminent starvation. How about a couple of omelets?"

"Kid stuff." Foxy peeked over her shoulder. "Do you cook?"

"Only if I fall asleep at the beach."

"Get me a skillet," she ordered, trying to look disgusted.

The Lancelot Matthewses enjoyed their wedding supper of omelets and coffee at the kitchen table. Outside, the darkness was complete, with the rain still pattering and the moon a prisoner of the clouds. Time was lost to Foxy. It might have been seven in the evening or three in the morning. The feeling of timelessness was soothing, and wanting to prolong it, she ignored the watch on her wrist. Beneath her light conversation, her nerves were struggling to reach the surface. She chided herself for having them, attempted to ignore them, but they remained, under the veneer of confidence. She toyed with the rest of her eggs as Lance divided the last of the pot of coffee between them.

"That's why you're so thin," he commented. When Foxy looked up blankly, he went on. "You don't take enough interest in food. You lost weight during the season. I watched it slide off you."

Foxy shrugged away the pounds but dutifully applied herself to the rest of her eggs. "I like to eat in restaurants as the exception rather than the rule. I'll gain it back in a couple weeks." She smiled up at him. "I do have a growing interest in a hot bath, though."

"I'll take you up," he said and rose. "Then I'll go out and get the bags. The rest of the luggage should arrive by tomorrow."

Foxy rose, too, and began to stack the dishes. Though she knew it was foolish, she felt her nerves rise with her. "You don't have to take me up, just tell me which bath to use. I'll find it."

He watched her back as she set the dishes in the sink. "The second door on the right's the bedroom, the bath's through there. Leave the dishes," he ordered.

Foxy started to refuse, but his hand on her shoulder gently persuaded her to forget her qualms. She needed a few moments alone to collect her wits. "All right," she agreed, then turned with a nod. "I won't be long. I imagine you'd like a bath after the driving you did today."

"Take your time." They left the kitchen together and walked down the main hall. "I'll use another bath."

"Fine," Foxy said as they parted at the end of the hall. *How polite we are,* she thought as she fled up the stairs. *How terrifyingly married.*

In the bedroom, a pair of French doors opened out onto a balcony. The walls were covered with a rich cream wallpaper with dark trim along the floor and ceiling. The furniture was a mixture of periods and styles; Hepplewhite, Chippendale, Queen Anne, and the result was both exquisite and natural. Set into the far wall was a white brick fireplace with a marble mantel; there were logs waiting to be lit within it. Foxy decided Mrs. Trilby must be efficient. The bed was a high four-poster and was covered with a midnight-blue silk counterpane. An heirloom, she knew instantly, probably priceless. She caught her bottom lip between her teeth. This was the sort of thing she would have to learn to deal with—more, to live with.

I'm being an idiot. I married Lance, not his money, not his family. Bride's nerves. I wouldn't feel so awkward and tense if I'd had more experience. Foxy's gaze strayed to the bed again before she took a deep breath and looked down at her hands. Her wedding band glinted back at her. Ignoring the fluttering in her stomach, she began to undress. In her slip, she walked into the bath and discovered more proof of Mrs. Trilby's efficiency. Fresh towels were laid out along with a collection of fragrant soaps, oils, and bath salts. The tub itself was sunken, large enough for two, and Foxy's skin tingled at the thought of languishing in it.

As the hot water began to run she experimented with scents and oils. The room grew rich with steam and fragrance. She began to enjoy herself. Thirty minutes later, she stepped out of the tub, her muscles loose, her skin pink and scented. Choosing a mint-green towel, she wrapped it like a sarong around her body. Lulled by the bath, she hummed lightly as she pulled the confining pins from her hair. It tumbled in a confused mass past her shoulders, and she ran her fingers through it in a vain attempt to set it to rights. *There'll be a brush and a robe in the bags,* she told her reflection. *Surely Lance has brought them up by now.* Leaving her hair carelessly tangled, Foxy opened the connecting door and walked into the bedroom.

The room was lit by the warm glow of china lamps and a crackling fire. It was the scent and sound of the burning wood that caused Foxy to glance toward the fireplace. She was halfway into the room before she saw him. With a small sound of surprise, she clutched at the towel that was tucked loosely over her breasts. Dressed in a black kimono-style robe, Lance stood beside a round, glass-topped table. He paused in the act of opening a split of champagne and studied every inch of his wife. With her free hand, Foxy pushed at her steam-dampened curls.

"Enjoy your bath?" he asked, opening the champagne without taking his eyes from her.

"Yes." Making a quick search, Foxy spotted her cases. "I didn't hear you in here," she said, knowing her voice was not quite its normal pitch. "I was just going to get my brush and a robe."

"Why?" Deftly he poured two glasses of the sparkling wine. "I like you in green." Foxy's fingers tightened on the towel as he smiled. It was the wicked, devilish smile that always pulled at her. "And I like your hair when it's not quite tamed. Come." He held out a glass. "Have some champagne."

It was not as Foxy had planned it. She knew she should have been dressed in the peignoir Pam had given her. She should have been alluring and confident and ready for him. It had not been in her plans to greet her husband on their wedding night clad in only a bath towel with her hair flying every which way and a look of stunned surprise on her face. She obeyed him, however, accepting the wine in the hope that it would soothe the sudden dryness in her throat. As she started to lift the glass to her lips, he reached out and took her wrist. Her pulse throbbed desperately under his fingertips.

"No toast, Foxy?" he said softly, the smile still lingering on his lips. His eyes remained on hers as he took a step closer and touched his glass to hers. "To a well-driven race."

She lifted her glass warily, watching him as she sipped. The champagne was ice cold and thrilling on her tongue.

"Only one glass tonight, Fox," Lance murmured. "I don't want your mind clouded."

Her heart hammering, Foxy turned away. "This is a lovely room." She hastily cleared her throat and moistened her lips. "I've never seen so many antiques in one place."

"Are you fond of antiques?"

"I don't know," she answered as she moved around the room. "I've never had any. You must like them." The last word was only a whisper as she turned around and found him directly behind her. There was something eerie about the soundless way he moved. She would have taken a quick step in retreat, but his hand circled her neck.

"It appears there's only one way to get you to hold still." With the merest pressure of his fingers, he brought her to her toes and firmly covered her mouth. Foxy felt the room dip and sway. His tongue teased the tip of hers before it traced her lips. "Would you like to discuss my Hepplewhite collection?" he asked. From her limp fingers, he took the half-filled glass of champagne.

Foxy opened her eyes. "No." Even the short word was difficult to form as her gaze strayed to his mouth. In an instant he was kissing her again, and the passion built, shuddering through her. She was clinging to him without having been aware of moving at all. The towel slipped unnoticed to the floor. With a low sound of pleasure, Lance buried his mouth against the curve of her throat while his hands ran over her heated skin. She felt the pain of desire and pressed closer to him. "Lance," she murmured as the blood drummed in her head. "I want you. Love me. Love me now." The words were lost under his mouth as it returned urgently to hers. "The light," she said breathlessly as he lowered her to the bed.

His eyes were dark and compelling. "I want to see you."

His body fitted itself to hers. He did not love gently. She had not expected gentleness, she had not expected patience. She had expected quick heat and urgent demands, and she was not disappointed. His hands moved roughly over her, exploring before they possessed. From her lips, his mouth trailed down along her throat, hungry always hungry, as it journeyed to her breast. Foxy moaned with trembling pleasure as he flicked his tongue over her nipple. The ache of desire spread from her stomach. His hands were bruising, arousing as they wandered down her rib cage, lingering at her waist and hips as his mouth continued to ravish her breast.

She began to move under him, a woman's instinct making her motions sensual and inviting. Lean and firm, his hands massaged the sensitive skin of her inner thigh, and her muscles went lax, her joints fluid. She learned that he made love as he had raced—with intensity and absorption. There was a ruthless, steady dominance in him, a power that demanded much more than submission. Surrender would have been too tame a response. More, she discovered her own power. He needed her. She could feel it in the urgency of his hands, taste it in the hunger of his mouth. She heard it as he spoke her name. They were tangled together, flesh against flesh, mouth against mouth while it seemed the only reality was dark, moist kisses and heated skin. The faint scent of wood smoke added something ageless and primitive.

As her body tingled under his hands she began to make her own explorations. She discovered the hard, rippling muscles which his leanness had disguised. As she moved her hands to his hips Lance groaned against her mouth and took the kiss deeper. His hands grew wild, desperate, and she tumbled with him into a world ruled by sensation. The pleasure was acute, so sharp, it brought with it a hint of pain. There seemed to be no part of her that he did not wish to know, to enjoy, to conquer. She locked her arms tightly around his neck, burying her mouth against his throat. His taste filled her until champagne seemed a poor substitute. Here was something dark and male she had yet to learn, and she traced the tip of her tongue over his skin, exploring, discovering. Passion was building beyond anything she had imagined possible. Both emotionally and physically, her response was absolute. She was his.

Her breath was clogging in her lungs, passing through her lips as moans and sighs. Desire reached a turbulent peak when she whispered his name. "Lance." His mouth took hers with fresh desperation, cutting off her words. He shifted on top of her, urging her legs apart with the movement.

The pleasure she had thought already at its summit, increased. Passion came in hot, irresistible waves, overpowering her with its tumultuous journey until all need, all sensation focused into one.

The dawn approached slowly. She was still wrapped tightly in his arms when the hiss of rain lulled her to sleep.

CHAPTER 10

Foxy felt content. A dull red mist behind her lids told her the sun was falling on her face. With a small sigh, she allowed sleep to drift slowly away. She remembered the ease of Saturday mornings when she had been a young girl. Then she would lie in bed, dozing blissfully, knowing there was nothing but pleasure in the day ahead. There would be no worries, no time schedules, no responsibilities. School and Monday morning were centuries away. Foxy drifted on the edge of consciousness with the sensation of being both protected and free—a combination of feeling that had not been hers for a decade. She inched closer to it and clung.

There was a weight around her waist that added to her sense of security. Beside her was warmth. She snuggled yet closer to it. Lazily her lids fluttered open, and she looked directly into Lance's eyes. The past was whisked away as the present took over, but the sensation she woke with remained. Neither she nor Lance spoke. She saw by the clearness of his gaze that he had been awake for some time. There was no hint of sleep in his eyes. They were as sharp and focused as hers were soft and heavy. His hair was tousled around his head, reminding her that it had been her fingers that had disturbed it short hours before. They continued to watch each other as their mouths moved closer to linger in a whisper of a kiss. The thought that they were naked and tangled together seeped through Foxy's drowsy contentment. The arm around her waist was firm in its possession.

"You looked like a child as you slept," he murmured as his mouth journeyed over her face. "Very young and untouched."

Foxy did not want to tell him that her thoughts had been childlike as well. As his fingers traced her spine she began to feel more and more as a woman. "How long have you been awake?"

His hand roamed with absentminded intimacy over her hip and thigh. Reminded that his touch the night before had not been absentminded, she felt her drowsiness swiftly abating. "Awhile," he said as he tightened his arm to bring her yet closer. "I considered waking you." His eyes roamed to her sleep-flushed cheeks, to the rich confusion of her hair against the pillowcase, to the full softness of her untinted mouth. "I rather enjoyed watching you sleep. There aren't many women who can manage to be both soothing and exciting the first thing in the morning."

Foxy arched her brows deliberately. "You know a great deal about women first thing in the morning?"

He grinned, then nuzzled the white curve of her neck. "I'm an early riser."

"A likely story," Foxy murmured, feeling her contentment mixing with a more demanding sensation. "I suppose you're hungry." She felt the tip of his tongue flick over her skin.

"Oh yes, I have quite an appetite this morning." He caught her bottom lip between his teeth. Desire quickened in Foxy's stomach. "You have the most appealing taste," he told her as he teased her lips apart. "I'm finding it habit forming. Your skin's amazingly soft," he went on as his hand moved to cup her breast. "Especially for someone who appears to be mostly bone and nerve." He ran his thumb over its peak and watched her eyes cloud. "I don't think I'm going to get enough of you anytime soon."

He was leading her quickly into passion with quiet words and experienced hands. His touch was no longer that of a stranger and was all the more arousing for its familiarity. She knew now what waited for her when all the doors were opened. She learned and enjoyed and shared. The morning grew late.

It was past noon when Foxy moved down the staircase toward the main floor. She moved slowly, telling herself that the day would last forever if she didn't hurry it. She wanted to explore the house, but firmly turned toward the kitchen. The other rooms would wait until Lance was with her. She had only taken two steps down the hall when the doorbell rang. Glancing up the stairs, Foxy concluded that Lance could hardly be finished showering and decided to answer the bell herself.

There were two women standing on the sheltered white porch. One look told Foxy that they were not door-to-door salespeople. The first was young, around Foxy's age, with warm brunette hair and a rosy complexion. She had a youthful beauty and frank, curious brown eyes. Her clothes were casual but expensive: a tweed suit with a fitted jacket and flared skirt softened by a silk blouse. Supreme confidence was in her every move.

The second woman was more mature but no less striking. Her hair was white and short, brushed back from a delicately pale face. She had few lines or wrinkles, and her not inconsiderable beauty depended more on her superb bone structure and cameo coloring than on the prodigal application of makeup. Her ice-blue suit matched her eyes; its simplicity cunningly announced its price. It occurred to Foxy in the instant they studied each other that her face was quite lovely but expressionless—like a painting of a lovely landscape executed without imagination.

"Hello." Foxy shifted her smile from one woman to the other. "May I help you?"

"Perhaps you'd be good enough to let us in." Foxy heard the distinct Boston cadence in the older woman's voice before she breezed into the hallway. More curious than annoyed, Foxy stepped aside to allow the younger woman to cross the threshold. Standing in the center of the hall, the matron stripped off her white kid gloves and surveyed Foxy's straight-leg jeans and loose chenille sweater. The air was suddenly redolent with French perfume. "And where," she demanded imperiously, "is my son?"

I should have known, Foxy thought as the cool blue eyes examined her. *But how totally unlike her he is. There's not even a shade of resemblance.* "Lance is upstairs, Mrs. Matthews," Foxy explained and tried a fresh smile. "I'm—"

"Well, fetch him then," she interrupted with an imperious movement of her hand. "And tell him I'm here."

It was not the rudeness as much as the tone of contempt that fanned Foxy's temper. Careful to guard her tongue, she spoke precisely. "I'm afraid he's in the shower at the moment. Would you care to wait?" She employed the tone of a receptionist in a dentist's office. From the corner of her eye, she caught the look of amusement in the younger woman's face.

"Come, Melissa." Mrs. Matthews flapped her gloves against her palm in annoyance. "We'll wait in the living room."

"Yes, Aunt Catherine." Her tone was agreeable but she flashed Foxy a look of mischief over her shoulder as she obeyed.

Taking a long breath, Foxy followed. She took care not to

search the room like a newcomer, deciding that Catherine Matthews need not know she had seen little more than the bedroom of Lance's house. Her eyes fluttered over a baby grand piano, a Persian carpet, and a Tiffany lamp before moving back to the queenly figure that had settled into a ladder-back chair. "Perhaps you'd like something while you wait," Foxy offered. Hoping her tone was more polite than her thoughts, she tried the smile again. She was aware of the fact that an introduction was in order, but Catherine's air of scorn persuaded her to hold back her identity. "Some tea perhaps," she suggested. "Or some coffee."

"No." Catherine set her leather envelope bag on the table beside her. "Is Lancelot in the habit of having strange young women entertain his guests?"

"I wouldn't know," Foxy returned equably. Her backbone stiffened in automatic defense. "We haven't spent a great deal of time discussing strange young women."

"I'm quite certain that conversation is not why my son enjoys your companionship." Placing both hands on the ends of the chair's arms, she tapped a manicured finger against the polished wood. "Lancelot rarely chooses to dally with a young lady because of the prodigiousness of her vocabulary. His taste generally eludes me, but I must say, this time I'm astounded." With an arch of her brow, she gave Foxy a calculated look. "Where *did* he find you?"

"Selling matchbooks in Indianapolis," Foxy tossed out before she could prevent herself. "He's going to rehabilitate me."

"I wouldn't dream of it," Lance stated as he walked into the room. Foxy was instantly grateful to see that he was dressed much as herself: jeans, T-shirt, and bare feet. He gave Foxy a brief kiss as he moved past her to greet his mother. Bending down, he brushed the offered cheek with his lips.

"Hello, Mother, you're looking well. Cousin Melissa." He smiled and kissed her cheek in turn. "I see you're lovelier than the last time."

"It's good to see you, Lance." Smiling, Melissa made a flirtatious sweep with her lashes. "Things are never dull when you're around."

"The highest of compliments," he replied, then turned back to his mother. "I imagine Mrs. Trilby told you I was coming in."

"Yes." She crossed surprisingly slender, youthful-looking legs. "I find it quite annoying to hear of my son's whereabouts from a servant."

"Don't be too annoyed with Mrs. Trilby," Lance countered carelessly. "She probably thought you knew. I intended to call you at the end of the week."

Catherine bristled at his deliberate misunderstanding of her meaning. When she spoke, however, her voice was cool and expressionless. Watching her, Foxy recalled Lance saying how the Bardetts were always civilized. *In their own fashion,* Foxy mused, thinking of her initial encounter. "I suppose I should be grateful that you intended to call me at all since you appear to be involved with your—" her eyes drifted to fasten briefly on Foxy "—guest." She lifted her brow, arching it into a smooth, high forehead. "Perhaps you would send her along so that we might have a private conversation. Since Trilby isn't here, she might make a pot of tea."

Foxy, knowing she would explode if she stayed, turned with the intention of locking herself into the bedroom until she could be trusted again.

"Foxy." Lance spoke her name mildly, but she recognized the underlying tone of command. Eyes flaming, she turned back. Lance casually crossed the room and slipped his arm over her shoulders. "I don't believe you've been introduced."

"Introductions," his mother cut in, "are hardly necessary or appropriate."

Lance inclined his head. "If you've finished insulting her, Mother, I'd like you to meet my wife."

There was total silence. Catherine Matthews did not gasp in alarm or surprise but merely stared at Foxy as if she were a strange piece of artwork in a gallery. "Your wife?" she repeated. Her voice remained calm, her face devoid of emotion. Folding her hands in her lap, she turned her eyes to her son. "When did this happen?"

"Yesterday. Foxy and I were married in the morning in New York. We drove up directly afterward for—" the grin flickered in his eyes as he kept them on his mother "—an informal honeymoon."

He's enjoying this, Foxy realized as she heard the amusement lace his voice. She knew, too, by the ice in Catherine's that she was not.

"One hopes Foxy is not her given name."

"Cynthia," Foxy put in distinctly as she grew weary of being referred to as an absent participant.

"Cynthia," Catherine murmured thoughtfully. She did not offer her hand or cheek for a token embrace or kiss; instead she carefully studied Foxy's face for the first time, obviously considering what could be done to salvage the situation. *I'm the situation,* Foxy realized with a quick flash of humor. "And your maiden name?" Catherine demanded with an inclination of her head.

"Fox," she told her with a mimicking nod.

"Fox," Catherine repeated, tapping her finger on the arm of the chair again. "Fox. The name is vaguely familiar."

"The race driver Lance sponsors," Melissa supplied helpfully. She stared at Foxy with undisguised fascination. "I suppose you're his sister or something, aren't you?"

"Yes, I'm his sister." The bold curiosity in her voice made Foxy smile. "Hello."

Mischief streaked swiftly over Melissa's face. Like Lance, Foxy noted, she was enjoying the encounter. "Hello."

"You met her on a—a…" Catherine's fingers waved as she searched for the proper term. "A race-car track?" The first hint of fury whispered through the words. Foxy stiffened again at the expression of contempt that was turned on her.

"I could do with some coffee, Fox, would you mind?" At Lance's calm request, she tossed her head back to flame at him. "Melissa will give you a hand," he continued, nearly cutting off her explosion. "Won't you, Melissa?" He addressed his cousin, but never took his eyes from his wife.

"Of course." Melissa rose obediently and crossed the room. Trapped, Foxy fought down the surge of temper. She turned, leaving Lance and his mother without another word. "Did you really meet Lance on a racetrack?" Melissa asked as the kitchen door swung behind them. There was no guile in the question, simply curiosity.

"Yes." Struggling with fury, Foxy managed to keep her tone level. "Ten years ago."

"Ten years? You had to have been a child." Melissa settled down at the table while Foxy scooped out coffee. Sunlight poured through the windows, making the drizzling rain of the day before only a memory. "Now, ten years later, he marries you." Elbows on the table, Melissa made a cradle out of her hands and set her chin on it. "It's terribly romantic."

As she felt her anger taper off Foxy blew out a long breath. "Yes, I suppose it is."

"I wouldn't worry too much about Aunt Catherine," Melissa advised, studying Foxy's profile. "She wouldn't have approved of anyone she hadn't handpicked."

"That's comforting," Foxy replied. Wanting to keep busy, she began to brew a pot of tea as well.

"There'll also be a large contingent of women between twenty and forty who'll want to murder you," Melissa added as she crossed her silk-covered legs. "There hasn't been a shortage of hopefuls for the title of Mrs. Lancelot Matthews."

"Marvelous." Foxy turned to Melissa and leaned back against the counter. "Just marvelous."

"You'll meet the bulk of them socially in the first few weeks," Melissa told her cheerfully. Foxy noted that like Catherine's, Melissa's nails were perfectly tended. "Of course, Lance will be there to guard against unsheathed claws at parties and dances, but you'll have to be alert during charity functions and those lovely luncheon meetings."

"I won't have time for much of that sort of thing," Foxy told her with undisguised relief. Turning away, she managed to locate an appropriate cream and sugar set. "I have my work."

"Work? Do you have a job?" The utter incredulity in her voice caused Foxy to turn back again and laugh.

"Yes, I have a job. Isn't it allowed?"

"Yes, of course, depending…" The tip of Melissa's tongue ran slowly along her teeth as she considered. "What do you do?"

"I'm a freelance photographer." Leaving the kettle on to heat, Foxy joined her at the table.

"That might do well enough," Melissa said with a thoughtful nod.

"What do you do?" Foxy countered, growing intrigued.

"Do? I…" Melissa searched for a word, then smiled with a gesture of her hand. "I circulate." Her eyes danced with such blatant good humor, Foxy was forced to laugh again. "I graduated from Radcliffe three years ago, then I took the obligatory Grand Tour. My French is flawless. I know who's tolerable and who's not in Boston society, how to get the best table at the Charles, where to be seen and with whom, where to buy shoes and where to buy lingerie, how to order creamed chicken for fifty Boston matrons, and where the skeletons are buried in the majority of closets. I've been mad about Lance since I was two, and if I wasn't his cousin and ineligible, I should certainly despise you. But I couldn't have married him in any case, so I'm going to like you very well and enjoy watching you twist a few noses out of shape."

She paused to catch her breath but not long enough for Foxy to get a word in. "You're fabulously attractive, particularly your hair, and I would imagine when you're suited up, you're devastating. Lance would never have chosen anyone with ordinary good looks. And of course, there's your tongue. You certainly set Aunt Catherine down a peg. You'll have to keep it sharp to get through the next weeks unscarred. But I'll help you. I enjoy watching people do things I haven't the courage to do. There now, your kettle's boiling."

Slightly dazed, Foxy rose to take it from the burner. "Are all Lance's relatives like you?"

"Heavens no. I'm quite unique." Melissa smiled with perfect charm. "I know a great number of the people in my circle are bores and snobs, and I haven't any illusions about myself." She shrugged as Foxy began to steep the tea in a porcelain pot. "I'm simply too comfortable to give them a black eye now and again as Lance does. I admire him tremendously, but I haven't the inclination to emulate him." Melissa tossed her hair casually behind her shoulder, and Foxy saw an emerald flash on her hand. "There are times Lance does things strictly to annoy the family's sensibilities. I believe he might have started racing with that in mind. Of course, he became quite obsessed with it for a while. And still, he's involved with designing and building cars rather than driving them…" Melissa trailed off, studying Foxy with thoughtful brown eyes.

Hearing the speculation in her voice, Foxy met the stare and spoke without inflection. "You're thinking perhaps he married me to again annoy the family's sensibilities."

Melissa smiled and shrugged her tweed-clad shoulders. "Would it matter? You took first prize. Enjoy it."

Both women turned as the prize strolled into the room. His eyes flickered over Foxy, then settled on his cousin. "Mother's anxious to get along, Melissa."

"Pooh." She wrinkled her nose as she rose. "I'd hoped all this would make her forget about the meetings she's dragging me to. I suppose she told you there's a party at Uncle Paul's tomorrow night. They'll expect you now."

"Yes, she told me." There was no enthusiasm in his voice, and Melissa grinned.

"I'm looking forward to it now. I expect Grandmother might even put in an appearance…under the circumstances. You really know how to keep them off balance, don't you?" Melissa winked at Foxy before she crossed over to Lance. "I haven't congratulated you yet."

"No," he agreed and lifted a brow. "You haven't."

"Congratulations," she said formally, then rose on her toes to peck both of his cheeks. "I like your wife, cousin. I shall come back soon whether you invite me or not."

"You're one of the few I don't draw the bolt against." Lance gave her a quick pinch on the chin. "She'll need a friend."

"Don't we all?" Melissa countered dryly. "We'll go shopping soon," she decided as she turned back to face Foxy. "That's a quick way to get to know each other. I'll see you tomorrow night," she continued before she moved to the door, "for your trial by fire."

Foxy watched the door swing to and fro after Melissa. "I'm feeling a bit singed already," she muttered.

Lance crossed the room and cupped her chin in his hand. "You seemed to hold your own well enough." His eyes grew serious as he studied her face. "Shall I apologize for my mother?"

"No." Foxy closed her eyes for a moment, then shook her head. "No, it isn't necessary. And as I think back you did try to warn me." She opened her eyes and shrugged. "I suppose you knew she wouldn't approve."

"There's very little I do my mother approves of," he countered. He traced his thumb over her jawline while his eyes remained on hers. "I don't base anything I do on her approval, Foxy, least of all my marriage to you. Our lives are our own." His brows lowered into a frown, and he kissed her, hard and quick. "I asked you before," he reminded her, "to trust me."

With a sigh, Foxy turned away. The air seemed suddenly thick with the scents of coffee and tea. "It appears we didn't manage our few days of peace." Picking up the teapot, she poured the contents down the sink. She felt his hands on her shoulders and straightened them automatically. Nothing was going to mar her first full day as his wife. Whirling, Foxy threw her arms around his neck. "We still have today." All the anger melted along with her bones as Lance covered her offered mouth with his. "I don't think I want any coffee now," she whispered as their lips parted and met again. "Do you?"

For an answer, he grinned and drew away. Before she realized his intent, Foxy was slung over his shoulder. Laughing, she pushed the hair from her eyes. "Lance," she said with a mock shiver as he swung through the kitchen door. "You're so romantic."

CHAPTER 11

Foxy considered dressing for her first social evening as Mrs. Lancelot Matthews equal to dressing for battle. Her armor consisted of a slim tube top and loosely pleated evening pants in pale green. Standing in front of the full-length mirror, she adjusted the vivid emerald hip-length jacket and fastened it with a thin gold belt. Deliberately she set about arranging a more dramatic style for her hair.

"If they're going to stare and whisper," she muttered as she pinned up the back of her hair, "we'll give them something to stare and whisper about." Using her brush lightly, she persuaded her curls to fall in soft disorder around her face. "I wish I was built," she complained with a glare at her willowy reflection.

"I'm rather fond of your construction," Lance stated from the doorway. Startled, Foxy turned and dropped the brush. Looking casually elegant in a black suit of the thinnest wool, he leaned against the jamb. His eyes trailed over her in a lazy arch before returning to lock on hers. "Going to give them their money's worth, are you, Foxy?"

She shrugged carelessly, then stooped to retrieve her brush. As she turned away to place it on her dresser she felt his hands descend to her shoulders. "My mother got under your skin, didn't she?"

Foxy toyed with the collection of bottles and jars on the dresser's surface. "It's only fair," she parried. "I got under hers." She heard him sigh, then felt his chin rest atop her head. She kept her eyes lowered on her own restless fingers.

"I suppose I should have apologized for her after all."

Foxy turned, shaking her head. "No." With her own sigh, she offered an apologetic smile. "I'm pouting, aren't I? I'm sorry." Determined to change the mood, she stepped back a bit and held out her hands, palms up. "How do I look?" Below the fall of curls, her eyes were saucy and teasing.

Catching her wrist, Lance spun her into his arms. "Fantastic. I'm tempted to forgo dear Uncle Paul's little party. I'm very possessive of what's mine." His mouth lowered to rub against hers. "Shall we play truant, Foxy, and lock the door?"

She wanted badly to agree; his mouth promised such delights. To keep the scales balanced, she drew her face away from the warmth of his lips. "I think I'd like to get it over with. I'd rather meet a cluster of them at one time than meet them in dribbles."

He brushed his fingers through her hair. "Pity," he murmured. "But then you always have been a brave soul. I believe you should have a reward for valor before the fact." He slipped his hand into his pocket, then held out a small black box.

"What is it?" Foxy demanded, giving him a curious look as she accepted it.

"A box."

"Clever," she muttered. After opening it, Foxy stared down at two shimmering diamonds shaped like exquisite tears of ice. "Lance, they're diamonds," she managed as she lifted wide eyes to his.

"So I was told," he agreed. The familiar crooked grin claimed his mouth. "You suggested once I buy you something extravagant. I thought these more appropriate than Russian wolfhounds."

"Oh, but I didn't mean for you to actually…"

"Not all women can wear diamonds," he said, moving lightly over her protest. "It takes a certain finesse or they look overdone or tawdry." As he spoke, he took the gems from the box and fastened them to her ears. His touch was smooth and practiced. Lifting her chin with his fingers, he critically studied the result. "Yes, it's as I thought, you're well suited. Diamonds need a great deal of warmth." He turned her so that she looked into the mirror. "A lovely woman, Mrs. Matthews. And all mine." Lance stood behind her, his hands on her shoulders.

The mirror reflected a pose of natural affection between husband and wife. Foxy's throat clogged with emotion. I'd trade a dozen diamonds, she thought, for a moment such as this. When her eyes met his in the mirror, her heart and soul were in them. "I love you," she told him in a voice that trembled with her feelings. "So much that sometimes it scares me." Her hands reached up to grasp his with a sudden desperation she neither understood nor expected. "I never realized love could scare you, making you think of all the what-ifs there are in life. This has all happened so fast that when I wake up in the mornings, I still expect to be alone. Oh, Lance." Her eyes clung to his. "I wish we could have been an island a little while longer. What are they going to do to us? All these people who aren't you and me."

Lance turned her until she was facing him and not his reflection. "They can't do anything to us unless we let them." Gently his mouth lowered to hers, but her head fell back, inviting more. His arms tightened as the kiss grew lengthy and intimate. "I think we'll be a bit late for Uncle Paul's party," Lance murmured as he changed the angle of the kiss, then teased the tip of her tongue with his.

Foxy pushed the jacket from Lance's shoulders, working it down his arms until it dropped to the floor. Slowly she moved her hands up the silk front of his shirt while her mouth answered his. She felt his response in the tensing of his muscles, in the strength of his hands as they moved to her hips. Locking her arms around his neck, she strained closer. His lips moved to her hair, then her temple, until they burrowed at her throat. His warm musky scent mingled with hers, creating a fragrance Foxy thought uniquely their own. She slipped out of her shoes. "Let's be very late for Uncle Paul's party," she murmured and sought his mouth again.

Foxy found her imagination had not been sufficiently extravagant in its picture of Paul Bardett's party. Her first misconception had been the number of people. In attendance were more than double her most generous estimate. The elegant old brownstone on Beacon Hill was packed with them. They thronged the tiny elegant parlor with the Louis XVI furniture, strolled on the terrace under the Chinese lanterns, moved up and down the carpeted staircase. Foxy was certain that every exclusive designer from either side of the Atlantic was represented, from the most conservative sheath to the most flamboyant evening pajamas. During her seemingly endless introductions to the vast Matthews–Bardett clan, she was treated to smiles, handshakes, pecks on the cheek, and speculation. The speculation, as the kisses and the smiles, came in varying degrees. Sometimes it was vague, almost offhand, and other times it was frank, direct, and merciless. Such was the case with the senior Mrs. Matthews, Lance's grandmother. Even as Lance introduced them, Foxy saw the faded blue eyes narrow in appraisal.

Edith Matthews was not a flamboyant countess from Venice. Her sturdy, matronly figure was clad decently in a tasteful black brocade relieved only by a small ruching of white lace at the throat. Her hair was more silver than white, waved carefully away from a strong-boned face. Foxy studied her in turn, wondering if there had once been beauty there, masquerading now behind the mask of age. With the countess, she had been certain, the beauty was still very much alive in the vibrant green eyes. The clasp of Mrs. Matthews' hand was quick, firm enough though the skin was thin, and the eyes told Foxy only that she was being considered: acceptance was being withheld.

"It appears you've cheated us out of a wedding, Lancelot," she said in a quiet voice, raspy with age.

"There seems to be no shortage of them each year," he countered. "One shouldn't be missed very much."

She shot him a look under brows Foxy noticed were thin and beautifully arched. "There are those who have been rather looking forward to yours. Well, never mind," she went on, waving him away with a queenly flick of her fingers. "You will do things your own way. You'll live in the house your grandfather left you?"

Lance was smiling at the gesture she had used. It had been employed in exactly the same way for as long as he could remember. "Yes, Grandmother."

If she recognized the teasing lilt to his voice, she ignored it. "He would like that." She shifted her eyes to Foxy. "I have no doubt he would have liked you as well."

Accepting this as the highest form of approval she would receive, Foxy took the initiative. "Thank you, Mrs. Matthews." Impulsively she bent and brushed the wrinkled cheek with her lips. There were soft scents of lavender and talc.

The beautifully arched brows drew together, then relaxed. "I'm old," she said and sighed as if the thought were not unpleasant so much as unexpected. "You may call me Grandmother."

"Thank you, Grandmother," Foxy replied obediently and smiled.

"Good evening, Lancelot." Foxy's pleasure faded as she heard Catherine Matthews' greeting. "Good evening, Cynthia. You look lovely."

Foxy turned to face her and saw the practiced social smile. "Thank you, Mrs. Matthews." *Manners at ten paces,* Foxy reflected, and thought pistols might be preferable. She watched Catherine's eyes flicker, as dozens of others had that evening, over the diamonds on her ears.

"I don't believe you met my sister-in-law, Phoebe," she said smoothly. "Phoebe Matthews-White, Lancelot's wife, Cynthia."

A small, pale woman with a nondescript face and hair the color of a lead pencil held out her hand. "How do you do?" She pushed her gray-framed glasses more securely on her nose and squinted her birdlike eyes. "I don't believe we've met before."

"No, Mrs. Matthews-White, we haven't."

"How odd," Phoebe said with mild curiosity.

"Lancelot and Cynthia summered in Europe," Catherine put in as she gave Lance an arched look.

"Henry and I stayed at the Cape this year," Phoebe confided, easily distracted from her curiosity. "I simply hadn't the energy for a trip to Europe this season. Perhaps we'll spend the holidays in St. Croix."

"Hello, Lance!"

Foxy turned to see a woman in delicate pink embrace her husband. Her photographer's eye detected a perfect model. She had what Foxy labeled the Helen of Troy look—classic delicacy with a sculptured, oval face. Her eyes were deep blue, round, and striking, the nose small and straight over a Cupid's bow mouth. Her figure was as classic as her face, richly curved and enticing in a simple silk sheath. Foxy saw the face in soft focus against the background of white satin—a study of feminine perfection. She knew the woman would photograph magnificently.

"I just learned you were back in town." The Cupid's bow brushed over Lance's cheek. "How bad of you not to have let me know yourself."

"Hello, Gwen. You're lovelier than ever. Hello, Jonathan."

Foxy glanced just beyond Gwen's right shoulder and saw the masculine version of her classic looks. These eyes, however, were not on Lance, but on her. His profile was magnificent, and her fingers itched for her camera.

"Catherine," Gwen said as she tucked her arm in Lance's. "You simply must persuade him to stay this time."

"I'm afraid I could never persuade Lancelot to do anything," Catherine returned dryly.

"Foxy." Lazily, Lance circled his fingers around her wrist. "I'd like you to meet Gwen Fitzpatrick and her brother Jonathan, old family friends."

"What a perfectly dreadful introduction," Gwen complained as her sapphire eyes roamed Foxy's face. "You must be Lance's surprise."

Foxy recognized the cool speculation and responded to it. "Must I?" She sipped at her glass of champagne. Still, she thought, the face is lovely regardless of the woman within. It has so many possibilities. "Have you ever modeled?" she asked, already formulating angles and lighting.

Gwen's brows arched. "Certainly not."

"No?" Foxy smiled, amused at the chipped ice in Gwen's tone. "What a pity."

"Foxy's a photographer," Lance put in and cast her a knowing glance.

"Oh, how interesting." Skillfully, she drenched the words in boredom before turning her attention back to Lance. "We were all simply stunned to hear you were married, and so suddenly. But then, you always were impulsive." Foxy struggled to remain amused. Again the round blue eyes shifted to her. "You must share your secret with those of us who tried and failed."

"You only have to look at her to learn the secret," Jonathan Fitzpatrick stated. Taking Foxy's fingers, he lifted them to his lips, watching her over her own knuckles. "A pleasure, Mrs. Matthews." His eyes were appealing and insolent. Foxy grinned, liking him instantly.

"How charming," Gwen murmured as she sent her brother a frosty glance.

"Hello, everyone." Stunning in red silk, Melissa popped up beside Foxy. "Lance, I simply must borrow your wife a moment. Jonathan, you haven't flirted with me once tonight. I'm terribly annoyed. You'll have to see if you can charm me out of the sulks as soon as I get back. Excuse us, won't you?" Beaming smiles in all directions, Melissa maneuvered Foxy through the crowd and onto a shadowed section of the terrace. "I thought you might like a breather," she commented as she adjusted the cuff of her sleeve.

"You really are unique," Foxy managed when she caught her breath. "You're also right." As she set the glass of champagne down on a white iron table, she heard the wind whispering through drying leaves. The approaching winter was in the air. Still, she preferred the light chill of fresh air to the growing stuffiness inside.

"I also thought a little road mapping might help you." Melissa carefully checked the cushion of a chair for dampness before sitting.

"Road mapping?"

"Or who's who in the Matthews-Bardett circle," Melissa explained and daintily lit a cigarette. "Now." She paused again as she blew out a stream of smoke and crossed her legs. "Phoebe, Lance's aunt on his father's side—relatively harmless. Her husband is in banking. His main interest is the Boston Symphony, hers is 'doing what's proper.' Paul Bardett, Lance's uncle on his mother's side—very shrewd, occasionally witty, but his life revolves around his law practice. Corporate stuff, very dry and very boring if he corners you. You met my parents, Lance's cousins by marriage on his father's side." Melissa sighed and tapped the ash of her cigarette on the terrace floor. "They're very sweet really. Daddy collects rare stamps and Mother raises Yorkshire terriers. Both of them are obsessive about their respective hobbies. Now, about the Fitzpatricks." She paused and ran the tip of her tongue over her upper lip. "It's best if you know Gwen was the front runner in the 'Who Will Finally Bag Lance Matthews Contest.'"

"She must be very annoyed," Foxy murmured. She walked to the edge of the terrace where the shadows deepened. With sudden clarity, she was reminded of the night of Kirk's party when she had sought out the scent of spring; the first time Lance had kissed her, on the glider in the moonlight. "Were they…" Foxy shut her eyes and bit her lip. "Were they…"

"Lovers?" Melissa supplied helpfully, taking a sip at Foxy's wine. "I imagine. Lance seems quite the physical sort to me." Glancing over, she studied Foxy's back. "You're not the jealous type, are you?"

"Yes," Foxy murmured without turning around. "Yes, I think I am."

"Oh dear," Melissa said into the champagne. "That's too

bad. In any case, that was Chapter One, this is Chapter Two. Oh, and as for Jonathan." Melissa finished the wine and gently crushed her cigarette under her heel. "He's a dangerous flirt and hopelessly charming and insincere. I've decided to marry him."

"Oh." Foxy turned back now and stared at her strange fountain of information. "Well, congratulations."

"Oh, not yet, darling." After rising, Melissa carefully brushed out her skirts. The pearls at her throat gleamed white in the moonlight. "He doesn't know he's going to ask me yet. I shouldn't think the idea will occur to him until around Christmastime."

"Oh," Foxy said blankly, then frowned at the empty glass Melissa handed her.

"You're perfectly free to flirt with him," she added generously. "I'm not the jealous type at all. I believe I'd like a spring wedding, perhaps May. A four-month engagement is perfectly long enough, don't you think? We'd best go back in," she said, linking her arm with Foxy's before she could answer. "I have to begin enchanting him."

CHAPTER 12

During the next week, Foxy established a routine. On a search through the house, she had located the perfect site for her darkroom. Her time was absorbed with the clearing out of a basement storage room, arranging for her equipment to be shipped from New York and altering the room to suit its new function. Lance's days were spent in his Boston office while Foxy spent hers relocating her career base. Before she could continue with the creative aspects of her work, there were practicalities to be seen to. There was cleaning, plumbing to be installed, equipment to be set up. During the transition, Foxy was grateful that Mrs. Trilby proved to be efficient indeed, and quite proprietary about the top three stories of the house. She left the basement to Foxy without a murmur of protest. But there was no doubt in Foxy's mind that the tiny, prim lady in crepe-soled shoes would have snarled like a tiger if she had interfered with the working routine of the living quarters. Foxy left the polishing of the Georgian silver to Mrs. Trilby while she set up her enlarger and bathing tanks. The arrangement suited them both.

Foxy alternated work in her darkroom with solitary explorations of the city. She shot roll after roll of film, recording her impressions and feelings with her camera. She became reacquainted with loneliness. It surprised her that after so many years of thoughtless independence, she should so strongly need another's company. Knowing Lance's business needed careful attention after his months on the road helped her to keep any complaints to herself. Complaints, in any case, were something she rarely uttered. Problems were made to be worked out, and she was accustomed to doing so for herself. The loneliness itself was fleeting, forgotten when she and Lance were together, dulled by her fascination with the city which was now her home. When loneliness threatened, she fought it. Work was her panacea, and Foxy indulged in it lavishly. Within a week, her darkroom was operable, and the prints of the racing season were half completed.

As she studied a set of drying work prints Kirk jumped into her mind. Had it only been three weeks since the accident? she mused as she brushed her hair away from her eyes. It seemed like a lifetime. Wasn't it, in essence? In some strange way, Kirk's accident had been the catalyst that had altered her life. The world she existed in now was far removed from the one she had known as Cynthia Fox. With an unconscious gesture, she fingered her wedding ring.

Hanging wet and glossy, a print of the white racer as it would never be again caught Foxy's attention. She had highlighted it, muting the background into a smudge of varied colors without shape. It had been an unconscious tribute to her brother as she had once thought of him—indestructible. Abruptly a flood of homesickness overwhelmed her. It was an odd sensation and a new one. There had been no truly consistent home in her life in over ten years. But there had been Kirk. Impulsively Foxy left her work in the darkroom and rushed up the steps to the first floor. Hearing the hum of the vacuum in the upstairs hall, she ducked into Lance's study.

Closing herself in the room, she dropped into the chair behind Lance's walnut desk and picked up the phone. In moments, the lines were clicking between Massachusetts and New York.

"Pam!" Foxy felt a quick rush of pleasure the instant she heard the quiet, southern voice. "It's Foxy."

"Well, if it isn't Mrs. Matthews. How are things in Boston?"

"Fine," Foxy replied automatically. "Yes, fine," she repeated, unconsciously adding a nod for emphasis. "Well." She sighed and settled back in the chair with a laugh. "Different certainly. How's Kirk?"

"He's doing very well." Pam's voice continued lightly. "Impatient, naturally, to get out of the hospital. I'm afraid you've missed him just now. He's down in X-ray."

"Oh." Her disappointment was clear, but Foxy pushed it away. "Well, how are you? Are you managing to keep Kirk in line and maintain your sanity?"

"Just barely." Pam's laugh was easy and familiar. Foxy smiled with the pleasure of hearing it. "He'll be sorry he missed your call."

"I missed him all of a sudden," Foxy confessed with a small shake of her head. "Everything's moved so fast in the past few weeks, sometimes I almost feel like someone else. I think I needed him to remind me I was still the same person." She stopped and laughed again. "Am I rambling?"

"Only a tad. Kirk's not only reconciled to your marriage now, but quite pleased about it. I think he's talked himself into believing he arranged the entire thing between races." Pam waited a beat, then continued in the same tone. "Are you happy, Foxy?"

Knowing Pam had meant the question seriously and not as casual conversation, Foxy took a moment to answer. She thought of Lance, and a smile coaxed her lips upward. "Yes,

I'm happy. I love Lance, and on top of that, I'm lucky enough to love the house and Boston. I suppose I've been a bit lost, especially since Lance is back at his office. Everything here is so different, at times I feel I've stepped through the looking glass."

"Boston society can be a wonderland of sorts, I imagine," Pam replied. "Have you been spending your time chasing white rabbits?"

"I've been working, my friend," Foxy countered in a tone that reflected her raised brows. "My darkroom here is now fully operable. I'll be sending you the prints in a week or so. I'll send you numbered work prints. If you need more copies, or want something enlarged or reduced, give me the number."

"Sounds good. How many prints do you have so far?"

"Finished?" Foxy's brow furrowed as she considered. "A couple hundred if you count the ones I have drying."

"My, my," Pam remarked. "You have been a busy one, haven't you?"

"Photography has become not only my career but my salvation. It saves me from luncheons." There was a smile in her voice now as she settled back into the deep cushion of the chair. "I went to my first, and my last, earlier this week. Nothing and no one will induce me to go through that again. I'm simply not cut out for *functions.*"

"Ah well," Pam comforted with a cluck of her tongue. "They will probably carry on without you. I take it you've met Lance's family by now."

"Yes. He has a cousin, Melissa, who's really a character. I like her. His grandmother was rather sweet to me. For the rest—" Foxy paused and wrinkled her nose "—there's been everything from casual friendliness to rank disapproval." Pam could all but hear the shrug in her voice. "I'm looking at this first round of social obligations and introductions as kind of a pledge week. After it's done, I'll know them, and they'll know me, and that will be that." She grinned. "I hope."

"Lance's mother is a…formidable lady," Pam commented.

"Yes," Foxy agreed, surprised. "How did you know?"

"My mother and she are slightly acquainted," she answered. Foxy was reminded that Pam had been born and bred in the world she had found herself thrust into by marriage. "I met her myself once when I was covering a story on art patrons." Pam recalled her impression of an elegant, aristocratic woman with cool eyes and beautiful skin. She remembered no warmth at all. "Just keep your feet planted, Foxy. It'll all settle in a few months."

Toying with the brass model of a Formula One that served as a paperweight, Foxy sighed. "I'm trying, Pam, but I do wish Lance and I could just lock the doors for a while. Our honeymoon was interrupted before it had really begun. I'm selfish enough to want a week or two alone with him while I'm getting used to being a wife."

"That sounds more reasonable than selfish," Pam corrected. "Maybe you'll be able to get away once he's finished designing this new car for Kirk. From what I gather, it's a bit complicated because of some new safety features Lance is working on."

"What car?" Foxy demanded softly as she felt her blood turn cold.

"The new Formula One Lance is designing for Kirk. Hasn't he told you about it?"

"No, no he hasn't." Foxy's voice was normal but her eyes were dull and lifeless as she stared down at the polished surface of Lance's desk. "I suppose it's for next season."

"That's why they're pushing to move it along," Pam agreed. "It's practically all Kirk can talk about. He's hoping to fly into Boston as soon as he's out of here so that he can be in on it before it's a finished project. The doctors seem to feel his avid interest in the car is a good motivation for getting him back on his feet quickly." Pam rambled on while Foxy stared without seeing anything. "There's no doubt he's cooperating so well with his therapist because he wants to walk out of here by the first of the year."

"If he's not on his feet," Foxy put in slowly, "they can lift him out of his wheelchair and strap him into the cockpit." Though it cost her some effort, she managed to keep her voice carefully level. "I'm sure Lance would have no objections."

"I wouldn't be surprised if Kirk tried to arrange it." Pam made a sound that was half laugh, half sigh. "Ah, well. What I would like, if you can do it, are some shots of the new car. Seeing as you have an in with the head man, you should be able to get close enough to take a shot or two. I'd especially like a few at the test track when it's progressed that far."

Foxy shut her eyes on the headache that was beginning to throb. "I'll do what I can." *Will I never get away from it?* she wondered and squeezed her eyes tighter. *Never?* "I have to get back to work, Pam. Give Kirk my love, will you? And take care of yourself."

"Be happy, Foxy, and give our best to Lance."

"Yes, I will. Bye." With studied care, Foxy replaced the phone on its cradle. The cold shield over her skin remained, stretching out to extend to her brain. There was a void where her emotions might have been. Anger hovered on the edge of her consciousness, but failed to penetrate. Kirk's accident replayed in her head, not with the smooth motion of a movie, but with the quick, staccato succession of a slide show. Each frame was distinct and horrible.

There were countless grids in her memory, countless wrecks. They came back to her in a montage of cars and drivers and pit crews all jumbled together in a throbbing mass of speed. She sat, swamped by the largeness of Lance's chair, and remembered all of ten years as the light shifted with evening. Outside, the temperature began to drop with the sun. When the door to the study opened, Foxy turned her eyes to it with little interest.

"Here you are." Lance strolled into the room, leaving the door open behind him. "Why are you sitting in the dark, Fox? Don't you get enough of that in your fortress in the basement?" Moving to her, he cupped her chin in his hand and kissed her. The gesture was casual and somehow possessive. When he received no response, he narrowed his eyes and studied her face. "What is it?"

Foxy looked up at him, but her eyes were shadowed in the dimming light. "I just talked to Pam."

"Is it Kirk?" The quick concern in his voice melted the shield that covered her. Under it was the boiling fury of betrayal. She struggled to remain objective until she understood. "Are you concerned about his health?" she asked, but drops of anger burned through the words.

Frowning at the tone, Lance traced her jaw with his finger and felt the tension. "Of course I am. Has there been a complication?"

"Complication," she repeated tonelessly as her nails bit into her palms. "That depends on your viewpoint, I suppose. Pam told me about the car."

"What car?"

The blatant curiosity and puzzlement in his voice snapped her control. Knocking his hand from her face, Foxy rose, putting the chair and her temper between them. "How could you begin designs on a car while he's still in the hospital? Couldn't you even wait until he can walk again?"

Understanding replaced the puzzlement on Lance's face.

He made no attempt to close the distance between them, but when he spoke, his voice was patient. "Fox, it takes time to design and build a car. Work was begun on this months ago."

"Why didn't you tell me?" She tossed the words at him, more annoyed than soothed by the patience in his tone. "Why were you keeping it from me?"

"In the first place," he began, frowning as he watched her. "Designing cars is my business, and you're aware of it. I've designed cars for Kirk before, you're aware of that, too. Why is this different?"

"He was nearly killed less than a month ago." Foxy gripped the supple leather of Lance's chair.

"He crashed," Lance said calmly. "He's crashed before. You and I both know that there's always the chance he'll crash again. It's a professional risk."

"A professional risk," she repeated while fresh fury grew in her eyes. "Oh, how like you! That makes it all neat and tidy. How marvelous it must be to be so impersonally logical."

"Be careful, Foxy," Lance said evenly.

"Why are you encouraging him to go back to it?" she demanded, ignoring his warning. "He might have had enough this time. He had Pam now, he might…"

"Wait a minute." Though shadows washed the room, Foxy had no need to see his face clearly to recognize his anger. "Kirk doesn't need any encouraging. Accident or no accident, he'll be back on the grid next season. It's no use trying to delude yourself, Foxy. Neither a wreck nor a woman is going to keep Kirk out of a cockpit for long."

"We'll never be sure of that now, will we?" she countered furiously. "You'll have one all ready for him. Custom fit. How can he resist?"

"If I didn't, someone else would." Lance's hands slipped into his pockets as his voice became dangerously quiet. "I thought you understood him...and me."

"All I understand is that you're planning to put him into another car, and he's not even able to stand up yet." Her voice became desperate and she dragged an impatient hand through her hair. "I understand that you might have used your influence to persuade him to retire, and instead—"

"No." Lance interrupted her flatly. "I won't be held responsible for what your brother chooses to do with his life."

Foxy swallowed hard, struggling not to cry. "No, you don't want the responsibility, I can understand that, too." Bitterness spilled over and colored her words. In the dimming light, her eyes glittered both with anger and despair. "All you have to do is draw some lines on paper, balance some equations, order some parts. You don't have to risk your life, just your money. You've plenty of that to spare." Her mind began to spin with a cascade of thoughts and accusations. "On a different level, it's a bit like the casino in Monte Carlo." Foxy raked her hands through her hair again, then gripped them together, furious that they were trembling. "You could just sit back and watch the action, like some...some overlord. Money doesn't mean very much to someone who's always had it. Is that how you get your satisfaction?" she demanded, too incensed to realize that his very silence was ominous. "By paying someone to take the risks while you sit back in safety and watch?"

"That's enough!" He moved like lightning, giving her no chance to evade him. In an instant, he had pulled her from behind the chair until he towered over her. "I don't have to take that from you. I did my time on the grid and quit because it was what I wanted to do." Temper was sharp in his voice, hard in the fingers that gripped her arms. "I retired because I chose to retire. I'll race again if I choose to race again. I don't justify my life to anyone. I pay no one to take risks for me."

Fear over the thought of Lance taking the wheel again coated her anger. Her voice trembled as she fought to suppress even the possibility from her brain. "But you're not going to race again. You're not—"

"Don't tell me what I'm going to do." The words were clipped and final.

Foxy swallowed her terror and spoke with a desolate calm. Once again, she felt herself being shifted to the back seat. With Kirk, she had accepted the position without thought, but now, waves of anger, frustration, and pain spilled through her. "How foolish of me to have thought my feelings would be important enough to matter to you." She started to move past him, but he stopped her by placing his hands on her shoulders. The gesture itself was familiar enough to bring an ache to the pit of her stomach.

"Foxy, listen to me." There were hints of patience in Lance's voice again, but they were strained. "Kirk is a grown man, he makes his own decisions. Your brother's profession has nothing to do with you anymore. My profession has nothing to do with us."

"No." Calmly she lifted her eyes to meet his. "That's simply not true, Lance. But regardless of that, Kirk will drive your car next season, and you'll do precisely what you want to do. There's nothing I can do to change any of it. There never has been with Kirk, and now my position's been made clear with you. I'm going upstairs now," she told him quietly. "I'm tired."

The room was dark now. For some moments he studied her in complete silence before taking his hands from her shoulders. Without speaking, she took a step back, then moved around him and walked from the room. Her footsteps were soundless as she climbed the stairs.

CHAPTER 13

Morning came as a surprise to Foxy. She had lain awake for hours, alone and unhappy. Her conversation with Pam played over in her mind, and the argument with Lance came back to haunt her. Now she awoke, unaware of having fallen asleep, and the morning sun was streaming onto the bed. Lance's side of the bed was empty. Foxy's hand automatically reached out to touch the sheets where he would have slept. Some warmth still lingered on the spot, but it brought her no comfort. For the first time since their wedding night, they might have slept in separate beds. They had not woken tangled together, to drift into morning as they had drifted into night.

The heaviness that lay on Foxy did not come from sleep but from dejection. Arguing with Lance was certainly not a novel occupation to her, but this time Foxy felt the effects more deeply. *Perhaps,* she thought as she stared at the ceiling, *it's because now that I have more, I have more to lose. He's probably still downstairs. I could go down and… No.* Foxy interrupted her own train of thought with a shake of her head. No, there was too much here to be resolved over morning coffee with Mrs. Trilby hanging over his shoulder. *In any case, I could use the day to sort things out.*

Mechanically Foxy rose and showered. She took her time dressing, though her choice of cords and a rag sweater were simple. As she dressed, she mentally outlined her schedule. She would work on the racing prints until eleven, then she would walk to the public gardens and continue on her new project. Satisfied with her agenda, she moved downstairs. There was no sign of Lance, and though she told herself it was for the best, she lingered by the hall phone a moment, undecided. No, she told herself firmly. *I will not call him. We can't discuss anything rationally over the telephone. Is there anything to discuss?* she wondered and frowned at the phone as if it annoyed her. Lance seemed clear enough on his opinion of our positions last night. *I won't accept it,* she told herself staunchly, still staring at the phone. *I will not accept it. He can't go back to racing.* She swallowed the iron taste of fear that had risen to her throat. He couldn't have meant that. Squeezing her eyes tight, Foxy shook her head. *Don't think about it now. Go to work and don't think about it.* She took a deep breath and turned her back on the phone.

After confiscating a cup of coffee from the kitchen, Foxy closeted herself in her darkroom. The prints still hung on the line as she had left them. Without consciously planning to do so, she pulled the print of Kirk's racer down and studied it. *A comet,* she thought, remembering. *Yes, he is a comet, but doesn't even a comet have to burn out sometime? There'll be other pictures of him next year, but someone else will have to take them. Maybe Lance will arrange for that, too.* A sharp, frustrated sound escaped her. *I can't think about all of this anymore.* She pulled down the dry prints, then began to work on a fresh roll of film. Time passed swiftly and in such absolute silence that she was jolted when a knock sounded on the door. Foxy frowned as she went to answer it. Mrs. Trilby had never ventured into her territory.

"Melissa!" she exclaimed as her frown flew into a smile. "What a nice surprise."

"It's not dark," Melissa said with a small pout as she moved past Foxy and into the room. "Why is it called a darkroom if it isn't dark? I'm disillusioned."

"You came at the wrong time," Foxy explained. "I promise it was quite dark in here a couple of hours ago."

"I suppose I'll have to take your word for it." Melissa slowly walked down the line of new prints Foxy had hanging. "My, my, you really are a professional, aren't you?"

"I like to think so," Foxy answered wryly.

"All so technical," Melissa mused as she wandered around the room and scowled at bottles and timers. "I suppose this is what you studied in college."

"I majored in photography at USC. Not Smith," she added with a lift of brow. "Not Radcliffe, not Vassar, but at that little-known institution, the state college."

"Oh, dear." Melissa bit her lip but a small portion of the smile escaped. "Some of the ladies have been giving you a bad time, I take it."

"You take it right," Foxy agreed, then wrinkled her nose. "Well, I suppose I'm just a nine days' wonder. They'll forget about me soon enough."

"Such sweet naïveté," Melissa murmured as she patted Foxy's cheek. "I'll let you hold on to that little dream for a while. In any case," she continued, briskly brushing a speck from her pale blue angora sweater. "There's a dance at the country club Saturday. You and Lance are coming, aren't you?"

"Yes." Foxy didn't bother to suppress her sigh. "We'll be there."

"Buck up, darling. The obligations will taper off in a few months. Lance had never been one to socialize more than is absolutely necessary. And—" she smiled her singularly charming smile "—it's such a marvelous excuse to go shopping." Melissa gave the room another sweeping glance. "Are you all done in here?"

"Yes, I've just finished." Foxy glanced at her watch and gave a satisfied nod. "And right on schedule."

"Well then, let's go shopping and buy something fabulous to wear Saturday night." She linked her arm with Foxy's and began to lead her from the room.

"Oh no." She stopped long enough to close the darkroom door behind her. "I went on one of your little shopping safaris last week. You invaded every shop on Newbury Street. I haven't taken my vitamins today, and anyway, I have a dress for Saturday. I don't need anything."

"Good grief, do you have to *need* it before you buy it?" Melissa turned back from her journey to the stairs and gaped. "You only bought one little blouse when we went shopping before. What do you think Lance has all that lovely money for?"

"For a multitude of things, I'm sure," Foxy replied gravely. Still, a smile tugged at the corners of her mouth. "But hardly for me to spend on clothes I have no need for. In any case, I use my own money for personal things."

Melissa folded her arms and studied Foxy with care. "Why, you're serious, aren't you, pet?" She looked puzzled as she lifted her shoulders. "But Lance has simply hordes of money."

"I know that. I often wish he didn't." As she started to climb the stairs to the first floor Melissa took her arm.

"Wait a minute." Her voice had altered from its brisk good humor. It was quiet now, and serious. "They really are giving you a bad time, aren't they?"

"It doesn't matter," Foxy began, using a shrug to toss off the question.

"Oh, but I think it does." Melissa's hand was surprisingly firm on Foxy's arm. She kept Foxy facing her on the narrow stairway. "Listen to me a minute now. I'm going to be perfectly serious for a change. This business about you marrying Lance for his money is just typical nonsense, Foxy. It doesn't mean anything. And not everyone is saying it or thinking it. There are some morons who carry on about status and bloodlines, of course, but I never pay much attention to morons." She smiled when she paused for breath, but her eyes remained grave. "You've already won over a great many people, people like Grandmother, who's no pushover. And you've done that by simply being yourself. Surely Lance has told you how many people are pleased with his taste in wives."

"We don't discuss it." Foxy dragged her hand through her hair with a sound of frustration. "That is, to be more exact, I haven't said anything about his less friendly relations. It hardly seems fair to hound him with complaints."

"Is it fair for you to stand quiet while a scattered few toss rocks at you?" Melissa countered, lifting a brow uncannily as Lance did. "Martyrdom is depressing, Foxy."

Foxy grimaced at the title. "I don't think I care much for that." Shaking her head, she gave Melissa a rueful smile. "I suppose I'm being too sensitive. There've been so many changes all at once, and I'm having a hard time juggling everything."

Melissa linked her arm with Foxy's again as they mounted the stairs. "Now, what else is there?"

"Does it show?"

"I'm very perceptive," Melissa told her carelessly. "Didn't you know? My guess is that you and Lance had a tiff."

"Your term is a bit mild," Foxy murmured as she pushed open the door to the first floor. "But we'll go with it."

"Whose fault was it?"

Foxy opened her mouth to blame Lance, closed it again on the thought of blaming herself. She gave up with a sigh. "No one's, I suppose."

"That's the usual kind," Melissa said briskly. "The best cure is to go out and buy something fabulous to boost your ego. Then, if you want to make him suffer, you can be coolly polite when he gets home. Or—" she gestured fluidly with her hand "—if you want to make up, you send Mrs. Trilby home early and have on as little as possible when he gets here."

"Melissa." Foxy laughed as she watched her retrieve her coat and purse from the hall stand. "What a lovely way you have of simplifying things."

"It's a gift," she said modestly, studying her reflection in the antique mirror. "Are you going to be fun and come shopping with me, or are you going to be horribly industrious?"

"I think," Foxy mused thoughtfully, "I've just been insulted." On impulse, she leaned over and kissed Melissa's cheek. "You tempt me, but I'm very strong-willed."

"You're actually going to work this afternoon?" The look she gave Foxy was filled with both admiration and puzzlement. "But you even worked this morning."

"People have often been known to work an entire day," Foxy pointed out, then grinned. "It can get to be a habit…like potato chips. I'm starting a series of photographs on children, so I'm off to the park."

Melissa frowned as she slipped into her short fur jacket. "You make me feel quite the derelict."

"You'll get over it," Foxy comforted as she ran a curious finger down the soft white pelt.

"Of course." Melissa swirled around and kissed both of

Foxy's cheeks. "But for a moment, I feel guilty. Have a nice time, Foxy," she said as she swung out the door.

"You too," Foxy called over the quick slam. With a laugh, she pulled her own suede jacket from the closet. In a lighter frame of mind, she swung her purse over one shoulder and her camera case over the other. As she turned she all but collided with Mrs. Trilby. "Oh, I'm sorry." *Crepe-soled shoes,* Foxy thought with an inward sigh, *should be outlawed.*

"Are you going out, Mrs. Matthews?" Mrs. Trilby stood stiffly in her gray uniform and white apron.

"Yes, I have some work planned this afternoon. I should be back around three."

"Very good, ma'am." Mrs. Trilby stood expressionless in the archway as Foxy moved to the front door.

"Mrs. Trilby, if Lance…if Mr. Matthews should call, tell him I…" Foxy hesitated, and for a moment the unhappiness and indecision was reflected on her face.

"Yes, ma'am?" Mrs. Trilby prompted with the slightest softening of her tone.

"No," Foxy shook her head, annoyed with herself. "No, nothing. Never mind." She straightened her shoulders and sent the housekeeper a smile. "Goodbye, Mrs. Trilby."

"Good day, Mrs. Matthews."

Foxy stepped outside and breathed in the crisp autumn air. Though her MG had been shipped from Indiana and now sat waiting in the garage, Foxy opted to walk. The sky was piercingly blue, empty of clouds. Against the unrelieved color, the bare trees rose in stark supplication. Dry leaves whirled along the sidewalk and clung to the curbs. Now and then, the wind would whip them around Foxy's ankles until they fell again to be crunched underfoot. The crisp perfection of the day lifted her spirits higher, and she began to formulate an outline for the project she had in mind.

Mums were still stubbornly beautiful throughout the public gardens. There were flashes of rich color along the paths where rosy-cheeked children darted and played. The afternoon was fresh and sharp. Babies were rolled along in carriages or strollers by their mothers or uniformed nannies. Toddlers practiced the art of walking on the leaf-carpeted grass.

Foxy moved among them, sometimes shooting pictures, sometimes striking up a conversation with a parent, then charming her way into the shot she wanted. She had learned from experience that photography was more than knowing the workings of a camera or the speed of film. It was the ability to read and portray an image. It was patience, it was tenacity, it was luck.

She lay on her stomach on the cool grass, aiming her Nikon at a two-year-old girl who wrestled with a delighted bull terrier puppy. The child's blond, rosy beauty was the perfect foil for the dog's unabashed homeliness. A pool of sunlight surrounded them as they tussled, finding each other far more interesting than the woman who crawled and scooted around them snapping a camera. The dog yapped and rushed in circles, the child giggled and captured him. He escaped to be cheerfully captured again. At length, Foxy sat back on her heels and grinned at her models. After a quick exchange with the girl's mother, she stood, prepared to load a fresh roll of film.

"That was a fascinating performance."

Glancing up, Foxy found herself facing Jonathan Fitzpatrick. "Oh, hello." She tossed her hair behind her back, then brushed a stray leaf from her jacket.

"Hello, Mrs. Matthews. A lovely day for rolling in the grass."

His smile was so blatantly charming, Foxy laughed. "Yes, it is. Nice to see you again, Mr. Fitzpatrick."

"Jonathan," he corrected and plucked another leaf from her hair. "And I'll call you Foxy as Melissa does. It suits you. Now, may I ask what it is you're doing, or is it a government secret?"

"I'm taking pictures, of course." With a grin, Foxy continued to load her camera. "I make a habit of it, that's why I'm a photographer."

"Ah yes, I did hear that." As she bent her head over her work, the sunlight shot small flames through her hair. With admiration, Jonathan watched them flare. "Professional, are you?"

"That's what I tell the publishers." Finished, she closed the camera and gave Jonathan her attention again. The resemblance to his sister was striking, yet she felt no discomfort with him as she had with Gwen. He was, she thought on another quick study, an exact opposite of Lance: fair and smooth and harmless. Instantly annoyed with her habitual comparisons, she gave him her best smile. "I'm working on a project with children at the moment."

Jonathan studied her, taking in the easy smile, the large gray-green eyes, the face that became more intriguing each time it was seen. He completed his examination in a matter of seconds and decided Lance had won again. This was no ordinary lady. "May I watch awhile?" he asked, surprising them both. "I have the afternoon free. I was just crossing to my car when I spotted you."

"Of course." She bent to retrieve her camera case. "But I'm afraid you might find it boring." Turning, she began to walk in the direction of the Mill Pond.

"I doubt that. I rarely find beautiful women boring in any circumstances." Jonathan fell into step beside her. Foxy cast him a sidelong look. He had the smile of the boy next door and the profile of an Adonis. Melissa, Foxy mused, is going to have her hands full.

"What do you do, Jonathan?"

"As I please," he answered as he slipped his hands into the pockets of his leather jacket. "Theoretically, I'm an executive in the family business. Import-export. In reality, I'm a paper shuffler who charms wives when necessary and escorts daughters."

Humor sparkled in Foxy's eyes. "Do you enjoy your work?"

"Immensely." When he looked down with his easy grin, she decided he and Melissa were ideally suited for each other.

"I enjoy mine as well," she told him. "Now stand out of the way while I do some."

There was a bench by the pond where a willow dipped into the mirrorlike water. A woman sat reading while a chubby toddler in a bright red jacket tossed crackers to paddling ducks. Nearby, an infant snoozed in a stroller in a square of sunshine. A forgotten rattle hung limply in the curled fingers. After exchanging a quiet word with the woman on the bench, Foxy set to work. Taking care not to disturb him, she captured the delight of the toddler as he threw his crumbs high in the air. Ducks scrambled for the free meal. The boy squealed with pleasure and tossed again, sometimes sampling a cracker himself while the ducks vied for the soggy offering. She translated the sound of his laughter onto film.

Using sun and shade, she expressed the peace and innocence of the fat-cheeked infant. Changing angles, speeds and filters, she altered moods and heightened emotions, until, satisfied, she stopped and let the camera hang by its strap.

"You're very intense while you work," Jonathan commented as he moved up to join her. "You look very competent."

"Is that a compliment or an observation?" Foxy asked him, then snapped on her lens cover.

"A complimentary observation," Jonathan countered. He continued to study her profile as she secured her equipment.

"You fascinate me, Foxy Matthews. I find you one more reason to envy Lance."

"Do you?" She looked up, revealing a guileless interest that surprised him. "And are there many others?"

"Scores," he said promptly, then took her hand. "But you're at the top of the list. Is it true your brother's Kirk Fox and that Lance snatched you from the racing world?"

"Yes." Foxy was immediately on guard. Her tone cooled. "I grew up at the racetrack."

Jonathan lifted a brow. "I've struck a nerve. I'm sorry." He ran his thumb absently across her knuckles. "Would it help if I said I'm curious, not critical? Lance's racing career also fascinates me, and I've followed your brother's as well. I thought you might have some interesting stories to tell." His voice, Foxy noted, was not like Gwen's; it was far too honest.

"I'm sorry." She sighed and moved her shoulders. "That's the second time today I've been overly sensitive. It's a bit difficult being the new kid on the block."

"You were a bit of a surprise." His touch was so light that Foxy had forgotten he still held her hand. "There are those who require everything well planned and predictable. Lance seems to prefer the unique."

"Unique," Foxy murmured, then shot Jonathan a direct, uncompromising stare. "I don't have any money, I haven't a pedigree. I spent my adolescent years around garages and mechanics. I didn't go to an exclusive college, and all I've seen of Europe is what I could squeeze in between time trials and races."

Watching her, Jonathan observed the tiny flecks of unhappiness in her eyes. Sunlight flickered through the willow leaves to catch the highlights of her hair. "Would you like to have an affair?" he asked casually.

Stunned, Foxy stepped back, her eyes huge. "No!"

"Have you ever ridden on the swan boat?" he inquired just as easily.

Her mouth opened and closed twice in utter confusion. "No," she managed cautiously.

"Good." He took her hand again. "We'll do that instead." He smiled, keeping her fingers tightly in his. "All right?"

Warily Foxy studied his face. Before she realized it, a smile began to tug at the corners of her mouth. "All right," she agreed. *Melissa will never be bored,* she decided as she let Jonathan lead her away.

"Would you care for a balloon?" His voice took on a formal note.

"Yes, thank you," she returned in a matching tone. "A blue one."

The next two hours were the most carefree Foxy had spent since she had begun her social duties as Mrs. Lance Matthews. With Jonathan, she glided on the Mill Pond, tucked in a swan boat with tourists and sticky-fingered preschoolers. They walked through the gardens eating ice cream with Foxy's balloon trailing on its string at their backs. She found him undemanding, easy to talk to, a tonic for depression.

When Jonathan pulled up in front of the brownstone, Foxy's mood was still light. "Would you like to come in?" She shifted the strap of her case onto her shoulder. "Perhaps you could stay for dinner."

"Another time. I have a dinner engagement with Melissa."

"Tell her hello for me." With a smile, Foxy opened her door. "Thank you, Jonathan." On impulse, she leaned across the seat and kissed his cheek. "I'm sure it was much more fun than an affair, and so much simpler."

"Simpler anyway," he agreed, then brushed a finger down her nose. "I'll see you and Lance on Saturday."

"Oh, yes." Foxy made a face before she slid from the car. "Oh, tell Melissa I totally approve of her plans for May." She laughed at his puzzled face, then waved him away. "She'll know what I mean." Slamming the door, she shivered once in the cooling air before moving up the path to the house. The front door opened as she reached for the knob.

"Hello, Foxy." Lance stood in the doorway. With a quick scan, he took in her smile, bright eyes, and blue balloon. "Apparently you've had an enjoyable afternoon."

Her buoyant mood left no place for remnants of anger from yesterday's argument. They could talk and be serious later, now she wanted to share her pleasure. "Lance, you're home early." She was glad to find him waiting and smiled again.

"Actually, I believe you're home late," he countered as he shut the door behind her.

"Oh?" A look at her watch told her it was nearly five. "I didn't realize, I suppose I lost track of the time." With the balloon tied jauntily to its strap, Foxy set down the camera case. "Have you been home long?"

"Long enough." He studied her autumn-kissed cheeks. "Want a drink?" he said as he turned and walked back into the drawing room.

"No, thank you." His coolness had seeped through Foxy's elated spirits. She followed him, calculating the best way to bridge the gap before it widened further. "We didn't have any plans for this evening, did we?"

"No." Lance poured a generous helping of scotch into a glass before he turned back to her. "Do you intend to go out again?"

"No, I…" She stopped, paralyzed by the ice in his eyes. "No."

He drank, watching her over the rim. The tension that had flown from her during the afternoon returned. Still, she could not yet bring herself to speak of Kirk or racing. "I ran into Jonathan Fitzpatrick in the public gardens," she began, unbuttoning her jacket in order to keep her hands busy. "He brought me home."

"So I noticed." Lance stood with his back to the wide stone fireplace. His face was cool and impassive.

"It was beautiful out today," Foxy hurried on, fretting for a way out of the polite, meaningless exchange. Warily, she watched Lance pour another glass of scotch. "There seem to be a lot of tourists still, but Jonathan said they slack off during the winter."

"I had no idea Jonathan was interested in the tourist population."

"I was interested," she corrected, then pulled off her jacket with a frown. "It was crowded in the swan boats."

"Did Jonathan take you?" Lance asked mildly before he tossed back the contents of his glass. "How charming."

"Well, I hadn't been before so he—"

"It appears I've been neglecting you," he interrupted. Foxy's frown deepened as he lifted the bottle of scotch again.

"You're being ridiculous," Foxy stated as her temper began to rise. "And you're drinking too much."

"My dear child, I haven't begun to drink too much." He poured another glass. "And as for being ridiculous, there are some men who would cheerfully beat a wife who spends afternoons with other men."

"That's a Neanderthal attitude," she snapped. She tossed her jacket into a chair and glared at him. "It was perfectly harmless. We were in a public place."

"Yes, buying balloons and riding on swans."

"We had an ice cream cone as well," she supplied and jammed her hands into her pockets.

"Your tastes are amazingly simple." Lance glanced briefly into his glass before lifting it and swallowing. "For someone in your current position."

Her shocked gasp was trapped by the obstruction in her throat. Absolutely still, she stood while all color drained from her face. Against the pallor, her eyes were dark with hurt. Swearing richly, Lance set down his glass.

"That was below the belt, Fox, I'm sorry." He stared toward her, but she backed away, throwing out her hands to ward him off.

"No, don't touch me." She took quick, deep breaths to control the tremor in her voice. "I've had to listen to the innuendos, I've had to put up with the knowing smirks and tolerate the sniping, but I never expected it from you. I'd rather you had beat me than said that to me." Turning quickly, she fled up the stairs. Before she could slam the bedroom door, Lance caught her wrist.

"Don't turn away from me," he warned in a low, even voice. "Don't ever turn away from me."

"Let go of me!" she shouted, trying to pull away from him. Before she thought about what she was doing, she swung out with her free hand and slapped him.

"All right," he said between his teeth as he locked both her arms behind her back. "I had that coming, now calm down."

"Just take your hands off me and leave me alone." She struggled for release but was only caught tighter.

"Not until we settle this. There are some things that have to be explained."

"I don't need to explain anything." She tossed her head to free her eyes from her hair. "Now take your hands off me, I can't bear it."

"Don't push me too far, Foxy." Lance's voice was as dark and dangerous as his eyes. "I'm running low on self-control, particularly after last night. Now calm down, and we'll talk."

"I don't have anything to say to you." Cold with fury, she stopped struggling and stared up at him. "I had my say yesterday, and you've had yours tonight. It looks like we understand each other well enough."

"Then we won't talk," Lance said harshly before his mouth came down on hers. With an iron grip, he handcuffed her wrists so that her frantic movements were useless. There was something calculating as well as brutal in the kiss. She recognized the same ruthlessness she knew him to be capable of in racing. Knowing her struggles were futile, she forced her body to go limp and her mouth to remain passive. "Ice won't work," Lance muttered and lifted her off her feet. "I know how to melt it."

As he began to carry her to the bed Foxy's passive acceptance disappeared. "No!" Desperately she tried to free herself from his arms. "Lance, don't, not like this." She pushed hard against his chest and felt herself falling. Her small cry of alarm was knocked from her as she hit the mattress. Before she could roll away, he was on top of her.

His body molded itself to hers. As she turned her head his hand locked on her jaw, holding her face still as his mouth took hers again. Quickly, as though her struggles were nonexistent, he began to undress her. There was determination without passion in his movements. He didn't look for partnership now, but for capitulation. Foxy's body heated to his touch even as she fought for freedom. Her sweater and jeans were tossed carelessly to the floor and the thin chemise she wore was no barrier against his hands. Her nipples were taut against the silk as he sought the sensitive hollow of her throat with his lips and tongue. She continued to struggle even as his hand moved down the silk to the flatness of her stomach. His fingers moved roughly over the top of her leg where the chemise ended.

Desire surged through her, weighing on her limbs as she pushed and twisted. She knew she needed to escape not only from him but from herself. Her movements brought only more arousal. With his tongue, he traced the peak of her breast through the chemise, catching it then between his teeth as her fingers dug into his shoulders. He exploited her weaknesses, explored the secrets only he knew until the fire kindled and flared. She responded. She arched against him now not in protest, but in answer. Hungrily her mouth sought his as her fingers fumbled with the buttons of his shirt. His skin was hot against her palms, his muscles tight.

Abruptly, his mood altered. His cool control vanished as a thunderous urgency took its place. Hooking his hands in the bodice, he ripped the chemise down the front in one sharp gesture. Foxy heard him curse her as his breathing grew as labored as hers. His hands were wild now, bruising over her naked skin while his mouth was hard and demanding. Control was lost for both of them. There was only sensation, only need, only the dark pleasure of damp flesh and deep kisses. But even as he took her, even as she gave herself without reservation, Foxy knew neither of them had won.

CHAPTER 14

It started raining early Saturday morning. Then the cold arrived and turned the rain to snow before afternoon. Alone, with the house rattling around her, Foxy watched it fall in thin sheets. The ground was still warm, and the snow melted even as it landed. It poured down quickly enough, but left no trace. *There'll be no snowmen built today,* Foxy mused and hugged her elbows. *I wonder where he could have gone.*

Lance had already left when she awakened, and the house was empty. Foxy knew that what had passed between them the night before had cost them both dearly. In the end, he hadn't taken her in anger, and she had given herself willingly. Desire had won over both of them but misunderstanding remained in its wake. Discovering herself alone in a cold bed had shot a shaft of gloom over her, which grew only sharper as the hours passed. The morning hours spent in her darkroom had been productive but had done nothing to alleviate her dilemma.

What's happening to my marriage? she asked herself as she stared out at the stubbornly falling snow. *It's barely begun, and it seems to be going nowhere. Like the snow out there,* she mused, and lay her fingers on the windowpane. *It just keeps disap-pearing. Could it be as fragile as an early snow, and as fleet-ing?* Foxy shook her head and cradled her elbows. *I won't let it be.* The sound of the phone had her whirling around. *Lance,* she thought instantly and raced to answer it.

"Hello," she said with anticipation ripe in her voice.

"Hiya, Foxy. How are things in the real world?"

"Kirk." Her disappointment was outweighed by her plea-sure. She dropped down on an ottoman and pushed the disappointment aside. "It's good to hear your voice." Even as she said the words, she realized how true they were. Her plea-sure increased and turned to happiness. "How are you?" she demanded. "Have you talked them into letting you out? Where's Pam?"

"I think marriage has slowed you down," he commented gravely. "Can't you think of anything to say?"

Laughing, Foxy tucked her feet under her. "Just answer any or all of the above questions, but start with the first one. How are you?"

"Pretty good. Healing. They might be persuaded to let me out in a couple weeks if Pam's willing to cart me back and forth for therapy." She could tell from the sound of his voice that his injuries were hardly uppermost in his mind. *Profes-sional risks.* She remembered Lance's words and bit down hard on her bottom lip.

"I imagine she could be persuaded," Foxy managed to say naturally. "I'm glad you're better." *I worry about you,* she told him silently, then smiled and shook her head. *He wouldn't like to hear that.* "I suppose you're getting bored."

"I passed bored last week," he returned dryly. "I'm getting so good at the *Times* crossword puzzles, I've started doing them in ink to show off."

"You were always cocky. Shall I send you some paste and

colored paper to keep you busy?" She kept her tongue in her cheek as she heard him snarl.

"I'll let that pass because I'm good-natured." Kirk ignored her laughter and continued. "So, tell me about Boston. Do you like it there?"

"It's beautiful." As she answered, Foxy glanced out the window. Flakes were falling in a white curtain and vanishing. "It's snowing now, and I suppose it'll turn cold, but I've done a lot of exploring. I'm rather anxious to see how Boston looks in the winter."

"How about Lance's family," Kirk demanded. "I can get a weather report from the newspaper."

"Well, they're..." She fumbled for words, hesitated, and ultimately laughed. "They're different. I feel a bit like Gulliver, finding himself an oddity in a world where the rules are all different. We're getting used to each other, and I've made a couple of friends." She smiled, thinking of Melissa and Jonathan. Remembering Catherine, she felt the smile slip a bit, and with a shrug began to trace a pattern on the ottoman with her fingernail. "I'm afraid his mother doesn't care for me."

"You didn't marry his mother," Kirk pointed out logically. "I can't imagine my sister letting herself get pushed around by a few Boston bluebloods." He spoke with such easy confidence that Foxy was forced to smile again.

"Who me?" she countered, accepting the strange compliment. "They grow 'em tough in the Midwest, you know."

"Yeah, you're a real Amazon." The rough affection in his tone made her smile sweeten. "How's Lance?"

"He's fine," she answered automatically. Nibbling on her lips, she added, "He's been busy."

"I imagine the plans for the new car have him pretty tied up just now." She heard the excitement creep into Kirk's voice and schooled herself to accept it. "It sounds like a beauty. I'm itching to get up there and see how it's going. Lance is a damn genius at a drawing board."

"Is he?" Foxy asked with a curious frown.

"It's one thing to come up with ideas, Fox. I have a few of those myself. It's another to be able to put them to practical use." He spoke with a hint of envious amusement, causing Foxy to consider another aspect of her husband.

"Strange, he doesn't seem the type for drawing boards and calculators, does he?"

"Lance isn't any type at all," Kirk corrected. "You should know that better than anyone."

Foxy paused a moment in thought. Her frown deepened, then softened into a smile. "Yes, of course, you're right. And I do know it, I've needed someone to remind me though. It's also nice to hear from my brother that my husband is a genius."

"He was always more interested in the mechanics than the race," Kirk added absently. "So, how are you?"

"Me?" Foxy shook her head to bring her attention back to Kirk. "Oh, fine. You can tell Pam I have the prints finished and I'll be sending them up to her."

"Are you happy?"

She heard the same seriousness in his tone she had heard when Pam had asked the identical question. "What sort of question is that to ask a woman who's only been married a few weeks," she countered lightly. "You're not supposed to come down to happy for at least a month."

"Foxy," Kirk began.

"I love him, Kirk," she interrupted, voicing some of her thoughts for the first time. "It's not always easy and it's not always perfect, but it's the only place for me. I'm happy and I'm sad, and I'm a hundred other things I wouldn't be if I didn't have Lance."

"Okay." She could almost see his nod of acceptance. "As long as you have what you want. Listen, I really called to let you know. Well, I thought I should tell you first...."

Foxy waited a full ten seconds. "What?" she demanded on an exasperated laugh.

"I asked Pam to marry me."

"Thank goodness."

"You don't sound surprised," he complained.

A grin of pure pleasure spread over Foxy's face. "Only that such a nifty driver could be so slow. When are you getting married?"

"An hour ago."

"What?"

"Now you sound surprised," Kirk stated, satisfied. "Pam wouldn't wait until I could stand up, so we got married right here in the hospital. I tried to call you before, but nobody answered."

"I was down in my darkroom." With a sigh, she drew her knees up to her chest. "Oh, Kirk, I'm happy for you. I'm not sure I believe it."

"I'm not sure I do either. She's not like anyone else in the world." Foxy heard the tone, recognized it, and blinked tears from her lashes.

"Yes, I know what you mean. Can I talk to her?"

"She's not here, she's out making arrangements for this place we're going to rent while I'm having my leg prodded. We're hoping to be in Boston by the first of the year so that I can keep an eye on Lance and my car, but we'll stay near the hospital till then."

"I see." *He'll never change,* she told herself and shut her eyes briefly. I was a fool to think differently. Everything Lance said the other night was true. Kirk will race as long as he's capable of racing. Nothing and no one could stop him. She clearly remembered the things she had said to Lance in the dimming light of the library. Guilt all but smothered her. Foxy switched the phone to her other ear and swallowed. "I'll be glad to have you and Pam here, even if it's only until the season starts." Understanding made acceptance easier.

"Will you be coming to Europe?"

"No." Foxy shook her head and made the break. "No, I won't be coming."

"Pam said she didn't think you would. Listen, they're coming in to poke at me again. Tell Lance that Pam and I expect him to break out some champagne when we get into town. The French stuff."

"I'll do that," she promised, relieved that he had let her go without a second thought. "Take care of yourself."

"Sure. Hey, I love you, Foxy."

"I love you, too." After cradling the phone, Foxy drew her knees closer and wrapped her arms around them. As she watched, the snow grew thinner until it was little more than a fine mist.

He doesn't need me anymore, she reflected before she realized the thought had been in her mind. It struck her as odd that she had not fully understood Kirk's need for her until it no longer existed. Their need for each other had been mutual, even when she had been a child. The link between them was strong, perhaps because of the tragedy that had left them only each other. *There'll always be something special between us,* Foxy brooded. *But he has Pam now, and I have Lance.* Resting her chin on her knees, Foxy wondered if Lance needed her. Loved her, yes, wanted her, but did Lance Matthews with his casual self-sufficiency, his easy wealth and supreme confidence *need* her? Was there something special about her that completed his life, or was she simply overly romantic and foolish in wanting to believe it was true? She found, to her surprise, that the answer mattered very much.

Abruptly Foxy's senses tingled. Lifting her head, she looked up to see Lance standing in the doorway. Moving quickly, she unfolded herself from the ottoman and stood. As she met his eyes every speech she had rehearsed, edited, and rehearsed that morning vanished from her mind. Foolishly she tugged her sweatshirt over the hips of her jeans and wished she had worn something more dignified.

"I didn't hear you come in," she said, then cursed herself for the inanity.

"You were on the phone." It was his quiet, measuring look. He stood watching her without a flicker in his eyes to hint at his thoughts. Nerves began to dance in her stomach.

"Yes, I… It was Kirk." She tugged her fingers through her hair, unable to keep them still, and inadvertently betrayed her tension.

In silence, Lance continued to scan her face. He came no further into the room when he spoke again. "How is he?"

"Fine. He sounds wonderful actually. He and Pam were married this morning." While making the announcement, Foxy began to wander around the room. She fiddled with priceless pieces of bric-a-brac and toyed with Mrs. Trilby's careful arrangement of fall flowers.

"That pleases you?" Lance asked, studying her restless movements before he crossed to the bar. He lifted a bottle of scotch, then set it down again without pouring any.

"Yes. Yes, very much." Taking a deep breath, she prepared to plunge into an apology for blaming him for Kirk's decision to continue racing. "Lance, I… Oh." As she turned, she found him directly in front of her. She backed up a step, surprised, and his brow lifted at her action. While Foxy dealt with feeling awkward and unsettled, Lance slipped his hands in his pockets.

"Apologies aren't my strong suit," he stated as she searched for a way to begin again. "In this case, however, I don't think it's possible to avoid the need for one." His face was closed against her searching gaze. His eyes were on hers, but they did not speak to her. "I apologize both for the things I said to you and for what happened. That hardly makes up for it, but you have my word, nothing like that will happen again."

His stilted formality only added to Foxy's strain. She knew nothing she had planned to say could be said to the polite stranger who stood before her. Dropping her eyes, she studied the pattern in the Aubusson rug. "No absolution, Foxy?" Hearing the softness in his voice, she lifted her eyes again.

The strain, she noted, was not all on her side. She saw the signs of a restless night in his face and was compelled to offer comfort. She lifted a hand to his cheek. "Please, Lance, let's forget about it. We've both said things these past couple of days that shouldn't have been said." Her eyes and mouth were grave as her palm brushed over his cheek. "I don't like apologies either."

Lance lifted his fingers and twined the tip of a curl around them. "You always were a strange mixture of tiger and kitten. I think I'd forgotten how disarmingly sweet you can be." His eyes were no longer silent as he looked at her. "I love you, Foxy."

"Lance." Foxy flung her arms around him and burrowed her face into his neck. At last, the tension inside her uncurled. "I've missed you," she murmured against his neck. "I didn't know where you'd gone, and the house seemed so empty."

"I went into the office," he told her as he slipped his hands under her shirt to caress the warm length of her back. "You should have called if you were lonely."

"I almost did, but I thought..." She sighed and closed her eyes, wonderfully content. "I didn't want it to seem as if I was checking on you."

"Idiot," he muttered, then tilted her head back and kissed her briefly. "You're my wife, remember?"

"You have to keep reminding me," she suggested and smiled. "I don't feel like a wife yet, and I don't know the rules."

"We make our own." This time when he kissed her, it was long and lingering. In instant response, her bones liquified. Her mouth clung to his, avid and sweet while his quiet moan of pleasure warmed her skin.

"I want champagne tonight," she murmured against his ear. "I feel like a celebration."

"For Pam and Kirk?" Lance questioned before he came back to her mouth.

"For us first," Foxy countered, drawing away far enough to smile at him. "Then for Pam and Kirk."

"All right. But tomorrow I want to go to the movies and eat popcorn."

"Oh yes!" Her face lit with pleasure. Her eyes danced. "Yes, something either terribly sad or terribly funny. And I want a pizza afterward with pepperoni."

"A very demanding woman." Lance laughed as he took her hand and lifted it to his lips. Suddenly his fingers tightened on hers. Sensing a dramatic change of mood, Foxy stared down at their joined hands. Slowly Lance turned hers to the side and examined the light trail of mauve shadows on her wrist. "It seems I owe you yet another apology."

Distressed that the stiffness was back in his manner, Foxy moved toward him. "Lance, don't. It's nothing."

"On the contrary." The coldness in his voice halted her. "It's quite a lot."

"Don't! I can't stand it when you're like this." Filled with frustration, Foxy paced around the room. "I can't deal with you when you're formal and polite." She whirled to face him, then whirled back to roam the room again. "If you're going to be angry, then at least be angry in a way I can understand. Shout, swear, break something," she invited with an inclusive sweep of her hand. "But don't stand there like a pillar of the community. I don't understand pillars."

"Foxy." A reluctant grin teased Lance's mouth as he watched her storm around the room. "If you knew how difficult you make things."

"I'm not trying to make things difficult." She lifted a pillow from the couch and hurled it across the room. "I'm trying to make thing simple. *I'm* simple, don't you understand?"

"You are," Lance corrected, "infinitely complex."

"No, no, no!" Foxy stomped her foot, furious that they were talking in circles again. "You don't understand anything!" Angrily she tossed her hair behind her back. "I'm going upstairs," she announced and marched from the room.

Going directly to the bath, Foxy turned on the water and let it steam. Carelessly she tossed a mixture of powders and scents into the tub and stripped. *He's an idiot,* she decided as she plopped into the oversized tub. Bubbles rose and frothed around her. *And so am I.* Seething with impotence, Foxy picked up a sponge and began to scrub.

I could probably stop loving him if I really put my mind to it. She scowled at the sponge then squeezed it mercilessly. *I'm going to stop loving him and work on hating him. Once I start hating him,* she concluded, *I won't be an idiot anymore.* As the door opened she glanced up sharply.

"Mind if I shave?" Lance asked casually as he strolled into

the room. He had slipped out of his jacket and now wore only his shirt and slacks. Ignoring her glare and not waiting for her assent, he opened the medicine chest.

"I've decided to hate you," Foxy informed him after he had removed the shaving lotion and begun to lather his face.

"Oh?" She watched his eyes shift in the mirror until they met hers. It infuriated her that they were amused. "Again?"

"I was good at it once," she reminded him. "I'm going to be even better at it this time."

"No doubt." The razor stroked clean over his cheek. "Most things improve with age."

"I'm going to hate you perfectly."

"Good for you," Lance told her as he continued to shave. "One should always aim high."

Beyond control, Foxy hurled the wet sponge and hit Lance between the shoulder blades. She felt a surge of satisfaction almost immediately followed by a surge of alarm. *He won't,* she decided grimly, *let me get away with that one.* Still, her eyes challenged his. Slowly Lance set down the razor and bent to pick up the sponge. Foxy's trepidation grew as he turned and walked to the tub. *He wouldn't drown me,* she thought, fending off a few pricks of doubt. Even as she debated the matter, Lance sat on the edge of the tub. She realized with some disgust that she had backed herself neatly into a corner.

Lance made no comment, only dropped the sponge back into the water with a plop. Distracted, Foxy glanced down. Before she realized his intent, his hand was on her head and she was sliding under the hot, fragrant water. Sputtering, she surfaced. Her hair dripped and frothed over her shoulders and into her face as she wiped the bubbles from her eyes.

"I do hate you!" she choked, pushing at her sopping hair. "I'm going to thrive on hating you! I'm going to invent new ways to hate you!"

Lance gave her a calm nod. "Everybody should have a hobby."

"Oh!" Incoherent with fury, Foxy tossed as much water into his face as she could manage. She braced herself for another dunking. To her utter amazement, Lance rolled into the tub in one smooth, unexpected motion. Bubbles spewed over the side. Her shock was transformed into hysterical giggles. "You're crazy," she concluded as she tried to keep herself from submerging under the rocking water. "How can I hate you properly if you're crazy?" Their bodies tangled together effortlessly. Her skin was slick and fragrant from the oil, and his hands slid over it, bringing her closer. His wet clothes were little more than nothing between them. "You're drowning me," Foxy protested as he shifted her. She swallowed bubbles and giggled again. "I knew you were going to drown me."

"I'm not going to drown you," Lance corrected. "I'm going to make love with you." He gripped her waist and nudged her up until her chin cleared the water. His fingers lingered, spreading over her stomach while his hand cupped her breast. There was a gentleness in his touch he rarely used. "Since you were sharing your sponge and water, I figured you wanted me to join you." He grinned as Foxy pushed dripping hair from his eyes. "I didn't want to be accused of being stuffy."

"You're not stuffy," she said softly. Her eyes reflected regret as they met his. "Lance…"

"No more apologies tonight." He closed his mouth over hers to shut it off before it could be formed. He took his hands on a slow, easy journey of her body, pausing and lingering, seducing with a quiet touch.

"We should talk," Foxy murmured, but the words were faint and without conviction. Her sigh was more eloquent.

"Tomorrow. Tomorrow we'll be sensible and talk and sort things through." As he spoke, his lips roamed over her face. His hands sought and touched and enticed. "I want you tonight. I want to make love with my wife." He moved his lips to her neck, tasting, before he caught the lobe of her ear between his teeth. Foxy shuddered and drew him closer. "Then I want to take her out and get her a little drunk before I bring her home and make love with her all over again."

His mouth returned to hers, demanding, then possessing, then demanding again. All sensible thoughts floated from Foxy's mind.

CHAPTER 15

Foxy began her work day much later in the morning than was her habit. It was nearly eleven before she had finished sorting and cataloging the prints. As she slid them into a thick envelope for mailing she thought over the last few months. For a moment, as she brought it all back into her mind, she could almost smell the hot scent of fuel, hear the high squeal of tires and roaring engines. Shaking her head, she began to seal the envelope. *I'm finished with all that now. It's behind me.*

Briskly she began to develop the film she had taken of children in the park and around Boston. In the back of her mind, the idea for a book was germinating, a collection of photographs of children. Instinct told her that some of the shots were exceptional. *More time,* she mused, *more variety. I'll have to haunt a few more playgrounds.* Patiently she worked through the morning and early afternoon, letting her fingers act as her eyes when the room was dark. Still, her mind continued to drift to Lance.

Foxy knew the night spent in lovemaking had not solved any of their true problems. Again and again, her thoughts returned to the possibility of Lance going back to racing. Again and again, she closed off the idea. *Coward,* she accused herself as she stood in the dark. *You have to think about it, you have to deal with it. I don't know if I can.* She pressed her fingers against her eyes and took a deep breath. *I have to talk to him. Sensibly. Isn't that what he said? Tonight we'll talk sensibly.* She reflected that they had done little of that since he had asked her to marry him in her motel room near Watkins Glen. It was time, she decided, to find out what each of them wanted from the other, and what each was willing to give.

Locked in the darkroom with a red bulb casting its pale light, Foxy discovered one of the answers for herself. As she moved prints from tray to tray and images formed on the paper, she began to understand fully what she had been looking for. The faces of children looked back at her, some smiling, some caught in temper tantrums or tears. There were sleeping infants, moon-faced toddlers, sharp-eyed preschoolers. Foxy hung the prints with a growing sense of serenity. She wanted children. She wanted a family and all that went with it. The home, the normality, the commitment of a structured family was something she found she wanted and perhaps had been afraid to ask for. A permanent home with the man she loved…Lance's children…family traditions. *Her* family's traditions.

Would Lance feel the same way? Foxy pushed the hair from her face and tried to think of the answer. She discovered that as long as she had known him, as intimate as they had been, she did not know. *We will have to talk about it,* she told herself as she studied the drying prints. *We will have to talk about a number of things.*

A glance at her watch told her she still had a few afternoon hours left. It was time, she thought, to finish her commitment to Pam and the racing shots. After gathering up her gear, she went upstairs to put a call through to Lance's office. The quick, efficient voice of his secretary answered.

"Hello, Linda, it's Mrs. Matthews. Is Lance busy?"

"I'm sorry, Mrs. Matthews, he's not in. Would you like to leave a message or is there something I could do for you?"

"Well, no, I… Yes, actually," Foxy decided with another glance at her watch. She wanted to get this done today. "He's working on a new car, a new Formula One for next season."

"Yes, the one your brother will drive."

"That's right. I'd like to get some pictures if I can."

"That shouldn't be a problem, Mrs. Matthews, if you don't mind a bit of a drive. Mr. Matthews and the crew have the car out at the track today for some testing."

"That's perfect." Foxy picked up the pad and pencil by the phone. "You'll have to give me directions. I haven't been out there yet."

Thirty minutes later, Foxy pulled up near the familiar sight of the oval track. As she stepped from the car the brisk breeze caught at her hair and blew open her unbuttoned jacket. The roaring sound of the engine reached her ears. Shielding her eyes with her hand, she watched the low red blur whiz around the track. The smell of hot rubber and fuel filled the air. *It never changes,* she thought and slipped the strap of her camera around her neck. She recognized Charlie with a group of men, wondered fleetingly where Lance might be, then set to work.

Foxy moved quickly. After choosing the best position for the shots, she selected a lens and set the camera. With quick turns of the controls and shifts of her own body, she snapped shot after shot. It was, she observed, a fast one. The car seemed like a ball of flame as it rounded a curve and sped down the straightaway. *It will suit Kirk,* she mused, easily able to picture him in the cockpit. *And Kirk will suit it.* Foxy straightened, pushing her hair behind her ears as she stood.

"Can't keep you away from the track, huh, kid?"

Turning, Foxy grinned into Charlie's scowling face. "I can't keep away from you, Charlie," she corrected. She plucked the smoldering cigar from his mouth and gave him a loud, smacking kiss. He shuffled his feet as she handed it back to him.

"Got no respect," he grumbled. He cleared his throat, then squinted at her. "You getting along all right?"

"I'm getting along just fine," she told him. Moving with an old habit, she rubbed her palm over his grizzled beard. "How about you?"

"Busy," he growled, but colored under his fierce frown. "Between your brother and your husband I got no time."

"Price you pay for being the best."

Charlie sniffed, accepting the truth. "Kirk'll be ready for the car when it's ready for him," he prophesied. "Shame we don't have two," he mused as he shifted his narrowed eyes back to the track. "Lance knows how to handle a machine."

Foxy started to make some comment when the full meaning of Charlie's statement sunk in. Her eyes flew to the track and locked on the speeding car. Lance. The iron taste of fear rose in her throat. She shook her head, trying to deny what her mind screamed was the truth. "Lance is driving?" she heard herself ask. Her voice sounded thin and hollow to her ears, as if it had traveled down a long tunnel.

"Yeah, regular test driver's sick." Charlie's answer was casual before he shuffled off. Foxy was left alone as the roaring sound of the engine droned on.

As she watched, the car did a quick fishtail on a curve, then straightened without any slackening of speed. Foxy's brow felt like ice. Queasiness knotted her stomach, and for a moment the bright sunlight dimmed. She chewed on her bottom lip and let the pain overwhelm the faintness. She stood helplessly while dozens of the crashes she remembered passed vividly in front of her mind's eye. *Not again,* she thought in desperation. *Oh God, not again.* He drove as he had always driven, with complete control and determination, not a comet, but a ruthless, cunning tyrant. Foxy began to shiver uncontrollably in the quick autumn breeze. *It'll be hot in the cockpit,* she thought as her fingers went numb on the strap of her camera. *Desperately hot, and all he sees is the track, all he hears is the engine. And the speed's like a drug that keeps pulling him back.*

Fear kept her frozen even after she heard the whine of the slowing engine. She stood straight and still as Lance pulled up near the group of men. Unstrapped, he unfolded himself from the cockpit, pulling off his helmet as he stood. He peeled off the balaclava then ran a hand through his hair. She had seen him make the same gestures after countless races on countless grids. Pain began to work its way through the cold fear. Her breath became irregular. Lance was grinning down at Charlie, and his laughter carried to her. His brow lifted at something Charlie said, and his eyes followed the careless gesture of the older man until they found Foxy.

For a moment, they only watched each other; husband and wife, man and woman, two people who had known each other for a decade. She saw his expression change, but took no time to decipher it. Tears were coming too quickly for her to prevent them. *I've lost,* she thought, and pressed her hands against the sides of her face. As Lance pushed his way through the group of men Foxy turned and ran toward her car. He called her name, but she wrenched open the door and tumbled inside. The only coherent thought in her mind as she turned the key was escape. Seconds later, she was racing away from the track.

It was nearly dark when Foxy turned down the street toward the brownstone. Streetlights flickered on. Lance's car sat at the curb rather than in the garage, and she pulled her MG

behind it. Foxy turned off the engine, and rested her forehead for a moment against the wheel. The two hours she
had spent driving had calmed her but left her enervated. She
took this time to gain back some strength. With slow, careful movements, she stepped from the car and moved up the
walk. Even as she reached for the knob, the door opened.
From either side of the threshold, they watched each other.

Lance studied her as if seeing her for the first time—thoroughly, carefully, with no smile to interfere with his concentration. His eyes were guarded but searching. The familiar
stillness was on him. She was reminded of the first night, at
Kirk's party, when she had opened the door to find him outside. He had looked at her in precisely the same way. *Will I ever
get over him?* she wondered almost dispassionately as she met
him look for look. *No,* she answered her own question. *Never.*

"Fox." Lance held out a hand to bring her inside, but she
ignored it, moving around him. Carefully she set down her
camera case but did not remove her jacket before she walked
into the parlor. Without speaking, she moved to the bar and
poured a snifter of brandy. Her decision had been made during her two-hour drive, but following through now was not
going to be easy. Foxy swallowed brandy, shut her eyes as it
burned her throat, then swallowed more. Lance stood in the
doorway and watched her.

"I've been down to your darkroom looking for you." He
frowned at the absence of color in her cheeks and dipped his
hands in his pockets. "I saw the pictures you had drying.
They're extraordinary, Foxy. You're extraordinary. Every time
I think I know who you are, I find another part of you."
When she turned to face him fully, he came into the room.
"I owe you an explanation for this afternoon."

"No." Foxy shook her head as she set the snifter down on
a table. "You told me before your profession had nothing to

do with me." Her eyes lifted and held steady on his. "I don't want an explanation."

He took a step closer. The shadows in the room shifted with the movement. "Well then, Foxy, what do you want?"

"A divorce," she said simply. Feeling the pressure of emotions rising in her throat, she spoke quickly. "We made a mistake, Lance, and the sooner we fix it, the easier it should be for both of us."

"You think so?" he countered. His eyes were level with hers.

"It should be easy enough to arrange," she returned, evading the question. "I'd like you to do it since you have lawyers and I don't. I don't want any settlement."

"Another drink?" Lance asked, and turned to the bar.

His casual tone had her eyeing him warily. "Yes," she answered, wanting to appear as composed as he. The room grew quiet save for the clink of glass against glass. With the decanter in hand, Lance crossed to Foxy and filled the snifter again. The sun slanted low in the window and fell at their feet. Foxy sipped, wondering with a flash of giddyness if they should toast their divorce plans.

"No," Lance said, then drank.

"No?" Foxy repeated, wondering now if he had seen into her mind.

"No, Foxy, you can't have a divorce. Can I interest you in something else?"

Her eyes widened, then narrowed at his arrogance. "I'll have a divorce. I'll get a lawyer of my own and sue you for one." She slammed down her glass. "You can't stop me."

"I'll fight you, Fox," he countered with easy assurance as he placed his glass beside hers. "And I'll win." Reaching out, he grabbed a handful of her hair. "I'm not going to let you go. Not now, not ever. I told you before, I'm a selfish man." Giving her hair a tug, he tumbled her into his arms. "I love you and have no intentions of doing without you."

"How dare you?" Furious, Foxy pushed against him. "How dare you think so much of yourself that you give no thought to my feelings? You don't know anything about love." She kicked out in frustration as her struggles got her nowhere.

"Foxy, you're going to hurt yourself." Lance locked his arms around her and lifted her off her feet. For a moment, she fought against him, then subsided. She shut her eyes, infuriated that she had to surrender on any level.

"Let go of me." Her voice came from between her teeth, but was quiet and even.

"Will you listen to me now?"

She jerked back her head, wanting to refuse. Her eyes were bright with anger and hurt. "I don't have much choice, do I?"

"Please."

The one simple word knocked her off balance. The word was in his eyes as well. Defeated, Foxy nodded. When Lance released her, she stepped away, moving to the window. The early moon was white and full and promising. Its light fell in showers over the naked trees and glittered over scattered leaves. Foxy thought nothing had ever seemed so lonely.

"I had no idea you were coming out to the track today."

Foxy gave a quick laugh, then rested her forehead against the glass. "Did you think what I didn't know wouldn't hurt me?"

"Fox." The tone of his voice persuaded her to turn and face him. "I didn't think at all, that's the point." He made a quick, uncharacteristic gesture of frustration. "I test the cars from time to time, it's a habit of mine. It didn't occur to me until I turned and saw you standing there how it would affect you."

"Would it have made a difference?"

"Damn it, Foxy!" His voice was hard and impatient.

"Is that an unreasonable question?" she returned. She began to wander about the room as she found standing still was impossible. "It doesn't seem like one to me. It seems perfectly justified. I've discovered something about myself in the past month. I can't be second with you." Foxy paused, taking a deep breath. "I have to be first, I can't ride in the back seat with you the way I've always done with Kirk. It's not at all the same thing. I want—need something solid, something permanent. I've been waiting for it my whole life. This house…" She made a helpless gesture as her thoughts came almost too quickly for the words to keep pace. "I want what it stands for. It doesn't matter if we leave it a dozen times a year to go to a dozen different places, as long as it's here to come back to. I want stability, I want commitment, I want a home, children. Your children." Her voice quivered with her feelings, but she turned, dry-eyed, to look up at him. "I want it all, everything."

Foxy turned away again and swallowed. She took two long breaths, hoping they would steady her. "When I saw you in that car this afternoon…" Emotions swamped her, and she shook her head before she could continue. "I can't explain what it does to me. Perhaps it's unreasonable, but I can't control it." Pressing the heel of her hand between her eyes, Foxy tried to speak calmly. "I can't live like that again. I love you, and sometimes I can't quite believe that we're together. I don't want you to be anything but what you are. And I know the things I want might not be what's important to you. But when I think about you going back to racing, I…"

"Why should I go back to racing?" The question was calm and curious.

Foxy moved her shoulders hopelessly. "You said you might the day I found out about Kirk's new car. I know it's important to you."

"Do you think I would do that to you?" This time the tone of his voice brought Foxy's eyes to his. "Have you been thinking that all this time?" He moved to her, then placed both hands on her shoulders. "I'm not interested in racing again. But if I were, I'd manage to do without it. I'm more interested in my wife, Fox." He shook her, but the gesture was more caress than punishment. "How could I consider racing when I know what it does to you? Can't you see you are first in my life?"

She opened her mouth to speak, but only managed to shake her head before he continued. "No, you probably don't. I don't suppose I've made things very clear. It's time that I did." He rubbed her shoulders lightly before he dropped his hands. "In the first place, I pressured you into marriage, taking advantage of Kirk's accident. I've had some bad moments because of that. Let me finish," he told her as she started to protest. "I wanted you, and that night you looked so lost. I snatched you into marriage and rushed you up to Boston without giving you any of the frills you were entitled to. The truth is, I was afraid you might get away, and I told myself I'd make it up to you after we were married."

"Lance," Foxy interrupted and lifted a hand to his cheek. "I don't need frills."

"Is this the woman who once compared a garage to Manderley?" he countered. He took her fingers to his lips, then let them go. "Maybe I need to give them to you, Foxy. Maybe that's why I was devoured with jealousy at the thought of you spending the afternoon in the park with Jonathan. I should have been with you. I rushed you into being my wife and never bothered to discuss the finer points." With his hands in his pockets, he turned away and roamed about the room. "It's difficult to be patient when you've been in love for nearly ten years."

"What?" Foxy stared at him, then slowly lowered herself to the arm of the sofa. "What did you say about ten years?"

Lance turned to her with his tilted smile. "Maybe if I had explained myself in the beginning, we could have avoided some of these problems. I don't know when I started loving you. It's hard to remember a time when I didn't. You were an adolescent with fabulous eyes and a woman's laugh. You nearly drove me out of my mind."

"Why...why didn't you tell me?"

"Fox, you were little more than a child. I was a grown man." With a laugh, he ran his hand through his hair. "Kirk was my best friend. If I had touched you, he would have killed me with perfect justification. No, I couldn't sleep that night at Le Mans because this sixteen-year-old girl was making me crazy. In the garage when I turned around and you all but fell into my arms, I wanted you so badly it hurt. Badly enough that I took my defense in cruelty. Driving you away from me was the only decent thing to do. God, you terrified me."

Shaking his head, he lifted Foxy's neglected drink. "I knew I had to give you time to grow up, time to form your own life. The six years I didn't see you were incredibly long. It was during that time that I started building cars and moved into this house." He turned and looked at her again. "I always pictured you here. It seemed right somehow. You belonged here with me, I felt it. I've never made love to another woman in this house." He set down the glass, and his eyes grew dark and intense. "There's never been anyone but you. Shadows, substitutes at best. I've wanted other women, but I've never loved anyone else. I've never needed anyone else."

Foxy swallowed, not certain she could trust her voice. "Lance, do you need me?"

"Only for day-to-day living." He moved to her, then ran

a hand down her hair. "I've learned a few things in the past weeks. You can hurt me." He traced a finger down the side of her throat as his eyes met hers. "I'd never considered that possibility. What you think of me matters. I've never given a damn what anyone thought of me before. You become more important to me in dozens of ways every day. And my need for you doesn't soften." He smiled slowly. "And you still terrify me."

Foxy returned his smile, feeling the blanketing warmth of contentment. "I suppose this sort of marriage will never be completely smooth and settled."

"I shouldn't think so."

"I suppose it'll always be somewhat tempestuous and demanding."

"And interesting," Lance added.

"I suppose when two people have been in love for as long as we have, they can be quite stubborn about it." She lifted her arms. "I've always loved you, you know, even through all the years I tried not to. Coming back to you was coming home. I want you to kiss me until I can't breathe."

Even as she spoke, Lance's mouth claimed hers. "Foxy," he murmured at length and rested his cheek against hers.

"No, no, I'm still breathing." Thirsty, her mouth sought his until he abandoned his gentle caress. Wild, turbulent, electric, their lips met over and over as the room grew soft with dusk. "Oh, Lance." Foxy held him tightly a moment, then lifted his face and combed her fingers through his hair. "How could we both be such idiots and not tell each other what we were feeling?"

"We're both new at marriage, Fox." He rubbed his nose against hers. "We just have to practice more."

"I feel like a wife." She wrapped her arms around his neck and pulled him close. "I feel very much like a wife. I like it."

"I think a wife should have a honeymoon," Lance murmured as he began to enjoy the privileges of a husband. "I should have told you that I've been spending a great deal of extra time at the office so that I could manage a couple of weeks away. Starting now. Where would you like to go?"

"Anywhere?" she asked, floating under the drugging power of his hands.

"Anywhere."

"Nowhere," she decided as she slipped her hands under his sweater. His back was taut and warm under her palms. "I've heard the service is great here." She smiled up at him when he lifted his face. "And I love the view." Reaching up and behind, Foxy found the phone and tugged it over her head. "Here, call Mrs. Trilby and tell her we've gone to…Fiji for two weeks. Give her a vacation. We'll lock the door and take the phone off the hook and disappear."

"I married a very smart woman," Lance concluded. He took the phone, dropping it on the floor with the receiver off. "I'll call her later…much later." Lowering his mouth, he rubbed it gently over Foxy's. "You did say something about children, didn't you?"

The eyes that were beginning to close opened again. "Yes, I did."

"How many did you have in mind?" he asked as he kissed the lids closed again.

"I hadn't thought of a number," Foxy murmured.

"Why don't we start with one and work from there?" Lance suggested. "An important project like this should be started immediately, don't you think?"

"Absolutely," Foxy agreed. Dusk became night as their mouths met again.

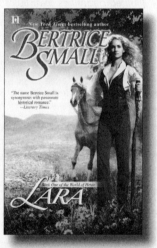

NORA ROBERTS

21876 BORN O'HURLEY	___ $14.95 U.S.	___ $18.95 CAN.
21885 THE MacKADE BROTHERS: DEVIN AND SHANE	___ $14.95 U.S.	___ $18.95 CAN.
21857 THE MacKADE BROTHERS: RAFE AND JARED	___ $14.95 U.S.	___ $18.95 CAN.
21873 SUSPICIOUS	___ $14.95 U.S.	___ $18.95 CAN.
21854 DANGEROUS	___ $14.95 U.S.	___ $18.95 CAN.
21812 MYSTERIOUS	___ $14.95 U.S.	___ $18.95 CAN.

(limited quantities available)

TOTAL AMOUNT $ _____
POSTAGE & HANDLING $ _____
($1.00 FOR 1 BOOK, 50¢ for each additional)
APPLICABLE TAXES* $ _____
TOTAL PAYABLE $ _____
(check or money order—please do not send cash)

To order, complete this form and send it, along with a check or money order for the total above, payable to Harlequin Books, to: **In the U.S.:** 3010 Walden Avenue, P.O. Box 9077, Buffalo, NY 14269-9077; **In Canada:** P.O. Box 636, Fort Erie, Ontario, L2A 5X3.

Name: _____
Address: _____ City: _____
State/Prov.: _____ Zip/Postal Code: _____
Account Number (if applicable): _____
075 CSAS

*New York residents remit applicable sales taxes.
*Canadian residents remit applicable GST and provincial taxes.

Silhouette®
Where love comes alive™